LOOSE
ENDS

A WILL HICKOCK MYSTERY

LOOSE ENDS

R.D. COPSEY

This is a work of fiction. Names, characters, organizations, places, events and incidents are either products of the author's imagination or are used fictitiously. Otherwise, any resemblance to actual persons, living or dead, is purely coincidental.

Copyright ©2023
R.D. Copsey
ISBN: 979-8-9926226-2-1(Print)
Cover Design by Deranged Doctor Design

Interior Design and Formatting:

E.M. TIPPETTS
BOOK DESIGNS

www.emtippettsbookdesigns.com

ALSO BY
R. D. COPSEY

Will Hickock Mystery Series
Loose Ends (Book 1)
Dead Man's Curve (Book 2)
Common Ground (Book 3)

The Long Way Home

For Cheri, my inspiration, my muse, my love.

CHAPTER 1

Notes floated up from his guitar like embers off his campfire. The flames flickered brightly, illuminating the grove of giant cottonwoods crowding the river where McKinley Creek roiled in off the rugged mountains to the west. The flat, sandy ground extended several yards out from the fast-flowing stream forming a natural basin in the ancient creek bed. Up on the steep bank at his back, silhouettes of aspens slashed the night sky into fragments studded with pinpoints of light. It was a perfect campground for a soft summer night.

Leaning comfortably against a weather-worn log, the fire shining in dark eyes that seemed to reveal a haunted soul somewhere deep inside, Will Hickock softly hummed a bluesy melody that had been rolling around inside his head for the past week, searching for lyrics to go with it. Hands that bore scars of hard work or abuse, or perhaps both, seemed too large for the instrument yet still plucked the strings with a delicate touch. His strong, angular face was handsome in a rugged kind of way, beneath dark, close-cropped hair. A faint scar ran from his left ear down the line of his jaw to his neck.

A fly rod leaned against a nearby tree and the well-used cast iron frying pan resting on a flat rock next to the fire held the remains of two good-sized trout. A few chunks of potato poked out here and there.

The melody suddenly eluded him, so he picked out the notes individually on his guitar, trying a couple of different chord progressions before frustration set in. He stopped playing and grabbed the bottle of Miller High Life standing in the sand next to his knee. Empty.

Resting his guitar against the log he rose to his feet and brushed the sand from the backside of his well-worn jeans and vaulted easily up the bank showing a strength and agility otherwise hidden by his long, lean body. He tossed the empty bottle into an old aluminum cooler sitting in the bed of his used-to-be-blue Dodge pickup and was about to pull a fresh beer from the half-melted ice when he noticed a distinct red-orange glow on the horizon off to the northeast. His face froze in the same intently curious expression it held when he was searching for the lost notes to his song moments before.

His first thought was military ordinance, but that was just instinct. He'd left all that behind in Iraq after his last deployment. Slowly, realization dawned. Fire! A sizeable one from the looks of it. His breath caught in his throat.

"Holy shit," he murmured, the words spurring him to action. He scrambled back down the bank, kicking apart the campfire as he grabbed the frying pan and ran to the creek. Scooping up a load of water he dumped it on the coals, stomping furiously on what was left of the logs to stanch the few remaining flames. No sense starting another fire. Then he grabbed his rod and the guitar and ran back up to the truck.

The headlights bounced violently as he raced along the rutted dirt road, revealing the sagebrush whipping past him on both sides in strobe-like fragments. As he drew closer the red glow grew bigger and more intense, spiking his anxiety. If the fire had cut off the road down Latham Canyon, he faced a long drive through dangerous mountain roads to escape in the other direction. But that wasn't what worried him the most. Other than a forest fire, the only thing in that direction that would burn that big was the Captain's place. The man to whom Will owed a debt that could never be repaid.

His mind raced back to the first time the old man had shown him the secret fishing hole he'd just left. He was only ten years old at the time. Hard to believe that was nearly twenty years ago. He could drive the narrow double-track road that followed the creek blindfolded now, which at this speed, in the dark, was just about what he was doing now.

The road cut behind the dark bulk of a high ridge silhouetted in the moonlight, and he scanned the surrounding mountainsides looking for hot spots but couldn't see any. The fire seemed to be contained down in the small valley he knew was just up ahead, which further confirmed his worst fears. He thought about the dried-out hay in that barn and those old bunkhouses out back that hadn't been used in over a decade and his stomach tightened. He smacked the steering wheel. "Damnit!"

Everything looked normal when he drove by earlier that evening on his way to fish for his usual Friday trout dinner. He'd thought about inviting the Captain along, as he often did, but today he just didn't feel like company. As was most often the case, Will felt most comfortable just being alone.

The road emptied him down onto the valley floor and the sight made him gasp. Instinctively, his foot came off the gas. The entire first floor of the old two-story wood-framed farmhouse was engulfed in flames, and they were rapidly licking their way into the second floor. They rose a good thirty feet into the sky, and cast an eerie orange glow a hundred yards out in all directions. Beyond that, all was darkness.

Just beyond the ranch house, the two low-slung bunkhouses were burning equally hot, already completely lost. He stomped on the gas pedal and roared across the narrow wooden bridge that crossed the creek onto the ranch proper. As near as he could tell there were no flames in the barn. Yet. What the hell could have started the house burning? And why wasn't anyone fighting the blaze?

He cursed himself for refusing to get a cell phone all these months. He just couldn't bring himself to be that available to other people all the time, especially since returning home six months ago after a decade as an Army Ranger. It didn't matter to him that some people put his attitude down to PTSD. Hell, he'd been that way all his life. It seemed like a lot of people were too quick to jump to that conclusion about combat vets anymore. The truth was, the vast majority of them became solid assets to their communities when they got home. It crossed his mind now that he hadn't thought there might be times when he would need other people available to him.

The truck slid to a stop as close to the house as he dared, and he jumped out. "Captain!" he shouted. "Captain, where are you?"

He ran toward the front door, but the heat was so intense he couldn't get within twenty feet. Even at that distance he had to shield his face. The entire front of the house was a wall of flame. He circled around to the side but couldn't see anything except more flames in the windows.

"Captain! Are you alright!?"

The fire had died down a bit in the back half of the house, and he was able to get close enough to see in a kitchen window. The room was a charred mess. A few flames still clawed at the cabinets and the exposed frame, but there was still no sign of the man who lived there.

He continued around to the back porch which, incredibly, was still standing. It looked as if the fire had attacked from the front of the house, but the flames hadn't spread enough to block access inside. He kicked open the screen door and made a dash through the open back door, shielding his face against the heat as he kicked the charred kitchen table to one side. He edged closer to the living room trying to get a better look inside. The room was solid flames, floor to ceiling. If the Captain was in there it was all over for him. Will could make out the couch and the easy chair, both charred black lumps, flames from the floorboards still licking at them. The television lay on the floor, its screen shattered.

A loud, creaking sound suddenly rose above the noise of the fire. The upper floor was starting to give way. He tried to stick his head through the archway to check the stairs, but the heat was too much. The creaking grew louder and the whole house shuddered. The living room ceiling began to sag, splitting timbers cracking like gunshots. Will ran back outside.

The roof had already collapsed onto the upper floor on one side of the house and now, with a horrible tearing and screeching, it gave way on the other side. The weight was too much for the upper floor. Helpless, Will could only watch as the rest of the house fell into itself with a thunderous crash, sending a torrent of embers into the night sky. All he could think of was all the memories they carried away with them.

Suddenly, he remembered the barn and sprinted back around the rear of the house. It was still intact, and he couldn't see any telltale smoke coming out anywhere. He ran to the pump that stood next to it. Jerking frantically on the handle, he filled the bucket that always sat there at the ready and tossed it on the side of the barn nearest the fire. He lost count of how many times he repeated the process before he finally heard a distant siren and saw flashing red lights coming up out of Latham Canyon to the east. As they roared onto the scene his tears finally came, and he fell to his knees praying that the Captain had somehow gotten out and gone for help.

CHAPTER 2

The young boy's concentration was intense as he struggled not to spill the pitcher of lemonade he carried from the house. A pair of mugs thick with freezer frost dangled from a length of twine looped around his neck. Up ahead, a tall, lean man in his late fifties, his dust-soiled t-shirt soaked through with sweat, was tossing hay bales up into the open barn loft off a flatbed truck.

When the man saw him coming a broad smile deepened the lines on his weathered face. Heaving the last hay bale up into the loft, he hopped off the truck and lifted the mugs from around the boy's neck with huge, work-hardened hands, exhaling a loud sigh as he rubbed them across his forehead. The frost instantly dissolved, running down his face, dripping from his long, pointed nose and chiseled chin. Wiping the liquid off with one hand he flicked it at the boy, who laughed with delight. The man threw back his head and laughed along with him, tousling the boy's hair with his still wet hand.

The first shafts of morning sunlight shooting up through the canyon that split the east end of the small valley hit Will square in the face, waking him in the bed of his pickup, where he lay on the foam pad he used for camping. Spring had turned to summer, but the nights were still cool in the southwestern Idaho mountains. He groaned and rolled over to get away from the blinding light. His stiff muscles screamed at the movement, but he ignored them, wanting only to drift back into his dream.

The smell of smoke triggered a more recent memory. One that caused him to sit up abruptly. The smell grew stronger, and when he saw the pile of charred rubble that was the Captain's house his stomach started to roil. He'd seen far worse during three tours in Afghanistan, but nothing that hit him as hard as losing the Captain. That was war. Things like this were not supposed to happen here at home.

Two of the posts that held up the porch roof were all that remained standing in front, blackened to jagged points, while in back the tiny, screened porch looked as if the fire had barely touched it. The old bunkhouses beyond were all but obliterated. The yellow crime scene tape that surrounded the entire area brought back the grisly vision of firemen hauling a black body bag out of the rubble. It had looked so small on the stretcher. Too small for a man the size of Wardell Linehart.

Will jumped down from his truck and scanned the steep heavily forested slopes surrounding the small valley, thinking how lucky they all were that the fire had not turned into a conflagration. His legs were unsteady, and he had to take deep breaths to keep his stomach down. He was bone tired, and emotionally drained. He hadn't been able to bring himself to leave when the fire truck arrived from Shambles and the volunteer crew went to work putting out the blaze. He had no idea when he'd finally crawled into his truck and passed out, but it was nearly dawn when the fire crew finally left, so he couldn't have slept more than a few hours.

He walked over to the barn, amazed that the largest structure on the property, barely twenty yards from the house, remained virtually untouched, and vaguely remembered his frantic efforts with the bucket before the fire crew had arrived. He stepped inside and immediately spotted a pair of tin pans sitting side by side near the barn door, empty save for a thick layer of soot.

Dusty. Poor guy must be totally spooked, Will thought. He never hung around the house much anyway, and if the fire hadn't scared him off all the sirens and lights and people sure as hell would have.

Will walked inside, past the ancient tractor the Captain used to clear deadfall from the creek, past the empty animal stalls to the tool shed next to a stack of dried hay bales in back where the big dog sometimes liked to sleep, but there was no sign of him.

Barely a year ago, not long after the Captain had finally retired, he'd found the young pup half starved, running wild in the forest, and nursed him back to health. Now fully grown, the giant Alaskan Malemute still wasn't too friendly toward people, although he was very protective of the old Sheriff. Dusty always seemed to know when someone was approaching the ranch long before any humans could tell. He would watch from a distance, as if making sure there was no danger, then disappear until they left. It was only in the last few weeks that Will's regular visits no longer spooked him.

He took the pans to the hand pump and washed them out, then filled one with fresh water and the other with dry food from a big bag the Captain always kept in the barn. He made a mental note to buy some canned food for the dog and instantly realized that Dusty, too, was now without his best friend in the world.

Stepping back outside he put two fingers along his bottom teeth and tried to whistle like the Captain had taught him. His shrill effort carried part way across the valley, but it was nowhere near the piercing call that Dusty was used to hearing.

"Dusty!" he yelled. "Where are you, boy?"

Will walked slowly around the barn calling out, shading his eyes against the sun that had just begun to bathe the forested slopes of the western mountains, searching for the familiar sight of the big beast bounding across the valley floor towards a sure meal. But nothing moved. Even the birds seemed to have taken leave of this place so recently visited by death. He wondered if the dog somehow knew that the Captain was gone for good and had taken off into the mountains, never to return. There was no doubt he could survive on his own, he pretty much did that anyway, but Will knew he would keep checking to see if the dog returned. The bond they both shared with the retired Sheriff was too strong to simply fade away.

Steeling himself, he circled the burned house, his mind searching in vain for an impossible clue that this was somehow not the right ranch, that it was just an old ruin, long since burned, and that his friend was still alive. All he saw were horrible visions of the night before. Flames leaped and roared in his mind's eye, and he felt once more the heat that prevented him from getting into the living room where he now knew the Captain had perished. Did he try hard enough last night? Could he have saved him? Why hadn't he taken him fishing instead of selfishly claiming the evening for himself?

His eye fell on two black lumps amid the rubble, the remains of the couch and the easy chair, the Captain's final resting place. Who could have done this? And why? The last question had haunted him more than all the rest since he saw one of the fire crew bring a badly scorched gas can over to Ben Roberts, the head of the volunteer fire department shortly after the blaze was extinguished and heard them discuss the likelihood of that the fire could have been arson.

A breeze, carrying the chill of early June, ruffled his hair and stung his nostrils once more with the smell of burnt wood and other things he didn't want to think about. He turned south so the west wind would no longer hit him from across the remains of the still smoldering house. As he did the breeze abruptly shifted, coming now from the south and bringing the scent of juniper and cottonwood from where McKinley Creek flowed past the ranch. Seeking respite from last night's tragedy he followed those familiar smells.

The heat from the fire had scorched the willows closest to the blaze, but beyond that initial damage, the resilient brush remained green. He had gone only a few yards when he noticed some peculiar marks in the dirt. A natural curiosity took over, one nurtured since he was a boy. Something had been dragged away from the house toward the creek. He stooped and studied the marks. There didn't seem to be any tracks indicating what, or who, had done the dragging.

"Everything leaves a trail," the Captain always told him, "it's the oldest writing known to man."

The old man had always encouraged Will to develop his natural instincts, insisting that they would come in handy later in life. It was one of many tecŠiques the Captain had employed to teach a young orphan boy to begin to think for himself. Will had never fully realized the value of those lessons until the day his patrol got lost in the desert near Mosul during his second tour and he was able to follow animal tracks to the nearest water hole, where they were able to get their bearings again. His lieutenant was still thanking him for saving their butts when they finally rotated back stateside months later.

The drag marks seemed to come from the house, but any more tracks in that direction had been obliterated by the firemen and their equipment. As he followed the marks toward the creek, another set of tracks emerged, heading off at a different angle. These were definitely human, made by what looked to be soft-sided hiking shoes. And they were fresh. He couldn't remember any firemen who weren't wearing boots of one kind or another, and since both sets of tracks were wiped out near the house, they must have been made before the firemen arrived.

Will's gut tightened. They could have been made by whoever started the fire. The son of a bitch who killed the Captain.

He lost the tracks momentarily in the thick brush along the creek, but after hopping a few rocks to the other side he quickly picked up the hiking shoes again, along with a set of the same tracks going the opposite direction. They led him to a small open space just off the road on the far side of a cottonwood grove completely hidden by tall willows. A perfect place to park if you wanted to sneak up on the house unnoticed. The ground was too hard for tires to leave much of a track, but there were skid marks where the killer had spun his tires, most likely when he left. Maybe the Sheriff could get something from that.

He followed the entry tracks back across the creek but lost them again in the willows. He was about to leave when a continuation of the drag marks caught his eye. A closer look revealed they veered left into the thicker part of the brush that lined the creek. Maybe not dragged, he suddenly thought, maybe more like a wounded animal trying to hide.

Suddenly there was a sound – or was there? He froze, listening hard. Yes, there it was again, a weird combination of moan and growl.

"Dusty?" he called out. "Is that you, boy?"

He moved more slowly now, working his way towards the creek, stopping every few feet to listen. Could he have been mistaken? Was it just the sound of the water on the rocks. No, wait. There it was again.

"Where are you, Dusty? Talk to me."

He pushed his way through the branches to the bank and there he was, lying in the water, his head resting on the rocky shore.

"Damn," Will breathed softly, dropping beside the huge form, "what the hell happened to you, boy?"

He touched the dog's shoulder, and the groan came again, but there was no movement. A trickle of dried blood ran down the side of the broad head, and when he touched it the dog made a weak attempt to snap at him.

"Okay, okay, I'll leave it alone."

His fur was coated with soot and when Will tried to get his arms underneath the animal to pull him from the water Dusty let out a painful whine. Will's hands came out black. The dog had been burned. That's why he pulled himself to the creek. That's why he was lying in the cool water. He lifted the front paws and saw that the bottoms were blackened as well.

"Poor guy," Will said softly, stroking him, "you tried to save him, didn't you?"

He had no idea how badly the dog was hurt, but he was still breathing. He had to get him out of here and down to a vet.

"I'll be right back, boy."

Dusty groaned once more as Will ran off. He grabbed an old horse blanket from the barn and pulled his pickup as close to the bushes as he could, then returned to the dog and spread the blanket along his back. Taking the front legs in one hand and the hind legs in the other, he gently rolled him over onto the blanket. The big dog seemed to float in and out of consciousness.

Will's stomach turned when he saw that most of the fur on the other side had been burned away. The skin was so caked with mud he couldn't tell how badly it was damaged. Part of him didn't want to know, but the mud seemed like it might be a good poultice, so he left it alone. He figured the killer must have managed to knock him out and left him to die in the fire, but the huge dog had miraculously pulled himself out of the burning house and down to the creek.

Cursing himself for not thinking about Dusty the night before, Will bent over to lift the wounded animal in his arms. He leaned in to speak some words of comfort and noticed several thin strands of what looked like black nylon fabric trailing out of the mouth. Grimacing, he spread the dog's lips apart. The strands were caught in his teeth. Examining them more closely, he noticed dark, red stains around base of some teeth and along the gums. Blood? Had Dusty bitten the killer?

Straining with the load, Will scooped up the huge dog and staggered to the truck, laying him on the foam pad in back as gently as he could.

"Okay, boy," he said softly, "let's get you to the vet now."

CHAPTER 3

Lights flashing, siren blaring, Sheriff Rodney Yeager drove the giant Ford Excursion up the narrow, winding, Latham Canyon Road like a madman. Deputy, J.D. Pacheko, gripped the center console between the seats with one hand and the hinged handle above the door so hard his knuckles were white.

"Jesus, Rod, slow down! You're going to get us killed."

"You didn't have to come along," snarled Yeager. "I said I could handle it myself."

"What makes you so sure he's the one who did it?"

"He's a Hickock. That's more than enough for me. Plus, he's been real quiet since he got back from the Army a few months ago. I wouldn't be a bit surprised if he's got combat issues."

"You mean like PTSD?"

"Whatever."

"Well, if that's the case, it's probably a good thing you've got some backup."

"I don't need backup for this punk."

Pacheko glowered at him. "The way you're driving it's more likely you'll need a witness."

He marveled at how his short, pudgy boss, despite his forty-something years of age, looked like a little kid behind the wheel of the huge automobile. Yeager's skinny moustache twitched fiercely as the big SUV slid around another blind curve on the inside lane. Pacheko cringed. Not even a week on the job and he was already wondering if he would live to regret it. Maybe some conversation would distract this madman.

"Chief Roberts said Hickock was pretty distraught when his fire crew left the scene."

"Then why'd he stay up there," Yeager shot back, "unless it was to destroy evidence. Roberts said it looked like arson."

"I understand Hickock and Sheriff Linehart were pretty close. Maybe he just wanted to grieve." Pacheko strained against his handholds as Yeager took another corner way too fast, spraying gravel off the edge of the road and down the steep bank into the rushing water of McKinley Creek a dozen feet below.

"Typical California. You want to be everybody's goddamn friend. But assholes like Hickock don't deserve friends."

Pacheko shook his head and gripped the handle tighter as the Excursion roared past the old smelter, a behemoth of concrete and steel, long since boarded up and deserted.

"Careful," Pacheko warned, "the pavement runs out around this next bend."

"I know that," Yeager snapped. "I was driving these roads long before any of you fucking tourists showed up."

"Look out!" yelled Pacheko

Yeager yanked the wheel hard to the right to avoid a blue pickup coming around the bend the other way and made the mistake of hitting the brakes just as the road turned to dirt. The pickup had no choice but to hug the bank on the inside of the curve while the huge Ford slid across the road in a cloud of dust, its nose dropping just enough down the steep embankment into the creek to raise its rear wheels off the ground. It hung there, teetering, like it was trying to make up its mind whether to go all the way over or not.

Will skidded to a stop and, once he started breathing again, let his brain catch up to the events of the last few seconds. A quick check through his rear window showed Dusty still unconscious on his sleeping pad. Turning back around, he could see the Excursion in his side mirror, high-centered on the ditch bank, its rear wheels spinning in the air. He was pretty sure he knew just what idiot was driving that tank like it was a sports car, and if he was right this was not going to be a pleasant encounter.

He climbed out and steadied his wobbly legs before jogging over to the Ford to see if anyone was hurt. Even before he got there, he could hear Yeager cursing a blue streak through the driver's open window. Then he heard another voice on the passenger side and decided to go around that way.

"I told you to slow down!" the man was shouting.

"It's not my fault if some fucking idiot can't hear the damn siren!" Yeager hollered back.

"Hey," yelled Will, slapping his hand on the side of the truck, "everyone all right in there?"

The passenger door opened and a tall, rangy man with a wild mop of blonde hair dropped down onto the ditch bank. Will had never seen him before, and the fact that he was wearing a sheriff's uniform made him even more curious.

"No," the deputy shouted back into the truck, "I'm not all right." He started to climb up the bank but slipped back down. "I'm thinking about suing for assault on a police officer."

Will held out his hand. The stranger took it and pulled himself up the embankment.

"Thanks."

"No problem," said Will.

Pacheko eyed Will's soot-stained clothes, but before he could ask a question, they heard the driver's door open, and Yeager's voice ring out.

"Hickock!? Is that you?"

They walked around the back of the truck to see Yeager scrambling up the bank on all fours.

"I might have known," he ranted as he reached the road and struggled to his feet. He jammed a wide-brimmed gray Stetson on his head and came face to face with Will. He was nearly a head shorter, even with the hat, and there were dirt stains on his shirt where his basketball-sized beer belly had dragged on the ground.

"What the hell were you thinking, driving like a maniac on this road?" he shouted.

"Me?" yelped Will. "You're the one doing sixty on the inside lane. What the hell was I supposed to do?"

Yeager ignored him, surveying the Excursion for damage. "You'll pay for every scratch, Hickock, and a fat fine on top of that for reckless driving."

"What! You're crazy if you think...."

"All right, all right," said Pacheko, stepping between them, "both of you just cool down. No one's fining anyone."

Yeager began to sputter an objection, but Pacheko got right in his face. "Remember what I said about a witness."

Yeager fumed, but kept his mouth shut.

"Now, what say we get this tank back on the road," said the deputy.

Yeager gave Will the evil eye, his hand resting on the butt of his holstered pistol as he watched them unhook the winch cable on the rear of the Excursion and run the line over to Will's pickup. Will looked the deputy over curiously.

"Who the hell are you, anyway?" he asked.

"Deputy J.D. Pacheko."

"Since when?"

"Almost a week now."

"How are you liking it so far?" Will smirked, as he hooked the line to his bumper.

Pacheko gave him a wry smile that sat crooked on his square jaw, then started the winch. Will climbed into his truck and held the brake pedal down to maintain the tension. The huge Ford slowly rose up the bank and back onto the road. Yeager walked around the Escalade checking the damage while Pacheko unhooked the winch cable and wound it back into its box on the Excursion. Will had barely stepped out of his truck again when Yeager drew his gun.

"All right, Hickock, spread 'em. Hands on the bed rail."

Will just stared at him.

Pacheko stopped rewinding the winch. "Sheriff, what the hell are you...?"

"Shut the fuck up, deputy."

Yeager walked up and shoved Will against his pickup hard. "Let's go, jerkoff, you've been there before."

He tried to spin Will around to face the pickup, but the younger man defiantly swiped the Sheriff's arm away. They stared each other down another moment, then Will slowly turned and placed his hands on the railing.

"What the hell's going on, Yeager?" Will asked over his shoulder.

"You're under arrest, that's what's going on," Yeager said, frisking him roughly.

"Arrest? For what? This can't be about your lousy driving."

"I'll tell you what it's about, Wild Bill." Yeager spat the name at him, obviously looking for a reaction, but Will just tightened his jaw and waited while Yeager finished patting him down.

"How about murder, destroying evidence, fleeing the scene? You want me to go on? Just what were you up to at the Captain's place last night?"

Will turned around and faced the Sheriff, his face a mixture of anger and disbelief, wanting nothing more than to punch the arrogant little shit in the face. He glanced over at Pacheko. From the way the deputy was staring daggers at the Sheriff it was easy to see that he didn't like what was going on, but he wasn't doing anything to stop it.

"Helping fight a fire." Will growled. "The Captain's dead. His place burned down last night, with him in it. What's the matter, no one bother to call you, Rodney?"

Will used the same nasty emphasis on the name that Yeager had used with his nickname and the Sheriff started to take a swing at him. Pacheko grabbed Yeager's arm and Will held his ground.

"You boys just don't play well together at all, do you?" said Packeko.

"You're done, Hickock," Yeager snarled. "I've got your ass good this time."

Pacheko struggled to hold on to the Sheriff. "If you don't cool down, Sheriff, I'm going to handcuff you to your damn car."

Yeager finally stopped struggling and Pacheko let him go. He took a couple of steps away, hitching his pants back up under his heaving belly. Will feigned a move toward him and the sheriff flinched so hard he lost his balance and stumbled back a step. Pacheko tried to wipe a grin off his face, but it didn't work.

"You want to tell me what he's raving about?" Will asked the deputy.

Pacheko cocked his head to one side and sighed. Yeager pulled out his handcuffs. Slowly the Sheriff's words began to sink in. Will was stunned.

"Come on, Rod, this is the Captain. Even you can't possibly believe I had anything to do with…"

"You're a Hickock ain't you? Since when do you need a reason to fuck up?"

Will looked to Pacheko for help, but the deputy just shrugged. "The Fire Chief radioed us on their way back to town. He mentioned you were up there when they arrived and still there when they left. The next thing I know we're in the car heading up the canyon like a bat out of hell."

"I was fishing up on McKinley Creek last night when I saw the fire. By the time I got there it was too late to do anything except try and save the barn."

"You call the fire department?" asked Pacheko

"I don't have a cell phone. But they got there not long after I did, so somebody must have."

His voice trailed off and he turned away to blink back some tears. Pacheko looked the other way, embarrassed. Yeager offered a sarcastic snort and started poking around in the bed of Will's pickup.

"Let's just see what we've got back here."

He flipped open the cooler, rattled the gas can strapped to the spare tire, looking disappointed that it was full, then his eyes fell on the horse blanket.

"What the hell's this?"

Before Will could answer Yeager leaned in and tossed the blanket open. He gagged, staggering back from the truck. "Jesus H. Christ on a crutch!"

Pacheko came over to see for himself and winced. "Shit," he groaned, "why didn't you just bury him?"

"Because he's alive. I was bringing him down to the vet."

"What!" cried Yeager, peering warily over the side of the truck bed.

Pacheko leaned in and laid a hand on the dog, who let out a moaning growl. Both he and Yeager jumped back.

"He's burned pretty bad on the one side, and he's got a crack on the head," said Will. "Either he was knocked out and left to burn, or maybe he went in after the Captain and something fell on him, but somehow he managed to drag himself down to the creek. And look at this."

He pushed back Dusty's lip and revealed the black strands in his teeth. Pacheko leaned back in. Yeager kept his distance, scowling.

"Looks like some kind of fabric," said the deputy.

Will pointed to the dark stains on the teeth and gums. "Could that be blood?"

Pacheko took a closer look. "Hmm, could be. The lab boys in Boise will tell us for sure. I've got an evidence kit in the truck. Good eyes, Hickock."

"Yeah, right," said Yeager, his curiosity working hard to pull him closer, but fear of the huge beast keeping him back. "If we hadn't caught you that evidence would be long gone."

"Think about it, dipstick," Will said evenly, "if I wanted to get rid of it, I could have cleaned it off up at the Captain's and no one would ever be the wiser."

"He's got you there, Sheriff." said Pacheko, returning with a packet of swabs and some plastic evidence bags. He took three samples of the red substance from Dusty's teeth and collected the black fabric strands, putting them all into separate bags and labeling them.

"Waste of time, you ask me," grunted Yeager.

"It's evidence, sheriff," chided the deputy. "Got to be handled properly if it's going to be effective." Pacheko pulled out another swab and turned to face Will. "If you don't mind, I'd like to take a DNA sample from you while we're here."

Will hesitated, fighting to keep his temper in check, then pulled up the sleeves of his shirt. "Check me out all you like, there's not a bite mark on me. You want me to strip?"

Pacheko looked over his arms, and Yeager peered around the deputy acting like he wasn't really interested but couldn't resist a peek.

"Interesting as that might be," Pacheko said, holding up a swab, "this is the surest way to put yourself in the clear."

Whether it was the crazy, crooked grin or the deputy's casual, friendly manner in the midst of a totally bizarre situation, Will relented. Pacheko rubbed the swab along the inside of his cheek and placed it in an evidence bag.

"Thanks," he said, then tilted his head in the direction of Dusty. "You better get him to the vet, pronto."

Will blinked. Pronto? Seriously? Who says that? "I thought I was under arrest."

"Damn right you are," Yeager snorted, grabbing Will's arm.

Pacheko stepped in front of him. "Give it up, Rod, we've got nothing to hold him on."

"What the hell do you know?" Yeager fired back, pulling his handcuffs off his belt. "You've barely had that badge a week. I'm still the goddamn Sheriff around here and I'm taking him into custody."

He grabbed Will's wrist and slapped a cuff on it. Will tensed, ready to fight, then saw Pacheko shake his head in disbelief at his boss's actions and relaxed. Yeager spun him around and cuffed the other hand behind him.

"What about the dog?" asked Pacheko.

"You're so fucking concerned you take him to the vet" Yeager snapped. I'm taking this mangy mutt to jail."

Will looked to the deputy for help as Yeager marched him off toward the Escalade, but all Pacheko could offer was a shrug. "I've got to tell you, Sheriff, it seems to me like you're taking this way too personal."

CHAPTER 4

Marcia Little Bird pulled her bright red Ford Fiesta into the parking lot behind the rectangular log building at the north end of Main Street promptly at 8:00 AM. Built in the 1920s, it originally housed the offices of the Latham Mining Company. When the company built their smelter a mile up Latham Canyon a decade later, the office personnel took up residence there. At that time the town was sorely in need of better jail facilities, so Latham generously donated it to the Placer County Sheriff's Department, along with the materials to add a sturdy cell block to one end of the building.

The full-blood Nez Perce woman was dismayed to find her usual parking spot occupied by a beat-up blue pickup. It was highly unusual for anyone to arrive at the office ahead of her and seeing this particular pickup in the lot aroused her curiosity in an *uh-oh* kind of way. A scowl furrowed her broad, smooth face, and her dark eyes grew even darker as she pulled into the spot next to the truck.

"Will Hickock, I swear..." she muttered to herself.

She unfolded her six-foot frame from the tiny Fiesta and made her way inside. A direct descendant of the famous Chief Joseph, who led the U.S. Cavalry on a three-month, 1,200 mile run for their money back in 1877, she carried herself with a regal bearing befitting of both her heritage and her fifty-five years. The sparse, open office space was empty, which surprised her a little, given the presence of Will's truck outside, then a smile tugged at the corners of her mouth, and she breathed a contented sigh. She thoroughly relished her alone time each morning before business took control of her day.

She dropped her purse on her desk, just inside the door, and flipped on the radio receiver, which stood next to it on a long, metal folding table, then eased over to fax machine and retrieved a stack of papers from the tray that had come in overnight. Shuffling through them, she placed most of the stack on the deputy's desk directly across the room from hers. A tall metal filing cabinet stood directly behind the neatly arranged desktop, and next to it a small bookshelf overflowed with a plethora of books and manuals addressing various legal and law enforcement rules and regulations.

Sheriff Yeager's desk was considerably larger than the other two and took up almost the entire end wall of the building. A small brass desk lamp occupied one corner, and a large brass nameplate mounted on an ornately carved wooden block stood dead center at the front. Other than that, the desktop was devoid of any files, paperwork or other clutter. The wall behind it held a head mount from a five-point Mule Deer buck, and a fifteen-pound cutthroat trout that the taxidermist had arranged with the body twisted and the mouth open as though it were in the midst of a battle with the fisherman.

She headed for the coffeemaker sitting on a small table next to the solid metal cell block door at the other end of the room. The moment she switched on the machine a voice startled her.

"Marcia, is that you?"

She jumped, looking around the room, then realized it came from inside the cell block. Fetching a set of keys from the deputy's desk, she unlocked the industrial dead bolt and swung open the heavy door. Her eyes went wide at the sight of Will locked in the first of three identical cells, their evenly spaced bars allowing anyone standing in the doorway to see inside all three of them. A second later she frowned.

"My, my," she scolded, "look what the cat dragged in. I thought that was your truck outside."

"Morning," said Will, trying to smile "I thought you were always the first one in."

"When am I not?" she grumped.

"You weren't here when he brought me in earlier."

"I've been up at my sister's in Lapwai the last few days. She's been feeling poorly." Noticing for the first time that Will was covered in dirt and soot she moved closer. "You look like hell, honey. What have you been up to that got you locked up in here?"

He started to speak, but the lump in his throat would not allow words to come. His head dropped and he slumped down on the cot against the back wall choking back a sob. Marcia's face went slack. "What the hell's happened, Will?

Deputy Pacheko parked next to Marcia's car and grabbed a grocery bag off the seat beside him as he exited the cruiser. He was still upset over the encounter with Will Hickock. Rod Yeager had only been Sheriff of Placer County for a little over a year, ever since Wardell Linehart retired, but he was the department's lone deputy for more than fifteen years before that. During his brief tenure in Shambles, Pacheko had come to realize that his new boss was a little too enamored with the power of his badge, but he'd never seen Yeager go quite as ballistic as he had earlier that morning when he arrested Will Hickock.

The first thing the deputy noticed when he stepped inside the office was that Marcia was nowhere to be seen. It was especially odd because her car was in the parking lot next to Will's truck. He knew she'd been out of town the past few days and was glad to have her back. She brought an air of calm to his otherwise tense workplace. He put the grocery bag down on his desk wondering where she might have stepped out to, and that's when he heard the crying.

The open cellblock door caught his eye and he instantly pulled his gun, making a beeline across the room expecting the worst. He burst through the door to find the door to the first cell wide open and Marcia sitting next to Will on the cot sobbing heavily. He had his arms around her awkwardly and it was immediately obvious that Will was trying to comfort her. Pacheko lowered his gun wondering what the hell had happened.

When Will looked up his cheeks were wet with tears as well. When he saw the deputy standing there looking bewildered, he shook his head gently. It suddenly dawned on Pacheko that Marcia couldn't have known about last night's tragedy. He'd heard enough about the former Sheriff in his short time on the job to know that no one in the community, except perhaps Will, had been closer to him than Marcia. She had been his right hand in the office for over thirty years. He slid his gun quietly back into its holder and respectfully backed out the door, quietly retiring to his desk.

As he listened to Will and Marcia cry and share stories about their friend, his mind started to drift back to the circuitous journey that had taken him from a tragedy of his own in California to the tiny town Shambles. Not only was he a long way from home, the locale and the lifestyle couldn't be more different from his former life. He quickly banished those thoughts. He had his reasons for ending up here, but they were not something he liked to think about, much less talk about.

It was a good ten minutes before the crying stopped. When Marcia finally emerged from the cellblock Pacheko tried hard to busy himself with paperwork. He failed, unable to resist casting a wary glance in her direction.

"What are you looking at?" she barked, grabbing a handful of tissues from a box on her desk and dabbing at her eyes.

"Nothing, ma'am," said Pacheko.

"Well, just keep on not looking at nothing."

"Yes ma'am."

"And how many times do I have to tell you to stop calling me ma'am? I've got a name, you know. You've been here almost a week, you ought to have learned it by now."

"Yes ma'…, I mean…"

"Never mind." She plopped down behind her desk and blew her nose.

Pacheko waited a bit to let her get settled, then asked, "Where's the Sheriff?"

"On his way to Boise."

"To see Chief Rankin, I assume." George Rankin was Chief of the State Police and in the hierarchy of Idaho law enforcement, Yeager's boss.

Pacheko nodded. "He called to tell them about the Captain and that the fire crew thought it looked like arson. Chief Rankin ordered him to come down immediately and give his crime scene report in person."

Marcia burst into tears again, holding her face in her hands. "I can't believe it. I just can't believe he's dead."

"I'm sorry."

She grabbed another tissue and wiped her eyes, sniffling, then turned a scowl on the deputy. "Don't be sorry. You want to be sorry for something, be sorry you locked that boy up on what has to be one of the worst days of his life."

"I didn't lock him up, the Sheriff did."

"Sadly, that doesn't surprise me."

"I told him I didn't think it was the smart thing to do."

She gave a grunt. "Rod Yeager's not often known for doing the smart thing.

"So I've noticed."

"It hasn't been easy for him, taking over when the Captain retired last year. He may not have shown it, but he respected that man as much as anyone. He always said he wanted to follow in his footsteps, but I think, deep down, he knew he could never measure up.

"He certainly doesn't seem to be much of a people person."

Marcia almost laughed through her sniffles. "Now there's an understatement."

"You should have seen the way he went off on Hickock up in the canyon, and for no real reason."

She sighed. "You couldn't to talk him out of it?"

"I tried, but he said at the very least the suspect was fleeing the scene."

"To save that poor dog!" she erupted, the tears starting up again. "More like a wolf, really, but he meant the world to Wardell."

"I dropped him off at the vet, then brought Will's truck here and took the cruiser up to the crime scene to meet with the arson inspector who drove up from Boise. From what he said it sure sounds like a murder to me."

"And Will helped them put out the fire the way I heard it," Marcia continued as if she hadn't heard him. "If he hadn't been there the barn would have been lost, too." She grabbed some more tissues and blew her nose again.

"Guess he told you what happened," said the deputy.

"Well, aren't you the observant one," she snapped. "Must be that fancy new criminal science degree you got tacked to the wall over there." Instantly regretting her tone, she gathered herself, letting out a deep sigh. "I'm sorry, J.D., I'm just a little worked up right now."

"That's all right," said the deputy, offering an understanding smile.

There was an uncomfortable pause. More tears leaked out and Marcia wiped her eyes with more fresh tissues. Pacheko waited until it looked like she was regaining her composure. "The Captain must have meant a lot to you."

"Thirty years we worked together." She nodded, sniffing once more. "He meant a lot to this whole town. But I doubt there's anybody around here he meant more to than Will Hickock. He raised that boy after his mama died. There is no way in hell he could be responsible for what happened to Wardell. That man was the only father he ever knew. What the hell was the Sheriff thinking?"

"Well, maybe it's because I'm so observant and all," Pacheko joked, hoping to lighten the mood, "but it's pretty obvious that he and Hickock don't get along."

Marcia rolled her eyes, but his lame attempt at humor seemed to calm her a bit. "Another understatement." She took a deep breath and tried to steady her nerves. "So, did you find anything up there that might tell you who did this?"

"Not really. The arson guy agrees it was started on purpose. He said it was pretty apparent that gas was the accelerant, and the fire crew found an empty gas can next to the house. They took some burn samples to test against any residue in the can, and they'll run the can for prints, but it was pretty burnt up, so I'm not holding my breath on that."

"What about the tracks?"

Startled by Will's voice, they both jerked their heads toward the cell block. Pacheko walked over to the open door.

"The only tire tracks we found around the place, other than the fire engines, are from the Captain's truck and yours."

"Check that little pullout on the road beyond the creek," said Will. Someone was parked there and left in a hurry. I followed a set of footprints from the house out through the willows to where they crossed the creek, and found another set leading back in. Some kind of hiking shoe."

"You listen to him, J.D.," Marcia said from behind another Kleenex, "he knows about tracks."

Pacheko looked confused and Marcia shot him a look. "Ok, I'll take a look."

"Looked like he waded the creek right near where I found Dusty," Will continued from the cell block.

"Poor Dusty," said Marcia, drying another flow of tears.

"What did the vet say?" asked Will.

Pacheko blew out a breath. "She said that dog's got one hard head. His skull was cracked but not fractured. With some rest, he should recover just fine. Turns out the burns were mostly superficial. Singed the fur off but didn't damage the skin too much. He said most of it will probably grow back."

"What about his feet?" asked Will.

"A little worse, but the vet said if he'll stay off them for a week or two, they should be fine."

"That's good news," Marcia said, brightening a bit. "Will said something about some fibers and blood in his teeth."

"Yeah, the Sheriff took those samples to the lab. We should get results on the blood and fiber back tomorrow. DNA will take longer."

"Why do you need Will's DNA?" Marcia asked, plainly upset. "It's plain to see there are no bite marks on him. And he wasn't wearing a black jacket, either."

"Relax, Marcia, this just makes it easier for us to eliminate him as a suspect and according to our boss, right now he's number one." She scowled at him. "And since you brought it up, why don't you start checking hospitals and clinics around here for anyone who came in with animal bite injuries or burns last night or this morning."

"You better believe I will." She nodded her head emphatically, as if to punctuate the statement. She took a big breath and put on a face that said it was game on. "Well, since it's not likely we'll see the sheriff again until tomorrow that leaves you in charge."

She tossed the cellblock keys across the room. Surprised, the deputy barely managed to catch them. "You can let Will go home now and get cleaned up. He's been through hell. Probably hasn't had anything to eat, either."

Pacheko suddenly remembered the grocery bag and picked it up. "I brought some…"

"And I'm late for work." Will called out from his cell.

He stood there a moment, holding the bag, unsure exactly how to proceed. Marcia stared him down expectantly. "Um, I'm not exactly sure I can do that, ma'am." He flinched. "I mean, Marcia."

"Sure you can," she said, with a dismissive wave of her hand. "I'd do it, but as dispatcher and office manager I'm not legally authorized to handle prisoners."

Pacheko hesitated, the look on his face saying the wheels in his brain were spinning frantically. Marcia gave him a scowl.

"Is he being held on any kind of legal charge, or is this just the Sheriff over exercising his authority again?" Pacheko gave her a shrug that said that latter was true. "That's what I thought. So go on," she urged with a wave of her hand, "it's not like he's going to run off. His mother raised him better than that, didn't she, Will?"

"Yes, she did," said Will. "And you've got my word on it, too, deputy."

"Trust me," Marcia whispered, "that's no small thing from him. Besides, he needs some time to grieve, and a jail cell is no place for that. I know where to find him if we need him."

"But what do I tell the Sheriff? He's not going to like it, not one little bit."

"I'll handle the Sheriff. By the time Chief Rankin gets through with him he'll most likely be in a much more receptive mood. Now get in there and unlock that cell."

They stared each other down for several moments, but Pacheko blinked first and headed for the cell block, not at all convinced that this was a good career move. He was searching the ring for the cell key when Will pushed the door open and stepped out.

"Thanks, deputy," he said. "I promise you won't regret this."

Pacheko's eyes went wide as it dawned on him that Marcia had not bothered to re-lock the cell when she left Will. He shook his head. Between Yeager's brusque attitude and Marcia playing loose with the rules, he was beginning to realize that his new job was going to take some getting used to.

Will gave Marcia a hug and scooted out the door. She sat down at her desk with a deep sigh and checked a list of phone numbers taped to the edge of her desk. "I'll give the medical clinic a call first." As she picked up the phone to dial, she noticed that Pacheko watching her. She'd seen that look before. "Something I can help you with, Deputy?"

He hesitated, then walked over to her desk. "What's the deal between the Sheriff and Hickock?" he asked.

Marcia looked up at him, one eyebrow cocked as she contemplated how to answer his question. "It's not really about Will," she finally said, "so much as it is his brother."

"Hickock has a brother?"

She sighed and put down the phone. "Pull up a chair, deputy," she said sternly. "It's time you had a little history lesson."

CHAPTER 5

It's never easy growing up with a name made famous by someone else. Ethan Hickock was a direct descendant of the 1870's lawman who was shot in the back during a poker game in Abilene, Kansas, and that's all it took to make him a fanatic about the Old West. Its myths and legends beguiled him early in life, and by the time he was twenty he packed up and headed for Nevada, lured by visions of instant riches in the gold and silver mines that were still producing more than a hundred years after the discovery of the Comstock Lode.

He soon discovered that mining was much harder work than he'd bargained for, and a lot less lucrative. His young wife LuAnn was a frail thing, and the transition from their comfortable Philadelphia family life to the raw Nevada desert, even in the early 1980's was not an easy one, especially being pregnant at the time. So, when Ethan heard that the smelter up in Shambles, Idaho was hiring he reluctantly opted for a steady paycheck and a roof over their heads in the company housing that came with the job.

She delivered their first child, a son, less than two months after arriving in the tiny town. The boy fulfilled a dream Ethan had nurtured for many years. He had always been disappointed that his parents didn't name him after his hero, Wild Bill, and he was determined not to let the same opportunity pass him by. But there was a problem. Their new son was displaying symptoms of tuberculosis. The doctor assured them this kind of thing showed up in newborns every so often, but that it usually went away after a few weeks. Fortunately, that turned out to be the case with the newest Hickock, but when it came down to the birth certificate, as far as Sam was concerned there was now only one name that was right for the boy – Doc Holliday Hickock.

He didn't tell LuAnn about it right away because he knew there would be hell to pay. Even after she found out she was still too weak to put up much of a fight. As it happened, the baby was healthy long before she was. It was all she could do to nurse the boy those first few weeks, and it was over a year before she was back to her old self again. As a result, she wasn't exactly thrilled at the prospect of getting pregnant again, especially not if her husband was going to pull another stunt like that.

"You might as well brand him like a steer," she used to say.

After that, sex became a rare commodity in the Hickock household. When she did give in to his advances it was with the greatest reluctance, and only after a careful check of the calendar and a steady supply of birth control. As the years went by, Ethan started hitting the bars after work, coming home late smelling of cigarettes and booze and God knows what else. He had never been a particularly kind man, and the drinking seemed only to exacerbate his dark side, often to the point of physical abuse.

This went on for a solid decade before LuAnn, either in a moment of weakness or a final, desperate attempt to save a marriage that probably wasn't worth saving, let Ethan have his way with her at an especially propitious time of the month. Once again, the pregnancy took its toll. She was sick almost the entire nine months. The doctor worried that she might not make it to full term.

Ethan stuck around just long enough to see his second son born and emblazon his birth certificate with the name Wild Bill Hickock, then he was off to seek his fortune in greener pastures. He was never heard from again, so the newborn was left with only speculation as to whether his father was just too dumb to realize their famous ancestor's real name was James Butler Hickock, or if he just named him Wild Bill out of spite.

Doc took Ethan's sudden departure a lot harder than LuAnn. She was simply relieved that she would never have to put up with his drunken rages or go through another pregnancy. But becoming the man of the house at age ten didn't sit well with the youngster. He had his father's mean streak, and constantly complained about having to help raise his little brother while his ailing mother took on one odd job after another to keep up the house payments. He blatantly ignored her repeated suggestions that he take on an after-school job to help out. They never had enough to eat, or proper clothes for the winter. And forget Christmas and birthdays, there just wasn't any money.

So, Doc took to stealing to get what he wanted. He would roam the small town, surreptitiously learning people's schedules, and hit their houses when he knew no one would be home. It was easy pickings, and safe – as far as burglary goes. He was clumsy at first, and got caught more than once, spending time for each offense at a juvenile detention facility known as the Ranch—a moniker acquired because the Placer County Juvenile Detention Facility was simply too troublesome to deal with. It was located up in a small valley three miles north of town on a small ranch owned by Sheriff Wardell Linehart. The Sheriff lived in his ranch house and the young men in his charge stayed in the bunkhouses out back. They served their time working the ranch except when they were in school, and Linehart always insisted his young charges continue their education, no matter what. He ran the Ranch with an iron fisted discipline, but when it came to ranch chores he worked right alongside the boys, earning their respect. No one knew exactly how it started, but one day some the boys started calling him Captain and the name just stuck.

Gradually, Doc became more proficient at his chosen craft. Being as young as he was, and always pleading the case of just trying to provide for his family, he never spent much time incarcerated. Never mind that he kept most of the money for himself.

By the time Wild Bill was five or six, Doc had started sneaking his little brother through crawl spaces and basement windows too small for him to enter so he could open up a house or a store. He always went off by himself to fence whatever loot they got, and no one ever knew little Billy was involved. Of course, the youngster never got a dime for his trouble, either. Doc always said he was just protecting his little brother; that if no money ever changed hands, he couldn't be connected to the robberies.

Since no one else was wise to Doc's scheme, there was no one to tell Wild Bill it wasn't all just a game. Doc encouraged the youngster with tall tales of how their ancestors made it on their own in the rough and tumble days of the Wild West, and since their father had left them high and dry, it was up to them to do the same. A man had to stand on his own two feet. It was the way of the world.

By the time LuAnn figured out what was going on, teenaged Doc was beyond her control. She was too weak and sick most of the time to do anything about it, and she couldn't bring herself to call the Sheriff on the only family she had left. Besides, she'd gotten used to the little presents Doc would bring home every so often, not to mention the occasional extra money he grudgingly contributed to the household from his ill-gotten gains.

If there was a scintilla of genuine love in Doc for his mother or his younger brother, it was well hidden. Still, when he got caught rifling the cash register in the general store on his sixteenth birthday, he stuffed Billy back in the crawl space before the deputies saw him and told them he was alone. The judge gave him six months at the Ranch, and he spent four before they let him off for good behavior.

He served his time like a man and, despite Sheriff LInehart's objections, managed to convince the parole board he had learned his lesson this time. He was going to stay in school and make his mother proud. Two weeks after his release the burglaries started up again. The Sheriff was pretty damn sure he knew who was behind Shambles' latest crime spree, but it wasn't easy catching him in the act.

All their lives people had made fun of their names, but Billy didn't mind. After all, the real Wild Bill Hickock and Doc Holliday were tough lawmen who helped clean up the West. Doc, on the other hand, always hated their father for putting such a curse on them, and their mother for not changing them after the old man was gone. He vowed he would do it himself as soon as he was old enough.

LOOSE ENDS

When Doc was seventeen, he realized that once he turned eighteen there would be no more juvenile court. If he got busted it was prison for him. He wanted desperately to leave his miserable life in Shambles far behind, but that took money. More money than they had ever gotten from robbing anyone in that one-horse, dying mining town. So, he planned one last big score. A deal that would get him enough to hit the road and never look back.

It was risky, and Billy was plenty scared when he heard about it. The youngster finally agreed to do it, but only if Doc promised to take him along when he left. Doc agreed, but he'd already figured out that the easiest way to pull off the job was to leave Billy holding the bag. As it turned out, neither of them expected things to go as wrong as they did.

The smelter outside Shambles paid its employees every Friday, in cash. A pair of armed guards brought the money up from the bank in town in an unmarked van to avoid suspicion. Doc's plan was simple – steal the van before it got to the smelter, hightail it over the mountains and disappear forever. He taught Billy to shoot the pistol their father had left behind, all the while assuring his little brother would never have to actually use it, except maybe to fire warning shots. Billy protested at first, but Doc told him how he'd be living up to his namesake, one of the best shootists the West ever knew.

"Wouldn't the old man shit green apples if he could see us now," Doc said as he blasted a pair of cans off a rock from twenty feet.

He plotted for weeks, following the van, studying its route and every move the two guards made until he knew their routine better than they did. They always seemed pretty relaxed on the drive up from town, usually smoking cigarettes and talking to one another, paying little attention to their surroundings. About halfway between town and the smelter there was a stretch where the road narrowed, winding between steep, rocky banks. On the fateful day, the van rounded one of the sharp curves to discover a big pile of rocks and railroad ties blocking the road. As soon as it stopped Doc and Billy swooped down out of the rocks, kerchiefs over their faces and hats pulled low, just like real old west outlaws holding up the stagecoach in a Roy Rogers movie.

The two guards were caught completely by surprise. Doc held the gun on them while Billy zip-tied their hands behind their backs. Then he marched them down to the creek and ordered them to sit down in the water, which was about two feet deep. They reluctantly did as they were told. The water came up to their chests and the current was such that without the use of their hands it was a struggle to remain upright.

He told Billy to keep them covered from a safe distance while he went to make sure the money was all there. But as soon as he hopped into the van he shouted, "So long, Cowboy," and drove it right up and over one side of the rock pile and off up the road.

Doc had done stuff like that before on jobs, just to give his little brother a scare, and give himself a laugh, so Billy stayed right where he was. The longer he obediently waited for his brother to come back he was getting more and more scared, and the guards were getting braver and braver. What he didn't know was that one of the guards had a pocketknife and had managed to cut the zip-ties behind his back under the rushing water. He secretly passed the knife to his partner, who signaled with a subtle nod when his hands were free as well.

Then, when Billy looked forlornly down the road a little too long one time, they jumped him. The gun went off in the struggle and one of the guards went down clutching his side, a red stain roiling down the creek as the current took his blood away. Billy was terrified. The other guard snatched the gun from him and shoved him face down in the creek while he handcuffed him and dragged him to shore. Then he a look at his wound. It wasn't serious, but it was bleeding quite a bit. They took Billy's shirt and tore it up to make a bandage, then the three of them walked back to town.

Billy told Sheriff Linehart everything he knew, which wasn't much. Doc had about a two-hour lead on them, but the Sheriff took out after him anyway. He called up in helicopter from Mountain Home Air Force base south of Boise and kept in radio contact. A few hours later, the chopper led him to a plume of smoke off an old logging road up near Sutter Pass, about ten miles above the valley where the Sheriff's ranch was.

By the time they got there, the van was nothing more than a smoldering mass of metal at the bottom of a deep ravine. Doc must have been too eager to make his escape and missed one of the sharp curves. It looked like the gas tank had exploded on impact. There wasn't much left of Doc, but Billy was able to identify a piece of shirt and a shoe they took from the badly burned body, and a gold ring his brother had particularly liked from one of his burglaries. The payroll money had burned, too, except for a few loose bills scattered around in the bushes.

LuAnn went off the deep end when she found out. She locked herself in the house and wouldn't answer the phone. She didn't even show up at the trial. Word was she couldn't even get herself out of bed. Because one of the guards had been shot, the Latham Mining Company lawyers pressured the judge to try Billy as an adult. Even though young

Billy admitted freely to the crime and apologized for his role in it he was convicted of armed robbery and sentenced to serve fifteen years.

Because he was only seven at the time he was sent to the Ranch to live until he was eighteen, at which time he would serve out the rest of his sentence in the state prison. The shock of losing both her boys was too much for LuAnn in her already weakened state. Just a few days after Will was sentenced, she was gone. Most folks said she died from heartbreak.

Even as he grew older and came to understand what they had been doing was wrong, he never got over the fact that his big brother had set him up to take the fall. It didn't matter that Doc was killed his betrayal didn't die with him. From that day forward Billy's hackles went up any time someone called him Wild Bill, or even Billy. He wouldn't even go along with William, his mother's preference. Finally, he settled on Will, and refused to answer to anything else. It would be a long time before he trusted anyone ever again.

CHAPTER 6

Tim Spangler, a short, stocky, very fit man in his early, already balding in hls early thirties, walked into the repair bay of Spangler Cyclery and noticed Will staring at the rear wheel of a bike mounted on a stand, absently turning the pedals. He stepped over and shifted gears, causing the chain to jump off the sprocket, jolting Will back to reality.

"See, the way it works," said Tim, "is you move the little levers and the gears change. Except on this bike, which is what you're supposed to be fixing."

"Sorry, Tim," said Will sheepishly, "I guess I drifted off."

Tim put a hand on his shoulder. "No worries," he said gently, "even half here you're still the best bike mechanic in town."

Will glanced around the tiny shop, crammed with bicycle parts and tools, and was relieved to see there was no one to witness his lapse. Tim gave him a sympathetic smile and put a hand on his shoulder. "How about a cup of coffee?"

They walked into the spacious warehouse-style showroom, where Tim's wife, Tina, a cute, hard-body brunette with a thick head of wavy brown hair, was talking to a customer about camel packs while another couple ogled the latest Tallboy Aluminum SPX. Will shook his head. It was one hell of a piece of equipment, but why anyone in their right mind would spend five grand on a bicycle was beyond him. They made their way up the stairs at the back of the vast room to the windowed office overlooking the sales floor. There were two desks placed at right angles in one corner, one neat as a pin, the other piled high with papers and catalogues surrounding a large computer monitor. Tim went straight to the coffeemaker on a long table in the opposite corner and poured two cups.

"Sorry," said Will, slumping into one of the chairs in front of the messy desk. "I just can't seem to get with it."

"Hey, you don't have to be here, you know," Tim said, handing him one of the cups and sliding behind his desk and setting his cup atop a stack of equipment catalogues. "I know what the old guy meant to you. That's why I told you to take a few days off. We can handle things around here. I can't even imagine what you must be going through right now."

"Yeah, you told me, and I appreciate it. I guess I was hoping work would take my mind off everything."

The bell on the front door jingled down below and Tim looked down in time to see four people enter the store. Tina threw him an anxious glance. The store was filling up and she needed help. Will picked up on the situation instantly and stood up. Tim started to protest, but Will held up a hand stopping him.

"Hey, no worries. Customers come first, I get it." He held up his cup. "Thanks for the coffee. Go get'em, boss."

"Listen," said Tim, "we're in good shape for the start of the season. The first big group doesn't come in for another week and you've already got almost all the rental bikes ready to go. It's Friday. Take off for the weekend. I'll see you on Monday."

"But there's still a lot of work to do."

Tim clapped him on the shoulder, and they started toward the door. "Go on, get out of here. Get lost up in the mountains, catch yourself some fish. It'll do you good to get out of Dodge for a while."

"You sure?" said Will, brightening.

Tim laughed. "That look of relief on your face just told me how sure I am. Besides, you're the best trail guide in town, and I want you ready to give those people a workout next week." He took back the cup of coffee. "Now scram."

"Thanks, Tim, I'll be ready to go on Monday, I promise."

"Of course, it'll cost you," Tim added, stopping Will halfway down the stairs. "Bring back a pile of those giant trout you're always bragging about and fire up that barbeque of yours."

Will grinned and was gone.

A minute later he was flying north on Main Street hooking his helmet strap with one hand and shifting gears with the other, feeling good about his decision to leave his pickup at home after he'd cleaned up from his stay in jail and ride his bike across town to work. A good hard trail ride sounded like just what he needed to ease the pain of losing his best friend.

The thought threatened to bring back a rush of memories, but he shook them off, taking in a deep breath and reveling in the warmth of the sunshine. It had been good bike weather for over a month, but he'd only ridden a dozen or so times. Instead of energizing him, the warm spring weather just seemed to make him lazier. Or maybe he was just getting old.

He banished that thought by pedaling harder, exhilarated by the wind in his face and the feel of muscles responding to the call. It had taken almost a year, but he finally paid off his Novara Komerade last month. Two thousand dollars was way more than he had any business spending on anything, much less a bike. Hell, it was worth more than his pickup. But during the warmer months it was his primary mode of transportation, and since it was necessary for his job, he could write it off as a business expense, so he figured it was worth it. Besides, the front and rear shocks made it ride like a dream.

There was only a smattering of cars on the streets, almost all locals, but in another two weeks it would be a very different story. He marveled at how the little town nestled in the elbow of a long dogleg valley carved out by the Middle Fork of the Boise River had changed during the ten years he'd been gone. He wasn't sure he liked all of it, but then he never was much for change anyhow.

The east side of town used to end a block past Main Street, but Sam Montforte changed all that. He was a no-account sheriff's deputy with a questionable reputation, and when Wardell Linehart was elected Sheriff, he promptly fired the ne'er-do-well. Montforte was forced to take a job as a security guard at the smelter to support his family, and the bad blood between them never died.

Then one fateful night, as the story goes, a couple of years after the smelter shut down, Montforte struck it rich at the crap tables down in Reno and decided to take up a career in real estate. Most folks saw two big problems with that idea. First, Sam didn't have brains enough to run a business of any kind, and second, there was no real estate market in Shambles.

Truth be told, there never was much glory in the tiny mining town at all. Folks always said it was a town that lived up to its name. Gold and silver brought the first miners to the California gold fields when the Comstock Lode was discovered back in 1859. Then, when gold was discovered in the Boise Basin a few years later, the flood of fortune-seekers moved north where big strikes around Idaho City and Placerville were keeping things plenty interesting. Shambles grew up a few miles east around the smelter that was built there during the next mining boom in the early 1900's.

The state naturally welcomed the smelter operation for the wealth of jobs it created, but the owners balked when they realized the closest law enforcement was over forty miles to the south in Boise. Adding to their consternation, Shambles was situated in Elmore County, and that Sheriff's office was over fifty miles away on rough dirt roads. The Boise County Sheriff's office in Idaho City was only twelve miles to the west as the crow flies but traveling the maze of mining and logging roads that wound through the rugged mountains in between made the journey more like fifty. With all the gold and silver passing through that area the folks in Shambles felt the need for some protection a little closer to home.

After haggling back and forth for several years, Henry Latham, the smelter owner, and his investors finally convinced the state legislature to carve out a chunk of Elmore and Boise Counties that covered the mining district surrounding Shambles and create Placer County. With Shambles as the county seat, the little town got their very own Sherriff's department. The following year they built the county courthouse right in the center of town. It was a thriving community for over eighty years until a series of unfortunate events finally closed the smelter operation for good in 1988.

Henry Latham had seen the end coming. The operation had been in his family for three generations, but by the late 1970's the entire mining industry was on the skids thanks to tough new environmental regulations. He held on for another dozen years or so, and then one day he just up and disappeared, leaving his wife and his business behind.

Latham had always been a well-respected man in Shambles, a pillar of the community, and most folks thought something tragic must have befallen the man. That is, until the auditors finally got things squared away and found the balance sheet was shy just north of ten million dollars. An investigation showed that Latham had been skimming from the miners for years and doing some fancy bookkeeping to cover it all up.

Wardell Linehart was still in his first term as Sheriff, and Shambles had never seen a crime of that magnitude. He brought in the State Police, even the FBI, but no one ever found a trace of Latham or the money, and the whole affair just slowly faded away into one of those outlaw legends the Wild West has always been famous for.

With no work at the smelter, and most of the mining claims either played out or close to it, people started leaving town like rats deserting a sinking ship. A few stayed on, mostly storekeepers who had supplied miners and ranchers in the area for decades and had everything they owned tied up in their businesses. Land prices fell through the floor.

Over the next decade, the population dropped nearly seventy percent, and Shambles was well on its way to becoming a full-fledged ghost town. But that didn't stop Sam Montforte. He started buying up all the property he could get his hands on. Most folks were happy to get anything at all out of their investments, and before long he ended up owning a big chunk of what was once a thriving downtown.

Everyone thought he was crazy, including his wife. When she couldn't talk him out of blowing their new-found fortune on worthless land, she left town with their daughter to rejoin her family back east somewhere. To add to the confusion, Sam had picked up a smart, ambitious young partner named Corinne Barker. Everyone said he'd finally found the brains for his business, and there were rumors that wasn't all there was to their partnership, but the town was still dying.

No one could figure out whether Sam had an honest-to-God vision of the future or whether it was just plain dumb luck, but when the Town Council unveiled its plan to revive Shambles, nearly twenty years after the smelter debacle, virtually all the property owned by Montforte Real Estate figured into it one way or another. He and Corinne had somehow managed to corner a real estate market nobody knew existed.

The plan revolved around capitalizing on a different kind of natural resource. The wild mountains surrounding Shambles offered just about any kind of outdoor recreation a body could want. Hunting and fishing had always been good, but it wasn't long before mountain bike enthusiasts began to discover the dozens of old mining roads and trails crisscrossing the mountains that were ready made for their burgeoning sport.

The miraculous transformation began right about the time Will graduated high school. Sheriff Linehart had literally raised the boy on the Ranch and based on his good behavior and good grades in school, along with calling in few favors, he managed to get Will's sentence reduced to time served. Will was relieved he didn't have to go to prison, but the reprieve came with the condition that he enlist in the military. The judge reasoned that it would instill a sense of discipline in the young man that would help ensure he continued his life on the right side of the law.

When Will left for Army boot camp, Shambles still looked just like it did the whole time he was growing up. The northwestern slope, known as the Hill, was still blanketed with rows of empty, cookie-cutter mining company houses where the smelter workers had lived, and virtually all the buildings on either side of Main Street's six whole blocks were still just as empty as when Montforte had bought them.

When he came home ten years later, he figured it would be like slipping back into a favorite pair of old slippers. After three tours as an Army Ranger in Iraq and Afghanistan, all he wanted to do was fade back into Shambles and become just another ghost in the ghost town. But in the interim, word had gotten out that the mother lode of trails in the historic old mining town constituted a paradise for two-wheel adventurers, and to virtually everyone's surprise, real, honest-to-God tourists started showing up.

At first it was just locals driving up from the Boise, Mountain Home and other southern Idaho communities but after a few years the Town Council's marketing efforts started to pay off, and folks from all over the Northwest began flocking in every summer, booking rooms in the new hotels and B&Bs that sprang up seemingly overnight, and spending money in shops and restaurants that began to fill up long-empty buildings along Main Street. New businesses began to sprout east and west of Main, all on Montforte land, making Sam and Corinne two of the richest and most influential people in town. The last few years, Shambles had even begun expanding beyond the original downtown.

Montforte had recently started promoting an exclusive new housing development called Spring Meadows Estates in the expansive flatlands along the river east of town. Three and five-acre plots, at prices no one from Shambles could afford, were being snapped up by people looking for vacation home property. Plans even called for a strip mall, featuring boutique shops and services for anyone who didn't want to drive the whole half-mile into town.

Five years ago, Tim and Tina Spangler were among those early out-of-state tourists. They fell in love with the area. Tim saw opportunity in the booming new tourist town. He convinced Tina to sell everything back home in Portland and open Spangler's Cyclery two blocks off the south end of Main Street, right next to the main trailhead. As the only bike shop in town, their investment began paying off almost immediately, and they quickly became one of the most successful businesses in town.

By the time Will returned, Shambles had officially risen from the dead. Mountain biking was by far the most popular activity, and the town was packed with riders from June through October. The only problem was no one had thought to organize the spider web of trails and roads into a system that people could understand. Will had grown up on those trails and knew them better than anyone else in town, so when he began offering his services as a trail guide his list of clients quickly grew. Recognizing a good thing when the saw it, Tim and Tina hired Will as their new Chief Trail Guide, but it didn't take long for them to discover he was also a whiz at fixing bikes.

Even now, cruising up Main Street, he still marveled at the makeover the town had received. Plain-faced buildings were restored with Old West facades and synthetic wood plank sidewalks had been installed. McCoy's Hardware became a Mercantile – the words on the big, red sign painted to look like they were made up of little logs, with a crossed pick and shovel at one end and a miner's gold pan at the other.

Nye's Department Store became a Country Emporium, and the soda fountain that occupied the front corner of the first floor added sarsaparilla to their menu. And even though Marv's Diner was serving the same food they always had, the names of all the dishes were changed to reflect the Old West theme everyone was now clamoring for.

The old Assay Office at the corner of Hill and Main had been home to a run-down Mexican restaurant until last summer. Now, a pair of young men maneuvered a ladder into place to hang a large wooden trout out front announcing the opening of a new flyfishing store. He made a mental note to check it out.

It wasn't as if Shambles really looked like this at any time in the past. It had been a dirt-poor mining town, not some western movie set. Will told Amy Sturgis, the local photographer who spent most of her time shooting tourists riding the trails, she ought to put some life-sized cutouts of JoŠ Wayne and other western movie stars around town so the tourists could have their pictures taken beside them. She just gave him that smarmy look she gave everyone who tried to make a joke at her expense and asked if he'd like to pose for one dressed as his namesake. That shut him up real fast. The one thing Will hated more than anything else was being reminded of his ancestry.

CHAPTER 7

Twenty minutes later, decked out in full riding gear, Will flew out of his driveway on his Novara. The Ridge Runner trailhead was just a block north of his house, and from there he could connect with over a hundred miles of trails and dirt roads that crisscrossed the foothills and mountains west of Shambles. It was one of the largest hiking and mountain biking trail systems in the northwest, and he knew almost every inch of it like the back of his hand.

He pushed hard up the first steep ascent, letting the sun warm him, feeling his muscles loosen and relax. Memories of the Captain caught up with him and he pushed harder, hoping to leave them behind. But they were still too raw, and as he dropped his bike to a lower gear, his mind also shifted, from sadness over his best friend's death to anger at whoever had murdered him. As a Ranger he'd witnessed enough interrogations and fought more than his share of hand-to-hand battles to conjure up images of what he might do to the murderer if he found him before the law caught up to him. He shifted gears again and pushed those thoughts out of his mind, knowing the Captain had taught him better.

His brain reeled through a montage of mug shots of all the boys he could remember who had spent time at the Ranch and any number of other criminals that had crossed the Sheriff's path during his three decades in law enforcement. But for the life of him he couldn't come up with one single person he thought capable of doing something so terrible to such a wonderful man.

By the time he reached the tree line his skin was prickling with sweat. He forced himself to stop contemplating theories about the murder and who might be responsible. The possibilities seemed endless, and he hadn't even been around for the last ten years of Linehart's tenure as Sheriff.

After a mile or so the slope leveled out somewhat, and he pumped hard up the Crossfire Trail, a long sweeping ridge that angled north and west, gradually rising above the trees. The air had cooled but sweat was rolling off him in rivulets. He welcomed the burn in his legs and arms and fought off more another onslaught of memories by pedaling harder. His breathing evened out with the terrain, growing deep and smooth, and one of his songs pushed its way into his consciousness. It seemed to match the rhythm of his pedals.

Why she left me I don't know
Wonderin' when I'll feel the blow
She said our love was on overload
She said goodbye, and on I rode

It was mid-afternoon by the time he reached the upper end of the wide circle known as the Ponderosa Loop that ran north and south around the outer edge of the trail system. His breathing was ragged, t-shirt soaked. Sweat ran freely down his face and neck and dripped out from under his helmet. He stopped on a rim and looked out over a fertile, oval-shaped valley about a quarter mile cross and nearly twice as long and the last twenty-four hours came flooding back over him like spring runoff down Latham Canyon.

At the south end sat the blackened skeletons of the bunkhouses and the Captain's house, flanked by the old red barn, looking almost out of place without the other structures. Funny how peaceful it all looked from up there. Visions of the fire flickered behind his eyes, but he fought them down. He took a long drink from his water bottle and squirted some more on his face as he waited for his breathing to settle back to normal.

The mountains of the Boise National Forest rolled away to the north, and eastward the distant peaks of the ragged Sawtooth Mountains rose majestically above the surrounding mountaintops. McKinley Creek wound its way down through the Ponderosa pine and Douglas fir that blanketed the rugged slopes that formed the western border of the valley.

A large grove of aspen and cottonwoods at the southeast corner of the ranch caused the creek to fork off and head east down Latham Canyon, dropping through a cut in the rolling hills where the south and east boundaries of the valley came together until it finally dumped into the Middle Fork of the Boise River on the far side of Shambles.

The road running past the ranch property was one of dozens that had been carved throughout these mountains by gold-hungry prospectors 150 years before. As it climbed up into the mountains beyond the valley it splintered along the ridges and into the canyons where those fortune hunters lucky enough to make a strike later widened it with wagons hauling their plunder out to the smelter. Once the gold played out, several of the fingers had been extended further up for use as logging roads. In time, a few of them connected with other logging roads that crept up from the Boise Basin on the other side of the mountains.

The valley was as beautiful a spot as any Will had ever seen. He couldn't blame the Captain for spending every dime he ever made to get his hands on it when he first came to Placer County. It was a damn shame someone had prevented him from enjoying it a little more than a year into his retirement, and Will vowed then and there to find whoever did it, no matter what it took.

A flash of sunlight reflecting off something down the valley caught his eye. It was gone as quickly as it came, but as he continued to scan the flat, open ground, he spotted a white pickup truck driving off the road and into the middle of the field north of the ranch. What the hell would someone be doing out there? He took one more drink of water and then dropped down a splinter trail that led to an old fire road on the backside of the Loop, which in turn connected to the main valley road. It was a tricky drop but one he had made many times before, and curiosity made him attack it aggressively.

Once he was on flat terrain, he sped up, and as he got closer, he could see a man kneeling in front of the truck a hundred yards out in the field, studying the ground. Will spotted the truck tracks where the man had pulled off the road and followed them out into the field. He felt on edge, as if he were confronting a trespasser. In fact, he was, but the Captain had never paid much attention to people poking around the ranch, so why should he?

He pulled up beside the big, new Dodge Ram 3500 and the man approached him out of the sun, forcing Will to shield his eyes. Even in silhouette he could see the man was well over six feet and built like a bull. A broad tan Stetson kept his face in shadow, but Will marked his well-worn cowboy boots and faded Levi's. He moved with the comfortable stride of someone used walking over rough country. He appeared to be around fifty, and though his smile was friendly enough, his dark eyes peering out from under bushy eyebrows told another story. Something about him made Will uneasy.

"Morning," said the man, a wide smile crinkling his weather-lined face. "Something I can do for you?"

Will felt his face flush, angry that the man had suddenly made him feel like he was somewhere he wasn't supposed to be instead of the other way around. "Yeah, you can tell me what you're doing out here."

The terse question didn't seem to faze the man.

"Just looking things over," he replied casually, pulling a can of chew from his shirt pocket. "Why do you ask?"

"This is private property. Who gave you permission?"

"Wasn't aware I needed any." He stuck a wad of chew inside his lip and wiped his hand on his jeans. "This your land?"

"No, but it belongs to a friend of mine."

The smile faded as he stuck the can back in his shirt pocket. "That would be Mr. Linehart. Please accept my condolences."

Will was surprised the man knew about the Captain's death. It hadn't even been twenty-four hours. Still, he knew word spread fast in a small town like Shambles. But despite the man's apparent friendliness Will felt like he was missing something.

"Sheriff Yeager said he thought it would be all right if I poked around out here for a bit," the man continued. "Don't mean any harm. I was just about to leave, anyway."

Will's protective instinct kicked in and he felt a sudden need to know more about this stranger. "What is it you're looking for? Maybe I can help."

"No thanks," said the man, spitting a wad of brown juice off to his left. "Like I said, I was just looking things over, Mr....?" He let the question hang, and once again Will felt like he was somewhere he shouldn't be.

"Hickock. Will Hickock. And you are...?"

The man gave him a half-smile and touched a finger to the brim of his hat. "Reckon I'll be on my way. Sorry for any trouble." He casually slid inside his truck and Will watched him drive off, trying to figure out what made him instinctively dislike the man. He took a walk around the area and noticed a few freshly pulled clumps of grass. The trail of dust from the white Dodge rose up past the barn as he disappeared down the canyon toward town.

CHAPTER 8

Will rode back up into the hills past the ranch and picked up the north end of Ponderosa Loop where it ran along a ridge that above Latham Canyon and the long-abandoned smelter. The giant concrete structure sat just under a mile up from town in the winding, narrow canyon carved by Miners Creek. Seeing it always brought to mind stories from his high school years about wild, all-night parties full of booze and drugs.

The Captain had tried for years to convince the Town Council that such goings-on were a bad idea. He believed they only served to create more young offenders in an already troubled town. The Council always agreed, but they never seemed to get around to taking any action. It took a drug overdose by a Council member's daughter to get them to let the Captain lock it down tight. Now the smelter was home only to the birds that nested in its rafters and whatever other critters could burrow or otherwise maneuver their way inside.

Will pulled up on a bluff overlooking the rambling hulk of a structure, still pretty much intact, sitting back from the road on a flat patch of ground about a hundred and fifty yards across that had been carved out of the steep side hill. From the outside, it resembled a giant warehouse, longer than a football field and over fifty feet high. The whole thing, including the rounded rooftop, was covered with thick, industrial-strength aluminum siding.

He was about to continue down the Loop trail away from the smelter when he heard a car coming up the canyon. A moment later the Sheriff Department's ageing black-and-white Chevy Impala rounded a curve and, to his surprise, pulled into the smelter turnout, disappearing behind the building. Curiosity got the better of him and he took a smaller, lesser-used track that dropped precariously down to the smelter parking lot.

As he started the descent a fresh bike track caught his eye. Someone had been down it recently and judging from the way the trail was torn up they were using too much brake, like an inexperienced rider might. The slope was steep, but a series of switchbacks kept it from being overly dangerous. It was a good early out for bikers coming up from town who didn't want to make a full day of it on the higher trail. A quick drop to Latham Canyon Road and they could coast downhill back to town on smooth pavement.

Will followed the fresh track off the trail and around the smelter to where the black-and-white was now parked. He figured the driver had to be Pacheko, the Sheriff was way too covetous of the big Excursion SUV to drive anything else. There was no way he wanted to confront Yeager again, but he was most likely still down in Boise reporting to the State Police. Assuming the arson inspector was right, the Captain's murder would set off alarm bells in every law enforcement office across the state.

He debated for a moment whether or not to venture inside. He'd had just about all he could handle with law enforcement already that day, but there was something about the way the new deputy stood up to his boss earlier that morning made Will curious to know more about him.

The huge sliding door that hung across the main entrance on a foot-wide steel rail was at least thirty feet square, big enough to let the giant ore trucks pull inside to dump their loads. A smaller, hinged wooden door mounted in the lower right corner stood ajar, a heavy chain and open padlock hanging from its latch. Will leaned his bike against the building and cautiously poked his head inside.

The only light streamed through two rows of large, mostly broken out windows that lined longer sides of the building about forty feet up, and it took a moment for his eyes to adjust. He peered around the huge, empty space but saw no one. Stepping inside he bumped the door, banging it against the wall. The sound amplified ten-fold in the empty space and brought forth a flutter of wings from the pigeons roosting in the rafters.

In a split second he was back in Iraq. His combat training immediately kicked in and he quickly took cover behind a wide concrete bunker as if he expected to be shot at any moment. It took a few moments for him to remember where he was, and he shook his head, surprised at how jumpy he was. The Captain's death and his subsequent arrest had obviously gotten to him more than he realized. When there was no reaction after a minute or so the adrenaline spike began to fade, and he stepped back out into the open.

He had seen the interior of the old relic only once before. He couldn't have been more than ten or twelve at the time, but he instantly recalled the musty smell of dust and bird droppings mixed with the lingering odor of cyanide and other chemicals that had leached into the soil during eighty-plus years of processing gold and silver ore.

The giant, architectural skeleton of rough-hewn, wooden beams that supported the walls and roof seemed even more massive than he remembered, and the spider web of catwalks that once gave workers overhead access to giant crushers, grinders, leaching vats and other equipment still looked dizzyingly high and precarious. At the far end of the building, slightly smaller beams framed a stack of boxy rooms, three stories high against the back wall. The first level sat up three steps onto a wide landing. A heavy wooden staircase rose to the upper two levels, then continued on up to connect with the catwalks above that. He tried to imagine what the vast space must have looked like in full operation.

The sudden shut-down brought about by Henry Latham's disappearance had caught investors and employees alike by surprise, and the ten million dollars he'd taken with him left them all high and dry. Will remembered his mother telling him that most of them had soon left town to find other work to support their families, but a small group of workers agreed to stay on to try and save what they could. Led by Latham's widow, Sarah, they declared the building and its equipment salvage, and sold off everything they could, distributing whatever money they received in equal shares.

The place had been stripped bare in a couple of years and the Latham Mining Company was dissolved. The only thing remaining was this shell of a building which apparently wasn't worth the trouble or the expense to tear down.

"Something else, isn't it?"

The voice, echoing out of the darkness at the far end of the building, made Will jump and suck in a mouthful of dusty air. Over his coughing, he heard a soft laugh float through the air, and he looked up to see Pacheko step into a shaft of sunlight on the landing.

"Sorry, didn't mean to scare you," said the deputy.

Will cleared his throat and started walking toward the deputy. "I thought maybe I startled you when I bumped that big door."

"That was you? I thought it was just the wind."

The deputy studied him as he approached wearing a curious expression that made Will feel inclined to explain his presence. "I was riding on the trail above when I saw you pull in. I was just curious what you'd be doing in this old hulk."

"I came by to check it out for Stu English," Pacheko said. "You know him?"

"Sure, everyone does. He's made damn sure of that by trying to buy up whatever property Montforte doesn't already own. Why's he interested in this place?"

"I don't really know. Marcia said he was very hush-hush about it. All he told her is that he wants to know if it's structurally safe."

Will took another look around at the exposed beams and metal shafts, thinking none of it looked too stable. "Safe from what? I doubt anyone's been in here since the Captain shut down the last party back when I was in high school."

The deputy looked around the vast space and smiled his crooked smile. "Yeah, I can see where this would be a righteous place for a kegger. But to answer your question, I have no idea. I guess Stu just wants to make sure he won't run into any man-eating jackrabbits."

Will couldn't help but grin as he watched the deputy make his way toward the rooms at the back of the landing. Where the hell was this guy from anyway, using words like righteous and pronto?

"I've been curious what the inside of this place looked like," Pacheko said shoving open a creaky door and peering into the darkness inside. "Ever been in here before?"

"Once, when I was just a kid," said Will, climbing up onto the landing. Pacheko's footprints were the only marks in the thick layer of dust that covered the broad wood planks, and virtually everything else. It didn't take an expert to realize that no one else had been here in many, many years.

"The Captain and I were out fishing when he got a call about a bunch of high school kids having a kegger up here. It was pretty common practice back then. He chased them all out and confiscated their beer."

"Ouch," Pacheko joked.

Will gave him a one-sided smile and the deputy cocked his head to one side, contemplating whether to ask the question on his mind or not. After a moment, he decided to go ahead. "You should probably know I looked up your file."

Will didn't know whether to feel betrayed or relieved. "I kind of figured you would, me being Yeager's number one suspect and all."

Pacheko gave a half-laugh. "Yeah, listen, about that…"

Will cut him off, anger flaring up in his cheeks. "So now you think you know everything there is to know about me?"

The deputy didn't seem to notice his harsh tone. "Not hardly, it's sealed. But you already knew that."

Will stifled a self-satisfied smile and stepped around him to look inside the room himself. It was completely empty. He reminded himself he needed to keep his anger in check. The deputy may be new in town, but he was a deputy after all. "Any luck with those other files you were going to check out?"

"Not yet. But going back thirty years will take some time." He waited for Will to come back out of the office. "Marcia tells me you and the Captain were really close."

Will felt tears well up in his eyes and turned away, his throat suddenly too tight to speak. Pacheko immediately regretted his decision. "Sorry," he said. "Too soon. I never was very good in the tact department."

Will sniffed, then wiped his eyes, turning to face the deputy. "It's all right," he conceded. "What else did she tell you?"

Pacheko cocked his head to one side. "Enough to know never to call you Wild Bill." He offered a shy grin that almost brought a smile to Will's lips. "Sounds like she knew your mom pretty well."

"Yeah, she was just about her only friend after…" He let the sentence trail off, lost in a memory.

"After the payroll robbery?" Pacheko ventured.

Will looked over at him, his eyes narrowing. "You said my file was sealed."

"Newspapers aren't."

Will took a deep breath. "Yeah, well, after that the whole town sort of shut her out of their lives. It wasn't exactly like she was on everyone's social calendar anyway, but even the folks who used to hire her for sewing or other stuff cut her off. Marcia was just about the only one who stuck by her."

"Must have been tough."

"Yeah, must have been. I wouldn't know, I wasn't around."

"What do you mean? Didn't they let you see her from time to time?"

"They would have, I guess, but then she…" His throat constricted again, and he stopped, not wanting to go there. "Just how much did Marcia tell you?"

"Pretty much the whole enchilada, up until you joined the Army. It couldn't have been easy for you, growing up incarcerated."

"The Ranch wasn't so bad, really. The Captain was a decent warden and it was good, honest work. I was way younger than anyone else there, so he kind of took me under his wing and pretty much raised me after that. Saved my life if you want to know the truth."

Pacheko pondered his next comment a few moments before speaking. "Your brother sounds like a real piece of work, leaving you there like that."

Will's nose wrinkled like he'd just picked up a bad smell. "I suppose you checked out his file, too."

Pacheko nodded. "Once he died the seal was broken. It's pretty thick for a guy who died before he turned eighteen. He was a busy boy."

Will grunted. "And that's just the times he got caught."

He walked over and stuck his head inside the other doorway off the landing, leaving Pacheko standing alone. This room was larger than he expected, stretching half the width of the building. Rusty metal lockers lined one wall, most hanging open, their contents long since gone. Pieces of broken wooden folding chairs were piled in one corner and a pair of tattered couches, springs sticking out of filthy cushions chewed apart by who knows what kind of varmint, sat opposite each other in the middle of the room.

He could almost hear the voices of workers eating a meal, playing cards, talking about their wives and girlfriends. He stepped back out on the landing and pointed to the upper offices. "Anything interesting up there?"

The question jarred Pacheko out of his thoughts. "I haven't gone up any further, but I'm guessing it's more empty rooms. Offices most likely. They cleaned the place out pretty well. Take a look if you want."

"No thanks, this place gives me the creeps. I keep thinking the whole thing is going to collapse any minute."

"Are you kidding?" Pacheko exclaimed gazing up at the rafters. "Those beams would hold ten times this weight. I've never seen construction like that. Looks like they just took whole trees and squared them off. It's amazing."

For some reason the deputy's apparent knowledge of construction surprised Will. Yet another layer peeled back on the new guy in town. Pacheko looked out over the vast space. "Imagine what it must have been like to work here."

"Yeah, long hours, low pay, breathing cyanide fumes all day. Sounds like a ton of fun."

Pacheko laughed and they made their way back to the entrance. As they stepped outside, Will spotted a set of tracks near the door that didn't belong to either of them and knelt down for a closer look.

"Looks like someone else was checking this place out."

Pacheko secured the door with the chain and padlock, then peered over Will's shoulder.

"These are bike shoe prints," Will said. "See the narrow heel? And those deep indentations at the front were made by toe clips."

"Yeah?" said Pacheko. He recaledl Marcia's comment about Will and tracks and leaned in for a closer look.

"I followed a fairly recent bike track down from the ridge," Will continued, pointing out that it ended right next to where Will's Novara was parked. The shoe tracks led from there to the door, where it looked like the rider stood for a while, no doubt checking out the padlock, then continued on down the side of the building.

"They're bigger than mine, and just as deep, so I'd say it was most likely a man. Looks like he favors his left leg a little."

"You're kidding me, right?" There was skepticism in his voice, but he walked over for a closer look.

"See that little twist in the left shoe," Will said, pointing. "He's probably got a slight limp."

"You can tell that?" The deputy leaned in, studying the marks in the dirt.

"It's easier to spot because of the mark left by the toe clip. Could be he's just sore from riding." He stood up and walked over to his bike. "You can see there where his bike tracks pick up again." A few feet beyond the end of the building they joined several other tracks headed for the canyon road. "A lot of riders come down this way and take the easy coast back to town on the pavement."

"I suppose you can tell what time he left, too."

Will frowned at the sarcasm. "No more than a couple of days ago."

Pacheko's eyebrows went up. "Seriously?" Will gave a nonchalant shrug, and the deputy shook his head. "You sound like one of those Indian scouts in the old westerns."

"You can thank the Captain for that, he was an expert tracker. Every time we went out fishing or hunting, he made me identify every damn mark on the ground. He was a fanatic about it. It wasn't enough to name the animal, I had to tell him how big it was, how old the tracks were, it drove me crazy but I learned. Getting it right was the only way to shut him up."

Will walked a wide circle around the smelter entrance and found a different set of footprints leading away from the smelter entrance to the other side of the deputy's cruiser. He motioned the deputy over. "What do you see?"

Pacheko knelt down and studied the tire tracks. "Now, vehicle tracks I've had some experience with. This is either a small truck or an SUV. Would I be right in saying they look new?"

Will nodded. "Not bad. Could be Stu. I'd bet the tire tracks will match his new Forester." He followed the boot tracks back to the smelter entrance, where they mingled with all the others. "These were made after the bike shoes. I'd say no more than a day ago."

"How the hell can you tell that?"

"See how the boots always overlap the bike shoes." He pointed to where the two sets of prints intersected. "And if you look closely, you can see much more detail in the hiking boot prints. The others have been worn down more by the wind."

Pacheko squatted beside him. "I can't see any difference."

"Neither could I when I first started doing this with the Captain."

The deputy looked skeptical. "You sure you're not just bullshitting me?"

Will shrugged. "It takes a while."

Pacheko studied the tracks again, getting his face right down on top of them, but came away shaking his head. "Pretty impressive I have to say."

Will smiled at the compliment. Pacheko stood up and brushed off the knees of his pants. "Well, I'd better be getting back to the office. The Sheriff's on his way back from Boise and wants me at tonight's Town Council meeting with him. Thanks for the lesson. Marcia was right, you do know your stuff."

Will watched him drive off, wondering what it was about this guy that made it so hard not to like him? The black and white disappeared down the canyon and Will climbed on his bike. He looked up at the hard climb back to the ridge trail and realized his legs were starting to stiffen up, so he opted for the easy out.

He was just about to turn onto the road when a white Dodge pickup roared around the corner and sped past him down the canyon. Will recognized the truck immediately and got a clear look at the driver's face beneath the straw Stetson. It was definitely the same guy he saw up at the Captain's place. For a split second he thought about following him, but there was no way he could keep up on his bike. He made a mental note to tell Pacheko about him and turned the Novara loose.

Moments later he was flying down the paved road, sitting tall, hands hanging by his side, steering through the curves with the weight of his body, feeling free. But he knew it the feeling wouldn't last forever. The weight of the Captain's death was right behind him, fighting to catch up.

I've been chewed up and spit out
Thrown down and laid out

LOOSE ENDS

But I keep comin' back for more.

I've been stood up and put down.
But I still keep turning 'round
Hopin' to see you comin' right back through my door.

CHAPTER 9

The sun was just dropping behind the western mountain peaks when Will flew out of the mouth of the canyon, but it would be another three or four hours until darkness enveloped the river valley far below them. It had been one hell of a day, and though the ride had worked most of the tension out of his body, his mind was still reeling with the loss of the Captain and Yeager's boneheaded accusation that he was the murderer.

He tried to push those depressing thoughts out of his head, but they just wouldn't go. At least, not all the way. Strange, he'd seen so much death, and caused so much during his deployments in the Middle East that he thought he'd be used to it by now. But this one had hit home hard. His sorrow went all the way into his bones, and it didn't feel like it was going away any time soon.

There were no cars to be seen so he took the right-hand turn onto High Street wide and hard, the rush of wind on his face giving him a momentary sense of freedom from the turmoil that had overturned his life. He coasted past the first block then hung a left on Second Street and turned onto the two cracked concrete tracks that constituted his driveway two houses down.

Even the oldest locals had forgotten how this section of town came to be called the Hill. The eight rows of almost identical small houses were originally bult to house workers at the Latham Mining Company. Miners were a transient lot, always moving from place to place in a vain search for that elusive big strike. Those diehards who refused to give up their search or, in some cases, simply had nowhere else to go, often ended up working in the smelter. If they couldn't afford to pay rent the company would gladly deduct it from their paychecks.

The company was also happy to sell the houses to those with the wherewithal to land a mortgage from the bank. Of course, back then the company owned the bank, too, so it didn't really matter much to them, one way or the other. A few, including Will's mother, LuAnn, were smart enough to realize that paying down a mortgage was a lot better than dumping money down the black hole of rent, never to be seen again.

She's always told them their father thought it was a waste of money, but the boys knew there were some things you just didn't butt heads with LuAnn about. It didn't matter who ended up with the money, what mattered was she would always have a home for her two boys. It took the better part of twenty years, but her plan finally worked out. For Will at least.

The houses were laid out in a loose grid covering the broad, open slope that swept up to the base of the mountains at the northwest corner of town. Each row contained four single-story one-and-two-bedroom homes. Over the years many had been replaced with brick structures to better withstand the test of time, but always on the same footprint of land.

Being situated on one of the uppermost blocks gave Will a spectacular view of Shambles, sitting peacefully in the long valley stretching away from town at both ends. When the sun rose over the eastern mountains each morning his was one of the first homes to be lit. It was the house he would have grown up in with his mom and brother, if fate hadn't intervened.

As long as gold and silver mining represented Shambles' primary source of income, every house on the Hill was occupied. When his father left, Doc was still too young to go to work, and Will had just been born. The company took pity on a woman trying to raise two young boys on her own and let them stay on as long as they kept up the mortgage payments.

When the smelter closed a few years later it didn't take long for the shabby houses to empty out. The mining company was scrambling to salvage what it could from its investment in the town and offered them up for a pretty good price. But in a town beginning its death throes, buyers were scarce and most of the homes were simply abandoned. LuAnn had nowhere else to go, so she took on any kind of work she could find to keep up the mortgage payments. He remembered with great fondness the night she announced over dinner that the final payment had been made and the house was all theirs. No matter what happened now, she had said proudly they would always have a roof over their heads.

Less than a month later one son was dead, and the other was incarcerated at the Ranch for armed robbery. Everything she had done—working two or three jobs at a time, battling all her health problems—had all been done for her boys, so they could live a decent life. Suddenly, that was all gone. What was the point of going on? It still gnawed on Will when he thought about the grief he and his brother had brought her. He blamed himself, even if he was only seven at the time, but he blamed Doc even more, and figured his brother got exactly what he deserved.

He leaned his bike against the side of the house next to his pickup, which was where the two-track driveway ended, and stepped out to the middle of a miniscule patch of front lawn to start his stretching routine. He'd learned the hard way that leg muscles not loosened after a long ride could develop persistent cramps, which in turn put odd stresses on the joints, especially the knees. Will's knees were a very important part of keeping his bills paid, not to mention achieving the solitude his soul craved, and he wasn't about to screw them up.

He spotted Stu English's red Subaru Outback parked in Marv Bowman's driveway a block down the street. He and Bowman were the last two holdouts on the Hill who owned their homes outright. No doubt Stu was making another offer to buy the place. Bowman owned Marv's Diner down on Main Street, and he was well past retirement age. If Bowman caved, Stu would really put pressure on Will to sell as well. Good luck with that. He was perfectly happy right where he was.

Stu was a Midwest transplant, one of a select group of newcomers Will liked to call leeches, who moved in to take advantage of the boomtown market created by a burgeoning tourist industry. He was convinced he was God's gift to salesmen and that Shambles was the shortest way to real estate nirvana. By the time he'd arrived in town, four or five years before Will returned home, Sam Montforte already owned pretty much all the prime land available in and around the town. But Stu wasn't daunted. He dug in and did his homework, then introduced himself to Sarah Latham.

Sarah was in her late fifties when her husband absconded with his ill-gotten millions two decades earlier, and she had never worked a day in her life. Henry had always taken good care of her, but after he was gone, all she had left was their four-bedroom home in an older, though still respectable part of town, and a few thousand dollars in a bank account. The son-of-a-bitch had left her high and dry, and she wanted him out of her life forever. She had Henry declared legally dead on the very first day following the seven-year waiting period required by law, and in the meantime, she hired a lawyer.

She knew Henry owned the Hill properties and the smelter operation outright, and by rights they should go to her, but some of the smelter investors had hired a lawyer of their own and claimed they were owed something for all the time and money they had put into the business. She didn't like the idea of them having to walk away with nothing any more than they did, so she offered to let them sell off all the smelter equipment, as long as she got an equal cut of the proceeds. An agreement was reached, and that, along with her Social Security benefits, had allowed her to scrape by over the years.

Through all this, no one had given the pitiful company houses a second thought, much less any kind of maintenance. They were basically worthless and growing more and more dilapidated as time went by. Not long after the mountain bikers started arriving, Stu showed up on her doorstep and convinced her that her ship had finally come in.

Of the thirty-two, single story houses, almost twenty were still livable. Four of those, including Will's, were privately still owned. With

Sarah's permission, Stu started investing some sweat equity, along with some of his own money, into fixing up several of the vacant houses, and marketing them as cheap rentals for the tourists. Business was good and as more and more mountain bikers poured into the area each summer demand for the houses continued to grow. Wisely, Stu poured some of their newfound wealth into repairing some of the other homes.

After a few years, Stu had made enough to begin buying the properties from the widow Latham a few at a time. Some thought he was taking advantage of an old woman who was pushing eighty, but she wasn't complaining. She had no children to leave anything to, the arrangement kept her in more than enough cash to live very comfortably, and Stu's real estate business kept growing. Everyone was happy, and the naysayers gradually faded away.

Stu had made several casual offers on Will's house since he'd come home, but Will wouldn't even discuss it. Where else was he going to go? At first, Stu passed it off by claiming that having a combat veteran in the neighborhood boosted his image in the community. Lately, though, there were rumors that once he owned the entire slope, he was planning to tear everything down and build a huge new development of some kind.

Stu never confirmed or denied the rumors, claiming it was all very hush hush, and his mysterious developer partners didn't want any details on the project released until he was ready to break ground. Will wasn't the only one who thought Stu might just be blowing smoke about his big plans. But to hear Stu talk, ten acres, right on the edge of the best mountain bike trail system in the northwest would be worth millions given the way the town was growing. Talk about your ship coming in.

Will finished stretching just as Stu pulled up in front of his house and leaned out the window. "Got a minute, Hickock?"

"How many times do I have to tell you, Stu," Will said as he strolled over to the car, "I'm not interested in selling."

Stu grinned. "Just thought you should know that old man Bowman just signed on the dotted line. That makes you the last man standing."

"And I plan on standing for a long time to come, right here on my own property."

"I might be able to come up a bit on my offer if it would get you off the dime."

"Since when?"

Stu leaned further out the window, a conspiratorial look on his face. "You never heard me say this, but I've got a developer out of San Francisco interested in this property. He and his partners have done more than a dozen developments in resort towns around the West. They've got very deep pockets."

"Give it up, Stu," said Will with a laugh. "I've heard the rumors. You're wasting your time."

"Hey, you don't ask, you don't get," Stu shrugged. "I see you've been out riding. Trails in good shape?"

"Yep, all ready for the onslaught. First big group comes in next week, and then it'll be Katie-bar-the-door for the next five months."

"Tell me about it," Stu said with a grin, "I'm already booking rentals into August." His expression grew serious. "Don't suppose you've seen any strangers poking around, have you?"

"What do you mean?"

"Ray Parker, down at the Town Council, let slip the other day that someone's been talking to some of the ranchers around here about oil and gas leases along the front. The Town Council's taking it up tonight. I'm headed down there now."

"Wasn't Sam Montforte pushing for some kind of exploratory drilling down in the foothills a while back?"

"Down there, yeah, but he's got way too much invested in this town to allow that to happen up here. I confronted him about it just last week and he got all up in my face. Said he would never jeopardize the town's new livelihood."

"I did run into a suspicious character up at the Captain's ranch today. Tall guy wearing a Stetson and cowboy boots, big white pickup, I told him it was private property, and he apologized and left. Funny thing, though, he wouldn't give me his name or tell me what he was looking for."

"What was he doing exactly?"

"Looked like he'd been pulling up clumps of grass."

"You think he could have been taking soil samples?"

"Maybe."

Stu smacked his steering wheel. "Damnit! It's not enough we've got a murder to kick off our busy season, now we've got the land men coming in. This could be a disaster."

"Land men?"

"These big gas and oil companies get a whiff of something, and they send in freelance geologists to start poking around, taking soil samples. The next thing you know we're the next big energy resource site. I've seen what happens when a bunch of damned drilling crews show up. They'll literally take over a town. The tourist business would be gone in a heartbeat.

"Along with your new development."

Stu slanted his eyes at Will. "Do not, I repeat, do not spread that around. It could kill the whole deal."

Will held up his hands. "Ok, ok, mum's the word."

"I appreciate that. A white pickup, you say?"

"Yeah, a big Dodge Ram. No signage on it that I saw."

Stu smacked the steering wheel again. "Damnit, I'd better talk to the sheriff." He punched the gas and roared off toward town.

Will wheeled his bike past his pickup and around to the back of his house. He opened the door on a small storage shed in the corner of his back yard and parked it inside, hanging his helmet off the handlebars. The back door of his house opened into a small, neat kitchen. The faded linoleum floor and countertops had been there since he was a boy, as had the square, wooden kitchen table and three matching chairs, that sat next to a window on the back wall. His mother's dishes and silverware were all still in the cupboards, but by the time he came home to stay a few months before, the stove and refrigerator were beyond salvage, and he had to replace them.

A narrow hallway next to the kitchen led to a tiny bedroom at the rear of the house that still held the bunk beds he and Doc slept in as boys. His mother's bedroom was at the other end of the hall at the front of the house and a small bathroom with barely enough room for a bathtub, sink and toilet occupied the space between. Will peeled off his sweaty shirt and turned on the shower head above the tub to let the water warm up. He still felt a little weird living in his mother's room, but he tried not to think about it. Tossing his riding clothes into a plastic laundry basket next to the closet he stepped back to the bathroom to shower.

He was barely eight when his mother died, and the loss hit him hard. Much moreso than the death of his brother. He was still angry with Doc for deserting him, even though he realized that had he fled with him he would most likely be dead now as well. Besides, Doc had never treated him like anything more than a tool to attain his own ill-gotten gains.

He knew his mother had always loved him and looked out for him. She'd tried to protect him from his brother's evil ways, even though she had been consumed by her illness and figuring out ways to keep a roof over their heads. Ever since he was arrested, he'd felt bad about disappointing her, and now that she was gone, too, the guilt was almost overwhelming. At the funeral, when they buried her next to Doc, he had never felt so alone and lonely in his young life.

As the sole surviving son, the house and its contents, had gone to him. The Captain had to drive him to town from the Ranch to meet with a lawyer and co-sign as the boy's guardian so Will could take ownership. The lawyer had suggested that, given Will's circumstances, they put it in a trust until he was of age. Still distraught over his mother's death, Will had simply shrugged and deferred to the Captain.

So, the house had been locked up and left alone until he came home from the Army six months earlier. All he had to do was sign some paperwork and the place was his. It wasn't much, but aside from a duffel bag filled with his Army uniforms, a couple pairs of jeans and a few t-shirts, it was all he had. For a while it felt weird living there all by himself, especially after being gone for so many years, but it was gradually starting to feel like home again.

After toweling off, a quick shave rid him of two days' worth of facial hair. He had hoped cleaning up would wash away some of his depression over the events of the last twenty-four hours, but although his body felt refreshed, the death of the Captain had caused a rip in his soul that he knew nothing but time would bring about whatever healing there was to be had. Back in the bedroom he slipped on a pair of jeans and grabbed a clean t-shirt from his chest of drawers, wandering into the living room as he slipped it over his head.

It was the largest room in the house, although large was something of a misnomer. A small picture window looked out onto the street in front of the house, and a well-worn couch from a long-ago era sat opposite, against the kitchen wall. Flanking it on the bedroom wall was an equally old and abused easy chair, and in the corner between them an antique end table held his mother's favorite porcelain lamp, its once-white shade now beige with age. A scratched and chipped wooden coffee table sat in front of them.

He was a fairly neat housekeeper, although there wasn't really much to keep tidy. Most of his mother's furniture was in pretty bad shape when he moved back in. He was able to salvage a few things, but the rest of it ended up in the dump. The replacement pieces he had picked up from a second-hand store in Boise and hauled up in his pickup hardly filled the place up, but his decorating budget was also on the downlow. Way down low.

. He'd been deployed for most of his time in the Army and given that he wasn't exactly what you'd call a social animal, he always stuck pretty close to the base wherever he was stationed, so he'd managed to save up a little money. The only thing remotely new in the room was the desktop computer he'd finally given in and bought after his bike was paid off. It sat atop a beat-up desk in front of the picture window next to the front door. He'd bought some songwriting software, but had yet to learn how to use it.

He sat down in the missing fourth chair from the kitchen table and woke up the computer. As usual, there were no new messages. He had taught himself to surf the net, sort of, but he was still having trouble with e-mail. Of course, it would help if he had someone to send a message to.

The faded wallpaper was still adorned with cheap prints of faraway places his mother had always wished she could visit. He kept them up because they reminded him of her, and he liked that. A small table next to the worn, overstuffed chair still held the small collection of family photos she had cherished. Any in which his father appeared had long since been removed, but there were a few shots of him and Doc as young boys, one with their mother, and two of his mother's parents, whom Will had never met in person. His only memories of them were fuzzy voices on a telephone held to his small ear as his mother urged him to say something to his grandpa and grandma.

Off to one side, and looking a little out of place, was a shot of Will and the Captain, taken after a particularly successful day of trout fishing. They each held a substantial string of trout. Will picked it up and gazed sadly at it for a while, remembering the day. He had been about nine or ten at the time, and still fairly new at the Ranch. It wasn't long after his mother had died, and he looked like a lost little boy standing next to the giant, smiling Captain. Damn, he was going to miss that old man.

CHAPTER 10

When Deputy Pacheko walked into the Placer County Courthouse in the middle of Main Street, the Town Council chambers on the first floor of the old stone building were packed, and the mood was hostile. The council members sat at a long table at the far end of the room. In front of that stood a podium and a microphone where a very uncomfortable Sheriff Yeager stood. Every seat in the room was taken, so Pacheko eased into an empty space along the back wall, nodding and smiling to the handful of people who gave the new deputy curious looks.

"Let me get this straight, Sheriff," said Clyde Peterman, council chairman and owner of the town's only insurance agency, "you're telling me you haven't heard one damn word about any of this?"

"Well, not exactly," Yeager hemmed. "There have been a few rumors…"

"Rumors!" shouted Councilman Mike Patterson, owner of the largest cattle ranch in Placer County. We've just heard from four different ranchers that they've been approached by one Marcus Fitch about selling their mineral leases. I'd say it's a hell of a lot more than rumors."

"Yes sir," said Yeager, "but as I understand it, no firm offers have been made. Hell, no one even knows who Fitch is working for. So far, he's just been asking around about who owns what, and whether or not anyone would be interested in allowing some exploratory drilling on their property."

"Drilling for gas," interrupted Councilman Ray Parker, owner of the Mercantile. "And we all know what that means."

"This isn't new," Yeager protested. "Corinne Barker's been talking about gas exploration on their foothills property for months now."

Stu English stood up, his face red and spoiling for a fight. "Drilling down in the desert is one thing, but all of these ranches are well up into the mountains. If we start opening up to this kind of exploitation, these gas companies will run rampant all along the entire front. Look what's happened along the eastern Rockies in Wyoming."

A discontented rumble ran through the crowd and Peterman banged his gavel. "Order, please, order. Mr. English, please take your seat. Your name is on the list, and we'll call on you in due time." He turned to Yeager. "Now, Sheriff," what does the law say on this. Does someone like Mr. Fitch need to file for a permit of some kind, or a notice of intent before he starts going around bothering folks like this?"

"No sir. There's no law against talking to folks. Unless someone files a complaint there's not a thing I can do about it."

The crowded room erupted again and Charley Evans, a rancher and cattle broker who was the senior member on the council spoke up. "Folks, please, let's just all take a breath here and calm down. As you pointed out, Mr. Chairman, we've heard from four different ranchers, including me. As far as we know we're the only ones this Fitch fella has talked to, and none of us have agreed to so much as a soil test as of yet. And you can be damn sure I won't be. Seems to me once Fitch enough pushback he'll move on."

Pacheko pushed himself off the wall and raised his hand. "Mr. Chairman."

Everyone turned toward the new voice, and the room went silent as a church on Monday. Peterman was taken aback as well, and it took him a moment to regain his focus. "Yes," he finally managed. "Deputy, uh…"

"Pacheko, sir, J.D. Pacheko."

"You have something you'd like to say, Deputy Pacheko?"

"Yes, sir. You can make that five ranchers. I got a call from Al Sorenson this morning that this Mr. Fitch had spoken to him about doing some tests on his ranch, and that he was asking about some the adjacent ranches, including the Linehart place."

The room was silent for a long moment. Pacheko leaned back against the wall and the crowd murmur began to grow in volume again. Peterman banged his gavel. "Please, let's keep it orderly, folks," he said.

Charley Evans cleared his throat. "Well, it seems to me like it might be a good idea to get this Fitch guy in here and find out just what his intentions are."

Noises of agreement swept the room. Peterman turned to the Sheriff once more. "You think you can handle that, Sheriff?"

Yeager looked nervous. "Fitch has been keeping a pretty low profile, Mr. Chairman. The only ones who have even seen him are the ranchers we've heard about tonight. He's not registered in any of our hotels."

"Hells bells," Evans retorted, "you're the sheriff, aren't you? Track the man down and get him in here."

"Yes sir," said Yeager. He stood there a moment, looking like he didn't know what to do next. When it became apparent that he was dismissed he hitched up his pants and stalked back to his seat, his eyes shooting daggers at Pacheko, who gave him a *what-did-I-do* shrug.

"Thank you, Sheriff," said Peterman, checking his notes. "We'll now take comments from our signup sheet." He looked up to see Stu English already making a beeline for the podium and held up both hands, letting out a sigh. "Have at it, Mr. English."

Stu stepped up to the podium and plopped down a thick notebook. The microphone boomed the sound throughout the room, causing everyone to flinch.

"Sorry," said Stu, adjusting the mic to his height. "I'd like to start off by adding to the report given by Deputy Pacheko."

"You've met this Fitch person?" asked Peterman.

"No sir. But just before I came to this meeting, Will Hickock told me he was up at the Linehart place earlier today and spotted a man walking around in the field. Sounds like it could be the same guy. Apparently, he had pulled up several clumps of grass, and I think he was taking soil samples. Hickock confronted him, but the man wouldn't say what he was up to, refused to even give his name. Hickock said he drove off in a big white Dodge pickup."

"I've seen a truck like that around town lately," said Mike Patterson. "Driver's a big man, wears a grey Stetson.

"There you go, Sheriff," Evans called out, "your first clue."

Laughter rippled through the room and Yeager fumed. He made a show of looking at his watch, then stood up and stalked out. On the way, he shot Pacheko another nasty look.

"The reason I'm here tonight," Stu went on, "and I hope I'm preaching to the choir on this, is that I don't think any kind of drilling is a good idea. We've spent almost a decade turning a dying town into a very successful recreational destination. How long do you think that would last if they started drilling wells along the front? Who wants to come up here and enjoy the great outdoors in the middle of a bunch of noisy damn wells running night and day?"

Pacheko noticed several heads nodding in agreement, but he also noticed others who didn't look convinced.

"Sure, it would bring more money to the area," Stu continued, "but it would also turn Shambles right back into the same kind of company town it was when the smelter was operating, with big, out-of-state corporations running everything and transient workers who aren't here to invest in our community. They just come to work and send all their money back home. The tourist trade will dry up and property values will drop like a hot rock. And once the gas companies are through with us, we'll be right back where we were 10 years ago, a dying ghost town."

The room was so quiet now Pacheko thought he could hear the wheels turning in every brain in the room. Stu let his words hang in the air a while before speaking again.

"All I'm saying is think long and hard about what you've built here in the last decade. It's more than just the investment we've all made, it's a lifestyle we've created, for ourselves and our families as well as for the tourists who come here to enjoy the freedom and beauty our mountains offer us all. I, for one, will be doing all I can to find out exactly what Mr. Fitch and whoever he's working for are up to. I hope you'll all do the same so we can put a stop to this kind of invasion once and for all. Thank you."

He picked up his notebook and stepped away from the podium. The room lit up with conversation. Peterman once again rapped his gavel in an attempt to regain control of the meeting and the councilmen shuffled their notes. Stu kept on walking past his empty seat and on out the door. Pacheko pushed off the wall and followed him outside. It was just dusk, and lights were starting to come on up and down the street. He caught up with Stu at his car.

"Nice speech."

Stu spun around, startled. "Oh, well, thanks deputy."

"For what it's worth, I agree with you."

"You mean about the drilling?"

"That, and what you said about the mountains. It's pretty darned peaceful up here. I'd hate to see that spoiled."

"Me, too," said Stu.

"You mentioned that Will Hickock said he saw this Fitch guy up at the Captain's?"

Stu nodded.

"When exactly was that?"

"Why, just before the meeting. I ran into him at his house, and he mentioned it."

"Did he happen to mention what he was doing up at the Linehart place?"

"When I saw him, he was just back from a bike ride. Said he was up inspecting the trails. He's a trail guide for Spangler's Cyclery, you know.

The crowds will start arriving any day now." He looked Pacheko over. "This will be your first summer in Shambles, right, deputy?"

"Yep," said Pacheko. "I'm looking forward to it."

"There's really nothing quite like it," Stu said with a gleam in his eye that left little doubt he was thinking more about the economic benefits than any other aspects of the tourism boom. He climbed into his car and Pacheko watched him drive away. Once the little Forester had disappeared, he looked back in the direction of the council meeting and considered going back inside, but decided he'd heard enough.

CHAPTER 11

Tommy Morrison was fresh off a brief stretch at the Ranch for possession of marijuana when he marched into Leon's Landing, the only bar in Shambles that had never closed its doors during all the bad years and talked old man Hutchinson into giving his new band a try. Never mind that they were all underage. It probably didn't hurt that he was dating Hutchinson's daughter, Libbie, but for whatever reason, Leon decided to give them a try.

Tommy and three friends showed up the following night, played a bunch of country rock cover songs. The crowd seemed to enjoy the music. Then they launched into some new songs Tommy had picked up from a friend he'd made while at the Ranch, and damned if folks didn't start clapping and hollering for more.

Leon had tried to book some of the bands that played Boise for special events over the years, but in those days, leaving the big city to play a tiny mountain town like Shambles was taking a step backwards career-wise, so Hardscrabble became the house band by default. By the time Shambles got itself turned around a few years later the group had become so popular that they rarely took a break.

When Leon retired, his daughter Libbie, took over the place. It was only natural since she'd grown up hanging around the place doing the odd chores when she was younger, then taken on waitressing duties until she was old enough to tend bar. The only thing that had changed since the new owner took charge was the name on the sign and a new coat of paint every few years.

There were no facades here, no pretensions, no attempt whatsoever at being anything other than what it was – a local bar. And like the blinking neon sign said, LIBBIE'S offered "Eats, Drinks, Live Music." Nothing more, nothing less. She and Tommy had been high school sweethearts, and when they tied the knot shortly after graduation the joke around town was that she only married him because her father couldn't afford to lose the band.

Will Hickock pulled into the dirt parking lot that surrounded the long, low, brick building that sat on a little hilltop at the south end of Main Street. It was already over half full, and as soon as he stepped inside, carrying his guitar case in one hand, he could see that the Friday night crowd had already begun to gather, and some of them looked like they'd started early.

Libbie looked up from behind the bar, pouring a pair of ice-blue martinis through a strainer. She was a classic redhead, with porcelain skin that never seemed to age and emerald-green eyes. She wore her usual black jeans and a t-shirt with the bar logo front and back.

Will had been dreading seeing her all day long. He knew it would be rough, and he was right. They both choked up the moment their eyes met. They'd known each other since high school and she and

Tommy were right up at the top of a very short list of people he called friends. He noticed she had put on a few pounds lately and wondered if she might be pregnant again. She and Tommy already had two, but they were great parents, and each one seemed to make them happier. She immediately made her way out from behind the bar with a towel in one hand and threw her arms around him. "Oh Will, I am so sorry."

He just stood there in a daze, unable to respond, fighting his own tears, the lump in his throat preventing any words from coming out. She pulled back and looked at him, tears streaming down her cheeks. Finally, he managed to find some of his voice. "Yeah, it's the shits, alright."

Libbie hugged him again. "I can only imagine how you must feel. We all know what he meant to you." Will could only nod. She stepped back, still holding onto his shoulders, and looked straight into his eyes. "Listen, I know you're the ultimate loner, but you don't have to get through this all by yourself. Anything you need, any time you want to talk, we're here for you. You know that, right?" Will nodded again. Libbie wiped her eyes with the bar towel. "Whatever you want tonight is on the house, okay?" she said giving him a soft smile.

Will tried to smile back, but he couldn't seem to make his face work. He couldn't even bring himself to wipe his wet cheeks. She noticed his guitar and her smile grew big. "You know Tommy loves it when you come to play."

He took a big breath and cleared his throat, finally managing to get some words out. "Thought maybe it would help some."

She gave his shoulders a squeeze. "Get you a beer?"

"Maybe in a while," he said, looking around the room. "He here yet?"

She glanced at the large clock above the cash register. It was just after six o'clock. A large sign next to it had a big red arrow pointed at the number two. Beneath it thick letters spelled out *Closing Time. No Excuses.*

"Any time now," she said, squeezing his hand.

As he made his way across the room to the stage several people greeted him with somber faces and soft condolences. He nodded his thanks and kept moving, trying not to show how uncomfortable the attention made him. He perched on a stool and tuned his guitar for a while, absently scanning the crowd across the empty dance floor. It was growing steadily, and he suddenly wished he had that beer Libbie offered. Rather than run the gauntlet of well-wishers back to the bar, he detoured past the row of booths along the wall that looked empty. He made it past the first two when a voice startled him.

"I was wondering if you might show up here tonight."

Tucked away in a corner of the third booth was the new deputy, wearing a red Forty-Niners jersey and baggy, neon-blue Hawaiian-print surfer shorts. He was leaning against the back wall with his feet up on the bench sporting flip-flops. In spite of how bad he felt Will almost laughed out loud. If Yeager could only see Shambles' newest law enforcement representative now.

"I take it you're off duty," he quipped.

The deputy just grinned and raised his half-full glass of beer, then waved his hand over the pitcher in the middle of the table and the empty glass next to it. "Buy you a beer?"

Will remained standing. "What made you think I might be here?"

"I asked around. Heard you like to play with the band from time to time. Figured this might be one of those times."

The last thing Will wanted right now was conversation, but his curiosity was piqued. He eased onto the bench opposite the deputy.

"All right," crooned the surfer, instantly producing the warm, easy smile that had charmed Will earlier that morning, the twinkle in his blue eyes visible even in the darkened booth. He pulled the empty glass over and filled it with a flourish.

"Pacheko, isn't it?" asked Will.

"That's right, but my friends call me J.D."

"What's that stand for?"

The deputy flinched slightly, then gave him a lopsided grin. "That's a long, ugly story, best left for another time." He slid the glass over to Will. "Listen, I wanted to say I'm sorry if I pushed too hard about you and the Sheriff Linehart earlier."

Will felt the lump return to his throat and only offered a nod. Pacheko's easy grin softened, putting Will oddly at ease. "He was quite the legend. I met him once, my first day on the job. He seemed like a real cool customer, kind of a throwback to the old wild west days."

The memories flooding Will's brain threatened to unloose another torrent of tears. Not something he wanted to do in front of a complete stranger. He sucked in a deep breath and fought to keep his composure. A part of him want to get up and leave, but a slightly larger part of him was curious what the deputy had to say. Pacheko seemed to sense his discomfort.

"Hey, I get it if you don't want to talk about it," he said. "I just thought since I'll be working the case, and you're the…well, since we'll probably be running into each other from time to time, it might be nice to get to know each other a little, off the record, so to speak."

Will took a sip of beer. "Does the Sheriff know you're talking to me?"

Pacheko laughed, then leaned in close, his voice dropping. "No, and if he found out we both know he wouldn't be too happy."

There was an uncomfortable pause, and both men took a drink of beer. Pacheko seemed to be struggling with where to begin. Will waited, trying to decide whether he enjoyed watching him squirm, or whether he was just as uncomfortable himself. He was surprised when he settled on the latter. Something about this guy made him want to find a connection.

Finally, Pacheko spoke. "I'll be up front with you, Hickock, I've been checking you out. Everybody I've talked to today seems to think you're an honest, stand-up guy. And no one wants to believe you had anything to do with Linehart's murder."

Will stiffened, feeling his face grow hot. "That's because I didn't."

Pacheko raised his hands and leaned back in the booth. "Okay, okay, all I'm saying is that, even though I don't know you at all, my gut is telling me you didn't do this. From what I've learned, you knew the Captain better than most around here, so I'm asking you if you'll help me figure out who did."

Will relaxed back against the booth and took another drink of beer, studying the deputy's face. He didn't quite know what to make of the surprising offer. His own gut was telling him he could trust the new guy, but the part of him that fought against letting anyone into his life couldn't help but wonder if he was being set up.

"What exactly is it you want me to do?" Will asked warily.

"Just keep your eyes and ears open for now and let me know if you hear anything." He leaned in again, resting his elbows on the table.

"Look, I realize this is a little unorthodox." Will snorted and Pacheko chuckled. "Okay, maybe a lot unorthodox. But you need to prove your innocence, and I want to keep my job. Sheriff Yeager's not the easiest guy to get along with, but believe it or not, I'm starting to like this town. Seems to me you've got a good thing going here with the mountain biking and all."

Will took another drink of beer. "Ok, I'll play along. For now. Only because I want to catch whoever did this more than you know. But trust works both ways, you know. If you want my help, you need to tell me what you know."

Pacheko poured himself another glass of beer, then held up the pitcher, looking at Will, who pushed his glass over. "For starters," he said, topping off Will's glass, "this afternoon the arson inspector confirmed the fire was fueled by gasoline, which also confirms we're looking at a murder."

Will took a long drink of beer to keep his throat from closing up. Pacheko was watching him closely. "You okay?" he asked. Will nodded, and the deputy continued. "The autopsy report came in a couple of hours ago. The body was too burned to tell much of anything, but the left side of his skull was caved in pretty good. Could have happened when the second floor crashed down on top of him..." he let the sentence hang.

"But you think someone killed him first," said Will. It was a statement, not a question.

"The Medical Examiner says there was no smoke in his lungs, which means he wasn't breathing when the fire started. So, yeah, more than likely the blow to his head happened before."

Will struggled to get his mind around the idea. "Who the hell would do something like this? Everybody loved the Captain."

"Apparently not everybody," Pacheko deadpanned. "I've been looking through a pretty long list of people he arrested, not to mention all the kids that spent time at that detention center of his, but so far, no one is jumping out at me."

"Yeah, but this is Shambles for Christ's sake. The only crime we ever have around here is drunk driving, stolen mountain bikes and a few small-time drug arrests."

"Speaking of stealing, could robbery have been a motive? Maybe the Captain caught him in the act and the thief killed him, then he burned the place to cover his tracks?"

"I don't know what they would have been after," said Will. "The only thing of any value on his place that I know of is the land. He put every dime he ever made into paying off that mortgage. The house and barn aren't worth anything to speak of, and after the juvenile facility shut down, he didn't put a whole lot of effort into keeping those bunkhouses up."

The lump in his throat suddenly felt the size of a baseball and he had to clear his throat to continue. "He made the final payment and retired a little over a year ago, not long before I got back. He said all he wanted to do the rest of his life was take it easy."

Will grabbed a napkin to staunch the tears that threatened to flow again. Pacheko ran his finger around the rim of his glass, waiting. Will could tell he had something else he wanted to say. "What?" he asked, looking defiantly into the deputy's eyes.

Pacheko thought about it another moment, then blurted it out. "Look, it's pretty obvious Yeager's got it in his head that you did it."

"That's bullshit!" Several heads at nearby tables turned at the sudden explosion. Will lowered his voice. "That man was the only father I ever had. I'd never do anything to hurt him."

"Yeah, Marcia was pretty firm on that point, too. But Yeager's got a burr up his butt for some reason."

"That's been there since he was a whiney little kid and my brother used to beat the shit out of him on a regular basis." Pacheko's eyebrows went up and he looked at him, waiting for more. "What, Marcia didn't fill you in on that, too?"

"Nope. I guess she must have felt like it wasn't her place." He waited a moment to let Will's anger subside. "Look, all I'm interested in is finding out what happened to Sheriff Linehart. So, we still good?"

Will took a breath. "Yeah, I guess.

Pacheko leaned back and took a swig of his beer, letting the tension ease. "Personally, I always try to keep an open mind and let the evidence write the story before I offer an opinion one way or the other. I just thought you ought to know what he's spreading around."

"Yeager's an asshole."

"Well, I can't disagree with you there," he said with a chuckle. "And it's pretty obvious he doesn't like you much, either."

"I've been on his usual suspects list since way before he ever made deputy."

"Let me guess, it has something to do with your brother."

Will clenched his jaw. "Ok, look, Yeager and my brother hated each other with a passion since before I was even born. Doc, just because he had a mean streak a mile long, and Rod, because he knew all the bad shit Doc was up to but could never prove any of it. Hell, he grew up wanting to be a cop just because he dreamed of nailing Doc one day.

Ask him about it sometime. I'm sure he'll be more than happy to fill you in."

A loud squawk from the bandstand grabbed everyone's attention. The band was plugging in and turning on, getting ready for their first set of the evening. Will noticed the place had filled up considerably since he'd come in.

Pacheko cocked his head in the direction of the stage. "I like their stuff. That lead guitar is pretty good."

"Tommy? Yeah. He's gotten a lot better the last few years."

"I take it you two go back a while."

Will studied the deputy, wondering whether he was really just an easy-going guy doing his job, or whether he should listen to echoes from his past, whispering that people in general were not to be trusted. It was tough being a loner in a small town, where everyone knew everyone and everything about them, but Will had always managed to keep a low profile, thanks in no small part to spending his formative years in detention whenever he wasn't in school.

Since he'd returned from the Army, the few people he considered friends respected him for who he was, not for anything that had happened in the past. Pacheko was a cop, and that made him naturally nosy, but something about the easy way he operated made Will feel almost comfortable, despite the fact that he was their number one suspect.

"Tommy and I met at the Ranch," he said, looking for a reaction. Pacheko didn't so much as blink. "It was back in high school. Tommy was there for three months one summer for possession of pot. He was a natural on the guitar, an excellent finger picker even then. I was always hanging around watching him, so he taught me how to play. By the time he left I'd learned enough to make up melodies for the lyrics that are always running around in my head."

The deputy looked sideways at him. "A songwriter, too? Very interesting."

"When he started the band, he insisted I play rhythm guitar. I never liked performing, and they left me in the dust musically pretty quick, but I've managed to write a few tunes they like, and it's fun to get together and play with them now and again."

Tommy gave him a wave from the stage, and several other faces looked his way offering a nod or a tip of the glass. At least they weren't stopping by the table offering condolences, but maybe that's because of who he was sitting with. Suddenly the lump was back in his throat, and he drank deeply trying to wash it down.

Pacheko waited patiently. His cop instincts were telling him to keep pressing, but his people instincts were telling him to take it slow with this one. He took another sip of his beer.

"I didn't think it would be this hard," Will muttered, half to himself. Realizing Pacheko heard it, he was instantly embarrassed.

The deputy's eyes went sad. "It's a bitch. Trust me, I know."

Something in the way he spoke the words caught Will's attention. "Sounds like you've got your own story."

Pacheko grunted. "Don't we all. But life goes on, and if we don't move with it, we die ourselves, little by little."

"Yeah, I suppose so," he said with a sigh. "I just can't believe he's gone."

As soon as he said it, his breath caught in his throat. He was surprised at himself. He never exposed his emotions like that to anyone, much less a stranger. He wanted a way to change the subject, and Pacheko helped him out.

"I was glad to hear that dog's going to be all right."

Will breathed a sigh of relief. "Dusty, yeah. I appreciate you taking him to the vet."

"Good thing as it turns out. The vet said he wouldn't have lasted much longer without treatment. I've got Marcia checking all the hospitals and doctors in the area for anyone who might have come in with animal bites." He gave a snort. "I sure as hell wouldn't want anything that size coming after me. Whoever it is must be hurting pretty bad right now."

Will took in a deep breath and let it out, remembering. "He's mostly wild. The Captain found him starving to death as a pup and nursed back to health not long after the juvenile center shut down. He'd never had a pet before that I knew of, and I remember thinking it wasn't like him. Ever since he lost his family, he'd always been alone."

Pacheko looked at him over his raised glass. "Sounds like some of that might have rubbed off," he said with a grin.

A small smile escaped Will's lips. "I told him it was just because he missed having all us kids around. Anyway, once Dusty got healthy, he started hanging around the ranch every so often."

"He looked like he could be a pretty formidable beast on his better days."

"He still spends most of his time off in the mountains. One summer the Captain didn't see him for almost a month. Thought he'd run off for good. But as soon as the nights started turning cold again, back he came, and looking none the worse for wear. I don't know what he's going to do with the Captain gone."

"You're not going to take him?"

"I'm not sure he trusts anyone but the Captain. Besides, I don't think he'd take too well to living in town."

"Yeah, I could see where that might cause some problems."

Pacheko's face opened up with that happy-go-lucky grin and Will was surprised to discover he was feeling more relaxed. The band started tuning up and he slid out of the booth.

"Thanks for the beer, but I think the best medicine for me tonight is a little music."

"Soothes the savage beast," Pacheko said, tipping his glass. "Oh, I almost forgot. I checked that pullout up at the ranch."

"Did you find the tire tracks?"

"There wasn't much there, like you said, but I took some photos. I haven't had time to see if the computer can find a match. But that's not all."

Will sat back down.

"I found those other tracks you told me about. You were right, they do look like soft hiking boots of some kind. They were kind of mushy because the creek bank was muddy, but I took photos of a couple of the clearer ones just in case." He cocked his head. "You don't smoke, do you?"

"That's one nasty habit I'm happy to say I never picked up."

"How about the Captain?"

"Used to roll his own, but he gave it up years ago. Why?"

"I found a cigarette butt hung up on a willow branch down by the creek next to that turnout. No telling how long it's been there." He shrugged. "It's probably nothing, but I'm having it tested it for DNA just to be sure. Anyway, thanks for the tip."

Will made his way to the stage and Tommy lunged at him seizing him in a long hug and clapping him hard on the back. Tommy never did anything halfway. He had the blocky build of a linebacker, and his long arms and broad shoulders nearly squeezed the air out of Will. Tommy was a few inches shorter and his dark brown eyes and thick, dark eyebrows under a mop of dark curly hair gave him a perpetually fierce look that would have served him well on the football field, had he not chosen other pursuits. At the moment he looked fiercely sad for his friend.

He tried to speak, but words would not come. Will smiled managed an understanding smile and said, "Let's get to it." Tommy gave him a curt nod in return and a minute later they kicked into "High Desert Ramble," one of Will's first songs and still a band favorite. Will lost himself in the driving rhythm, pumping chords in time with the drums and bass, floating free on Tommy's soaring guitar licks. Free of the crowded bar, free of Yeager and his petty theories, free of Shambles and all his troubles.

They said don't go,
Don't take the gamble.
I said I'm gone
On a desert ramble

CHAPTER 12

Loud pounding dragged Will out of a deep sleep. It took him a while to realize someone was beating on his front door. He shook his head to clear the cobwebs, and the memory of the previous night came flooding back. After their last set the bar closed and Tommy had insisted he come over to their house and work on a new tune he'd been struggling with lately. He had a brief vision of Libbie tossing him a pillow and blanket and telling him he was in no shape to drive home.

The pounding grew louder, more insistent. He rolled over and saw his alarm clock read 7:00 AM. He remembered getting up to take a piss at Tommy's and deciding to head home. Dawn was just beginning to break, so that couldn't have been more than a couple of hours ago. Who the hell could be at his door at that hour?

He stumbled to his feet and slipped into his jeans, and as he headed for the door the pounding came again, this time with a voice. "Open up, Hickock, I know you're in there!"

Will groaned. Yeager. What the hell did he want now? He opened the door just as the Sheriff was raising his arm to pound some more. He immediately shoved Will back into the living room and barged in.

"What the…" Will began.

"Shut up, Hickock," barked the sheriff. "You're in a world of shit. Your past just came back to bite you on the ass big time."

Will fell back onto his couch. "What's the bug up your butt this time?"

"You want to tell me where you were last night?"

"Not really."

"Don't get smart with me, I've got another dead body on my hands and given your history with him, right now you're looking pretty good for it."

That cleared the last of the cobwebs and Will sat up straight. "Dead body? What are you talking about?"

"Just tell me where you were last night."

"I played down at Libbie's until closing, then we went over to Tommy's house. I just got back here about a couple of hours ago and went to bed."

"Naturally they'll vouch for you."

"Why wouldn't they, it's the truth."

"We'll see about that. Meantime I'm taking you in. Get some clothes on."

"On what charge?"

"The murder of Sam Montforte."

Marcia Little Bird smiled when she arrived to find the parking lot behind the Sheriff's office completely empty. Maybe she could finally get some work done. She hummed a happy tune as she went inside and headed straight for the coffee machine.

"Mind making me a cup while you're at it?"

She jumped, dropping the box of phony sugar she was digging through, and whirled around to look for the source of the voice, but no one was there.

"Sorry if I scared you."

Recognition flooded her face, and she blew out an aggravated breath, realizing it had come from the cell block. "Will Hickock, I swear..."

Retrieving the cellblock keys, she swung the metal door open and frowned at him, sitting on the cot in the first cell. Again. "You're starting to make a habit of this, young man."

"Yeager woke me up this morning and arrested me again. What is it with that guy, Marcia?"

She shook her head. "What for this time?"

"Apparently, Sam Montforte was killed last night.

She gasped. "What the hell's going on in this town?"

"His house was burned, just like the Captain's, so I guess Yeager figures I must be good for this one, too.

"You don't sound too concerned."

"That's because I've got a rock-solid alibi."

"Which he didn't bother to check, I'm guessing."

Will snorted. "Said he had things to do, and I could cool my heels here until he got around to it."

"I swear, that man will be the death of me. That makes no kind of sense at all. You'd think with him being in charge now he'd start acting a little more Sheriff-like."

"I don't think his version of Sheriff-like is necessarily the same as everyone else's."

"Not where you're concerned, that's for sure." She shook her head. "Some folks just don't know when to let go of a grudge." She bustled back into the office, leaving the connecting door open. "Let me get some coffee going and we'll get this thing sorted out."

"This new guy, Pacheko, " Will called after her, "what do you think of him?"

"J.D.? Oh, he's a sweetheart. Why?" She turned on the coffee machine, grabbed the empty pot and went into the bathroom in the corner next to the cell block. "Don't tell me he's on your case, too?"

Will heard the sound of water running in the sink. "Kinda the opposite, actually. Where'd he come from, anyway?"

"California. Santa Cruz, I think he told me. Used to be some kind of pro surfer, I guess."

"You're kidding me," Will said with a snort. "How the hell did he wind up here?"

The water shut off and Marcia re-emerged from the bathroom. "I asked him that, straight out, but he wouldn't talk much about it. He did show me a medal he won in some big competition. Keeps it in his desk drawer."

"He sure dresses like a surfer when he's off duty."

Marcia laughed. "Doesn't he, though. He showed up here his first day to pick up his uniforms looking like he just stepped off a beach somewhere. You should have seen the look on the Sheriff's face."

They both laughed, though Will's was considerably more sarcastic. Marcia dumped some coffee in the tray above the heating element, the poured the water from the pot over it and stuck the empty pot underneath. A moment later, dark liquid began dripping down into it.

"Why all the questions?" she asked.

"Just curious. I ran into him down at Libbie's last night."

She waited, but there was only silence from the cell block. "And?" she finally prompted walking back and standing in the open door.

"He mostly wanted to know more about me and the Captain." Will debated whether to tell her that the deputy had asked him to help with the investigation and decided the fewer people knew about that, the better. "You know if he got the report back on the blood and fibers in Dusty's mouth?"

"Damnit, Will, you know I can't be giving out active case information, especially to..." She stopped short, embarrassed.

"The prime suspect?"

She stepped back into the cell block and he could see she was blushing. "You know I don't believe for a minute that you had anything to do with the Captain's death, or Sam Montforte's for that matter."

"Tell that to Yeager."

"Yeah, well, we both know he's got a mind of his own, don't we?"

"That's the understatement of the year. And all the more reason I need to see that report."

She looked sideways at him, but Will could tell she was thinking about it. He gave her a wounded puppy face, which only made her frown deepen.

"Don't you try that look on me, Will Hickock. I knew your mother way too well. Besides, if the Sheriff caught me, I could lose my job."

"Okay, so just tell me what it said."

She feigned being offended. "How would I know? I'm not allowed to read those things."

Will gave her a not-buying-it look. "Come on, Marcia, I need to know where I stand here."

"Go ask your new pal, J.D.," she tossed over her shoulder as she went back to check on the coffee.

Will frowned. "He's not my pal." Then his tone softened. "I just figured that since you know I had nothing to do with any of it, and since you're the one who really runs things around this office, you might be willing to cut me a little slack."

She blew out exasperated breath. "And if you think that weak attempt at flattery is going to get you anything you can think again."

Will went silent, and Marcia allowed herself a smile. She poured two cups and went back to the cell block.

"Thanks," Will said as she handed one of the cups to him through the bars. "It's almost worth being in here just to get a cup of your coffee."

Marcia rolled her eyes and sighed. "If we did get that report back, and you never heard me say we did, and if I read it, which I'm not saying I did, there's a pretty good chance it might have said it was a microfiber of some kind, probably from a windbreaker-type jacket. Satisfied?"

"What about the blood?"

"Human, Type A."

Will face filled with worry. He was Type A, although so were a ton of other people. Still, it ticked off another item on Yeager's checklist of reasons Will was guilty. Rather than mention it to Marcia, he immediately changed the subject. "He also said you were checking hospitals and doctors for dog bite victims."

"Nothing there at all, and I even checked Boise and Mountain Home."

"See how easy that was? Yeager and the surfing champ will never be the wiser."

"Don't you bet on it," she said. "J.D.'s as smart as they come. That boy knows his stuff."

"At least that makes one of our esteemed law enforcement officers."

"Yeah, well, the Sheriff is still the Sheriff, so I suggest you watch your mouth around him. I let you finagle a little information out of me because I care about you. Yeager wants to pin these murders on you whether you're innocent or not, and you know damn well why."

The words came down hard, but they rang true, but his answer did nothing to mask his dislike of the man. "Because I'm the last reminder of what a piece of shit he really is."

"Listen Will, I've been running this office since Sheriff Linehart first got elected, and if the spirits are willing, I'll be here long after that…" She bit down on her words. "…after Sheriff Yeager is gone. But you need somebody with a lot more clout than me on your side if you expect to just walk away from all this."

"And you're suggesting the rookie?"

"Just because he's new in town doesn't mean he can't tell which way the wind blows. He's not afraid to challenge the Sheriff, but he's walking a fine line between doing what's right and pissing off Yeager just enough to get himself fired. If he's opening up to you about this mess, maybe it's because he's willing to give you the benefit of the doubt."

"Or giving me enough rope to hang myself," countered Will.

"Either way, it just might be that you two could help each other out. I know you always like to fight your own battles, but maybe it's time you started trusting someone."

Will's eyes grew sad. "The people I trust seem to have a way of dying."

Marcia shook her head. "I hear you," she sighed. "And I know you lost some friends as a Ranger, too. But you can't give up on people, Will. You're home now, and you've got people here who love you." Will sighed and nodded as he finished off his coffee. "You want another cup?"

He handed his mug through the bars and she went back into the office. "He sure is keeping the Sheriff on his toes, though," she said with a little giggle. "Speaking of which, I don't suppose he said where he was going?"

"Nope," said Will, "but I'd guess he's out at the crime scene. Probably wants to make sure his deputy doesn't find anything that might incriminate anyone else."

"Didn't you say you've got an alibi for last night?"

"Hell yes," wailed Will. "I slept over at Tommy and Libbie's house until after five this morning. I told Yeager that."

She returned and handed him a full cup. "Let me get J.D. in here, and I'll give Libbie a call and see if we can get you cut loose."

"Thanks, Marcia."

"Don't thank me yet. Libbie's an honest woman, but that Tommy's a rascal. Given his history with our illustrious sheriff, I wouldn't be surprised if it took a lot more than their word to get you out of that cell.

CHAPTER 13

Tommy and Libbie were there in less than twenty minutes, Tommy bursting through the door in full linebacker mode and looking more fierce than usual. "What the hell, Marcia!?" he exclaimed.

Libbie put a hand on his shoulder, attempting to calm him down and gave Marcia an apologetic look. Marcia broke out her wide, warm smile and gave then both a hug, which Tommy accepted only grudgingly. "Thank you for coming down,"

"Are you kidding me?" said Tommy. "What the hell was Yeager thinking?"

"I can't believe the Sheriff," said Libbie. "Why would he just arrest him without even checking with us first."

"All he had to do was make a call," Tommy said, heading into the cell block to talk to Will.

"I know," said Marcia, "but communication isn't exactly his strong suit."

Libbie lowered her voice. "Tommy is really worried about Will. We heard he's a suspect in the Captain's murder, too? How is that possible?"

"How about a cup of coffee?" said Marcia.

"Great," said Libbie. "I can't remember the last time I was up this early." She followed Marcia to the coffee machine. "What the hell's going on around here, Marcia?" she asked. "Two murders, in two days?"

"Tell me about it. I haven't seen the sheriff so riled up since I don't know when."

The door opened and Pacheko walked in, his jacket and face streaked with soot. Marcia instinctively looked behind him to see if he was alone.

"Good thing you called my cell," the deputy said. "Yeager would have picked it up on the radio."

"Don't I know it," Marcia said with a smirk. "He must not have been very happy when you wanted to leave the crime scene."

"He wasn't, but I told him the lab report on the blood and fiber samples was in and I needed to pick it up."

"But that report came in before he left this morning."

"Gee, I must have forgotten to mention it to him," Pacheko said with a sly grin.

Tommy came out of the cell block. "It's about damn time. Can we get him out of there now?"

Pacheko ignored the jibe and stuck his hand out to Tommy. "Glad to finally meet you. You play a mean guitar."

Tommy hesitated, surprised at the deputy's friendly attitude. "Thanks," he said, shaking the deputy's hand, his anger dissipating somewhat. Libbie and Marcia exchanged a smile.

"And you're Libbie," Pacheko continued, shaking her hand as well. "Best burgers I've ever tasted."

Libbie blushed a little. "Glad you like them. Now about Will…"

"Yeah, of course. We just need you both to fill out a report and sign it." Marcia handed them each a yellow legal pad and a pen, ushering them to separate chairs. "If each of you would write down your own account, to the best of your knowledge, of the time Will spent with you last night we'll get this taken care of."

"Then Will's free to go?" asked Tommy.

"Assuming you can vouch for his whereabouts the entire night, yes."

"Damn right we can. After the bar closed, we jammed until almost four in the garage out back of our house."

"Don't want them waking up the kids," Libbie interjected.

"We had a few more beers, so Libbie wouldn't let Will drive. He slept on the couch."

"And you're sure he was there the whole night?"

"I got up to go to the bathroom about five-thirty," said Libbie, "and he was sneaking out the door, trying not to wake us."

"Did you speak to him?"

"We just waved. Then I went back to bed."

"No way he could have snuck out earlier in the night and come back?"

"I'm a pretty light sleeper, but anyone would have heard that truck of his starting up. It sounds like a meat grinder."

"What time did the fire happen?" Tommy asked.

"Fire Department got the call about two-thirty this morning."

"We were still jamming. I can bring you three other witnesses."

"Sounds like you're covered, then," said Pacheko. "Just write it all down and sign it. Be sure to include the names of the other witnesses, and their phone numbers if you have them. I doubt we'll need to bother them, but just to be on the safe side."

They went to work, and Marcia came over with the cell keys. "The sheriff's going to have a cow, you know."

"Yeah, but it's the right thing to do," said Pacheko, grabbing the cell block keys from his desk. "He never should have arrested him in the first place without checking his alibi."

"I'm liking you more and more, Deputy Pacheko," she said with a grin.

"Thanks, Marcia. The feeling's mutual."

The radio squawked and Yeager's voice blasted out. "Dispatch, this is Sheriff Yeager, over."

Marcia exchanged a look with Pacheko, then walked over to the radio console and picked up the microphone, flipping a switch.

"Dispatch here, over," she said crisply.

"Where the hell's that deputy of mine?"

Pacheko shook his head and waved his hands indicating he wasn't there.

"He just left a couple of minutes ago, Sheriff. Should be headed your way now, over."

"Well then why the hell doesn't he answer his damn radio," shouted Yeager.

"No idea, Sheriff, over," said Marcia.

"I just got a call from Chief Rankin at the State Police. He's mad as a hornet about this. Now I've got to drive all the damn way back down to Boise again to give him another report. You keep trying Pacheko until you get him. Tell him to call me asap with that lab report on the damn dog and to inform me immediately, and I mean immediately, on anything he finds out at Montforte's place. You got that?"

"Ten-four, Sheriff," said Marcia. "I'll give him the message as soon as I can, over and out."

Pacheko gave Marcia a thumbs-up as she switched off the radio, then disappeared into the cell block. A moment later he returned with Will in tow.

"Thanks guys," Will said as Libbie wrapped him in a hug. Her expression told him how sorry she was. It was the same look she had when he first saw her at the bar the night before and he felt a tug of emotion once again. Tommy quickly tamped that back down with a wisecrack.

"I can't believe that jerk-off actually tossed your ass in jail," he groused, clapping him on the back.

"You two finish up those reports," said Marcia. "I'm going to need all the documentation I can get when the sheriff gets back and finds his prisoner gone."

Libbie and Tommy resumed their writing. Will strolled over to Pacheko at his desk. It was spotless. No family pictures, no personal effects of any kind, just a plastic tray with a neat stack of forms and a plain wooden nameplate that read Deputy Sheriff J.D. Pacheko.

"I appreciate this," he said. "You'll probably get your butt chewed for it."

"If that's all I get I'll be lucky," said the deputy, his eyes twinkling. "But he's the one not playing by the rules."

"I suppose the fire at Montforte's destroyed everything?"

"Not quite. The front half of the house is pretty much toast, but some of the back rooms have less damage. Another half hour and it all would have been gone. It was set up to look like Montforte was killed in the fire, just like the Captain, but the fire department got there in time to recover the body before it was too badly burned. They said it looked like he was beaten and cut up pretty bad.

"You're kidding me," said Will, his eyes going wide.

Pacheko nodded. "Any ideas on who might have wanted him dead?"

Will shook his head. "I remember hearing back in the day that some people were pissed off about a few of his real estate deals, but I was too young to pay much attention to that kind of thing. The only people I stayed in touch with while I was in the Army were Tommy and Libbie, and the Captain. Montforte's name never came up. All I've heard since I got back is that he's richer than ever."

"Yeah," mused Pacheko, "a lot of good it'll do him now."

"Well, thanks again," said Will reaching out his hand. "Next time, the beer's on me."

Pacheko's grin went wide, and he shook Will's hand firmly. "I'll hold you to that. "But right now, I'd better get back to work." He took the papers in his hand over to Marcia. "These are the lab reports the Sheriff was asking about. Will you give him a call and relay the information?"

"I've been wondering when these would come in," she said, feigning surprise.

Pacheko rolled his eyes at her and turned back to Will, who stifled a grin. "By the way, do you know your blood type?"

"A positive." He said, shooting a sideways glance at Marcia, who caught it and immediately stuck her nose in the report.

Pacheko looked back and forth between the two. He was about to say something when the front door opened and a very agitated Stu English burst in, dressed in his standard blue blazer, a pale blue dress shirt open at the collar, khaki Dockers, and the spanking clean hiking boots he wore to try and give himself an outdoorsy image. Truth was, Stu never got too far off the beaten path. The only time those boots saw dirt was when he was showing a client an undeveloped property. He made a beeline for Marcia. "The Sheriff in?"

"Nope."

"Shit," he spat, stomping his foot on the floor.

Marcia gave him a dark look and Stu's face turned red. Will and Pacheko both wiped off smirks.

"Sorry," Stu muttered, "but it's important. Do you know if he sent someone by to check on the smelter yet? My client is very anxious to get a look at it."

"The old Latham smelter?" Tommy chimed in. "Man, we used to have some parties in that place back in the day. You wouldn't believe..." Libbie put a hand on his arm, shaking her head, and he went back to writing his report.

Pacheko spoke up. "I was up there yesterday. Walked around inside. I'm no engineer, but it seems safe enough for a tour."

"Great," said Stu, his expression brightening. "I'll let my client know." He spotted Will his eyebrows went up. "What are you doing here, Hickock? Someone steal your bike or something?"

Will just stared at him. "Or something, yeah."

Stu gave him a puzzled look. Marcia cleared her throat. "Just who is this mysterious client of yours, anyway?"

Stu looked around the room, seeming to notice Libbie and Tommy for the first time, and turned to her all business again. "I'm afraid I can't tell you that. He prefers to remain anonymous until the deal is in place. He flew back to San Francisco yesterday to meet with his bankers and take care of some other business, but he wants to see the smelter as soon as he gets back. I'd like to get the key so I can check out the inside for myself, first."

"I'm afraid you'll have to get that from the Sheriff, Mr. English," said Marcia. "But he's a little busy today. Seems we've had another murder."

Stu was instantly contrite. "Yeah, I heard about that. I'm sorry."

"Where did you hear about it already?" Pacheko cut in.

"Over at the coffee shop earlier this morning. Everyone in town's talking about it. Sam Montforte was a force to be reckoned with. I remember when I first…"

"I'm afraid the Sheriff's gone down to Boise this morning, Marcia interrupted. "I don't know when he'll be back."

He checked his watch again and headed for the door. "Soon as you hear from him, tell him to call my cell."

As soon as he was gone, Marcia shook her head. "I swear, that boy's wound so tight something's going to explode one of these days."

"What's he so stressed about?" asked Will.

Marcia chuckled. "According to Stu, his big shot developer is thinking about turning the smelter into a fancy health club with a pool, weights, climbing wall, the whole shebang, as part of his Hill development."

Pacheko snorted. "You ask me, the only way to fix that place up is with a case of dynamite."

Everyone nodded in agreement. Pacheko started to leave and then thought of something else. He paused, contemplating how much trouble it would land him in, and then decided to go ahead and find out. "You mind walking me out to my car, Hickock. I'd like one more word with you."

Marcia gave Will a no-clue shrug as Pacheko led him out the door and into the parking lot, looking around to make sure they were alone. They got to the cruiser and the deputy stepped in close, speaking in low tones.

"This is a very unofficial request, If you get my drift," he said, eyebrows raised, "but since the Sheriff's out of the picture for the day, would you be willing to come out to the Montforte place and take a look around?"

Will was confused. "What for?"

"I was impressed with your tracking skills yesterday. Now that your alibi checks out, officially, we need to find something that will help us point this thing in some other direction."

"You mean now?"

"Time is our enemy at a crime scene. Evidence tends to disappear faster than you'd think."

"What would Yeager say about his prime suspect poking around a crime scene?"

Pacheko shrugged. "You heard him, he's on his way to Boise. What he doesn't know won't hurt him."

Will thought about it, but before he could answer, Tommy and Libbie came out, with Marcia right behind them.

"How about some breakfast?" said Libbie. "I'm starved."

"Yeah, let's head over to Marv's," said Tommy.

"Count me in," said Will.

Pacheko cocked his head to one side and looked at Will. "Maybe later, then."

"Yeah," said Will. "Maybe later." He hurried to catch up with Tommy and Libbie, but as he watched the deputy climb into his cruiser, he couldn't help but wonder whether his request for help came with ulterior motives.

CHAPTER 14

The sun was well up as Will pedaled his bike east out of town. After the big breakfast with Tommy and Libbie all he really wanted to do was sleep, but he had to admit he was curious. Sam Montforte wasn't the most popular guy in Shambles, but he couldn't think of anyone who would have a reason to murder him any more than the Captain. Even as he rode, he was having second thoughts about helping Pacheko, but Marcia's comment about trusting someone had worked its way to the surface and begun to gnaw at him. She was right, of course, but that didn't make it any easier to swallow.

In the months since he returned to Shambles, he'd created a comfortable little cocoon for himself. Work, home, and the occasional trip to Libbie's to play with Hardscrabble had become his entire world. As long as he didn't let anyone get too close, his past remained just where it belonged, in the past. So what if he was a loner? He liked it that way; no attachments, no responsibilities to anyone except himself. He was doing just fine, why did he need to start trusting someone? Yet here he was, ignoring all that as he turned onto the road into Spring Meadows.

He often marveled at how the development looked nothing like the rest of Shambles. If the river stone columns supporting a massive wrought iron sign arching across the entrance wasn't enough, the white vinyl corral-style fences that divided the three and five-acre lots sure did the trick. There were still quite a few unsold lots, but the homes that had already been built were typical of most mountain resorts, with lots of stone and wood beams. They all had manicured, well-landscaped lawns, and a few even had swimming pools out back. Most of them had three-car garages with plenty of room for toys like bikes, ATV's, hunting or fishing gear, and at least one outbuilding that served as either a tack room or a pool house. No sir, nothing at all like the Shambles he grew up in.

He pulled up to Sam Montforte's house, or what was left of it, on a three-acre lot right along the river taking note of the Bureau of Land Management truck parked next to the police cruiser. He leaned his bike against the cruiser and hung his helmet on the handlebars.

Pacheko stepped out of the house, a smile on his face. "I'd be lying if I said I wasn't surprised to see you." He checked his watch. "How was breakfast?"

"Excellent. I almost went home for a nap. I didn't get a lot of sleep last night. But you got me curious."

"I appreciate you showing up," the deputy said, switching to his cop face. "Just remember, we need to keep it on the down low. If the Sheriff…"

"Well, I'm sure as hell not telling him." They stared each other down a few moments before Will broke a smile. "And I figure I can buy you off with a few beers."

Pacheko grunted. "Yeah, but I'm not the only one here."

"So I noticed. Since when did the BLM start working on police investigations?

"Since Dolores started taking forensic science classes down at Boise State. She's pretty sharp, and I can use all the help I can get."

"I might have some ideas about how to buy her silence."

J.D. laughed. "I want to be there when you tell her that."

"Tell me what?"

They both turned to see Dolores Esperanza walking down the driveway toward them looking like she had been poured into her trim, green and gray uniform. She was in her mid-thirties, but she looked a good ten years younger. Her smooth, olive skin almost seemed to glow. Black hair cut short and ragged, laced with blonde highlights, stuck out from under her brown baseball cap with the triangular BLM logo on the front. Full, pouty lips made her dark brown eyes look hard, but there was mischief in them as she approached.

Will tried to hide his embarrassment by wiping the sweat off his face with his shirt. Pacheko held on to his poker face, waiting to see how Will would answer her question, but she saved him the trouble. "What's he doing here?" Doesn't he know he's suspect numero uno?"

"He knows," said Pacheko.

She gave Will a look that was only half sympathetic. "Then he's not nearly as smart as I gave him credit for."

Will tilted his head in Pacheko's direction. "He didn't mention I have a solid alibi for this one?"

A smile tugged at the corners of her mouth. "He might have."

"You think I killed the Captain?" Will asked.

She gave him a wink. "Nah, I know how tight you two were. But from what I hear, you and old Sam did have your differences."

Pacheko shot a questioning look at Will, which he avoided.

"That was a long time ago," Will objected, "and I paid for it. Why would I want to stir all that up again?"

"You tell me?" asked Dolores.

"The short answer is I wouldn't. I've already had more than enough trouble with the law in my life."

"All the more reason your butt should be as far away from here as possible," said Dolores.

"Relax, Dolores," Pacheko cut in, "I invited him."

She shot him a surprised look, her dark eyes flashing with questions. "You what?"

Will cut in. "I figure my best way out of this is to find Yeager another number one suspect."

"This is an official investigation," Dolores scolded Pacheko, "we can't have civilians poking around. If Yeager finds out…"

"It's my ass on the line here, Dolores," Will interrupted. "And you aren't exactly official here yourself, are you?"

Dolores looked to Pacheko for support, but he just shrugged and said, "He's right. Besides, he's got skills, and another pair of eyes wouldn't hurt. He did find us a damn good lead at the Captain's place."

"You mean the dog?" she said, grimacing. "Eww, that must have been sick."

The two men laughed. Dolores gave them a nasty smirk, then shook her head and breathed a deep sigh that indicated her reluctant acceptance. The swelling against the front of her shirt drew both men's eyes. Dolores was the kind that didn't mind looks but pity the poor fool who got out of line with his hands. Her preferred form of exercise was karate, and she had a third-degree black belt to prove it. Rumor was a few years back Yeager had found out the hard way once. And only once.

"I'll probably regret this," she said, "but all right. You owe me, Hickock, big time."

Will smiled. "Anything, Dolores. You just name it." He was joking, but only halfway. He may not be the sharpest tool in the shed when it came to women, but he'd had his share of flings in the Army. They were all brief, mostly due to the way the Army moved people around, but that was just fine with him. Getting too attached was anathema to a loner like him.

She gave him a look that let him know there wasn't a chance in hell of getting what he had in mind, then held up a small, plastic bag. "Found these over behind the pool house."

Pacheko took the bag and held it up. Inside were two relatively fresh cigarette butts. "Did Montforte smoke?" he asked.

"That's just it," she said, "he had asthma. Wouldn't allow a lit cigarette within a hundred yards if he could help it. Could be just a couple of party guests stepped out there for a smoke, but…" She let her voice trail off.

"The killer waited around to watch it burn," said Will.

Pacheko handed the bag back to her. "Good work, Dolores. The lab said the creek washed away any DNA evidence we might have gotten from the one I found at the Captain's, but If we can get something off these we can check it against the blood from Dusty's teeth."

"Can you show me where you found those?" Will asked.

She nodded and they headed back toward the pool house. Pacheko went back inside wondering how deep a hole he had dug for himself with Yeager this time and thinking the waves back in Santa Cruz were starting to look pretty damn good right about now.

Dolores led Will to the back yard. Next to the medium-sized swimming pool was a small structure built to look like a miniature version of the main house, complete with a little porch along the front side and a pair of large windows flanking the front door. Will glanced in through the windows as he passed by and saw an open room with a pair of couches against the walls and a wet bar at the back next to a door that led to what he presumed were dressing rooms beyond. Yes, indeed, life had been good to Sam Montforte. Until now.

She pointed out where she had found the butts, near the back corner of the little house. There were tracks from Dolores's boots all over the area, but he quickly picked up another set that led up the side of the hill rising up west of the house. He pointed them out to Dolores.

"Seriously?" she said. "Those could be from anybody."

"So you think the killer just drove up into the driveway and walked up to the front door with a can of gas?" She gave him a frown that he thought was more cute than mean, and he stifled a smile. "That tall clump of brush on top of the hill would make a good surveillance spot. What's on the other side of it?"

"Haven't got the foggiest," she replied, heading back toward the house.

Will watched her go for a moment, shaking his head at the thought of asking her out on a date, then started following the tracks up the hill. As he suspected, they led right into the thick brush. He followed the trail of broken branches, picking up the same footprints again on the other side where there were additional sets, older, and all made by the same waffle-soled hiking boots.

He found multiple sets of tire tracks running to and from a narrow dirt road that ran past two empty five-acre lots below the backside of the hill in the direction of the entrance to Spring Meadows. The tracks all looked to have the same tread, and the width of the tracks told him they were all likely made by the same big truck or SUV. Whoever it was had come back multiple times. No doubt the killer wanted to learn Sam's movements in order to determine when he would be home alone.

It didn't take long to find the initial boot tracks leading down to Montforte's house. They were noticeably deeper, as they would have been with the extra weight of a full gas can or two. Something struck him as familiar about them and he knelt down to study a particularly clean print. He puzzled over it for a while but couldn't come up with anything, then followed them down the hill to the front of Sam's house. Pacheko appeared out of the dark maw that used to be the front of the house carrying several evidence bags, which he placed next to a case on a charred metal table standing near what used to the front porch.

"You found something?" asked the deputy.

"This guy's not too careful about covering his tracks," Will said, pointing up the hill. There's a road along the back side of that hill. Wouldn't take much to four-wheel it up to the top from there. Looks like he was up there more than once, parked behind all that tall brush. I can't tell for sure, but it could be the same tire track from the pullout at the Captain's."

Pacheko started walking towards his car. Will caught up to him.

"I've also got footprints coming down over here and going back up over by the pool house. They look to be the same size as the tracks at the Captain's, but he wore different boots this time."

"You're assuming it's the same person," said Pacheko.

"Two murders in two days? What are the odds we're dealing with two different killers?"

"Good point," Pacheko conceded. Opening the passenger door, he pulled out a Nikon D-9 digital camera.

Will gave a low whistle. "The sheriff's department is looking pretty high tech these days. I can't believe Yeager sprang for that."

"He didn't," Pacheko said. "It's mine."

Will was about to make a smart remark, but Pacheko was already heading up the hill. He hurried to catch up again. "If the tire tracks match, I'd bet it's the same guy. There are some pretty clear prints in the open patches between clumps of cheat grass."

Pacheko stopped and took several shots of the boot prints, then moved up the hill to the tire tracks and took some more shots. "These are a lot cleaner than the one at the Captain's, I should have no problem getting an ID."

As they headed back down to the house, Will took in the devastation caused by the fire. He'd been so focused on the tracks that he hadn't noticed before. The roof was completely gone over the front half of the house, and most of the walls in the living room had either burned through or been knocked down by the fire fighters. The fire hadn't done quite as much structural damage in the back of the house, although from where he was standing it looked like nothing was left untouched. He thought of the ranch house, and the Captain, and felt his throat start to close up again.

Pacheko noticed his interest. "The fire trucks got here pretty fast," he said, "so they were able to limit the damage somewhat. The body wasn't burnt as bad as Linehart's. The M.E. found contusions on his wrists and ankles that suggest he was tied up, and then beaten. There were knife wounds on his chest and abdomen."

"You mean like he was tortured?"

"Could be," he shrugged. "We'll know more after the autopsy." He stopped Will at the front door. "Whoa, this is as far as you go."

"Come on," Will protested. "You asked me out here to help, so let me help. Tracks are tracks, they don't have to come from feet or tires. We had to check out plenty of enemy hideouts in Iraq. I know how to spot things that are out of place."

Pacheko thought hard about it, then blew out a long breath. He reached into the evidence case and reluctantly handed Will some latex gloves and a pair of blue fabric booties. "Why do I have the feeling I'm going to regret this."

Will just smiled and slipped on the gloves booties as he followed Pacheko inside the house. "Anything in particular I should be looking for?"

"It's pretty basic. We just need to go over every square inch and note anything that looks suspicious. Not the most exciting job in the world."

"I'm up for anything that will help catch this bastard."

Pacheko broke off a piece of charred wall timber at the entry to the front of the house and it immediately crumbled to black dust in his hand. "See how this wood is fried completely?" He led Will back to the rear of the kitchen and broke off another piece of wood. "And how this isn't burned all the way through? That's a good indication some kind of accelerant was used here."

"So, someone doused the front wall with gas or something."

Pacheko nodded. "Only the front of the house, just like the Captain's."

"Arson doesn't sound like anyone local. Everyone around here would be too concerned with starting a forest fire."

"First time for everything," Pacheko said with a shrug. "He led Will into the den at the back of the house, where Dolores was snapping photos of the blood stains on a heavily singed couch that sat in the center of the room facing a giant flat screen TV, its screen shattered. She looked up, surprised to see Will, and started to say something, then decided against it, shaking her head and going back to taking pictures.

Will took one look at the couch and felt his stomach turn. He quickly looked away. "Why wouldn't he start the fire back here? Seems like he'd want to make sure the body got burned up to hide the torture marks."

"Good question. Looks to me like he did douse those bookshelves a bit. Maybe he started at the front and didn't have much left by the time he got back here, but we don't want to jump to any conclusions." He led Will back to the kitchen. "Dolores has this area covered. You start in here and I'll work the living room. If you find anything, don't touch it, just give me a holler."

Will stepped carefully around the debris that covered the floor as he began his inspection. He worked his way through several rows of drawers below the charred cabinets along one wall, finding nothing of interest. He stood up, scanning the thick granite countertop, now cracked in several places from the heat. At the far end, a wood block holding a set of carving knives caught his attention. "Hello."

Pacheko's head popped around the corner. "Got something?"

"I'm not sure," said Will, looking around the room. "One of these knives is missing. A big one, from the size of the empty slot. I don't see it anywhere around."

"Maybe it's in the dishwasher."

Dolores came in from the den. "Looking for this?" she said, holding a large, bloody carving knife carefully between two gloved fingers. It matched the kitchen set.

"Where'd you find it?" asked Pacheko, coming over for a closer look.

"Stuffed down in the couch springs," she said. "Probably thought it would burn up with everything else. Looks like he used this to cut Sam up."

"We'll know for sure when we check the blood," said Pacheko. "Maybe we'll get lucky and find a print."

"What would Sam have that's worth getting tortured for?" asked Will.

"I don't know," Pacheko shrugged. "Maybe a land deal gone bad?"

"Either way, I'd bet money it wasn't anyone from around here," said Dolores, slipping the knife into an evidence bag and sealing it. "Sam may have been a crusty old fart, but I can't think of anyone in Shambles who would do something like this." She looked directly at Will. "What do you think, Hickock?"

Will met her challenging gaze and chose not to comment, instead deferring to Pacheko. "The only stranger in town I've heard about lately is this Marcus Fitch guy who's been talking to some of the ranchers about exploratory drilling for gas. Got some folks pretty fired up."

Will perked up. "That's the guy I saw up at the Captain's. Drives a big white Dodge truck."

Pacheko nodded. "Town Council really wants to have a talk with him, but no one seems to know how to find him. He's not registered in any of the local motels."

"I've seen a big white Dodge parked out behind the Montforte Real Estate office a few times over the past week or so," said Dolores. "Wyoming plates."

"That's got to be him," said Will.

"Makes sense," Dolores continued. "Sam's filed for half a dozen resource leases with me over the last several months on a piece of land he owns down in the foothills."

"But why would Fitch kill the only man around who's willing to do business with him?" Pacheko countered.

"He couldn't be the killer," Will said flatly. Pacheko and Dolores stared at him, waiting for an explanation. "He's way too big to have made the footprints at either crime scene."

"That doesn't mean he isn't involved," said Pacheko. "He could have an accomplice." He turned to Dolores. "You know of anyone else who's filed for permits?"

"Not on BLM land," said Dolores. "I only know about Sam's property because he traded us a prime acreage over by Featherville for it a few years back. I can't speak for any other private landowners, but they may not even know it's being done. These land men can be real sneaky. They don't even have to notify landowners when they file for oil and gas leases."

"You mean they can just buy a lease right out from under your nose?" exclaimed Will.

"There are rules, but if you're not paying attention, yeah, it's possible."

"Do me a favor, Dolores," said Pacheko," next time you see that pickup at Montforte's office, or anywhere else, give me a call."

"Sure," said Dolores. She went off to find another evidence bag and Will continued his search of the kitchen.

Pacheko returned to the living room, kneeling down to rummage through the contents of a blackened set of built-in shelving that had collapsed onto the floor, but he found himself distracted. Something was troubling him. It took him a minute or so to work out what it was, and when he finally did, he sat back on his knees and called into the kitchen. "What did Dolores mean earlier about you and Montforte having differences?"

Will's shoulders slumped and he let out a big breath, but he didn't answer. All his life he'd been suspicious of other people. He always figured that, growing up the way he had, it just came with the territory, but it had definitely kept him from getting too close to anyone. The Captain used to tell him that it was because he didn't see himself as trustworthy, but the way Will saw it, the less people knew about him, the easier it was to blend in and go unnoticed.

Part of him would just as soon forget he was alive before his eighteenth birthday, but even after he got back from the Army the old stories about his past still surfaced from time to time. Most of them had become exaggerated beyond the point of belief over the years, and some were just bald-faced lies, but a few others held enough truth to make him less than comfortable with the way some folks looked at him.

After being gone for ten years all that had finally begun to fade away. Now these two murders were digging it all back up again, whether he liked it or not.

"You playing shrink or cop?" Will finally asked as he rounded the corner into the living room just in time to see Pacheko place a charred chunk of something into a plastic bag and seal it up.

"Any cop worth his salt is a little of both."

Part of Will wanted to believe that Pacheko was just fishing, but the look in his eyes told him the deputy had found a scent.

Pacheko looked up at Will. "Wouldn't have anything to do with that payroll robbery, would it?"

Will stayed silent again, waiting to see if the deputy would reveal just how much he knew. Pacheko put more samples in another bag and finally continued. "The ME also told me he noticed an old scar on Montforte's right side. Said it looked a lot like a bullet wound."

Will dropped his chin to his chest and hung his head, shaking it slowly. "You're like a dog with a bone, aren't you? You get hold of something, and you just don't let go."

"Not if I can help it."

Will set his jaw and turned to face the deputy. "Okay, Montforte was the payroll guard I shot. There. You satisfied now?"

"Getting there," Pacheko said with a grin.

CHAPTER 15

Funerals weren't usually a big deal in Shambles but laying Placer County's beloved Sheriff Wardell Linehart to rest brought the everybody out. There must have been close to five hundred, all dressed up in their Sunday best. It was a beautiful day with bright blue skies and a handful of puffy white clouds drifting past the mountain peaks. The summer tourist season wouldn't kick in full bore for another couple of weeks, but the population of the tiny town had swelled with folks from all over the county and beyond, come to pay their last respects to the man who more than anyone else had represented law and order in and around Shambles for almost four decades.

The little Presbyterian church in the center of town couldn't begin to hold all the mourners, and the overflow milled around outside in the warm sunshine, listening to the organ music that drifted out from inside and looking anxious, as if they were about to witness some kind of miracle or something. Like maybe the Captain was going to rise up and stroll right out those polished oak doors dancing to the Resurrection Blues.

Inside, Sheriff Rod Yeager planted himself in the front pew, right on the aisle, trying hard to look important sitting next to the spit-and-polished State Police Chief George Rankin and a dozen other officers from various law enforcement agencies around the state, all long-time colleagues and friends of the former Sheriff. The Sheriff wore his dress uniform, brass polished, pants creased, his snakeskin cowboy boots rubbed to a high gloss, and a brand-new black Stetson on his lap, but few, if any gave him so much as a glance.

Will sat two pews back at the far outside end, trying to be as inconspicuous as possible, though he felt anything but in the new blue blazer he bought for the occasion. He was uncomfortable enough in khakis and a clean white shirt without the damned necktie choking him. He fought to keep himself from tugging at it, and renewed his promise to himself that he would not cry.

He'd been extremely uncomfortable entering the church, not because he wasn't much of a believer in organized religion, but because of the looks he was getting from the other people in the room. He knew how fast rumors spread in a small town like Shambles, and he had no doubt that Yeager had been bragging about how he'd already caught Linehart's murderer. He avoided as many eyes as he could, unable to tell whether they felt sorry for him because of his relationship with his old friend or if they were suspicious that he might have been the one who killed him.

The Reverend had asked him if he would like to say a few words, but he firmly declined. Speaking in public was way outside his comfort zone. Besides, his feelings for the Captain were far too personal to share with any of these people, no matter how close they had been to the man he loved like a father.

Flanked by a State Police color guard, Pastor Michael Brannigan—Reverend Mike to nearly everyone in town, Presbyterian or not—gave a stirring eulogy. He spoke of Wardell's service in Korea, which had won him a Silver Star, and how the tragic death of his wife, Mary, during the still-birth of their first child had driven him from his lifelong home in Ohio to seek a more favorable fortune in the gold and silver mines of Idaho. And every head in the church nodded somberly when he spoke about how lucky they were that the Captain had never struck it rich as a miner and ended up taking on the job of sheriff to make ends meet.

Will had heard the story of LInehart's arrival in Shambles a hundred times, of his signing on as a Sheriff's deputy because he was dead broke after several failed mining attempts, and the smelter wasn't hiring. He knew by heart how Linehart's natural investigative instincts, what the Captain called his "nose for trouble," that had helped him rise from deputy to Sheriff in just two short years.

Will also knew it was the Captain's love of kids, as much as his longing for the family he never had, that drove him to persuade the Placer County purse-tenders to help him buy out a dying ranch operation in a scenic valley three miles up in the mountains north of town so that youngsters who went astray could be given a chance to find the right path again by working off their sentences there instead of languishing in the county jail. And he knew it was Linehart's innate ability to talk anyone into almost anything that convinced many of his friends in law enforcement to volunteer their off-duty time as guards and counselors over the years.

Sheriff Yeager was the next to speak. He'd been appointed by the Town Council to finish out Linehart's term when he finally decided to retire a little over a year ago. Yeager was the only deputy and by default the only other person in the area remotely qualified to take on the job. No one was very happy about it, but no one else seemed to want it badly enough to step up and prevent Yeager from taking over. The Captain had managed to keep his deputy's laziness and short temper in check for the most part, but those unfortunate traits had resurfaced increasingly in the year since he'd become Sheriff.

Linehart ignored the Council's pleas to hang around long enough for them to conduct a proper search for his replacement. He'd made up his mind to leave, and by God he was leaving. He was going to do nothing but fish, and hunt, and enjoy the rest of his life. No one ever suspected that life would end so soon.

Will watched out of the corner of his eye as Yeager made his way to the podium, hitching his pants up under his belly. The thin line of moustache on his lip was beginning to show some grey, and it twitched nervously as he made a brief, halting statement of how the Captain had been a role model and a mentor to him, and taught him everything he knew about law enforcement, and how proud he was to be following in such hallowed footsteps. He concluded his mercifully brief remarks by thanking the Town Council for trusting in him and promising that to do his best to live up to the high standards the Captain had set.

Will could not hide a smirk. Leave it to Yeager to make it all about himself. The row of law enforcement officials in front seemed to breathe a collective sigh of relief when the Sheriff finally stepped down.

Last, but not least, Reverend Mike introduced the Idaho State Police Chief. George Rankin tucked his hat under one arm as he walked up to the podium. He was a tall, lean man, his close-cropped hair greying at the temples, and looked dashing in his dark blue uniform, his chest adorned with medals. He proceeded to praise Sheriff Linehart, both as a good friend and as an exemplary law enforcement officer, telling the people of Placer County how blessed they were to have had such a man as a leader in their community. He spoke of the overwhelming opposition Linehart had overcome to turn the Ranch into an extremely successful juvenile rehabilitation facility that had turned hundreds of young boys from a dark path in life back toward the light. Thanks in no small part, he intoned in an deep, serious voice, to the Captain's philosophy that hard work will make any man better, and there is no harder work than running a ranch.

He related how his good friend Wardell had found the property for sale and struck a deal with the State Land Board to purchase it, with the State paying a percentage of the mortgage as long as it operated exclusively as a juvenile facility. Linehart had run it successfully for over twenty years, until legislative budget cuts did away with funding. With the detention center gone, the ranch still needed running. As luck would have it, the mortgage had been paid off the previous year and Wardell was able to run it by himself.

Rankin broke the solemn mood with a story about how one particular inmate at the Ranch, who happened to be from Mississippi, had taken to calling Wardell "Captain" just to try and get his goat. Rather than a harsh response, Wardell chose to take it as a sign of respect and began calling the inmate "Cool Hand Luke" for the duration of his stay. The ploy worked. Luke went on to a successful, honest life, but the name he planted on the Sheriff stuck, and it had since become the title by which nearly everyone knew and respected him.

The Chief praised Wardell for having the courage to stand up for what was right, despite ongoing attempts by bureaucrats and politicians to dismiss his pet project as a waste of time and money. He thanked Linehart posthumously on behalf of all the young men and women whose lives were better today for having spent time there. He went on to cite several examples of people who, after rocky beginnings brought them a stay at the Ranch, had gone on to make something meaningful of their lives.

He recognized a number of those examples in the audience, and to a man they were nodding their heads in agreement. He couldn't help but notice the Chief's gaze settle on him for a brief moment, too, and by the time Rankin was finished, there wasn't a dry eye in the house. Will battled his emotions throughout the proceedings but somehow managed to keep them from getting the best fo him. He knew it was foolish, but part of him felt like the Captain would be proud of him for keeping his promise.

As soon as the service ended, the County Coroner Ed Stubbins, who doubled as the Funeral Director, hustled down the aisle and ordered everyone waiting outside to line up along the front walk out to the street. Then he directed the pallbearers to march the casket between the rows of bereaved townsfolk to the hearse, which he'd parked clear down at the corner of the block, so each and every one of them could say a final farewell to a pillar of their community.

Sheriff Yeager was carrying one of the rear handles on the coffin, and when he saw the size of the crowd outside, his moustache started to twitch again. His beady eyes darted around suspiciously, and for a moment it looked like he might abandon the casket and launch into crowd control. He might have, too, if Reverend Mike hadn't laid a calming hand on his shoulder and whispered a reminder of the priorities at that particular moment, pointing out that everyone was, after all, pretty well behaved.

Yeager reverently lowered his head, hitched up his pants with his free hand, and continued the solemn march oblivious to the stifled grins and snickers of his fellow pallbearers and several onlookers. Will adjusted his grip on the opposite handle and fell back into step, trying hard not to look over at Yeager.

The Sheriff had been damn near apoplectic when he found out Will was going to be one of the pallbearers. He'd actually told Reverend Mike he wanted Will removed from the list, but the reverend just gave him a scowl, then turned on his heel and walked away. He even tried pleading his case to the rest of the men asked to serve, but got no support there, either, which had made Will breathe a little easier. As much as he disliked Yeager, he wasn't about to be left out. And truth be told, they needed every man they had. Even burned to a crisp, the Captain was not a light load.

CHAPTER 16

Most of the crowd chose not to make the journey to the tiny cemetery perched on a gently sloping hillside west of town. Knowing how close Will and the Captain had been, Stubbins had asked him to pick a final resting spot for his friend, a request he was honored to fulfill.

He'd chosen a plot at the highpoint of the graveyard near one of the ancient ponderosa pines that surrounded the grassy field. He liked to imagine the Captain laid out comfortably, the mountains rising majestically behind him, gazing out over the small, rough-shod mining town that had become his home, and on across the wide valley to the Middle Fork of the Boise River that ran southwest toward the high desert. He smiled to himself at the thought that the only thing missing was a six-pack of his favorite Miller High Life for the Captain to enjoy on his trip to eternity.

Once the casket was placed on the crossbars above the grave and the State Police color guard had marched into place at its foot, Reverend

Mike took up the Bible once more. Apparently, he hadn't preached his fill in church and proceeded to read several more passages from the good book before he finally wound down. Then the color guard fired off a 21-gun salute, and somebody played a recording of "Taps over a small, tinny speaker placed next to the grave." As the last, mournful trumpet notes rang through the surrounding peaks, the small crowd began to drift away with them, talking quietly and shaking their heads at the sadness of the whole affair.

After accepting condolences from a few of the townsfolk who remembered him, Will lingered, not wanting to say goodbye to the man who'd raised him since he was seven years old and taught him right from wrong. He stared down at the coffin resting in the bottom of the grave and wished for the thousandth time he had stopped that evening and taken his old friend fishing with him. If only he hadn't been so selfish the Captain would be alive right now and they'd be drinking beer and swapping stories of the good old days.

Will couldn't stop his eyes from welling up. Even as he'd watched the firemen haul the body out of the charred ranch house, he wouldn't let himself believe the old man was dead. When that rationalization wore off, he got angry—at himself for not somehow preventing it, at the Captain for leaving him, and finally at the rest of the world for allowing such a tragedy to occur in the first place. Now he realized they were all just abstract excuses that only postponed the inevitable realization. The Captain was gone, and he would never be back.

The dam broke. Tears flowed freely and Will felt his body shudder as the first sob worked its way to the surface. As it escaped, he felt his knees start to buckle. A strong arm wrapped around his shoulders and held him upright. He couldn't look up to see who it was, but through his tears he could make out a Bible clutched against vestments.

"It's all right, son," Reverend Mike said softly, "let it out. It had to come sometime and now is just as good as any."

Will had no idea how long he let himself be held like that, sobbing and sniffling. When he finally pulled himself together again, Reverend Mike gave him one last gentle squeeze and let him stand on his own.

Abe Wilson, the cemetery caretaker, and his gravedigger Stanley had already started shoveling dirt into the grave. As Will stared, transfixed, at the coffin slowly being covered up, two sharply pointed toes on a pair of snakeskin cowboy boots stepped into his field of vision at the opposite edge of the grave, poking out from under tan uniform pants. Will looked up as Yeager gave Abe and Stanley a look that sent them over to their truck for a smoke, then removed his new Stetson and held it over his protruding belly, as if to hide the fact that the buttons on the bottom of his blue dress uniform shirt were straining so much that his white undershirt showed through.

"He was a good man," said Yeager. "Best law officer I ever knew."

The lump in Will's throat was still too big to allow any words past, so he just nodded. There was a moment of silence as the sheriff stared down at the coffin paying his last respects, then he sighed deeply and spoke again.

"I just don't understand it." He let the words hang in the still air. They hovered low over the grave between them like a balloon that wasn't quite out of helium. Finally, Will looked up and found the sheriff's small, dark eyes bearing down on him. He knew Yeager was baiting him, but he was in no mood for games.

Finally, Yeager spoke again. "But don't you worry, I'll figure out who did it." The stare hardened. "And when I do, I promise you'll be the first to know."

A nasty retort was right on the tip of Will's tongue, but he wasn't about to let his temper get the best of him. Not here. Not today. Not in front of the Captain.

"Jesus, Sheriff, lay off." Pacheko said, stepping up beside Yeager and casting a sympathetic glance Will's way. His uniform was rumpled and covered with dirt and soot marks, indicating he'd been working at the crime scene.

Will had asked around, but no one seemed to know much about J.D. Pacheko except that he came from California and had a master's degree in Criminal Justice from Boise State University. That alone put him miles ahead of his boss, who barely got through high school, and provided plenty of reason for the withering look the sheriff shot at his subordinate.

"What the hell are you doing here, Pacheko? I thought I told you to work out at Montforte's place."

The deputy just shrugged it off. "I was, and I found something I thought you ought to know about."

"Whatever it is, it can wait until I get back to the office!" Yeager snapped. "This here ain't none of your damn business."

"This isn't the time or the place, Rod," the deputy deadpanned quietly. "Linehart's barely in the ground, for Christ's sake."

The Sheriff's accusing scowl shifted back to Will. He looked like he wanted to say something more, but after a glance down at the half-covered coffin, he stuffed his hat back on his head and stomped off toward the parking lot.

The deputy offered up his crooked grin. If it wasn't for the uniform, you'd swear he was just some California surf bum with his unkempt straw-colored hair and deep blue eyes that, at the moment, seemed to offer an apology. "He sure doesn't like you."

Will snorted. "The feeling's mutual."

"I guess everyone's a little on edge today."

"Yeah, I guess."

The sound of the Excursion roaring to life in the distance drew their attention and they both watched it tear away, tires spitting dirt.

"Thanks for that," said Will.

The blue eyes went soft, and the deputy looked down and shuffled his feet. "Look, I don't feel too comfortable discussing things right here over the man's grave and all. Besides, the sheriff will be looking for me back at the shop. But if you ever feel like talking, anytime, you just give me a shout, okay?"

Will didn't really hear the man, didn't look up to see him leave, or pull out of the empty parking lot in the department's black-and-white Chevy cruiser. He just stood there, staring out at nothing, feeling the sorrow that had gripped him the past few days morph into a new kind of anger deep inside. His jaw tightened and his hands clenched into fists so tight his knuckles went white. After several moments he began to feel lightheaded, and he realized he hadn't been breathing.

Reaching out for support, his hand found the handle of a shovel sticking up from the pile of dirt next to the grave. He stared at it for what seemed like minutes as he took several deep breaths, then he slowly removed his blazer started to fill the grave. The more he shoveled, the more the idea of someone killing the Captain ate at him and the faster he worked, until he was breathing hard and sweat ran down his face.

Abe and Stanley stood over by their truck, watching him curiously. After a while, they both lit another cigarette.

CHAPTER 17

An hour later, Will pulled into his driveway and came to a stop where the twin concrete strips ended beside his house. He looked a mess. His new pants were streaked with dirt, his shirt sweat-soaked from filling the Captain's grave. Much to Abe and Stanley's surprise, he even helped them cover it with sod. He grabbed his blazer and necktie, both of which thankfully remained stain-free, from the seat next to him and slid out the door, feeling an extreme need for a shower.

The sound of a small engine slowing down out front caught his ear and he walked around the front corner of the house just as Hilda Jackson stuck her daily deposit of junk mail in his box. They exchanged a wave, and she was off, paying his appearance no mind. By the time he reached his mailbox she was already past Bowman's and rounding the next corner, headed for Ray Parker's place three streets over, his next closest full-time neighbor, and owner of the country store cum mercantile.

Ray had sold out to Stu English a few months ago and was waiting for his new house to be completed over in Spring Meadows so he could move in. Apparently, Stu's desire to transition into commercial real estate fostered considerably more generosity than his offers for residential plots like his. Given Stu's recent success acquiring Marv Bowman's place, it wouldn't be long now until he would be Hilda's only stop on The Hill. As expected, the stack of envelopes he retrieved from his mailbox contained numerous offers for credit cards, cruises, and other "deal of a lifetime" sales pitches. Except for one.

Will had dealt with lawyers only twice in his life. The first time was when he was remanded to the Ranch after the payroll robbery, and the second was when he inherited his mother's estate. The name printed in bold, black letters on the upper left-hand corner of the envelope brought both those memories back into sharp focus: *Arvin Melville, Attorney at Law*. Will studied it apprehensively as he walked back to the house.

Melville was Shambles' oldest resident. Hell, he was ancient when he'd executed the transfer of Will's mother's house after her death some twenty years before. It was the only time Will had ever met the man. Rumor had it he was born in Shambles, but no one had ever been able to verify it. Records from the early twentieth century in a town this small were sparse, to say the least, and in many cases non-existent. He seemed to recall hearing that the old codger had finally retired from practice several years ago, at the ripe old age of eighty-something. He stared at the plain, white envelope with its stark, black lettering, wondering what part of his past had caught up with him this time.

As he stepped inside, hunger gripped him, and he remembered he hadn't felt like eating before the funeral, so he skipped breakfast.

Dropping the mail on the kitchen table, he peeled off his sweaty shirt as he walked over to his refrigerator. He kept it well stocked with fresh vegetables, fruits and juices, along with the obligatory six-pack of Miller High Life. Kitchen duty had been a regular part of the chore rotation during his years at the Ranch, but his true appreciation for the skills he'd acquired there hadn't come until he began living on his own and realized how much money he could save by cooking for himself.

Will was not a fast-food guy. Unlike most kids, he hadn't grown up on the stuff. When he was little, they could never afford it—not that McDonald's or Burger King had ever thought about setting up shop in Shambles—and at the Ranch it most certainly was not an option. He pulled out a carton of milk then reached into the cupboard for a box of Kellogg's Mini-Wheats and a bowl and a minute later he sat down to a heaping bowl of cereal covered with sliced banana.

In the Army a lack of funds limited him to the mess hall, where the food actually wasn't bad, but like the vast majority of his fellow soldiers, he was never much of a fan of the MRE's they were issued whenever he was deployed. By the time he returned home he favored a healthier diet of cereals, fruit and salads, but he was by no means a vegetarian. His freezer always held a ready supply of steaks and burgers, and his fishing skills provided fresh trout whenever he had time to get out and catch them. The propane grill in his backyard bore a decidedly well-used look.

As he ate, he reflected on his time back in Shambles after a decade serving his country. Since his return, he'd pretty much kept to himself, as was his habit, and to his mind he'd been a model citizen. All the more reason his recent arrests had caused a nagging irritation to take up residence in the back of his brain.

His penchant for staying out of trouble at all costs had always played into his reputation as a loner all his adult life, but he didn't mind. It seemed like every time he let someone get too close it always ended badly. Sooner or later, they would ask about his past, and on the rare occasion when he told them they would either get real distant and eventually stop seeing him altogether, or they would feel sorry for him, in which case he would get real distant and eventually stop seeing them altogether. Somewhere along the line he'd just stopped trying.

The Captain was an exception. When Will first moved back to Shambles, before he started guiding for the Spanglers, he relied on odd jobs to keep the bills paid, and he often had to depend on his fishing and hunting skills to put food on the table. The old Sheriff had helped him out on both scores, paying him to help with chores around the Ranch from time to time, and reintroducing him to the hunting and fishing spots they used to visit when Will was growing up. Naturally that also meant renewing Will's tracking lessons, and the bond that had developed between them during their years together at the Ranch flourished anew.

They'd been quite the pair back in those days, the young boy and the old codger. A couple of loners who enjoyed the same passion for the outdoors. Truth was, each filled a hole in the other's life. The old Sheriff became the father Will never had, and Will was the son Wardell always wanted. When Will left for the Army, it was the only time he had ever seen the Captain shed a tear. Will felt his emotions rising and fought back the memory, forcing his mind back to the present.

This business with Yeager was more irritating than anything else. He didn't think it was likely he'd ever actually be charged with anything, despite Yeager's animosity toward him. Still, there was a good possibility that he might need a lawyer at some point. And there was that damned letter staring him in the face, daring him to open it. The dare continued to lay on the table while he washed the dishes. He tried to ignore it while he stripped to his shorts in the bedroom but finally, he couldn't stand it any longer and decided the shower could wait. He sat back down at the kitchen table in his underwear to confront whatever awaited him.

He opened the envelope slowly, holding it at arms' length as though the bad news might explode like one of the IED's he had seen ruin so many lives in Iraq and Afghanistan. Inside was a single sheet of crisp, white paper with the same stark black letterhead that was on the envelope. Typed neatly below, over Arvin Melville's elaborate, if shaky, signature, was a single, brief paragraph requesting a meeting at Will's earliest convenience to discuss a matter of great importance "to both of us."

Will scratched his head and read the letter again. Hell, the man had retired before Will ever came back to town. What could possibly be important to both of them? A chill ran down the back of his neck, another skill he'd picked up in the Rangers, and something that only happened when trouble was in the vicinity.

CHAPTER 18

Half an hour later, showered, shaved, and dressed in a fresh blue polo shirt and his best jeans, Will emerged from his bedroom. He read the letter twice more before stuffing it in his pocket and walking out the back door. The drive across town took less than five minutes. The sun had dropped behind the western peaks and the light was just beginning to fade. He was halfway to Melville's office before it occurred to him that he probably should have called ahead to make an appointment.

What the hell, he thought, it wasn't like the man still had a pack of clients filling up his day. But then, what if he only worked mornings? What if he was bedridden, or sick? He almost talked himself into going back home and calling, and for another, decidedly briefer moment he found himself wishing he'd given in and bought a cell phone like everyone was always bugging him to do. By then he was turning onto Highland Drive, the showplace of Shambles, the only street in town that could truly be called historic. He figured he was committed now.

Only two blocks long, the street was lined with huge old two and three-story mansions, built by the lucky few who struck it rich in the mines over the years. Almost all the houses had been well maintained as monuments to what the town used to be, and since the tourism renaissance had hit town, a few had been completely restored. Lawns were green and manicured, paint was clean and fresh, trees neatly pruned. Most had become swank office space for successful businesses like the Baker & Baker, a husband-and-wife law firm that had sprouted up three or four years back, and Stu English, who had set up shop in the old Walters place on the corner just a year after he moved to town. Only a handful were still private homes.

Melville had always run his business out of the grand, three-story Georgian mansion that dominated the second block, where his family had lived ever since they built it sometime around the turn of the twentieth century. Apparently, the good folks of Shambles had always felt the need for a good lawyer. Will pulled up in front of the huge house and suddenly felt like he should have worn his new blazer, maybe even the tie. Too late now, he thought climbing out of his truck. He just wanted to get whatever this was over with.

The imposing marble sign planted in the front yard was engraved with Melville's name in the same bold, black letters that appeared on the letterhead now residing in Will's pocket. It was surrounded by a colorful, freshly tilled bed of tulips and petunias and Will couldn't help but wonder if the old man still did his own gardening. Two giant blindingly white pillars towered over him as he climbed the broad steps leading up to an expansive porch that ran the length of the house. It took a full five strides to reach the wide black double doors that must have been ten feet tall.

He started to knock, then noticed a large brass knob sticking out from the wall just to the left of the doors. He gave it a pull and a series of chimes rang softly inside. After several nervous moments, he was about to pull the knob again when the door cracked open about a foot. He waited, but no one appeared. Finally, a gruff voice bellowed from inside.

"Well, don't just stand there, come on in."

Will pushed the door open and eased inside. A wizened old man sat in a wheelchair, dwarfed by a huge foyer open to the floor above. He was dressed in a tan suit, his crisply starched white shirt set off by an old-fashioned string tie with a large, polished agate cinched up to the collar. A shawl hung loosely around his shoulders. Wisps of thin, grey hair surrounded his bald pate, matching the wild eyebrows that glowered over dark, sunken eyes.

His bony hands tugged at the wheels of his chair, backing himself slowly away from the door. He looked extremely weak, but his eyes were startlingly alive. They darted over every inch of Will, taking in each detail, then suddenly shifted as they caught sight of something behind him.

"Shut the damn door," he barked in a surprisingly commanding voice, "you're letting the heat out."

Will gave the huge door a push. The sound of it closing echoed off the polished wood floors and up the sweeping staircase that led to a wide second-floor landing. Will's eyes followed the sound, and he was awed by the size and magnificence of the place. The old man noticed Will staring.

"Kinda like a museum, ain't it?" he said, forcing a grunt that might have been intended as a laugh.

It was as if Will had stepped back in time a hundred years. The furniture, paintings and photographs were all from another, much older era. Even the wallpaper looked like something out of an old movie, and yet, absolutely everything appeared brand spanking new, as if it had just come off the showroom floor. The one concession to modern tecŠology was a small metal platform attached to an electrical track embedded in the wall that ran up the stairs.

"It's always been this way," said Melville, "ever since my father built it in nineteen ought-eight. Just the way my mother, God rest her soul, left it."

Will tore his eyes away from a series of black and white photographs depicting Shambles during the boom times. "You're Arvin Melville?" he stammered.

"Who the hell were you expecting, Popeye the sailor man?"

"No sir, I…"

"Surprised to find me alive, huh? Well, I've got news for you. I feel the same way every morning when I wake up." He appeared to laugh, but the only sound that came out was a faint wheezing, then he leaned forward in his chair. "But it helps to live in a house where everything's older than I am." He smiled, showing neat white rows of dentures that looked a little too big in the gaunt, wrinkled face.

Will smiled back, amazed at such clarity and wit coming from a body that appeared so frail. He was so overwhelmed by the man and the place he could not think of a single thing to say. Melville stared at him a moment, then cocked his head to one side. "

Spit it out, boy, time's a wasting. What do you want?"

The force of the demand shocked Will to action and he pulled the letter from his pocket. "I, uh, got this…" he began softly, his voice trailing off as he held the paper out in front of him. He noticed his hand was shaking slightly.

Melville cupped a hand to one ear. "What's that? You've got what?"

Will cleared his throat. "This letter."

"A letter, you say. Who's it from?"

"It's from you."

"Me. What the hell did I send you a letter about?"

"It says you want to discuss a matter of great importance to both of us."

"I said that? Let me see that thing." He suddenly wheeled himself forward and grabbed the letter, then fumbled in his pockets for his glasses, which were hanging on a lanyard around his neck. "What did you say your name was?"

"Hickock. Will Hickock."

Melville's whole face lit up and he forgot about the glasses.

"Wardell's boy! Well, why the hell didn't you say so? I ain't seen you since…hell, I can't remember when."

"When I inherited my mother's house over on the Hill."

"That right?" Melville struggled to remember, then gave up. "Where the hell you been?"

"The Army, mostly."

A memory seemed to spark to life in the old man. "Yeah, I seem to remember Wardell sayin' something about that." His face suddenly went sad. "Damned shame about Wardell, the way he went and all. Any idea who done it?"

Will shook his head.

"Figures with that no account we got for a Sheriff now. Wardell would've had the bastard behind bars long before this."

The sudden, spirited reference to the Captain threatened a rush of emotion, but it vanished as quickly as it came and Will felt relieved that he'd finally gotten his grief under control. He wanted to say that he would damn well find out who did it, but instead he just smiled and nodded, feeling the quiet confidence of his Ranger persona taking charge. Melville looked him over again.

"Wardell's boy," he repeated softly, smiling again. "Well, kiss ol' Rosie, if this ain't a day! Wheel me into my office, son."

Will stepped behind the chair and stood there, not knowing which way he should go.

"Come on, I ain't got all day. Through there," Melville ordered, pointing a bony finger toward an ornate archway beneath the landing.

Will pushed the chair under the arch into a wide hallway with highly polished hardwood floors. The walls were lined with portraits of statesman-like men and elegantly dressed women. His mind was bubbling over with curiosity, but he was halfway down the hall before he could find his voice.

"Are all these your family?"

"Damned if you can't speak a full sentence," Melville responded, slapping the armrest with his hand. "We'll have us a conversation yet." He jabbed his arm toward another archway at the end of the hall. "In there," he barked.

Will steered him into a large corner room with tall windows lining the two outside walls. Lace curtains, tied apart at the midpoint, gave way to a spacious view of the mountains towering above the western edge of town. The other two walls were covered, literally, with dozens of degrees, certificates, awards and photographs, many of which showed a younger Melville with various distinguished-looking men. Will was sure he recognized some of the faces from his high school history books. He noticed more than a few of the photos included the Captain.

An ornately carved wooden desk sat atop a beautiful oriental rug. Will felt the chair slow to a crawl as its wheels sank into the deep pile. He strained to keep going, but Melville took over with a surprising show of strength and wheeled himself behind the desk. Aside from a small lamp, a brass nameplate, and an upright pen set with an engraved brass plaque—yet another award—only a leather-lined blotter and a set of cut-glass coasters adorned the glistening desktop. The office, like the rest of the house he had seen so far, gave the eerie impression that the old man had already died, and the museum was open for tourists.

Melville slapped Will's letter on a yellow legal pad atop the blotter and pulled open a file drawer on one side of the desk.

"Don't just stand there like a statue, son, pull up a chair," he said.

Will slid into one of three wooden chairs lined up across the front of the desk, sitting opposite Melville who was lifting a thick file from the drawer. After he finally located his glasses—not without some difficulty—and perched them on his nose, he began arranging papers from the file in a neat row in front of him.

"I don't hold much with funerals anymore," he said. "Reminds me too much of my own impending doom, I suppose." He peered at Will over his glasses. "I'm assuming Reverend Mike did him proud."

"Yes, sir, he did," Will managed.

Melville gave a curt nod and went back to arranging his papers. When he was finished, leaned back in his chair with a sigh, looking over his glasses at Will. "You have no idea why you're here, do you, son?"

"No sir," said Will.

Melville smiled softly and shook his head. "That would be just like Wardell."

"What's this got to do with the Captain?"

"He never was one to talk about personal matters."

"Not while I knew him."

"Which was how long, exactly?" asked Melville.

"First time I met him was when he arrested me."

Melville's bushy eyebrows shot up, then he frowned and began shuffling through the papers.

"Ah, yes, I remember now. You'll have to excuse me, it's been some time since I've had occasion to read his file." He pulled out a sheet of paper and scanned it. "That would have been after you attempted to rob the smelter payroll with your brother at gunpoint." He stopped reading and peered over his glasses again. You were, what, eight years old at the time?"

"Seven," said Will.

Melville grunted softly and continued reading. "Your mother died shortly afterwards. You were confined to the juvenile facility known as the Ranch until your eighteenth birthday, at which time you were released for good behavior, and proceeded to join the Army for..." The eyebrows went up again. "...ten years. Ranger. Three tours in Iraq. Decorated for bravery, Bronze Star." He paused and looked up at Will. "Doesn't exactly read like the resume of a career criminal."

"The Rangers taught me some hard lessons, but it was the who Captain really turned my life around. He showed me I could become a useful member of society instead of just looking out for my own personal gain, like my brother."

"That would be one Doc Holliday Hickock," said Melville, reading again, "killed in that same robbery attempt. Interesting choice of names."

"My father fancied himself some kind of wild west expert. I never knew him. He ran off right after I was born."

"Leaving you with an interesting moniker of your own." He peered over his glasses again. "Is this correct on your birth certificate? Wild Bill Hickock?"

Will nodded, red-faced and fuming in his chair. He hated that name with a passion. If Melville noticed, he gave no indication. "Any relation?" asked the old man."

"So the story goes. I've never bothered to check."

"Hmmm. I can understand the Wild Bill connection, but Doc Holliday?"

Will sighed, trying to keep his frustration in check. "It was the tuberculosis."

"I beg your pardon?"

"Doc was born with a mild form of childhood tuberculosis, and my father..."

"Same disease that took the original Doc Holliday."

"He grew out of the disease, but the name stuck."

Melville gave him a wry smile. "Your father must have been and interesting fellow."

"I guess that's one way of putting it," said Will. "I really wouldn't know."

The old attorney paused and studied him a moment. "Well, Bill..."

"I go by Will now."

Melville seemed startled by the firmness of his response. He looked down at the papers again and cleared his throat. "Yes, I see that here now. Well, Will, let's get down to brass tacks."

Melville picked up one of the documents from the row of papers in front of him and placed it in front of Will.

"That is Wardell Linehart's Last Will and Testament." Will stared at the document. "From the look on your face I'm going to assume Wardell never said anything about it to you."

Will started to speak but there was suddenly a lump in his throat, so he just shook his head. He felt his eyes tear up and he looked away.

Melville respectfully went back to arranging his papers. "I miss him, too, son. He was my last true friend on this earth."

Will noticed the old man's eyes were damp as well. "How well did you know him?"

"We had occasion to meet in the courthouse quite often while he was still a deputy. I liked him. He had spunk. He didn't sugarcoat his opinions and was never afraid to stand up to any man in the name of justice. I campaigned for him when he ran for Sheriff, and we became friends. When he bought his ranch from the state, the legalities proved too much to handle by himself and he was forced to ask me for assistance."

Melville chuckled at the remembrance before continuing. "It pained him a great deal, and despite my protests he insisted on paying my full fee. I donated it to his next campaign, which made him even madder."

Will had to laugh, nodding at a memory of his own. "When I got back from the Army, I bought him a new fishing rod, to thank him for…everything."

"For taking a young boy who had strayed onto a dark path and guiding him back to the light?" asked Melville.

Will smiled. "He was always fond of that phrase." Melville nodded in agreement. "He did that for a whole lot of us at the Ranch, but any time anyone tried to thank him he always said he was just doing his job, and he didn't want anything in return. When I gave him the rod, he got so damned mad I thought he was going to pop a vein."

"What did you do?"

"I got mad myself and walked out, left the rod laying on his kitchen table. A couple of days later he called and asked if I wanted to go fishing. When I showed up, he pulled out the new rod and proceeded to catch his limit in less than an hour. He never said another word about it, but every time we went fishing after that he always brought that rod."

Melville chuckled. "Did he ever take you to his secret spot, up above the Ranch where McKinley creek comes out of the mountains?"

"Ever since I was 10. He swore me to secrecy. Said he'd never told another soul. How do you know about it?"

"Who do you think showed it to him?"

They shared a laugh, and a silence settled over the room as the two men remembered. Finally, Melville spoke. "He thought the world of you, young man."

Will looked down at the document. "It says that in there?"

"Not in so many words, but he told me so himself many times."

"Well, the feeling was mutual," Will replied.

"I can see that. And that's why it's a pleasure for me to inform you that Wardell left everything he had in this world to you."

Will's jaw dropped open and his eyes grew wide as saucers.

Melville smiled. "I know it's bit of a shock."

"You…you mean the ranch?" Will stammered.

Melville nodded. "Lock, stock and barrel. It's completely paid off, too. That, along with his truck and a few thousand in the bank was all he had except for his pension, which unfortunately can't go to you because he never officially adopted you."

"Holy shit," Will breathed softly, feeling his throat close up and his eyes grow wet. So much for quiet confidence. He gripped the arms of his chair, taking in a few deep breaths as he absorbed the shock. Melville didn't seem to notice.

"I'm sorry to say he didn't have any insurance on the house, but Wardell being, well, Wardell, he naturally didn't have any debts either. The paperwork's all right here. Take all the time you want looking it over. Take them home and study them if you want. Once you sign these documents, I'll notarize them, and it's all yours. Course you'll have to file for a new deed on the property and transfer the truck title, but that shouldn't take more than a week or so. I can walk you through it if you like."

Melville sensed Will was no longer listening to him and looked up to find his client sitting back in his chair with a very troubled look on his face. "Something the matter, son?"

Will just sat there, staring out the window, eyes glazed over, as if he hadn't heard a word he said. "You still with me, son?"

After another few moments, Will snapped out of it and leaned forward, onto the desk. "Can I ask you a legal question, sir?"

"Certainly."

"Once I sign those papers, this all becomes public knowledge, right?"

"Not if you don't want it to. Your signature simply says that you've read the will and understand the contents. I have to register that notification with the county, but the details of the will are not public. However, once you file for a new deed or take any other legal action to claim any of Wardell's property, you do create a public record."

"That's good, because I think it would be best if we kept this just between the two of us, just for now, if that's possible."

Melville sat up and cocked a suspicious eye toward him. "You mind if I ask why?" he queried.

Will took a deep breath and let it out slowly. "Does any of this conversation fall under attorney-client privilege?"

"Anything you say to me here in this room will go no further without your express consent." He leaned over his desk, looking Will in the eye. "What is the point you're trying so hard to get to, son? Just spit it out."

"Well, at the moment, I'm kind of a suspect in two murders."

Melville's bushy eyebrows shot up so hard he fell back against his chair. It took him a moment to recover from the shock. "What the hell does that mean, *kind* of a suspect," he asked. "You're either a suspect or you're not. Which is it?"

"It's complicated," hedged Will.

"That's what lawyers are for, son, sorting out complications. Now, why don't you just tell me what the hell's going on. Maybe I can help."

Will explained the events of the last few days in as much detail as he could. When he was finished, it was Melville's turn to stare out the window.

CHAPTER 19

The last wisps of pink clouds trailed over the peaks as darkness began to descend over Shambles. Deputy Pacheko, dressed in his off-duty clothes, wheeled his vintage 1969 candy apple red Camaro convertible into the parking lot at Libbie's. It felt good to be out of his uniform. Always wary of parking lot door dings, he took a spot near the back, away from the other cars lined up closer to the front door.

The last few days had been frustratingly unproductive. The files on Sheriff Linehart's past arrests had come up empty. Every single one of the more than thirty individuals he managed to track down had left town as quickly as possible after their incarceration and, to a person, expressed a sincere desire never to cross paths with Wardell Linehart again. Many of them had continued their criminal ways in other parts of the country, but a surprising number had turned their lives around and, as far as Pacheko could tell, had not had any subsequent arrests.

Marcia had double-checked every hospital and clinic in southwest Idaho, but no one had any record of treating anyone for dog bites. She even checked a long list of pharmacies looking for suspicious purchases of bandages and antiseptic. No luck there, either. There were no prints on the knife Dolores found, but the blood type did match Montforte's, which was no surprise. The deputy asked the lab to expedite the DNA tests to confirm that, as well as any results that might come up on the cigarette butts found at the scene.

The tire tracks on the hill above the victim's house were a match to the ones Will had found in the turnout near the Captain's place, but they were a generic Firestone heavy-duty tire that could be found on a dozen or more brands of SUVs and trucks. The only good news was that in the three days since Sam Montforte was killed there had been no new murders.

He and the Sheriff had canvased the entire town looking for anyone who had a problem with either the Captain or Montforte and come up empty. Although he wasn't sure exactly how much investigating Yeager had actually done. His boss seemed to be even more distant and on edge than usual. When he was in the office, which wasn't a lot, he kept his head down claiming he was busy with paperwork and wanted to be left alone.

Both he and Marcia had expressed their skepticism on that score numerous times to one another in private. Their suspicion was that the Sheriff was in way over his head. He didn't want to accept the fact that there had been two murders in his town in the space of forty-eight hours and he was hiding out, hoping it would all just go away.

To make matters worse, the whole town was in full prep mode for the official opening of the mountain bike season and the imminent arrival of the first onslaught of tour groups. Coming on the heels of Wardell Linehart's murder and the celebration of the former Sheriff's life, most folks didn't seem ready to cope with another violent death. In short, they had no suspects. Except for Will. And as much as his gut was telling him Hickock wasn't involved, at the moment the recently returned Army vet was all they had.

It wasn't until he got to the entrance that he noticed Will's truck parked right next to the front door. Stepping inside, he stopped to let his eyes adjust to the dim light. Libbie was busy behind the bar, as usual, and Tommy was wrangling a new keg into position underneath the row of beer taps. Both pool tables were in use, and a few customers he had come to recognize as regulars were perched on their usual stools at the bar.

"Don't you two ever take a night off?" he said as he slid onto a stool.

Libbie looked up and smiled. "Well, if it isn't our new deputy." She flipped the Pabst Blue Ribbon tap with one hand and scooped up a glass from the sidebar with the other, sliding it expertly under the stream of beer before a single drop hit the drain. "What was it? Paduka?"

"You remember what beer I drink, but not my name?"

"Names don't pay the bills."

"I hear that," he said with a grin. "It's Pacheko, but most folks call me J.D."

Tommy stood up behind the bar and closed the cooler door. "What's that stand for?"

"That story is reserved only for very close friends. And even then, I'd have to be pretty damn drunk."

"Well then," said Libbie, sliding the full glass over to him, "I guess we're just going to have to become friends, J.D. Pacheko."

"Watch out for this one, deputy," said Tommy said with a sly grin as he hefted the empty keg onto a two-wheeled cart, "she has a way of finding out all your dirty little secrets."

Libbie swatted him on the butt as he wheeled away the empty keg, then glanced down at Pacheko's Forty-Niners jersey. "Is that the only shirt you own?"

"Nope, but it's the most comfortable."

"Ought to be, I haven't seen you wear anything else, except your uniform."

"Guess I'm not much of a clothes horse."

"Hey, even a horse changes his outfit once in a while."

A tall, lanky young man stepped up to the bar with an empty pitcher and Libbie drifted off to pour him a refill. Pacheko spun around on his stool, leaning back against the bar and sipping his beer as he gazed over at the pool tables. Three cowboys were engrossed in a serious game of cutthroat at one of them. Three bills lay side by side on one corner of the table awaiting the winner. At the other, a stocky twenty-something took the fresh pitcher of beer his tall buddy brought from the bar and filled the glasses of the two young ladies in their company, both of which had the trim, hard bodies of young mountain bikers and wore tight, cut-off jeans that showed a lot of leg.

Bikers, he surmised, in early to hit the trails before the crowds arrive. One of the girls noticed him watching and said something to her friend. They both offered him a smile, and when he tipped his glass in their direction they started to giggle. That got him a nasty look from their escorts and J.D. decided to turn his attention elsewhere.

Scanning the room, he noticed Corinne Barker in one of the near booths along the wall. She was all smiles and talking up a storm to the young couple across from her as she showed them something on a tablet computer. No doubt photos of a home they were considering. He shook his head. Not much grieving going on there.

His eyes continued down the row of booths until he spotted someone sitting alone in the last one. By the way the man was slumped over the table he was either asleep or drunk. Something about him looked familiar, and then he remembered the beat-up blue truck parked outside.

"He came in a couple of hours ago," said Libbie, suddenly appearing behind him again. "He looked kind of dazed, and his eyes were all red. I asked him if he was okay, but he just ordered a pitcher and a double shot of tequila and made a beeline for that booth. He's been there ever since."

Pacheko gave a low whistle. "I guess losing the Captain has been pretty rough on him."

"Yeah, but this is something else."

"What makes you say that?" She gave him a look that said if he was any kind of cop he would know. "Okay, so why tell me?"

She gave him a sideways look, contemplating what she was about to say. "I pride myself on being a good judge of character, J.D. Pacheko. It kind of goes with the job." She leaned across the bar and looked him in the eye. "You seem like a straight shooter to me, so I'll be straight with you. I know you and Yeager have Will tapped as your number one suspect in these murders." Pacheko started to object, but she wasn't finished yet. "But I'll tell you right now there's no way in hell he had anything to do with either one of them."

"Well, since we're going to be friends and all, just between you and me, I don't think he did it either."

She stepped back and scrutinized him with narrowed eyes. "Are you bullshitting me?"

Pacheko grinned. "No, ma'am, I would never do such a thing. Especially to someone who knows everybody's dirty little secrets."

"And don't you forget it either," she said with a wry grin.

"So, tell me, who do you think the culprit is?"

She sighed and leaned on the bar. "I haven't got a clue. I'm sure there are plenty of guys the Captain pissed off in his time as Sheriff. But it's been more than five years since the Ranch closed down and this town's always been pretty quiet as far as crime is concerned."

"What about Sam Montforte? From what I've heard he was never too well liked around here."

"Sam made his share of enemies over land deals, and he was never a very friendly guy to begin with."

Pacheko tilted his head toward the front booth where Corinne Barker was getting up to leave. She was a plain, pear-shaped woman, with narrow shoulders, wide hips and sharp features that were unfortunately emphasized by straight, shoulder-length brown hair which she continually tucked behind her ears. She tugged down the front of her dark blue business jacket and smoothed the front of the matching slacks.

"Apparently, his partner didn't feel that way, or so I've heard," he said

"Yeah, I've heard those rumors, too." She laughed softly. "Corinne's a real piece of work."

She mulled over the idea for a moment as they watched her shake hands warmly with the young couple and hand them a brochure.

"Actually, I wouldn't put it past her," Libbie continued. "But if she was sleeping with Sam, it was because she had the right, shall we say, incentive. She a sly one, but she's more of a devious plotter than a risk-taker. She and Sam have had a pretty good thing going here for a long time, and the way this tourist thing is catching on, it only looks to get better. Honestly, I don't see what she'd have to gain."

"How about control of the Montforte empire?" asked Pacheko.

Libbie snorted. "She's been running that for quite a while now. Sam never was the brains behind it, just the legend that struck it rich in a gold town long after all the gold was gone. Don't get me wrong, he was plenty smart, but I could never see him managing the day-to-day affairs of a business the size of Montforte Real Estate."

They watched Corinne say her goodbyes to the couple and make a beeline out the door like she had someplace important to be. She kept her eyes straight ahead, offering not so much as a nod to anyone as she left.

Libbie watched her go. "But I guess I could see how him being gone would free her up to do whatever she wants with the company."

"She come in often?" Pacheko asked.

"Funny you should ask," said Libbie. "Tonight's the first time I've seen her in here for quite a while. And that was her second meeting in a row."

"Yeah? Who was the first?"

"Big guy. I never saw him before. Dressed like cowboy. Wore a big grey Stetson."

Pacheko perked up. "Another potential buyer, you think?"

"Didn't look like it. They were all business. For a minute, it looked like they were arguing about something, but then they calmed back down and he left. The young couple came in and joined her a little while later."

"Don't suppose you saw what the big guy was driving?"

"Nope." Her curiosity was piqued. "Mind if I ask why you want to know?"

He smiled at her natural inquisitiveness. "Just something that came up at the City Council meeting the other night. Do me a favor, will you? If he comes in again give me a call. I'd like to talk to him."

"Sure thing."

Pacheko took a sip of beer and looked back over at Will slumped over in his booth. He was about to ask her another question when he remembered his criminology professor preaching that the best way to learn was to listen, so he took another sip of beer instead. It only took a moment for Libbie to pick up the slack.

"Will may have his issues," Libbie continued, "but in spite of his past, he's no criminal. Tommy always said it was Will who kept him from going crazy during his time at The Ranch."

"How's that?"

"In spite of the Captain's good intentions it was still a jail. There were all kinds of bad choices just begging to be made for anyone who spent time there, and plenty of truly bad individuals to help you make them. Tommy could just as easily have gone back to selling pot when he got out, but Will's interest in the guitar kept him focused on what he really wanted to do. You could say teaching Will how to play saved his life. I know Tommy feels that way."

"Sounds like you know Will pretty well."

She laughed. "Nobody knows Will Hickock well, not even the Captain, God rest his soul. He's always been a loner. Given his upbringing I guess it's no big surprise, but the other night I noticed he actually seemed to open up to you."

"Yeah, sometimes I have that effect on people."

He grinned over his beer glass and Libbie blushed as she realized how much she had been talking. "Damned if you don't," she said with a laugh.

Pacheko looked over at Will again. "How much has he had to drink?"

"I've poured him two more double tequilas since that first one, and I see the pitcher is almost gone. I asked him twice if he wanted something to eat, but he just shook his head. Last time I snuck these off the table." She pulled a set of car keys up from behind the bar. "He never even noticed."

"From the looks of him you'd better hang onto them tonight."

She put the keys back under the bar. "Planning on it."

The deputy watched Will a while, then drained his beer and let out a long sigh. "Give me another pitcher and a couple shots of that tequila." She gave him the sideeye but he just shrugged. "Sometimes you've got to fight fire with fire." She frowned but started drawing beer into a fresh pitcher. "And send over a couple double cheeseburgers with lots of fries."

"Now you're talking," Libbie said, smiling as she poured the shots. He picked up the drinks and ambled across the dance floor to Will's booth.

"Is this a solo party or can a latecomer crash?"

Will glanced up at him briefly, saying nothing, then went right back to staring at something far off. Pacheko wasn't sure if Will recognized him or not, but after a brief wait, he slid into the booth opposite him, setting the full pitcher and shots of tequila between them. "Looks like I've got some catching up to do."

"Look," Will began, his tongue thick, "I'm really not…" His voice trailed off.

"Very sober," Pacheko finished for him. "That's fairly obvious."

Will grunted. Pacheko took it to be a laugh, but only because the corners of his mouth turned up a fraction.

"You're right about that," Will mumbled. "But I've got a very good reason."

"Well, since you seem to be in a reasonably good mood, I'll assume it's nothing bad."

"That depends on how you look at it.

"How do you look at it?"

Will started to speak, but nothing came out. He took in a deep breath and rubbed his face with both hands, then squinted across the table through red, bleary eyes. "What the hell are you doing here, anyway?" He looked down at the deputy's clothes and squinted like he wasn't sure if he was seeing correctly. "And why are you dressed like that?"

"I just got off work. Came in for a burger and a beer. Libbie said you were acting kind of strange, so I came over to see if there was anything I could do."

Another grunt. "I'm afraid it's already been done."

"What's that?"

Will looked at him sideways for a moment, as if he was unsure whether he should answer the question. Pacheko waited patiently, and finally Will blew out a breath and slumped back in the booth. "You know that motive Yeager's been looking for?"

"You mean for the murders?"

Will nodded and took a drink of beer, spilling some down his shirt. He shook his head and laughed under his breath. "I just got it handed to me on a silver platter. "

Pacheko's eyes narrowed. "What do you mean?"

"Are you going to drink those?" Will asked, pointing at the two shots of Cuervo?

"Don't you think you've had enough for one day?"

"No way, man, I'm celebrating," Will said, snatching up a shot glass and holding it high in a challenge.

Pacheko laughed in spite of himself. "That seems pretty obvious, but celebrating what?"

Will just stared at the deputy, still holding the shot glass up between them, daring him. Pacheko could see there was still some resolve behind the glassy eyes, so he picked up the other shot, clicked it against Will's glass, and downed it. He grimaced and quickly chased the burn rolling down to his stomach with a gulp of cold beer.

"First one's the worst," said Will with a sloppy grin, then he downed his shot and set the glass down hard on the table. "It's all downhill from here. How about another one?"

J.D. took another long swig of beer. "Not until you tell me what the hell's going on with you."

Will's expression morphed back and forth between sadness and anger as he spoke. "It's just not fair, that's all. He was only retired for one damn year, after more than thirty years on the job. All he wanted to do was enjoy his ranch, do a little fishing, and some asshole has to…"

He squeezed his eyes shut, failing to hold back the tears that streamed down his cheeks. At first, he was pissed off that he'd opened himself up like that, then it seemed as though he didn't have the energy to fight it. "You probably think I'm some kind of baby, crying like this."

Pacheko shook his head. "Not on your life. I've been there myself a time or two."

Will squinted at him, trying to find the lie in his words. When he culdn't, he took a deep breath and blew it out. "He was a good man, you know. A crusty old fart but a damn good man. Best sheriff this county ever had."

He grew quiet and started to drift off again, and J.D. felt the need to keep him talking. "Yeah and now look what we're stuck with."

Will huffed. "Rodney fucking Yeager. It's no secret he's never had the brains for the job."

"No, but he does have a natural, god-given talent for rubbing people the wrong way."

That brought a short, staccato laugh from Will, then he was silent again, his gaze reverting to the faraway stare. "You know, when I was at the Ranch, the Captain used to take me fishing at his secret spot. He made me swear never to tell anyone. Said he'd get in big trouble if the brass found out he was taking one of the inmates off fishing. But you know what I think?"

"Nope. What?"

"I think he was lonely. He just wanted some company."

"Why do you think he picked you?"

"Hell if I know. He always used to say he saw something in me, that I could be better than what circumstance dumped on my plate. Maybe he just felt sorry for me because I was the youngest kid out there. I guess I'll never know now, but I'll tell you one thing, those times together created some kind of bond I never felt before in my life, not even with my mom. And it stayed strong, too, even after ten years in the Army. I guess we both needed what it brought us, but for different reasons. God knows we both had holes in our lives that needed filling."

He wiped away another tear and took another drink of beer. "Damn," he said. "I never talk about this stuff. I must be drunk."

"I heard a rumor to that effect."

They both laughed, and Will looked him straight in the eye, his gaze steady, sizing up the deputy as if he was debating whether or not to say something. Pacheko raised his eyebrows, waiting. At that moment, the food arrived.

Half-an-hour later, Pacheko slid his basket across the table to Will, who greedily finished off the last remaining fries. "Feeling better?" he asked.

They were the first words he'd spoken since the food arrived. Will, on the other hand, had unloaded, talking almost non-stop about his visit with Melville, liberally lacing the tale with more stories of the Captain and the Ranch. He finished the last of his fries and noticed Pacheko trying to hide a grin.

"Damn," he said, shaking his head, "guess I rambled on for a while there. Sorry about that."

"It's a hell of a story," said Pacheko.

"Yeah, well, it is what it is. Anyway, thanks for listening."

"Sometimes it's good to get stuff off your chest."

Will scrunched his eyebrows at the deputy. "I've never been much of a talker," he said, "so why is it I keep unloading all my crap on you?"

Pacheko laughed. "Listening is part of the job description."

Will gave him a wry smile. "I'm not so sure I should have told you about inheriting the Ranch. Yeager will have a field day with that. But you're right, it does feel good to get it all out."

"And it does give you a hell of a motive, I have to say." He gave Will a wink. "But under the circumstances I think we can keep this between the two of us for right now."

Libbie appeared and cleared their food baskets. "You boys behaving yourselves over here?"

"Trying to," said Pacheko.

Will polished off his beer and belched again. His eyes were now at half-mast. The food was taking effect.

"You know," he said, sounding more tired than drunk now, "I don't remember the last time I peed." He slid clumsily out of the booth, almost falling when he tried to stand up.

"You need any help?" asked Pacheko.

"Hell no," Will protested, steadying himself on the table.

They watched him stagger down the row of booths, putting a hand on each one as he passed to keep himself balanced, until he disappeared into a doorway marked Bucks next to one marked Does.

He going to be alright?" asked Libbie.

"It's been a rather momentous week for our young friend. I think he just needed to unload a little."

Libbie stacked the baskets on one arm and scooped up the empty pitcher. "I'll expect a full recounting, with all the juicy details."

"Yes ma'am," Pacheko answered with a smile, and she headed back to the bar.

Will stumbled back from the bathroom, tripping as he approached the booth. The deputy caught him as he fell.

"Whoa, cowboy, I think it's about time I took you home."

Will jerked out of his grasp with fire in his eyes. "Don't ever call me that."

Pacheko was shocked at the sudden outburst. "Call you what?"

"Cowboy. Doc used to call me that," he growled, his anger apparent but unable to reach the surface through all the alcohol. He took a step, but his balance was gone, and he had to grab the booth for support.

"No problem," said Pacheko. "What say I give you a ride home?"

Will gave him a blank stare, as though he was trying to remember where he was or how he got there. "Probably a good idea," he mumbled, "since I can't hardly stand up."

Pacheko cracked up, then Will joined in, and the two of them stood there laughing, the anger gone, its reason forgotten. The deputy clapped him on the shoulder. "Come on, my car's outside."

They started unsteadily for the door, Will holding onto Pacheko for support.

"Just don't call me cowboy," muttered Will.

As they made their way past the bar, J.D. said, "Put this on my tab, will you, Libbie?"

"What tab?" she said with a grin, mouthing the words *thank you.*

CHAPTER 20

A smile brightened Libbie's face as Will came through the door the next afternoon just after five wearing his riding clothes and looking wrung out. He slid gingerly onto a stool at the bar, and she reached for a beer glass.

"Can I just get some water, please," he said with a tired grin.

She gave him an understanding smile and scooped some ice into a glass, the twinkle in her eyes signaling a sarcastic comment. Tommy beat her to it, his voice booming across the room as he approached from storage room past the far end of the bar. "Back for a little hair of the dog?" He clapped Will on the shoulder as he slipped onto the stool next to him.

"No way," Will groaned, holding up his hands. "Just picking up my truck."

You always were a glutton for punishment. Sure you don't want a beer? Maybe a shot of Cuervo?" Tommy's laugh lit up the whole room, and Will couldn't help but chuckle.

"Not today, Tommy," he said. "Last night was enough to hold me for quite a while."

He drained the glass of water Libbie slid in front of him.

"You look beat," she said, snatching up the glass and refilling it. "Been out riding?"

"Yeah, the first big tour group comes in next weekend, and Tim asked me to give the trails one final check."

She grimaced as she slid the full glass across the bar to him. "Given the condition you left here in last night, that must have been painful."

Will waved her off. No, it was a good thing. I needed to sweat out some of that damn tequila."

Tommy laughed again and Will took a long drink of water. Libbie retrieved his car keys and tossed them onto the bar. Will smiled. "When I couldn't find those this morning, it took me a minute to figure out you might have them. Getting home is a little fuzzy, though."

"You can thank our new deputy for that," said Libbie with a grin. "He practically had to carry you out of here."

The fog began to lift slowly. "Yeah, I kind of remember that now. Did he buy me a tequila?"

"And a burger."

"Probably saved your life, right there, bro," laughed Tommy. "You were feeling no pain."

"You two were chatting away for about an hour over there," Libbie said.

Will looked surprised. "Really? That part's still pretty foggy. Must have been about Montforte's crime scene. I was helping him out the day after he was killed."

Libbie refilled his glass and placed it back in front of him. "Damn shame. I can't say I really liked old Sam, but he sure did a lot for this town."

"Wait a minute," Tommy cut in, looking surprised, "you were at the crime scene? Helping how?"

Will shrugged. "Apparently, he appreciates my tracking skills. I found some footprints and a tire track up at the Captain's, so he asked me to take a look around Montforte's place."

"And?" prompted Tommy.

"There were some tire tracks on the hill overlooking his place, and boot prints to and from. He took some pictures."

"Cool. What else did you find?"

Will shook his head. "I probably shouldn't be talking about an ongoing investigation."

"I'm assuming Yeager wasn't in the vicinity," Tommy said with a grin.

"Hell no, and you never heard me say I was anywhere near there, either."

"What Yeager doesn't know won't hurt him."

"What the hell's going on around here, anyway?" asked Libbie. "I can't remember when there was one murder in this town, much less two right in a row. People are freaking out."

Will shook his head sadly. "Yeah, and Yeager still thinks I'm good for both of them."

"Aw, he's just being his usual asshole self," said Tommy. "Everybody knows there's no way you would have hurt the Captain. And as for the night Montforte died, we've got thirty or forty witnesses that saw you playing with us right up until closing, and the whole band was jamming with us at our place after."

"Who the hell could be doing this?" asked Libbie. "And why?"

"I have no idea," Will said, "and I'm pretty sure Yeager and his new deputy don't, either. All I want is to get Yeager off my ass."

"He never has liked you, has he? said Libbie.

"It was Doc he hated with a passion," Tommy chimed in.

Will grunted. "When we were kids, it was Doc's personal mission to make his life miserable. He loved pranking the guy. It was easy to see why, though, Rodney was a dick even back then."

"Now he's got a badge and it's payback time," Tommy scoffed. "And since Doc's not around anymore, his little brother will fill the bill. Guys like him get off on abusing their power any way they can."

"That new deputy seems nice enough," said Libbie. "Dresses a little funny, but folks seem to like him."

"Yeah, he does have a way about him, I guess," said Will.

"He must not agree with Yeager about you being a suspect if he asked you to help out at Montforte's."

"What's that old saying," said Will, "keep your friends close and your enemies closer."

"I don't know," she said, shaking her head, "he doesn't seem like the devious type to me."

Tommy frowned. "He acts all friendly, but there's something about him. Am I the only one who thinks it's a little suspicious that he showed in town up just before all this went down. I mean, who is this guy? Where did he come from, anyway?"

A thought struck Will. "Somebody new in town," he said, half to himself.

"What do you mean?" asked Tommy.

Will waved him off. "Just something Dolores said."

"Hey, this is me you're talking to. I can see the wheels in that brain of yours spinning like you were heading down Tomcat Trail with no brakes."

Will hesitated. "It's probably nothing." But the thought wouldn't leave him alone. "You think you could do some checking for me?"

"On the deputy?" asked Tommy. "Hell yeah. I'll get Thumbs on it. He can find out anything about anybody on that super-computer of his. It'll be just like the old days back at the Ranch, us against Rodney."

"Oh great," groaned Libbie.

"What?" said Tommy.

"You and Thumbs going after the sheriff and his deputy with your history? What could possibly go wrong?"

"Aw, babe."

"I'm not kidding. You think Yeager is trouble, you do anything that will get your ass sideways with the law again and I'll give that word a whole new meaning for you." Will laughed through his nose, choking on the water he was drinking. Tommy feigned being hurt. "Don't give me that look," Libbie continued, "you've got responsibilities now, here and at home. Those two boys don't need to see their father locked up."

"I know, babe, I know" Tommy soothed. "Don't worry, it's just a little research, that's all."

She rolled her eyes, her gaze landing on the front door and here expression sobered. "And speaking of the law."

They looked over as Pacheko entered wearing neon green shorts and his standard Forty-Niner shirt, only this time it was the white road jersey instead of the red home field version. He spotted Will and smiled.

"I'll just make myself scarce," said Tommy, tossing Will a conspiratorial wink as he left.

"Evening, J.D.," Libbie said as Pacheko took a stool next to Will. "What can I get you?"

"Evening, Libbie. I'll have a beer, please." He glanced at Will's glass of water, a twinkle in his eye. "Still feeling the effects?"

"Last night is not something I want to repeat any time soon," said Will.

Libbie brought Pacheko's beer. He took a drink, then turned to Will with a more serious look. "I'm glad I ran into you. I keep meaning to apologize for the way Yeager's been treating you in all this." Will shot him a sideways look that was more than a little skeptical. Pacheko smiled. "No, I mean it. He was totally out of line the other night, arresting you without checking your alibi first. I mean, that's just standard procedure."

Libbie raised her eyebrows at Will and busied herself down the bar.

"I appreciate that," Will said, "working for him can't be easy."

"Let's just say he's something of an acquired taste."

Will laughed. "First you get Rodney as a boss, then two murders right in a row. You're really getting a baptism by fire on his job."

Pacheko shook his head. "You know, when I took this job right after graduation, I thought, small town, no crime to speak of, I'll just be able to kind of ease into law enforcement."

"Yeah? How's that working out for you?"

Pacheko just grinned. "Actually, it's been pretty damned interesting. I'm finding out I really do like the work. And I'm learning this town has some pretty cool people, too."

He took a drink of his beer and Will looked at him sideways. "Has Marcia been giving you more history lessons?"

Pacheko laughed. "Not exactly. She did tell me about how your tracking skills saved your squad in Iraq. I thought she was feeding me a line, but now I've seen you in action."

"Yeah, we got lucky that day. It could have turned out a lot worse."

"Don't suppose you'd like to fill me in?"

Will's eyes went cold. "Not really."

Pacheko grinned. "Okay, no war stories, I get it, the strong silent type." He took another drink. "Look, I know a lot of you vets don't like to talk about what happened over there, but if you ever feel the need to unload, I'd really be interested in hearing about it."

Resentment creeped into Will's voice. "What for, cheap thrills?" PacÕo frowned and took a long swig of beer. When he looked back at Will, his expression was stone cold serious. "My brother was over there a few years ago. He promised to tell me all about it when he got back. But he never did."

Will's face went slack. "Shit," he sighed. "I'm sorry to hear that."

"Yeah, me, too. I guess you saw a lot of that in ten years."

"Too much."

They drank in silence for a while, each lost in their own memories. Finally, Pacheko spoke up. "You know, I keep hearing about this juvenile facility Linehart ran, but nobody's told me what exactly went on up there."

"That wasn't part of Marcia's history lesson?"

"Nope, says she doesn't like to talk about it."

"I'm surprised Yeager hasn't mentioned it. He always liked to tell everyone how he was the one who kept all of us in line up there once he became a deputy."

"In case you haven't noticed, lately he's not exactly been a forthcoming kind of guy. Hell, he's hardly ever around. Always off on some kind of *official business*," he said, making air quotes with his fingers. "Or so he says."

"The Ranch was a kind of work-rehab program for young offenders back in the day," Will began. "We raised cattle, a few horses, grew alfalfa and hay to feed them, had a huge vegetable garden, chickens, some goats, all taken care of by the inmates and overseen by the Captain. When the smelter closed things got pretty tough for most of the families who stayed around here. A lot of kids got into criminal activities. Some were actually trying to help their families make ends meet, but most of them just did it for something to do.

Then everyone started leaving town and once the population got low enough, I guess the Ranch sort of outlived its usefulness. When the state finally shut it down, there was no way the Captain could keep everything running on the place and still handle being Sheriff. He leased most of the cropland and cattle range out to other ranchers just so he could make his payments on the place. The day he finally got the mortgage paid off, was the day he decided to retire. He always said he wanted to get the garden going again, but now…"

His voice trailed off. After a few moments, Pacheko's curiosity got the best of him. "How much time did you do up there, exactly?"

Will's first instinct was to tell him it was none of his damned business, but he bit his tongue and turned away, only to find Libbie staring at him as she put a fresh beer in front of Pacheko. "In for a penny, in for a pound," she said.

"He'll find out sooner or later, anyway."

He took a long swallow of beer, then turned back to Pacheko. "Ten years."

Pacheko's eyes went wide, and his glass came to a sudden halt just before it reached his mouth and beer splashed onto the bar. He pushed his stool back to avoid getting doused with the mess. Libbie grinned and tossed him a bar towel.

"See," she said with a grin. "It was worth it just to see that look on his face.

"My sentence was for fifteen. I was remanded to the Ranch until I turned eighteen, then I was scheduled to be sent down to the State Penitentiary outside of Boise. When I graduated high school, the Captain got my sentence reduced to time served for good behavior. At the judge suggested that joining the military would be a lot better for me than going to prison. I took the hint."

Will slid off his stool and Pacheko stopped wiping up the spilt beer. "Wait a minute," he said, "you can't just leave me hanging like that. What's the rest of the story?"

"You couldn't get my file unsealed?"

"I couldn't even find it. Seems to be missing."

"What!" exclaimed Will.

"Interesting," said Pacheko, taking note of his reaction. "Yeager was just as surprised as you. And Marcia claims to know nothing about it, either. Any idea where it might have disappeared to?"

"How the hell would I know? The state closed down the Ranch just a few years after I left for the Army."

Pacheko sighed. "The way Yeager keeps files I'm not too surprised. You don't suppose the Captain would have had it up at the ranch, do you?"

"I don't know why, but if he did, it's gone now for sure. As far as I know he kept all that kind of stuff at the office here in town."

Pacheko nodded grudgingly. "Guess that'll have to hold me for now." Will started to leave. "So, the reason I tracked you down here today..." Pacheko continued, letting the thought hang as he took another drink of beer. Reluctantly, Will slid back onto his stool. "I was going to tell you last night, but you weren't focusing real well."

Will gave him a smirk and Pacheko smiled softly. "Those photos of the tire tracks at Montforte's paid off. That skid mark you found up at the ranch didn't give us much to go on, but as near as we can tell, they're a match."

"What does that mean?"

"Unfortunately, not much. It's a pretty common brand. Comes standard on several makes and models."

"Like a big, white Dodge Ram?"

"That's one of them, but it doesn't necessarily mean Fitch has them on his truck, even if I could find it. That guy's been keeping a very low profile. One thing though, this tread model only came out this year, so odds are it's a new truck or SUV. I've got Marcia checking on late model sales and rentals during the past three months in a five-hundred-mile radius."

"What about the footprints?" asked Will.

"You were right about them being the same size as the one's you found at the Captain's, but it's a different type of shoe, so that doesn't help narrow it down much."

"At least you've still got the cigarette butts."

"I'm pretty confident we'll get some DNA off the ones from Montforte's, but the one from the creek at the Captain's was all but worthless."

"Are they at least the same brand?"

"Yeah, we've got that going for us, but it won't mean much in court. You said you never smoked, right?"

Will shook his head. "I never could stand the things."

"Not even pot," Libbie interjected, placing a fresh beer in front of Pacheko. "Though God knows Tommy tried back in the day."

Will quickly interjected. "But he's been off that since he did his stint at the Ranch."

Libbie put her hand on Will's. "You're one of the big reasons for that, you know. You got him to focus on his music."

Will shrugged. "Once he figured out how much better he played when he wasn't high, he never looked back."

She squeezed his hand and moved off to answer the call of another customer.

"I hesitate to ask," said Pacheko, "but exactly how much information did you manage to charm out of Marcia during your stay in jail the other night?

"We had a nice chat, why?

"She might have let slip that you found out something about the report from the vet."

Will turned up his palms and shrugged. "I have no idea what you're talking about."

Pacheko frowned. He obviously didn't believe Will, but he went on anyway. "It was pretty much what we suspected. We can assume the nylon strands were from clothing of some kind, possibly a windbreaker, but without something to match it to there's no way to tell exactly."

"Which would indicate the nylon is from clothing worn by the killer, and Dusty chewed the hell out of him."

"If so, he must have treated the wounds himself. We haven't found any doctor or hospital or clinic that has treated dog bites in the last month. And half the town is probably type A."

"Me included," Will blurted out without thinking, blushing as he realized his admission. "But you probably knew that already."

"Actually, I didn't." He paused a long moment, letting Will squirm. "Until Yeager told me."

Will frowned. "Very funny."

"I pointed out to him that you don't have any dog bites. That stumped him, but I don't think it took you off his list."

"I'm not surprised." He stepped off the stool. "Well, I'm headed for bed."

"I still owe you a beer for coming out to Montforte's the other day. You were a big help."

"Tell Yeager that." He stopped. "On second thought, don't."

Pacheko grinned and tipped his glass as Will headed for the door.

CHAPTER 21

Shambles hadn't seen two funerals in the same year since anybody could remember, but here they all were again, barely than a week after the Captain was buried. A large crowd had gathered on another beautiful spring morning to listen to Reverend Mike wax philosophic about another mainstay of their small community.

Sam Montforte may have been revered for entirely different reasons than Wardell Linehart, but he was revered all the same. The only difference between the Captain's funeral and this one was the lack of law enforcement and a twenty-one gun salute. Yeager was there, of course, in full dress uniform, his pointed-toe snakeskin boots gleaming in the sunlight, black Stetson held reverently over his pot belly.

The lone bench beside the grave held Corinne Barker, dressed in a tasteful, expensive-looking black dress and a wide-brimmed hat. Every so often her hand would slip up underneath the thin black veil that hung down over her face it to dab at her eyes with a tissue.

Seated next to her was an attractive blonde woman who appeared to be in her late twenties. Her ice blue eyes darted among the crowd as if she wasn't sure she was in the right place. The rest of the attendees stood scattered around the grave, mourning the loss of a man many of them didn't even know, yet somehow felt they must pay some measure of respect because of his standing in the town.

Will stood further up the hill, near the Captain's grave wearing his new navy-blue blazer for the second time, hoping no one would notice him, or worse, talk to him. His white shirt and khakis had been cleaned and pressed, or at least someone had made a half-assed attempt at pressing them. He'd only decided to come to the service at the last minute, and was still questioning the wisdom of showing his face at the funeral of a man he had been accused of killing, alibi or no.

His mind drifted back to the night he got drunk at Libbie's after learning he was the Captain's sole heir. His memory of events was still foggy, but pieces of his conversation with Pacheko had been drifting back to the surface the past few days and he was feeling nervous about whether he may have told the deputy more than he should.

Speak of the devil, Will thought as Pacheko stepped up beside him. He couldn't help staring at the deputy's stylish grey sport jacket, pale blue dress shirt and dark slacks. The surfer had miraculously transformed into someone who looked like he just walked out of the latest issue of GQ magazine. Pacheko gave him a nod and adjusted his dark blue silk tie. They watched in silence as Reverend Mike ran down a long list of good deeds the deceased had done for the community. When he returned to the scripture, the deputy leaned over to Will.

"You know," he said softly, "Montforte never impressed me as being all that smart." Will grunted in assent. "So how did he manage to build that seed money into a real estate fortune?"

"Two words," whispered Will, "Corinne Barker. She joined up with him right out of Real Estate school, only a few years after she graduated high school."

"I didn't realize she'd been in the business that long."

"No one seems to know how they met, but the story goes that Corinne always knew what she wanted and would do just about anything to get it. Actually, they were a pretty solid combination; her brains, his money."

Pacheko watched Corinne dab her eyes with the tissue again and thought to himself that the years had not exactly been kind to her. Even under the veil her narrow face looked almost gaunt, the lines around her eyes and mouth more pronounced than should be expected in a woman in her early fifties. The dark circles under her eyes could be attributed to grief over the loss of her partner, but they could just as easily have come from years of trying to maintain control of a growing real estate empire headed by a man who had as little regard for his money as he did for most people. She was tall and large-boned, a fact not easily hidden, even by expensive clothes and refined manners.

"You think they were,,,you know?" asked Pacheko.

"Rumor had it." Pacheko winced and Will grinned. "And if the rumors are true, it's probably one of the reasons his wife left him. She's lost some of her looks over the years but none of the brains. The way I've heard it, Montforte's name may be on all the signs, but she's always been the driving force behind their success."

"When I met with her to make the official notification of his death," Pacheko whispered, "she made it a point to tell me that even though Spring Meadows was supposed to be his swan song, it was really her baby all along."

"It might be interesting to know who Montforte left his money to."

"Maybe that's why his daughter showed up."

Will's gaze shifted to the young woman sitting next to Corinne and he felt a jolt of sudden recognition. Straight, blond hair flipped up just off her shoulders, a thin, straight nose angled perfectly between nicely defined cheekbones and translucent skin accented by a soft red lipstick. The clothes didn't look particularly expensive, but she wore them well. Long, elegant legs extended out from a charcoal-grey suede skirt that finished just above the knee, a nicely tailored navy-blue shirt accentuated her slender, yet curvaceous body.

He blew out a breath softly. "I didn't recognize her," said Will. "She was still in high school when her mother left Sam and took her back east somewhere."

"Must take after her mother," said Pacheko, "she sure doesn't look like Sam." Will stifled a laugh.

In contrast to Corinne, Carla Montforte was surprisingly stoic. Her eyes were sad, but dry, and they wandered over the crowd as if she were trying to locate someone she knew. She didn't appear to be paying much attention to the service, and the emotionless, almost inquisitive look on her face could be interpreted either as surprise at the large turnout or wondering whether the person who wanted her father dead was among them.

"She's never been back until now?" asked Pacheko.

"Not that I know of," said Will. "No reason to, I guess. Given the reasons her mother left him they probably weren't too close."

"She doesn't exactly seem all broken up," Pacheko observed. "She looks about your age. Was she in school with you?"

Will nodded. "She would have been a year or two behind me."

Pacheko felt like there was something missing in Will's response. "She doesn't look like the type you'd forget."

"Yeah, well, I didn't exactly have much of a social life."

Pacheko started to say something, then decided it would be best to change the subject. "What about the ex-wife?"

Will shrugged. "If I remember right, she was only a couple of years younger than Sam. Given his age difference with Corinne, it's no wonder the divorce wasn't exactly amicable."

Reverend Mike wrapped up his sermon and the casket slowly began to descend into the grave. Everyone stood silent, watching it drop. The only sounds were the grinding of the battery-powered motor that operated the pulleys and Corinne Barker's sobs. When the motor stopped, Corinne eased up to the edge of the grave and dropped in a single white rose she'd been holding. She shook Reverend Mike's hand and said something to which he smiled and nodded humbly, then she started up the hill directly toward Will and Pacheko.

The two men exchanged an apprehensive glance, each hoping the other knew what she was up to, but it was clear neither did. She marched right up to Will and handed him a business card. The tears had stopped completely, if they were ever real, and the look on her face was all business. "I know this isn't the time or place, Mr. Hickock," she said, "but we need to talk. I'd appreciate it if you would call me at your earliest convenience. It's very important."

Before Will could respond, she turned on her heel and walked off. Pacheko watched her go, then looked down at the card, then to Will, who offered only a shrug in response to the deputy's unspoken question. The crowd began to break up. Will stuffed the card in his shirt pocket and watched Corinne make her way through the rows of gravestones toward the parking lot. She passed Dolores Esperanza, who was lingering at the edge of the cemetery dressed in a nicely fitted black pants suit, scanning the departing crowd.

"Dolores looks like she lost someone," said Will.

"Killers are known to return to the scene of the crime. I asked her to come and help me check out the crowd. Turns out she's almost as good as you at spotting things that are out of place."

Will watched Pacheko eyeing Dolores and buried a smirk. "You know, almost every single guy in town, and most of the married ones, have been trying to get next to her ever since the BLM sent her up here three years ago. You shouldn't be too disappointed that you haven't gotten anywhere in just a couple of weeks."

Pacheko frowned at him, but Will was pleased to see that his remark had hit home. "If you have to know," he said, "there's nothing going on between us. She asked me to help her out with the criminology classes she's taking down at Boise State, and in return she helps me out on the job every once in a while. It's always good to have another set of eyes around, especially when they're anonymous. I'm not getting much in the way of help from our illustrious Sheriff."

Will noticed Yeager schmoozing a group of ranchers near the grave site. "You think the killer would actually show up here?"

"It happens a lot more than you'd think. That's why I wore civvies, so I could kind of blend in."

LOOSE ENDS

"You mean as opposed to your regular surfer look?"

Pacheko shifted nervously and adjusted his sport coat. "What, you think it's too much?"

Will shook his head. It's a cinch no one from around here will recognize you in those clothes. See anyone suspicious?"

"Nope, but it looks like Yeager did."

Will spotted the Sheriff staring at him from across the cemetery. He did not look happy. "Shit. Doesn't he ever give up?" he groused. "I think I'll just hang out up here until he's gone."

"Suit yourself," said Pacheko. "I'm going to check in with Dolores. See you later."

The deputy strolled down the hill past Yeager who continued to glare up at Will, daring him to come down. Getting no response, he finally headed toward his big SUV.

Will watched the Sheriff walk across the parking lot right past a white Dodge pickup parked next to Corinne's big blue Cadillac. She was giving an earful to someone he couldn't see standing behind the big pickup. Her arms were flying around like windmills, quite a contrast to her demure funeral behavior a few minutes before. He took a couple of steps sideways to try and see who she was so mad at, and a grey Stetson came into view.

Will recognized Marcus Finch immediately and looked around for Pacheko to let him know. He spotted the deputy on the opposite side of the parking lot with Dolores, who was already pointing him in that direction. When he looked back, he saw Corinne push past Fitch and get into her car. She pulled away fast, and Fitch followed close behind in his truck. Will saw Pacheko make a beeline for his Malibu and take out after them. Will knew it was smarter to keep his distance, but part of him wished he were with the deputy. He had a few questions of his own for the land man.

Abe and Stanley had started shoveling dirt into Montforte's now deserted grave and, finding himself alone, Will decided to pay the Captain a visit while he was here. Even though it had only been a week since the funeral, the fresh sod had begun to look more natural. If it wasn't for the new headstone, you'd think he'd been there for quite some time.

"It sucks not having you around," Will said to the gravestone. "No one to go fishing with." He smiled at the memory. "I guess what I really wanted to say was thanks for trusting me with the ranch." He brushed some loose soil off the top of the headstone. "You could have said something, you know. But then that wouldn't be you, would it? You always did get a kick out of seeing me totally blindsided."

He swallowed hard, his eyes welling up with tears. He pushed them back inside and cleared his throat, not wanting the Captain to see him crying. "I promise I'll take real good care of it." He paused, as if waiting for a response, then tapped his foot at a section of sod that was sticking up and let out a sigh. "I'll see you around."

He smiled down at the grave, then walked slowly down the row of headstones toward the pathway that led out to the graveyard entrance. A spooky feeling crept over him. Graveyards had always made him uncomfortable. His own mortality had been tested way more than he liked to think about during his years in the Army. It was not something he liked to dwell on, and he picked up his pace.

Near the end of the row, he stopped at the simple, unadorned headstone that bore his mother's name. Next to it stood Doc's, and he realized he couldn't remember the last time he'd been to out to see them. A sudden pang of guilt stabbed him, and he worried that it seemed he cared more about a cantankerous ex-Sheriff than he did about his real family. He had a feeling his mom would understand. Of course, Doc would be furious. But then Doc was the one who had left him holding the bag all those years ago.

He stood staring at the two graves, trying to think of something to say, but it had been so long, and he had changed so much. His mother, he knew, would be pleased at the way he turned out, but he could still hear Doc raging on about how they had to take care of themselves because no one else gave a damn, and how the only way they were ever going to get anything in life was to and take it.

Funny, he thought, I actually used to believe that. Thank God for the Captain, who showed him that no one was owed a good life, you had to go out and earn it.

"Death's a strange thing, isn't it?"

He spun around, startled by the voice. Carla Montforte stood just a few feet away. She kept herself from smiling at his reaction, but her piercing blue eyes twinkled in the sunlight. All Will could do was stare at her. She was even prettier up close. Her skin was smooth and alabaster white, and her eyes seemed to bore right into him. His heart was beating a mile a minute, and he fought to keep his cool. He hadn't felt this flustered since, well, since he could remember.

"How do you mean?" he finally managed.

"I don't know, it just seems strange to think about all these people lying here dead, people that you knew, and talked to, with nothing but these stone markers to tell anyone who they were."

Will looked back at the graves, her matter-of-fact response somehow making him feel more at ease. "I'm sorry about your father," he said softly.

Her face grew sad. "Yeah, me, too," she said. "It's funny, you never really think about these things until they happen." She looked at the name on the gravestone next to him. "Is that your mother?"

Will nodded. He wanted desperately to say something, but no words would come. He chided himself for his lack of fortitude. It wasn't that he was afraid of women, exactly. Well, okay, maybe he was, just a little. But he'd never had the chance to have any experience with them during his puberty years, and as a result he felt a distinct lack of confidence around them most of the time.

You were only what, seven or so when you lost them?" she asked.

He nodded, astonished that she remembered. "I used to come here fairly often," he said, "but since I got back to town, I haven't been by much for some reason. Even at the Captain's funeral the other day I didn't think to pay them a visit. I guess I came to think of him more as family than I did them."

She gave him a curious look, and he realized she would have no idea what he was talking about. He hoped she wouldn't ask. Instead, she cast a look back up at her father's grave. "My mother died last year, but she never would have come back for this anyway. Good riddance, she would have said."

Once again, Will could not find words. It was like his brain had just locked up. He wasn't kidding himself, though, he knew exactly why Carla Montforte had him so discombobulated, he just didn't know if he had the courage to dredge up long-lost memories.

She looked back at him, and her head tilted sideways, letting the light catch her eyes. "You don't remember me, do you?"

Mortified that he would say the wrong thing but not wanting to lose the opportunity to keep talking to her, he opted for, "Should I?"

She smiled a warm smile, as if a fond memory had just crept across her mind. "Not really, I suppose." She started to say something more, then thought better of it and turned to go. From some unknown place inside Will, panic rose. The words were out of his mouth before he even realized he'd said them.

"Could I buy you a cup of coffee?"

CHAPTER 22

Pacheko followed Fitch's pickup, which was following Corinne's Cadillac, straight to the Montforte Real Estate office. Fortunately, there was a lot of traffic as people left the cemetery, so he was able to use it as cover for the otherwise conspicuous Malibu. Corinne pulled into her personalized parking space on the three-car concrete pad in front of the single-story log building. It seemed somehow incongruous that the man who brought Shambles back from the dead should have chosen a piece of its past for a headquarters. Perhaps it served as a reminder to those building the shiny, new resort town all around it of how far they had come.

Fitch parked across the street and the deputy drove right on past, pulling into an empty spot down the block that left him half-hidden behind a big SUV. He watched in the side mirror as Fitch cautiously checked the surrounding area to make sure no one was watching, then caught up to Corinne as she was getting out of her car. He started to say something to her, but she shushed him hard and hurried on inside, looking around like she didn't want to be seen with him. He stood there a moment, fuming, then checked once more for anyone who might be watching before he followed her.

As soon as both of them were inside, Pacheko got out of his car and strolled casually down the sidewalk past the office. The door was still partially open and he heard Corinne's shrill voice all the way out on the sidewalk. She was seriously upset. Pacheko slowed down, trying hard not to make it obvious he was listening.

"How many damn times do I have to tell you we can't be seen together in public, Marcus? I can't afford to be connected to you and your dealings with the ranchers."

"Damnit, Corinne," Fitch shot back, "everyone already knows we're working together on your desert land. Besides, you're the one who asked me to start talking to the ranchers. This is a small town. Did you think word wouldn't get out?"

"Yes, eventually, but we need to delay it as long as possible. I want the entire front secured before we go public. If we're missing even one piece, it could all fall apart. There were some seriously pissed off people at that council meeting the other night."

The door slammed shut and their voices faded. Pacheko could see them through the big picture window in front as they moved toward the back of the building. He circled around to the alley where a several clumps of tall sawgrass allowed him to get close to the building without being seen. Conveniently, the window to Corinne's back office was open. Fitch was right on her heels as she entered and tossed her purse onto a chair in the corner. He tossed his hat on top of it.

"What are you worried about?" he said. "With Sam gone, you're the biggest landowner around these parts."

The comment seemed to placate her somewhat and her tone softened. "I know, but we still need a few more pieces of the puzzle."

"I'm making progress, but these ranchers are damned stubborn. I just need more time."

"That's not what I'm worried about. The Linehart ranch is the key to the whole thing."

"Don't blame me for that. You said that ranch was state property."

"I thought it was. I figured those soft-hearted bastards on the State Land Board just let him live there after the juvenile center shut down because he had no place else to go. It wasn't until he retired that I found out he had some secret deal to buy the place all along."

"So what? He's dead now. You said he had no heirs, so it will revert to the state, and you should be able to pick it up for a song."

"Yeah, well, that part of the plan went up in smoke yesterday."

"What do you mean?"

"Apparently, he left it all to that Hickock kid."

"What! How the hell did you find that out?"

"A friend at the courthouse told me Arvin Melville came in yesterday and registered Linehart's will. It's not public until Hickock files for the deed, but that's just a formality."

"Is that the guy you were talking to up at the funeral?" Corinne nodded. "That's the same kid I ran into when I was up there taking soil samples. You don't think he'll sell? Seems a young kid like that would welcome a big pile of cash."

"Hard to say. Linehart was like a father to him. The ranch may have sentimental value."

"Well shit, that sure as hell throws a wrench in the works."

"I'm no happier about it than you are, believe me."

"Without that valley to link the ranch properties on either side of it our plan becomes a hell of a lot more complicated, not to mention expensive, to pull off."

"I know, damnit, I know," she said, pacing back and forth in the small office. "On top of these damn murders and the mood at the council meeting the other night I've got Sam's little bitch of a daughter showing up asking all kinds of questions about the company."

Fitch looked concerned. "You think she's going to be a problem?"

"No, not really. I've pretty well convinced her that she has no claim to any of it, but she's a damn lawyer for Christ's sake! The last thing I need is for her to start digging around in all the deals Sam and I made over the years. I just think we need to lay low until things calm down a bit."

"Screw that!" shouted Fitch. "I've got sounding trucks scheduled to start working that desert land in just a couple of days. It'll cost a fortune to reschedule them, not to mention the time lost. No way. There's no going back now."

Corinne slumped back against her desk, looking like she was going to start crying again. Fitch blew out a breath and took her by the shoulders, his voice softer now.

"Look, Corinne, both of these murders have worked to our advantage. You can talk to Hickock, offer him the deal of a lifetime for that valley. And with Sam out of the way, there's no one who can stop us. I've just about got the ranchers where I want them. Most of t[heir mineral leases are set to expire next month. Once we secure those, we'll be set for life."

"But won't that throw suspicion on us for the murders?"

Fitch pulled up short and stared at her. "You said Sheriff Yeager had that under control. I thought he had a suspect."

"Not really."

"What the hell does that mean? Either he does or he doesn't."

"He's letting a personal grudge get in the way of doing his job. You'd never convince anyone in this town that Will Hickock killed Linehart, the man practically raised him. And Yeager said he has a solid alibi for Sam's murder."

Fitch stalked across the office. "Damnit, Corinne, you told me you and Yeager had this under control."

"We do, but now that new deputy is nosing around asking questions, and once those mineral lease deals go public it doesn't take a genius to see we have plenty of motive for both killings."

Emotion overtook her and she buried her face in her hands. The sudden flood of tears made Fitch uncomfortable. He shifted from one foot to the other, unsure what to do, then walked over and took her in his arms. "Calm down now, honey," he soothed, "they haven't got a damn thing on either of us."

She stared hard at him through her tears, looking more scared than angry. "Not on me, at least."

Fitch stiffened. "What the hell is that supposed to mean?"

She pushed him away and moved around the desk, giving herself some distance. "Oh, gee, I don't know, you come waltzing in here with this big plan that's going to make us both millionaires and all of a sudden the two biggest obstacles in our path are…taken care of."

His eyes narrowed and his jaw tensed. "Why Corinne, sweetheart, that sounds like you don't trust me."

She backed up, the scared look returning. "If there's something you'd like to tell me, Marcus, now would be a really good time."

He took a breath, then raised his hands and gave her a big smile, coming around the desk beside her, cupping her chin in his hand and looking her in the eyes. "Corinne, honey, trust me, you've got nothing to worry about."

His arms slid around her waist, and he gave her a kiss. She responded, but only for a moment before pulling away. "All the same, I just think it might be better to let the pot simmer until they find out who killed them. Once we're in the clear, no one can stop us."

He let her go, biting back his frustration. "You know it's going to destroy this town."

She spun around, facing him again. "I don't give a damn about the stupid town. Small business leases and selling lots for a few summer homes is nothing compared to what we can make off those gas leases. But until that happens, it's my meal ticket, and I'm not about to blow it before everything is in place."

Fitch sensed her resolve was weakening. He moved in to her again, brushing a lock of hair off her face. "Hey, stop your worrying now. Everything's going to be all right."

"I want it to be. You know I do, Marcus. But these damn murders, and now this hiccup with the ranch…"

"Hey, hey, hey," he said, pulling her close and nuzzling her neck. Her breathing quickened. "I told you we'd see this through together, and I meant it. You stick with me, and in another few weeks we'll be rolling in clover."

He kissed her again, and this time she didn't resist. She grabbed his head, holding his mouth to hers, her passion growing. Fitch's hands started pawing her and she rubbed her body hard against him. His hands slid down her backside and he lifted her onto the desk. Pacheko didn't stay for the rest. He slipped quietly back around the building and took off, his ears still burning.

CHAPTER 23

"I lied," said Will as soon as they sat down at a relatively quiet corner table in the Mountain Bean. The small coffee shop had opened up in one of the many vacant storefronts on Main Street soon after the biking boom hit town. As usual, business was brisk.

Carla smiled a mischievous smile, as though she knew exactly what he meant. It unnerved him, but he had committed himself now. "I do remember you," he continued. "Back in school everyone knew who you were."

"Yeah," she said, "crazy Sam Montforte's daughter."

"No," Will protested, "that wasn't what I meant at all." He wanted to say it was because she was the prettiest girl in school, but she cut him off with a laugh.

"Everyone thought he was nuts," she said with a sigh.

"Even your mom?"

"Especially my mom. It's why she jerked me out of school in the middle of my junior year and left him. They never had any money to speak of, and when he struck it rich down in Reno, she thought it was their ticket out of Shambles."

"So, it really was a gambling score?"

"That's what he always said. Mom believed him, so I did, too." She looked at him sideways. "Why?"

Will took a breath and then told her about the Captain's theory that it was a payoff from Latham for helping him skim from the smelter. She just sat there and listened, her face going sad. When the tears started, Will decided he'd better stop. "I'm sorry. I'm such an idiot. You just buried your father and here I am…"

"It's ok," she said, wiping her eyes.

"If it makes you feel any better, there was never any proof one way or the other."

"I guess it's just one more thing we'll never know about him." She grabbed a napkin and wiped her nose. "Well, wherever he got it, she never forgave him for blowing it all on worthless land in a dying town." She looked around the busy shop at the line of bikers waiting for their jolt of caffein before hitting the trails. "I wonder what she'd think if she saw it now?"

Will couldn't help but feel sorry for her. He knew only too well about loss and what it could do to loved ones and families. He felt a sudden urge to do something to help ease her burden. "What about you?"

She shrugged. "Mom used to say he was a hard man to love, but he always treated me with love and respect, and I loved him back. Still, even at that age I could see there wasn't much of a future for me in

Shambles. Mom was always talking about getting out of this place and chastising him for letting his daughter grow up without any chance for a better life. I could tell it hurt him, but he had his vision, and he wouldn't let go of it."

"Well, it finally paid off," said Will.

"Yes, it did, but not until after we were long gone. Mom had moved on, from him and from Shambles. She had some family back in Minnesota. They helped us get settled and Mom got a job. There was no way she was ever going back."

"What about you? Did you stay in touch with him?"

"He used to write me letters, and for while I wrote back. He sent some money for college, but his real estate thing hadn't really taken off yet, so it wasn't much. Then life just sort of took over. I had to get a job to pay for school, and classes kept me busy. The letters became birthday and Christmas cards and then gradually stopped altogether." She gazed out the window at the bustling street. "I guess he got busy, too."

"Yeah, the town has changed a lot."

She gave him the mischievous smile again. "You were the cute guy who got dropped off every morning and picked up every day after school by a sheriff's car. It drove me crazing wondering what was up with that, until someone told me you were an inmate at the Ranch."

Will felt his face redden. Yeah, that's a long and complicated story. Not really worth telling."

Her ice blue eyes twinkled with curiosity, but she didn't press. "Well, you obviously got out."

"When I graduated, I still had a few years left on my sentence. The Captain talked to the judge and he gave me a choice, prison or join the military and get my sentence reduced. So, I joined the Army. I kind of liked it, actually. In a lot of ways, it wasn't much different than the Ranch."

She laughed. "I guess I could see that. What did you do in the Army?"

"Ranger."

Her raised eyebrows and a simple tilt of her head said she was impressed. "It's funny, I don't really know you at all, but for some reason, I'm not surprised." She smiled at him, and he breathed a little easier. "You must have seen some action, then. Middle East?"

He nodded. "Three tours."

Her eyes went wide, but she seemed to sense he didn't want to talk about this, either. But the more he resisted, the more she wanted to know. "But you're back in Shambles now?"

"A few months ago. Decided I'd pushed my luck far enough with the Rangers, so I came back here to figure out what I wanted to do next."

"And you're still figuring?"

He smiled. "I guess you could say that."

The barista called out Will's name and he started to get up, but Carla put a hand on his arm. "Would you mind if we took those to go?"

"Yeah, sure," he said, trying to hide his disappointment, not wanting to let her go. "I'm sure you've got a lot of stuff to do."

She gave an embarrassed laugh, confusing him even more. "Actually, I was hoping I could talk you into showing me around a bit."

She smiled again, and suddenly all was right with the world. Will paid for the coffee and they piled back into his truck. As they drove down Main Street Will pointed out all the shops, restaurants, hotels and office buildings that now sat on her father's once worthless land. She barely said a word, just taking it all in. He could tell she was affected by the changes she saw, but he couldn't decidel whether she was pissed about missing out on her father's success, or proud of him for seeing what nobody else could all those years ago, that there was still a pulse left in the little mountain town.

Their conversation flowed easily, and much to Will's surprise she began to open up to him. She told him about her undergraduate years at Northwestern, then dropped the bomb that she had gone on to law school.

"You're a lawyer?" Will exclaimed.

She laughed at his shocked expression, then punched his shoulder. "You don't have to act so surprised," she said with mock disdain.

Will was instantly embarrassed. "No, I'm not…that is, it's just…"

"Not what you expected?" she finished for him, smiling.

"Honestly? No. But I'm impressed. Coming from a town like Shambles was back then, I'd say you've really done well."

She blushed. "Thanks. It took a lot of hard work. And I've got a lot of school loans to pay off, but I've got a good job with a great firm in Minneapolis."

"Putting criminals behind bars?"

"Not really. It's mostly corporate stuff—contracts, mergers, that kind of thing."

"I'm guessing that will come in handy dealing with Corinne on your father's estate."

She got a faraway look in her eyes and Will sensed he'd trod on unfavorable ground. They drove in silence a while. When the tour of town was finished, she hesitantly asked him to drive her by the house where she grew up. Will was happy to oblige. He wasn't ready for their time together to end. She seemed more and more apprehensive as he drove, and he wondered what memories of her childhood were being dredged up in her mind.

It was a dumpy little place on the west side of town, but the family who lived there now had kept it up well. As Will drove by there were a couple of little kids kicking a soccer ball around in the front yard.

"Wait, I don't understand," she said, looking confused.

"What's wrong," Will asked, pulling to a stop at the side of the road, "isn't this the right place? I thought…"

"It's the right place, but Corinne told me whoever killed my father burned the place down."

Now it was Will's turn to be confused, and he began to wonder exactly what Corinne had told Carla about her father's estate.

She pointed to the kids. "How long has that family been living here?"

"I'm not sure," Will replied. "Four or five years, I guess. Ever since he and Corinne started Spring Meadows."

She gave him a curious look. "What's that?"

"It's an upscale housing development along the river east of town. Sam and Corinne each built the first houses in it. She didn't mention that?"

She shook her head, looking confused for a moment, and then it seemed like a couple of puzzle pieces fell into place for her. "Can you take me there?"

"Now?"

"Yes, now," she said firmly. "I want to see it."

"Are you sure?" he asked. "It's still a...I mean, it hasn't been cleaned up or anything since..."

"I'm sure," she said firmly, crossing her arms and facing forward.

Will put the truck in gear and drove through town, feeling a little apprehensive himself now. But she proved tougher than he thought. Once past the initial shock of seeing her father's ruined house, she asked a ton of questions about the development. Will tried his best to answer them, but he had to defer to Corinne several times. He could see she was getting frustrated, and she finally noticed how uncomfortable he was becoming.

"I'm sorry, Will," she said. "It's not you at all. I really appreciate you taking the time to show me all this." She let out an airy laugh. "It's just so much to take in. When I was growing up, Dad was such a..."

She struggled for a word but couldn't find one. Will had a few in mind but kept them to himself.

"It seemed like he had no sense of money whatsoever," she continued. "Mom was always complaining about it. And now, to see everything he's built, and what's happened to this town, I guess I'm just a little overwhelmed."

"I can understand," said Will. "I felt the same way when I got back. It's almost like Shambles has risen from the dead. Your father played a big part in that."

"I wish I'd known. I wish I could have told him how proud of him I am."

She broke down and sobbed. Will didn't have a clue what he was supposed to do. He wanted desperately to try and comfort her somehow, but he couldn't bring himself to put an arm around her. He remembered the stack of unused napkins in the glove compartment he'd collected from getting coffee to go, so he gingerly reached across in front of her and pulled out a few. She took one and dabbed at her eyes. After a minute or so, the crying stopped.

"I'm sorry," she sniffled. "I didn't mean to…"

"It's okay," Will said, smiling. "Are you feeling any better?"

"Yeah, I think so." She blew out a breath. "I guess I needed to do that sooner or later. This whole trip has been so strange. When I first got the news, I wasn't going to come out here. I figured Corinne could handle everything. She was his business partner, and more, if you believe the rumors. I didn't think there was anything left for me in Shambles but a lot of bad memories."

"I get that," said Will, "but he was your father, good or bad."

"That's funny," she said, half smiling, "that's exactly what I told myself. So, I bought a ticket and here I am. I have to say, it certainly has not been what I expected."

He offered her another napkin, which she took, and dried her eyes one more time.

"You ready to head back to your hotel?"

"What, that's it?" she asked sarcastically. "You mean he only owned half the town?"

They shared a laugh, and she blew her nose again. Will started up the truck, and then remembered something. "Actually, there is another piece of land."

She laughed. "I was joking, Will."

"No, I'm serious. I heard he bought a chunk of desert land a while back, down in the foothills."

"Do you know where it is?"

"I'm pretty sure I can find it, but it's bit of a drive."

"I've got nowhere else to go," she said with a smile. "And I'm enjoying the company."

Will felt himself blush, and couldn't help smiling at her, wondering all the while where these new feelings were coming from. They picked up some sandwiches and drinks from Marv's Diner and ate as he drove south out of town. Gradually, the mountains began to give way to broad rolling hills and the forest transitioned to sagebrush and cheat grass. After about twenty minutes he turned off on a dirt road that ran along a high ridge and stopped at a pullout about two hundred yards in that gave them a view of the broad front stretching out below them to the south and east. The midday sun intensified the green of the fresh spring grass that blanketed the hills.

"Oh wow," she said, almost to herself. "I'd forgotten how beautiful this place can be."

They got out and walked around to the front of the truck. She climbed up on one fender and gazed out over a landscape virtually untouched by man for several millenia.

"From where we turned off the main road," said Will, his hand sweeping from the direction they had come all the way along the hills below them, "to where this ridge runs to ground further down there."

She looked at him, confused for a moment, then it dawned on her. "Oh, my god!" She traced the same sweep with her eyes, her mouth hanging open. He owns all that?"

"As I understand it, roughly from this ridge road down across the flats. I'm not sure exactly how far."

"But that must be hundreds of acres."

"Thousands, actually."

"I had no idea," she said, blowing out a breath. "It must have cost a fortune."

"You're asking the wrong guy," said Will. "I heard it involved some kind of land swap with the BLM. Only reason I know about it at all is that when they bought it, Sam apparently gave a big pitch to the Town Council about its potential for another trail system that could expand the resort."

"Sounds like those plans may be changing."

"You don't miss much, do you."

"It's a small town," she said, "all you have to do is listen. I've only been here a day, but everyone in Shambles seems to be talking about some kind of oil or gas project."

"You probably know as much as the rest of us, then. The whole thing just came to light in the last few days, but it's apparently been in the works for some time. As I understand it, Corinne talked Sam into hiring some kind of land man named Fitch to do some exploratory drilling all along this front to see if it has any potential for natural gas. It's far enough from Shambles that drilling probably wouldn't affect the resort.

"But if I what I heard is correct, this isn't the only place they're looking to explore."

"Yeah, I heard this Fitch guy has been talking to ranchers all over the county, trying to convince them they could all make a bundle if it pans out."

"And that would hurt the resort."

Will nodded. "To hear the Town Council talk, it would kill it." He looked over at her. "I don't suppose there's anything you could do about all this?"

She sighed. "As far as I know, everything dad had was tied up in his real estate business. I haven't seen a will yet, but according to Corinne, all the land is in both their names, and as far as she's concerned, she owns it all now."

"When did she tell you that?"

"I let her know I was coming for the funeral, and she offered to pick me up at the airport. Even arranged a fancy room for me at the Alpine Inn."

"Nice," said Will.

"That's what I thought. Then, on the drive up from Boise, she filled me in on her version of the future of Montforte Real Estate. Needless to say, I'm not included."

"That's pretty harsh," Will said with a frown. "Your father wasn't even in the ground yet."

"I thought so, too."

"Well, Corinne's never been one to mince words."

"She seems like a pretty hard case, alright. But I guess she's got a lot on the line, especially with this gas exploration and what it might mean for Shambles."

"So, I take it she won't be giving you a ride back to the airport."

Carla laughed. "Is that an offer?"

"Sure. Whenever you like?" She smiled. "But for now, how about I buy you some dinner?"

"That sounds nice, Will, but can I take a rain check? It's been a really long day with the funeral and all."

Will felt his face turning red. "Of course, I'm sorry. I didn't mean to be pushy or anything."

"No, I mean it about the rain check. I'll be around for a few days. I've got to go through all of dad's things. I'm meeting with his lawyer tomorrow to see if there's anything I need to do with his estate."

"Let me guess, Arvin Melville."

"How'd you know?"

"Trust me, it wasn't a tough call." He shook his head and smiled. "You're in for a treat."

She waited for him to elaborate, but he seemed to be thinking of something else. Looking back out across the ridge she marveled once again that all that land belonged to her father. When Will spoke again, it startled her.

"Listen, I'm having a few friends over for a fish fry tomorrow night. You could come if you like. That is, if you're free." She smiled again, amused at his clumsiness. He stopped himself and took a breath. "What I mean is, I'd really like it if you came."

Her smile was all the answer he needed. And that twinkle was back in those translucent blue eyes.

CHAPTER 24

Freewheelin'
That's good enough for me.
Freewheelin'
What comin' home was meant to be.

The sun was barely up, but Will was already well beyond the Ponderosa Loop and the rest of the official trail system, pedaling up a steep, barely perceptible track along the upper end of the tree line, Tommy's biking song ringing in his head. The rocky terrain made it hard work, and so did the single-wheel trailer he was hauling behind him. Strapped onto it, along with his fishing rod and a large backpack-style creel, was an even larger cooler. The sweat poured off him, soaking his shirt, but there was a smile on his face.

It had been a very long time since he had any reason to feel like his life was looking up. Coming home from the Army to a town radically different from what he expected only to be accused of two murders had done little to make him feel welcome. But between inheriting the

Captain's ranch and meeting Carla, he was beginning to think things might be starting to turn around. Now if he could just convince Yeager.

The trail ducked into the trees and leveled out as it traversed the face of the mountain, making the going somewhat easier. It led him to the base of a steep, narrow couloir with a broad creek crashing down through it in a series of spectacular waterfalls. He stopped and positioned his bike securely on the uphill side of a large pine tree, then unstrapped his rod and creel from the trailer, leaving the cooler where it was. He opened the lid and pulled out the large water bottle nestled next to a big bag of ice. After taking a long drink, he secired the bottle inside the creel, then slipped the straps over his shoulders and started climbing.

The incline was extremely steep, and he had to beat his way around and through the thick brush that lined both sides of the creek, but he moved up the couloir with relative ease, using rocks and boulders the roaring water had tumbled down the mountainside over time as steppingstones. Half an hour later, the ground began to level off and he made his way through the last of the trees into a giant, open cirque that held a pristine lake about a quarter mile across and almost perfectly round. It sat like a jewel at the base of several massive snow-capped peaks that shot straight up around it. This early in the season patches of snow still remained among the trees on the north-facing slopes.

He paused to catch his breath and take in the beauty of the spot, retrieving his water bottle and taking a drink, then started working his way around the edge of the lake. He hadn't gone twenty feet when he spotted a fresh boot track, and then another. His smile quickly faded. He hadn't noticed any tracks coming up the couloir, and there was no other way in short of a helicopter, which meant whoever was here must have come up the other side of the creek. He smiled to himself, knowing all too well that was doing it the hard way.

He scanned the shoreline. It seemed empty at first, and then he spotted a flash of fishing line as it swept out from behind a clump of willows about halfway down the lake. The fly on the end of the line lit lightly on the mirror-smooth water for only a moment before it was yanked back. Almost immediately it flashed out again, landing on another spot a few feet further out, where it lay, waiting.

Will took to higher ground and made his way around the lake, disappointment clouding his face. In a way, he'd always considered this lake his personal property. He'd never seen another soul here before, except the Captain, who had showed it to him in the first place, and who had welcomed any opportunity to accompany him before Will left for the Army. Sadly, by the time he returned, his mentor had gotten too old to make the climb.

Just ahead, the trees that populated the lower end of the lake came to an end. Will peered around the last big pine into the open cirque and spotted the other fisherman. His face was hidden by a ridiculous floppy hat. Its headband was studded with an incredible variety of flies, most of which were totally wrong for the types of insects that inhabited this area. It looked like he had gone into a fishing store and asked for one of everything.

His fishing vest was brand new, it's pockets bulging with what Will suspected was way more fishing gear than necessary. Spanking new hiking boots were more evidence, as far as Will was concerned, that this guy had no idea what he was doing. He couldn't help but wonder how such a rookie had gotten all the way up here, all alone.

The stranger made another cast, and Will had to admit his tecŜique wasn't bad. His wrist oscillated perfectly between ten and two as he teased the surface with the fly twice, three times, then let it gently settle onto the crystal-clear water. Will was about to announce himself when the man turned to place his next back cast. Recognizing Pacheko all decked out in that outfit almost caused Will to laugh out loud. The deputy still hadn't seen him, so Will waited until he was focused on his casting again, and then quietly worked his way down the slope until he was just a few feet behind him.

"I'm starting to think you're stalking me," Will said calmly.

Pacheko jumped like he'd been shot and jerked around, losing his balance on the boulder, his arms flailing frantically as he tried to keep himself from falling into the lake. He would have, too, if Will hadn't reached out and grabbed his arm, pulling him back upright. Pacheko hopped off the boulder onto solid ground and broke out that big grin.

"Whoa, that was close," he said, looking up at his rescuer. "How'd you do that?" Will cocked his head, not understanding. "Sneak up behind me like that. I never heard a sound."

Will smiled. "A little something I picked up on my tours across the pond. You don't learn to move quietly over there, you're dead. What the hell are you doing clear up here?"

"Yeager was starting to get to me. I had to take a break."

"I hear that," said Will. He watched the deputy reel in his line. "How'd you hear about this place?"

"Mike Patterson on the Town Council told me this lake had some of the best fishing around.

"Mike would know. He's hiked these mountains his whole life."

"I asked him about a map, but he said it was a no-name lake, whatever that is."

Will smiled. "It means it's not named on any map. Helps keep it from getting trampled by too many tourists. At least, that's the intent."

"So, this is one of those secret fishing holes you were talking about the other night?"

Will shrugged. "You might say that. The Captain brought me up here for the first time when I was twelve or thirteen. He always told me no one else knew about it, and that I should never tell anyone where it was."

"And you believed him?"

"Back then I did. It was pretty cool to have my own private lake. I used to wonder whether he was just pulling my leg, but in all the years I've been coming up here I've never seen another soul except the Captain. Until you."

"I can see why," Pacheko said with a grunt. "Getting up here is the hike from hell."

Will just smiled. "Welcome to Idaho."

Pacheko frowned at him. "What about you? Shouldn't you be working on bikes or clearing trails or something?"

"The boss gave me the day off, as long as I bring him some fresh trout."

Pacheko grunted, then thought of something. "How come I didn't see your campfire last night?"

"I came up this morning."

"From town? \ Are you kidding me? The sun's barely up. What did you do, fly up?"

Will laughed. "No, I biked up. There's a little trail off the Loop that gets you about halfway up the base of the couloir, then I hiked the rest of the way. The whole trip took about two hours."

"Now you tell me. Damn, it took me over five yesterday afternoon. I got lost twice and I was halfway up the damn creek with the waterfalls before I realized I should have been on the other side. It was damn near dark when I got to the lake. I've never been so glad to crawl into a sleeping bag on hard ground in my life."

Will couldn't help a chuckle, then they stood quiet for a while, soaking in the beauty of the alpine lake and the peaks surrounding it. Pacheko finally broke the silence. "Mike owns that big ranch north of the Captain's place, right?

Will grunted. "Big doesn't hardly say it. Isn't he one of the ranchers Fitch has been talking to?"

Pacheko nodded. "Why do you ask?"

"If Fitch finds gas on Montforte's foothills land, he won't stop there. He'll want more, and from what I've read about some of these land men, they don't care much who they step on to get it."

"You think Patterson will cave to him?"

"I can't see that happening. Their family's been on that land for four or five generations. But you never know. Money can be a powerful motivator."

The deputy turned and started another casting sequence. Will watched him drop his fly in the middle of a deep hole about ten yards offshore. After the third cast, Pacheko let it settle and reeled in a little line.

"From what I hear, everyone's waiting to see what happens with the Linehart ranch. Word is, if they get their hands on that, the dominos could start falling."

Will clenched his jaw. "Yeah, well, that'll never happen as long as I have anything to say about it." Pacheko flicked his fly off the water and back over their heads, dropping it in another spot a few yards further out. Will couldn't tell whether the deputy had heard him or not. He decided to test the water, so to speak. "But first I have to get out from under these murders."

Pacheko gave his line another flick and set the fly down again. "I'm working on that, but neither of them seems to be connected in any way. And I haven't found a single potential suspect who doesn't have either a solid alibi or no motive. The pieces of this puzzle just don't seem to fit together."

"Maybe you need more pieces."

"Yeah, that's another reason I came up here. Clear my head, maybe come up with a new angle."

"If I come up with one, I'll be sure to let you know. Right now, I've got some trout to catch." Will started to walk further around the lake, then stopped. "I'm assuming you've got a license, deputy," he said with a straight face. Pacheko gave him a smirk. "Oh, that's right, I forgot. You've got an in with the BLM."

"Ha!" barked Pacheko. "You know what a stickler for the rules Dolores is just as well as I do, Hickock. Don't worry," he said, patting his vest pocket, "I'm legal."

"What, no inter-departmental cooperation?"

"Not yet," Pacheko said with a chuckle, "but you just keep pushing that angle and maybe she'll get the idea one of these days." They shared a laugh. "Hey, that reminds me, is there some kind of limit up here?"

Will looked over Pacheko's outfit once more, suppressing a smirk. "I doubt you'll have to worry about it, they're pretty tricky."

"That sounds like a challenge."

Will just shrugged and moved off down the shore.

"Loser buys the beer," Pacheko called after him. Then he smiled and went back to his casting.

Will stopped at a rock outcropping that jutted out into the lake and began to set up his rod. The water was amazingly clear. He could follow the line of the cliff at least thirty feet down into the greenish-blue water. A whoop of excitement drew his attention back to Pacheko, who had just snagged a fat cutthroat. He watched as the deputy struggled to land the big fish, only to lose it a moment later. Finding a likely spot for his first cast, Will allowed himself a satisfied smile. This was going to be no contest at all.

They both worked their way around the lake in opposite directions, each lost in the pleasure of doing battle with trout instead of murderers, at least for now. The sun was straight overhead by the time they met up again, and Pacheko asked Will to join him for some lunch. He followed the deputy to his camp near the lower end of the lake where he produced a couple of energy bars from his pack. Will couldn't suppress a grin.

"This all you brought?" he asked.

"Ate the last of my stew for breakfast this morning. But I saved a couple of these for lunch." He pried open a pile of wet grass next to his tent and revealed six fat trout, all expertly cleaned. Will's jaw dropped open.

"You were right," Pacheko said with a grin, "they're sneaky little suckers." "You caught all those this morning?"

"Yeah, but I must have lost twice as many. How'd you do?"

Will smiled and opened his creel. It was brimming with cutthroat and rainbows.

"Whoa," said Pacheko, "must be more than a dozen. You can't be that hungry."

"I'm having a few friends over tonight for a little fish fry." He eyed Pacheko's catch. "You plan on eating all those for lunch?"

"Hell, no. I'm hoping the wet grass will keep them fresh long enough to get them back to my freezer, minus a couple for us, of course." He tossed several small branches on the remains of his campfire and blew on the embers to get it going again. Once it was burning brightly, he threw on a few more branches, then picked out two of his biggest trout and laid them on a flat rock next to the remains of his campfire.

"I'll doctor these up a bit and get cooking. Then I've got to be heading back. Yeager will be missing me."

Will nodded, looking down at his catch. "While you do that, I'd better take care of these."

He took the creel down to the lake shore and began cleaning his fish, keeping one eye on Pacheko as he produced a couple of sheets of tin foil and placed a fish on each. After rubbing each trout inside and out with a little olive oil and sprinkling salt and pepper on them, he pulled a lemon out of his pack and cut it into slices. He stuck a couple of slices inside each trout and wrapped them up in the foil. Then he spread the branches of the fire around forming a bed of red hot coals and laid the fish right on top of them. Will felt his mouth begin to water.

Once the fish started sizzling, Pacheko strolled down to the lake and offered to help clean the rest of the catch. Will was surprised to find himself cultivating a new respect for the deputy.

"Can I ask you a question?" Pacheko asked as he gutted a large rainbow. Will just kept working, which Pacheko took as a yes. "How the hell did Yeager ever get to be sheriff?"

"By default, pretty much," Will snorted. "He'd been deputy for so long I guess it was just the natural progression when the Captain retired. But there wasn't exactly a long list of candidates clamoring for the job, either." He looked over at the new deputy, his expression asking where this was going

"He acts righteously pissed about these murders," said Pacheko, "but I get the impression that it's not so much because of who was murdered, it's more because he doesn't have a clue where to start investigating."

"I can't say I'm surprised. I don't know when the last murder happened in Shambles, but it had to be long before even the Captain became sheriff."

Pacheko kept working for a while. "He doesn't seem to get along too well with most folks in town."

"You noticed," said Will sarcastically. "He's always had a natural tendency to rub people the wrong way. But most folks put up with him because of the badge."

"How about Corinne Barker?"

"I don't know. Why?"

"Seems like he talks to her quite a bit. For a while I thought maybe they had a little thing going on the side."

Will laughed, then shuddered. "Thanks a lot, now I'll never get that image out of my head."

Pacheko chuckled as got up and flipped over the fish on the coals.

"Yeah, I never really gave it much credence, but when I told him we ought to question her about Montforte's murder, he shut me down hard. Told me to leave her alone and focus on finding the real killer."

"Meaning me."

The deputy walked back down to the water and picked up another fish to clean. "Look," he said earnestly, "I know I'm new in town, and I may not know exactly which way the wind blows around here yet, but I've told you how I feel about that, and I haven't found anything to change my mind."

Will breathed a sigh of relief. "Thank you for that." He finished cleaning a big Rainbow and rinsed his knife off in the lake. "Stu English told me he thinks Corinne is the one behind all this gas business, and that Yeager is helping her stay under the radar."

Pacheko perked up. "When did he tell you this?"

"Just a couple of days ago, right before Montforte was killed."

The deputy stopped cleaning the fish he was holding and chewed on a thought for several moments. Will picked up another fish from the creel. Finally, Pacheko looked him in the eye. "I'm going to trust you here."

Will looked at him with a curious expression, which the deputy must have bought, because he proceeded to tell Will about following Fitch and Corinne to her office after Montforte's funeral. As he walked him through their conversation. Will's eyes got wider and wider, and when he heard the last part, his jaw dropped.

"You've got to be shitting me!" he exclaimed. "Corinne and Fitch?" He laughed. "Well, at least I can see her choosing him over Yeager." Pacheko laughed along with him, and Will had a new thought. "Hell, there's your motive right there. Fitch killed the Captain to free up his ranch land, and then murdered Montforte to give Corinne control of the business."

"I thought you told me she already controlled the business."

"Maybe he found out about Fitch and the gas deal and was going to expose them."

Pacheko blew out a breath. "I don't know. You said Fitch is too big to have made those footprints at the crime scenes?"

Will thought about it. "Yeah, he is, I guess. I still wouldn't rule him out."

They continued to clean fish in silence for a while, then a mental light bulb went on for Will. "Wait a minute. You said the Captain's ranch was the key to her plan. That's what she meant at the funeral when she said we needed to talk. But how the hell did she know I inherited it? According to my lawyer it's not supposed to be public record until I sign papers claiming the property."

"She told Fitch she had a friend at the courthouse who told her when Linehart's will was registered." He went back over to the fire and flipped the fish once more, then poked at them with a stick, testing to see if they were done. "I'm sure she's got connections all over town, but that doesn't really matter now. She knows, and she's none too happy about it. She claimed not to have any part in the killings, but she didn't seem too sure about Fitch."

"Doesn't matter, she's an accomplice, right?"

"If Fitch committed the murders, I'd say yes."

"Sounds like he as good as admitted it."

"Nah, he never really committed one way or the other. And the fact that I overheard their conversation without their knowledge makes it hearsay. That'll never hold up in court." He flipped the fish again. "Almost ready."

"Well, at least this might take some of the heat off me."

"I wouldn't hold your breath when it comes to Yeager. He seems pretty determined to convict you of something, he doesn't really care what."

"Sounds like you're fishing for another history lesson," said Will.

Pacheko shrugged. "You know what they say about campfires, they make for good stories. I was hoping you might give me your version of the famous payroll robbery."

Will looked hard at the deputy for several seconds, then glanced over at the frying pan. "Those fish done yet?"

CHAPTER 25

Pacheko finished off the last bite of his fish and put his plate down. "So, Montforte was the payroll guard who got shot, right?"

Will was surprised. "How'd you figure that?"

"Autopsy report said there was an old bullet wound along his right side."

Will gave a shrug of acquiescence, a smile tugging at the corners of his mouth.

"You must have freaked out when they jumped you."

"Not nearly as bad as when the judge announced my sentence," said Will. "If figured my life was over."

"And yet, here you are," Pacheko said with a grin.

"Thanks to the Captain. He kind of took me under his wing to protect me from getting bullied by some of the older boys. I guess he was hoping I could be diverted from the dark path my brother led me down."

"Seems to have worked."

"It took a while. I had a real chip on my shoulder at first. Doc always taught me that cops were not to be trusted, that they'd just as soon bust you as look at you. But the Captain was different. He listened. And he taught me the importance of hard work. Even though I was by far the youngest one at the Ranch, as long as I busted my butt just as hard as everyone else, I earned their respect."

"What about school?"

"It was part of the program. Besides working the ranch, we all had to go to classes every day. Everyone who was there through high school walked away with a diploma."

"You too?"

"Yep. The Captain was adamant about it. He said putting us kids back in society without an education wouldn't do anybody any good. We'd just revert to our old ways. Ask Yeager about it sometime."

"Yeager. Don't tell me he was at the Ranch, too?"

"Oh, he was there all right, but not on the inside. Not that he shouldn't have been for all the trouble he caused."

"That's right, he was a deputy back then."

"Not until a couple of years after I got there. And with Doc dead he decided to go after me." Pacheko gave him a questioning look. Will put down his plate and leaned back against a tree. "When Yeager was a kid, he tried to be a bully. I think it was to make up for his size. He was always too little to pull it off."

Pacheko let out a laugh. Will grinned and continued. "Nobody ever took him seriously, and it really used to piss him off. Doc was a year or so younger, but taller and meaner. Every time Yeager tried to give him a hard time, Doc just beat the shit out of him. Rodney used to try and get his older friends to gang up on Doc, but they were all scared of him. Yeager was just too stubborn to know any better.

"Some things never change," said Pacheko.

"Ain't it the truth."

"And once he got a badge, he could finally be the bully he always wanted to be. But just because he hated your brother, why take it out on you?"

"I think he always blamed both Doc and me for losing his first job."

Pacheko's jaw dropped. "Yeager was the other payroll guard?"

Will just shrugged and Pacheko laughed long and hard.

"What's so damned funny?" asked Will.

"I was just visualizing Yeager sitting in the middle of the creek with an eight-year-old holding a gun on him."

They both laughed this time, enjoying the image. Will tossed his fish bones onto the fire. "Listen, I've got a cooler down at the trail with my bike. If you want, I could haul your fish down on ice along with mine."

"In that case," said Pacheko, "why don't you just add them to the pile for your party."

"But I thought…"

"Like I told you, I came up here to clear my head. Besides, I'm not really much of a trout man. They'll just probably end up in my freezer way longer than they should."

"That's because you've never had trout the way I fix them."

Pacheko perked up. "That an invitation?"

"You caught them. I'd hate to see you miss out on eating some of them.

Pacheko's grin widened. "Thanks, Hickock. I'd welcome the chance to get to know some more of the people around here off the job, if you know what I mean. One thing I didn't count on when I became a cop, it kind of limits your social life."

"Sounds like you miss that," said Will.

"I'm not going to lie, in my former life I got out and about a lot more."

Pacheko started cleaning up the plates and Will stirred some water into the fire to douse the last of the coals.

"Out and about where?" asked Will.

"What do you mean?"

"I've practically told you my whole life story and I realize I don't know a thing about you."

Pacheko shrugged. "Not much to know, really."

"Now why do I not believe that?" He could see the deputy was getting uncomfortable with the questions, so he went to work himself, breaking down Pacheko's tent. "The way you dress, I picture you with a surfboard, long hair, bonfires on the beach, bikini babes all around..."

Pacheko gave a half-hearted laugh. "Yeah, well, there was a time when you wouldn't have been too far off."

Will waited, but nothing more came. "So, Marcia was right about the surfing thing."

"Yeah," Pacheko said, his voice almost sad. Then he suddenly changed gears. "But now here I am stuck in the middle of nowhere Idaho in this ridiculous outfit trying to out-fish a local who's been doing it all he life."

It was obvious the deputy's past was a sore subject, so Will gave up. "We better head out. I don't want to be late for my own party."

While Pacheko got his pack together, Will soaked some fresh grass in the lake and wrapped up the fish that wouldn't fit in his creel in a jacket he'd brought. As they headed back down the couloir, Pacheko followed in silence, paying strict attention to the precarious footing and marveling at how easily Will seemed to be handling the steep descent. Once they reached the switchback trail, the deputy spoke up suddenly. "Something's been bugging me."

His concentration broken, Will stumbled, grabbing a handful of willow branches to steady himself. "What's that?" he asked once he regained his balance.

"Montforte was tortured."

"What the hell was the killer was trying to get out of him?"

"It must have been something he wanted awful bad to go to those lengths.

"I wonder if Montforte told him what he wanted to know?"

Their conversation was silenced as the trail passed by a thirty-foot waterfall. They worked their way down past it, each lost in his own thoughts, until the trail led away from the creek again. "Assuming it's the same killer," said Will, "I've been wondering why this guy would go after the Captain?"

"You're right, two murders this close together would seem to indicate there's some kind of connection. You know the history better than I do. What could it be?"

"Montforte was a deputy back before the Captain came along, you know."

"So I heard. What of it?

"Story goes he wanted to be Sheriff, but the Captain took it away from him."

Pacheko's eyebrows went up. "Couldn't have made him too happy with Linehart."

"It gets better. Not long after the Captain became Sheriff he fired Montfort for being lazy and not doing the job. Montforte had to take the payroll guard job at the smelter. He always blamed the Captain for that. You notice he didn't show up at the funeral. There was never any love lost between those two."

"Okay," said Pacheko, "let's say that might give Montforte a motive to kill Linehart, but why now, after all these years? Besides, Montforte had it made a ton of money on his real estate deals, and that new housing development was bringing in even more. Why take a chance on screwing all that up?"

"Maybe the Captain finally found some evidence."

"Ok, but then who killed Montforte?"

"Maybe that brings us back to Corinne and Fitch."

Pacheko shook his head. "No, I'm not buying it. Too many maybes. Besides, there are too many similarities in the two murders. There's got to be a connection we're missing."

They dropped off the couloir slope onto the main trail and Will stepped past Pacheko to pulled his bike out of the brush behind the tree.

Pacheko saw the trailer and whistled. "Whoa, that's pretty slick. You got ice in that cooler?"

"Damn straight," said Will, removing the straps and opening the lid. He pulled out the bag of ice and dumped a layer on the bottom of the cooler, then put his fish inside. He emptied Pacheko's catch on top of them and tossed away the wet grass, then made sure the rest of the ice covered all the fish before strapping the lid back down. While he was attaching the creel and his pole to the top of the cooler, Pacheko shifted his pack on his shoulders uncomfortably. Will looked over at him.

"Just follow this trail going out. You should hit the Ponderosa Loop in about an hour, then just follow the signs back to the trail head."

"Yeah, thanks," the deputy said grudgingly.

Will got the bike and trailer pointed down the trail, then looked back at Pacheko. "Well, what are you waiting for?" he said with a grin. Strap that thing on top of the cooler so I can get going."

Pacheko's face lit up. "You serious?"

"You can pick it up at my house tonight. With any luck, you might make it down before all the fish are eaten."

CHAPTER 26

It was a beautiful June evening in Shambles. The sun had disappeared below the western peaks, but the afternoon heat still lingered, and the warm glow of dusk was settling over the little valley on the Middle Fork. Will's back yard was filling up with people and the sound of laughter bubbled up here and there. Strings of white lights glowed along the top of the fence giving the place a festive air.

Will was busy prepping the morning's catch on a table next to the grill, carefully dipping each trout in a big bowl of pasty batter and placing them side by side on a foil-covered baking sheet. Tommy and Libbie were happily kicking around a soccer ball with their two young boys, Ben and Matt, while Tim Spangler and his wife Tina talked about the latest bike tecŠology with a few more friends.

Aaron "Thumbs" Cooper appeared around the corner and held out a twelve-pack of beer. Will pointed to a large cooler next to the back door. Thumbs added his drinks to the others already on ice, then popped one open for himself and went over to talk with Tommy. Little

Matt saw him coming and kicked the soccer ball to him. Thumbs deftly deflected it to Ben, who picked up the ball and ran away, squealing with delight. Libbie took that as her cue to stroll over to Will.

"Need a hand?" she asked, dipping a finger in the batter.

Will swatted at her hand, but she was quicker. "Hey, keep away from my secret recipe. It's the only way I can get any of you people to come over to my side of the tracks."

She laughed and stuck the batter-covered finger in her mouth. "Mmmm, "this makes it well worth the trip. Are you ever going to tell me what's in it?"

"Nope. The Captain made me promise."

"And you always keep your promises?"

"Whenever I can, Lib," he said with a wry grin. "I just try not to make them too often."

She gave him a smile and a pat on the back as Tommy came over, an urgent look on his face. "Hey, we need to talk. Thumbs found something on your favorite deputy."

Libbie gave an exasperated sigh, but Tommy ignored her.

"No can do right now, Tommy," said Will. "I need to get these fish on the grill before the batter dries out."

Tommy looked down at the table full of fish, then back at Libbie, who rolled her eyes and stepped up next to Will. "Go ahead," she said, It doesn't look like there's much of a secret to this part."

Will reluctantly surrendered, wiping his hands on a towel as he followed Tommy across the yard to where Thumbs was putting on a show with the soccer ball for Ben and Matt. The two youngsters watched wide-eyed as he bounced the ball from one foot to the other, then up onto his forehead, ran it around his shoulders and let it drop, catching it expertly with one foot.

"There you go, rascals," he said as Tommy and Will approached. "You go work on that trick and I'll check on you in a little while."

Thumbs was a tall, lanky guy about six-foot-five, with long, stringy hair and an oafish look about him that belied his true talents. He'd been playing drums with Tommy's band for almost five years and his presence had definitely brought the rhythm section up a few notches. He also knew his way around computers, and was the group's go-to guy for anything high-tech. As a result, he had the hollow-eyed look of someone who spent too much time in front of a screen.

Playing music at Libbie's wasn't exactly the most lucrative job in the world, so he spent most of his time kicking ass on video gaming networks, where his reputation, as well as his stash of bitcoin, were both said to be considerable. In fact, it was his prowess with video games that earned him his nickname. He always said the two skills were the perfect combination. The gaming let him utilize his brain and delicate motor skills to the fullest, and the drums gave him a chance to work all the aggression and frustration that built up from long hours of gaming out of his system.

"Hey, Thumbs," said Will. "Glad you could make it."

"Appreciate the invite," he said with a grin, tipping his beer to his host.

Tommy was bouncing from one foot to the other. "Go ahead, tell him what you found," he urged.

Thumbs leaned into Will and spoke conspiratorially. "Seems as though our new deputy has a bit of a troubled past."

"What do you mean?" asked Will.

As if on cue, Pacheko walked in. As usual, his Forty-Niners jersey, neon surfer shorts and flip flops drew stares. Tommy spotted him immediately. "Damnit," he said under his breath, "speak of the devil."

Thumbs jerked up straight, looking as if he'd been caught, and snaked a long arm into the back pocket of his jeans. "I printed everything out," he said, handing Will a few folded pages.

Will slipped the papers into his pocket. "I'll take a look at this later. Thanks, Thumbs." He intercepted Pacheko at the grill, where Libbie was just slipping the baking tin loaded with battered fish onto the grill and lowering the lid. "Glad to see you found your way back."

"Had to," said the deputy, eyeing the fish on the table. "I wasn't going to let you take credit for catching all these." Will grinned. "But what the hell is that goop you're putting all over them?"

"That goop," said Libbie, "is what's going to make these the best fish you ever ate."

"That's high praise from the lady with the finest menu in town," said Pacheko. "My mouth's watering already."

"Thanks, Lib, I can take it from here," Will said, looking around for someone who obviously wasn't there. He checked the grill's thermometer, which read 400 degrees. "Perfect," he said, shooting Libbie a playful grin. "We'll make a fish fryer out of you yet."

Libbie swatted him on the shoulder and was about to make a response when something caught her eye across the lawn. "Oh my god," She exclaimed leaning around Will. "Is that who I think it is?"

Both men turned to see Carla Montforte standing at the end of his driveway looking extremely nervous and out of place. Will's face broke into a smile and walked over to greet her.

"Isn't that Montforte' daughter?" asked Pacheko.

"Damned if it isn't," said Libbie, who appeared to be in shock. "I didn't even know she was in town."

"We saw her at Sam's funeral. Will never told me he invited her."

She gave him a sly grin. "I always said he was a smart man." Pacheko acknowledged the jibe with a tilt of his head, and she took him by the arm. "Why we grab ourselves a beer and I'll introduce you around."

"I'd be much obliged," he said with a grin as they headed for the cooler.

Carla's face relaxed into a smile when she spotted Will coming across the lawn. "I'll be damned," he said. "You came."

"I almost didn't. Are you sure it's alright?"

"It's way better than alright," Will said with a grin. "Come on in."

"I brought this," she said, holding out a bottle of wine.

Will was instantly embarrassed. "Thanks, but I, um, I don't think I have anything to open it with."

She spotted the cooler overflowing with beer. "Don't worry about it, I'll just have a beer."

"Are you sure? I can try to…"

She laughed, enjoying his nervousness, and put a hand on his arm. "Relax," she soothed, "I'd really rather have a beer."

Her touch flustered him even more, but he managed to get a beer opened and into her hand. Libbie was just handing Pacheko a bottle as they approached. She took one look at Will and nearly burst out laughing. She had never seen him so discombobulated before. Pacheko and Will exchanged an uncomfortable look and Pacheko drifted off toward the other guests. Libbie turned to the new arrival. "You won't remember me, but…"

"Libbie Hutchinson?" Carla exclaimed. "Oh my god, how are you?" Libbie was genuinely surprised at the recognition but managed to shake Carla's outstretched hand. "Of course I remember you, from home-ec class. You always made the best food."

"She still does," said Will.

"It's Morrison now. I married Tommy," she said, pointing to where he and Thumbs were playing with the boys.

"The one with the dark hair? Yeah, didn't he used to play in a band, or something?"

"Still does," Will and Libbie both said at the same time. They all shared a laugh, then fell into an awkward silence.

Pacheko just stood there with a goofy grin on his face and Will finally took the hint. "And this is J.D. Pacheko, our new Deputy Sheriff."

"Please to meet you. Sorry for your loss," he said, extending a hand.

Carla shook it. "Thank you," she said, looking him over suspiciously. "I'm going to take a wild guess that you're not from around here."

Will and Libbie burst out laughing and Pacheko blushed. "I wouldn't exactly say that," he said, "I've been here a whole two weeks now."

They all shared a laugh and Pacheko started to leave. "Reckon I'll just mosey on over and talk to some of the other folks."

Will sensed that Libbie had more she wanted to say to Carla, so he excused himself as well. "I need to go check on the fish."

As soon as he was gone, Carla leaned in close. "I can't believe the way that guy dresses. Is he really a deputy?"

Libbie laughed softly. "I know what you mean, but he's a sweetheart. I love the way he talks, too. Must be a California thing." She took a drink of her beer and her expression turned somber. "I'm really sorry about your dad."

The words hung on the air for a moment, but then Carla smiled at her. "Thank you," she said sincerely. "I appreciate that. I haven't had any real contact with him for over ten years, so I guess I'm not really sure how I'm supposed to feel." She smiled at Will, who just stood there awkwardly, searching for something to say.

"Don't tell me those are your boys," said Carla, coming to the rescue. Libbie nodded proudly. "They're adorable."

"Why don't you come over and meet them," Libbie said, tossing Will a wink as they passed the grill. "We'll let the chef take care of his fish."

Libbie shuffled her off and Will breathed a sigh of relief. He grabbed his spatula and began gently turning the fish over to cook the other side. Pacheko walked up and placed a fresh beer on the table next to him. "You look like you could use one," he said, casting a glance toward Carla, who was shaking hands with Tommy.

"Is it that obvious?"

Pacheko grinned. "Tell me I'm wrong. You're jumpy as a fish out of water."

"I think she's out of my league."

"You don't know until you try." Pacheko looked down at the fish. The batter had turned a nice golden brown. "They look good," he said, "but I'm still not sure about all that goop."

"It hasn't failed me yet," he said, closing the lid and watching Libbie show off her boys to Carla.

"I was surprised to see her here," said Pacheko.

"She said she was sticking around town for a few days to deal with her father's estate, so I figured she might like a chance for her to get away from all that and enjoy herself."

"And you knew that how?"

"We met after the funeral," he said, ignoring Pacheko's raised eyebrows. "She remembered me from high school. We talked a while, and she asked me to show her around some of her father's land."

Pacheko grinned. "And naturally you were happy to oblige."

"What? No, I mean, that's not why…we just…"

The grin turned into a laugh, and Will decided to shut up. As he continued flipping fish, he noticed Pacheko scanning the yard.

"Expecting someone?"

"I asked Dolores to stop by. Hope that was okay."

"Sure, but don't hold your breath. Pacheko looked puzzled. "She's been invited to things like this before, but she never comes. Either she's tired of getting hit on all the time or she's just not very social."

Pacheko grunted and took a swig of beer. Will suppressed a grin of his own. "Give it time," he said, "this is a small town. You need to give folks a chance to get used to you."

"Yeah, I know how it is. Santa Cruz is a small town, too."

"I've been thinking about that. How did a surf bum like you end up a cop in a place like this?"

"After my brother was killed the surfing thing didn't seem so important anymore. I needed something different. Believe it or not, Boise State has a damn good criminal justice department. When I finished school, I needed a job. This was the first offer that came along."

"You don't miss California?"

"Not really."

Will waited, hoping the deputy would keep talking. The printout from Thumbs was burning a hole in his pocket. He lifted the lid on the grill again and Pacheko took a deep breath, changing the subject once again. "Damn, those smell good," he said.

"Yeah, I'd say they're done."

"Then let's eat!" the deputy boomed, loud enough for all to hear.

In moments, the grill was crowded with people holding out plates as Will scooped trout onto them. While Pacheko regaled everyone with tales of his high mountain adventure and how he'd caught most of the fish. Libbie busily directed everyone to another table that held loaves of warm garlic bread and a giant bowl of her famous potato salad, along with silverware and napkins.

Once the rush died down, she brought Will two fresh beers. "I can take if from here," she said. "There's a certain young lady who might be needing a rescue." she tilted her head, directing his gaze across the yard where Carla was being hustled hard by Stu English.

Will caught Carla's eye and she gave him a help-me look. "Thanks," he said to Libbie, "I appreciate you keeping an eye on her."

He took the beers and walked over to them. "You look a little parched," he said to Carla. "Sorry I've been neglecting you."

Her look of relief was a welcome sight. Will handed her a beer and clicked his bottle against hers. Stu immediately took the hint and backed off.

"I'm a big girl," she said with a coy smile. "Besides, you've been busy cooking. The fish are delicious, by the way. I've got to have that recipe."

"Good luck with that," said Stu. "Everyone in town has tried to figure it out, but no one's come close."

"Stu's been telling me all about his plans for the Hill," Carla said with a subtle roll of her eyes, "and how he's got some big San Francisco developer interested in the smelter of all things. Somehow, I just can't see that old monstrosity as a spa."

"More like a health club," Stu said. "The first time I saw this town I knew it was a gold mine. I always admired your father for having the vision to see what the town could become, but I was amazed he didn't see the potential for the Hill, too."

"When do you plan to start?" asked Carla.

"I'm hoping Hickock here might give me an answer to that question pretty soon."

Carla gave Will a questioning look.

"You're standing on the only piece of property on the Hill he doesn't own," Will said.

"Yet," countered Stu. "My last offer was more than generous, but he's still holding out."

"You're right," said Will, "it was generous." The sudden realization that he now owned the Ranch almost caused him to accept Stu's offer on the spot, but it was definitely not the time to open that can of worms. "But with the real estate market what it is in Shambles these days, it wouldn't be enough to buy another place, and I'm kind of partial to owning my own property."

"Can't say I blame you," said Carla. "I remember my father telling my mother over and over that owning your own land is the best investment anyone can have."

"No argument here," said Stu. "My new development is going to change this town in a big way and closing that smelter deal will be the icing on the cake."

"If he's so interested, how come nobody has met the guy?"

"He's been staying down in Boise. He says it's easier to keep in touch with his office and the bank that's financing the deal."

"So, it is a real deal, then?" asked Will.

"Looks that way," Stu beamed. "He's even more anxious than me, if you can believe that. He says he's bringing up an architect in the next day or so to talk about design ideas. Speaking of which, I need to let Deputy Pacheko know about that. Didn't I see him here earlier?"

They looked around, but Pacheko was nowhere to be seen.

CHAPTER 27

Pacheko rounded the corner on the ridge road above Sam Montforte's foothills property and spotted Dolores's BLM truck in the pullout. She was standing at the edge of the overlook with a pair of binoculars, scanning the rolling hills below. Pacheko pulled the black and white cruiser up next to her truck and got out. Dolores had sounded very official when she called, so just to be safe, he went home and changed into his uniform. She was focusing on something in the distance and acted like she hadn't even heard him arrive.

"Missed you at the party," he said.

"I'm not much of a party girl," she answered, without turning around

"So I heard."

That got him a nasty look, and he raised his hands. "Sorry, not trying to pry. None of my business."

She handed him the binoculars. "Take a look."

"What am I supposed to see?" he asked, adjusting the focus.

"Second row of hills, just up off the flats."

Pacheko panned the glasses slowly across the expanse, finally spotting three heavy trucks parked in the lee of a large rise. Several men were running cables up the ravine and across the lower slope. "Got 'em," he said. "Any idea who they are?"

"Seismic rigs," said Dolores, "from some drilling company. They've been doing tests most of the day. I got a call from Corinne about it this morning. Apparently, she isn't spending much time grieving over the loss of her partner."

"This is Montforte's land?"

"Yep, all four sections." Pacheko's blank stare caused her to smile for real this time. "A section is 640 acres, roughly a square mile."

Pacheko whistled. "That's over 2,500 acres."

She nodded. "Nice little chunk of land. Montforte swapped us about a thousand acres of forest land over by the Payette National Forest for it a year or so ago."

"What do you mean he swapped it?"

"Land swaps are a good way to consolidate parcels of land, usually to gain resource value, stuff like that. It's pretty common between government agencies and private owners. We thought he was getting the short end of the stick on this deal, until now."

Pacheko lifted the binoculars back up and found the trucks again. "What kind of tests?"

"They bounce sound waves down into the ground to map the rock formations, then look for potential gas deposits."

"You mean like sonar?"

She looked over at him and smiled. "Basically, yes. Impressive, deputy."

Pacheko shrugged. "A few years back the Navy used sonar to map the ocean floor around Santa Cruz. Interesting stuff." He lowered the binoculars. "But if this is all private land now, what's your interest?"

"All the land surrounding Montforte's is BLM. I'm just making sure they don't color outside the lines."

"And you called me because…" He let the question hang.

She tried to hide a shy smile. "With all the brouhaha about gas wells and mineral rights lately, I just thought you might be interested to know. Call it interagency cooperation."

Pacheko didn't hide his smile. "You could have told me all this on the phone."

She moved closer. "You've been so helpful with my studies, letting me work crime scenes and all. I just figured this was a chance to return the favor."

She put her hand on his arm and Pacheko felt his blood race. All he could think of was Will's comment about her not liking to get hit on. He was pretty sure that's exactly what she was doing to him, but he wasn't nearly so sure he should act on it.

Dolores let out a soft, throaty laugh. "That's what I like about you, Pacheko, besides being so damned cute you're about as unassuming as they come." She reached up and pulled his head down to her, kissing him hard.

The move caught him totally by surprise, but before he could overcome his shock and respond, she broke it off and walked away, causing another level of shock to set in. She walked around to the driver's door of her truck, then looked back at him, waiting. His mouth was working but no words came out. All he could do was stare at her. She gave him a moment, then frowned and started to get in. Finally, his brain started working again.

"Wait a minute!" he cried. She stopped. "What the hell was that?"

"You know why I don't like to go to parties?" she asked.

"Will says it's because guys are always hitting on you."

"That's part of it. But mostly it's because I like to be the one to decide who I'm going to be with, and when."

"And this was what, you asking me out on a date?"

She smiled at him and shrugged. "You figure it out." She got in and closed the door.

Pacheko walked quickly around the truck to her open window. "So why me?"

She laughed. "Oh, I've had my eye on you ever since you hit town, Deputy Pacheko. In case you hadn't noticed, you're not like a lot of the men around here."

"What the hell's that supposed to mean?" he sputtered.

"You've got something going on up here," she said, tapping her forehead with a finger. "You're not afraid to be who you are, even if it seems a little out of place. I like that in a man."

"Well, I have to tell you, District Supervisor Esperanza, that was some of the best interagency cooperation I've ever had the pleasure to be a part of. I hope it's something we can continue to practice here in Shambles."

She gave him a sly grin. "We'll see, Deputy. We'll see."

His phone rang just as she started up her truck. He was so flustered he had trouble getting it out of his pocket. Once he answered, Marcia was talking so fast and furious Pacheko couldn't get a word in edgewise.

The worried look that came over his face caused Dolores to stay put and listen.

"Where's Yeager?" he finally managed to squeeze in.

Her response was so loud he pulled the phone away from his ear and Dolores could hear it plain as day. "Where the hell do you think? Get your butt in here! Now!!"

She hung up. Dolores was so curious she was about to bust. "What the hell's going on?" Pacheko just sat there, stunned to silence. Finally, she reached out the window and gave him a shove. "Pacheko?"

He looked over at her, a combination of confusion and hurt on his face. "DNA came back on the blood from the dog's teeth and the cigarette butts at Montforte's."

"And…" she prodded.

"According to Yeager, they're both a match to Will."

Pacheko made it to the sheriff's office in record time. Yeager was strutting triumphantly around the office.

"I told you," he gloated as soon as Pacheko and Dolores walked through the door. "I told you he did it." He snatched the report off his desk and handed it to the deputy. "Maybe now you'll learn to trust experience and gut instinct."

Pacheko look at the papers and then to Marcia, who was fighting to keep her own temper. "He's in there," she said, tilting her head toward the cellblock. He tossed the report onto his desk and grabbed the keys.

"It won't do you no good to talk to him," taunted Yeager, following him across the room. "He denies it, of course, but DNA don't lie." Pacheko jerked the door open and stalked inside. The Sheriff strutted back to his desk, chuckling to himself, ignoring Marcia's angry glare.

Will sat on the cot in the first cell, fuming. Pacheko stood and stared at him until he finally looked up. "I trusted you," the deputy said evenly.

Anger flared in Will's eyes. "That son-of-a-bitch must have doctored the report," he spat. "I didn't do this, Pacheko."

"Then who, Will? Tell me who?"

Will just sat there, seething in silence. Pacheko stormed out of the cellblock, slamming the door.

"This doesn't make any sense," said Marcia. "He has an alibi for the Montforte killing. Tommy and Libbie…"

"Are lying through their teeth," Yeager chimed in. "That Morrison kid was at the Ranch with Hickock. Hell, they're still thick as thieves."

"Tommy's been clean for over ten years," Marcia shot back. "He's got a family now and a thriving business. Why would he jeopardize that?"

"Once you cross the line, you never go back," groused Yeager. "Not all the way. Their kind will cover each other's ass for anything." He turned to Pacheko. "You get down to that club right now and you bring him in. If he values his family at all, he'll change his story."

"Now wait a minute, Sheriff," said Pacheko.

"I've waited too damn long already. I let you climb all the way out on the end of the limb, Pacheko. Well, now it's broken off and you're down in the dirt with the rest of us." He strutted over and sat down behind his desk like a king on his throne. "Look on the bright side, Pacheko. We just solved two murders. And Will Hickock is finally going back where he belongs."

"I wouldn't be too sure about that, Sheriff."

Everyone turned to stare at Dolores, who sat at Pacheko's desk flipping back and forth between the pages of the DNA report. The room went dead silent until she finally looked up at them. "This isn't Will's DNA."

CHAPTER 28

Pacheko followed Will in the front door of his house to find Libbie and Carla cleaning up from the party. Everyone else was gone.

Libbie ran over and gave him a big hug. "What the hell is going on?" She turned to Pacheko. "Please tell me this was just another big mistake."

"Yeager still doesn't think so, but it looks that way," said Pacheko.

As he told them about the DNA report, Carla remained standing in the kitchen doorway nervously toying with a dishtowel. Will kept looking over at her, but she wouldn't meet his eyes.

"A familial match?" asked Libbie. "What does that mean?"

Carla spoke up for the first time. "It means someone related to Will."

"Has to be your father, right?" Libbie asked Will. "But he hasn't been seen around here for almost thirty years."

"Could be he had another kid no one knew about," said Pacheko.

They all looked to Will, but it was painfully obvious he did not want to talk about it. Libbie put her arm around his shoulders. "Well, I just knew it had to be a mistake."

"Sorry Yeager had to bust up your party," said Pacheko.

"Carla and I were the only ones left by then, anyway," said Libbie. "Then we got to talking and…well, anyway, we thought we might as well clean up a bit."

"Thanks," Will managed, still looking at Carla.

There was an awkward silence, which was broken by Pacheko.

"Miss Montforte, I wonder if you'd mind stopping by my office sometime tomorrow?"

Carla looked surprised. "Sure, I guess so. Can I ask what for?"

"It has to do with some activity on a piece of your father's land." Pacheko looked at Libbie and Will. "I don't know that this is exactly the time or place to discuss…"

"Whatever it is, I'd appreciate it if you told me now, Deputy. I have a meeting with Corinne Barker first thing in the morning and I can use all the information I can get about my father's holdings."

"Were you aware that there are drilling trucks on that piece of land down in the foothills? According to the BLM they're exploring for oil and gas deposits."

Carla looked surprised. "I know nothing about that, but I'll be sure to bring it up with Corinne in the morning. Thank you."

"Just thought you ought to know, ma'am."

Will got up and walked over to Carla. "I'm really sorry you had to get mixed up in all this."

She forced a smile. "I already was, thanks to my father. I'm not going to lie, I was pretty worried when I heard about the DNA."

"You don't really think I could…" Will protested.

"I didn't know what to think," Carla said. "I didn't want to believe it, but we've only gotten to know each other these past two days." She looked into his eyes. I'm just glad to see you're all right."

Will felt his heart skip a beat, but he could see she was upset. He tried to smile, but it was a weak effort. "Not exactly the way I was hoping the evening would turn out. I don't seem to be making a very good first impression."

"I'll admit I was pretty confused when the sheriff hauled you away, but after talking with Libbie, well, let's just say I'm really glad she was here." She finally looked him in the eye. "She a good friend, I hope you know that."

"Yeah, I do. She and Tommy saw me through some tough times back before I left for the Army." She looked away again, like she had something else to say but either didn't want to say it or was afraid to. Will waited, the tension between them building, then blurted out, "I'm really glad you stuck around."

She studied his face and Will wondered whether she was trying to decide whether or not she was glad, too. Finally, she seemed to come to a decision and smiled, for real this time, and Will began to breathe a little easier. Suddenly remembering they weren't alone, they looked around the room, but it was empty. Both Libbie and Pacheko had slipped out without either of them knowing it. Carla blushed, and Will fought back a grin.

"I'm sure Libbie was anxious to get home to her kids," he said, "and Yeager is probably keeping Pacheko on a pretty short leash since I foiled his plans to re-incarcerate me. Again."

She laughed softly. "Good thing, too. Otherwise, I'd be out a tour guide."

He grinned back at her, then leaned in slowly and gave her a tentative kiss. She didn't resist. The second time, she even kissed back, but then she pulled gently away.

"I think I'd better be getting back to the hotel," she whispered.

"Are you sure," he asked, stealing another kiss.

"Not really," she said, the beginnings of a smile breaking out, "but there's just a whole lot going through my brain right now."

Will took a step back. "I'm sorry if I was out of line. I probably shouldn't have done that."

Her face went serious. "Probably not," she said, giggling at the horrified look on his face, "but I'm glad you did." She kissed him again, then sighed. "I just need a little time to sort stuff out."

"Of course," said Will, suddenly unsure what to do with his hands. "I totally understand." She laughed at his nervousness, which made him laugh, too. "How much time?"

She laughed again. "How about until tomorrow? I still need a tour guide."

Will grinned. "Deal"

"In the meantime, I don't suppose it would be too out of line if you were to give me a ride back to my hotel."

On the drive downtown, Carla marveled at all the lights that now filled the little valley and how different it was from what she remembered. Will could relate and talked about how he felt when he first saw the changes on his return from the Army. She asked him about his family, and to his surprise, he found himself telling her about his life of crime as a young boy, the death of his brother and his mom, and how the Captain turned his life around. When he pulled to a stop in the Alpine Inn parking lot and turned off the engine, he realized he had been doing all the talking since they left his house and started to apologize.

"Don't, please," Carla said with a laugh. "It really was interesting."

Will blushed. "Seems like all I've done since we met is talk about me. I don't know much at all about you."

"Not much to tell, really."

"Somehow, I doubt that. Rumor back in high school was you were a real heartbreaker."

"What?" she squealed. "I was no such thing."

Will laughed. "You were the prettiest girl around. All the guys had a crush on you, and you wouldn't have anything to do with them."

Now she was the one blushing. "Including you?"

Will went silent. The question clearly made him uncomfortable, and she let it, for a while, then she giggled. "Truth is," she said, "I had a terrible crush on you."

Stunned, Will stared at her in disbelief.

"It's true," she said. "But whenever you weren't in class, you were gone. You never came to any dances or sports events."

"Not by choice, I can tell you that."

"Oh, trust me, when a kid gets dropped off at school by a sheriff's car every day, and picked up by another one after, people talk."

Will frowned. "Yeah, it didn't do a whole lot for my image."

"I asked my dad about it one day and he got really angry." Her voice deepened in an imitation. "Those Hickock boys are nothing but lowlife criminals. You damned well better stay away from that one or there'll be hell to pay."

They shared a quiet laugh.

"He ever tell you what happened that day?"

"You mean the payroll robbery? Yeah, he told me his version of it. But I always had trouble seeing a seven-year-old kid holding a gun on two grown men."

"Sometimes fear can make you do things you wouldn't even think about otherwise." He stared hard at her, considering whether he should ask the next question. He could see his gaze was making her uncomfortable, so he plunged ahead. "Did he tell you I shot him?"

He was prepared for a look of shock, but she just smiled, then reached across and put a hand on his arm. "He was pretty angry about it for a long time, but I think his pride was injured more than his body. Then one day, all of a sudden, he didn't want to talk about it anymore. I remember thinking it was kind of strange."

Will started to speak, but she put her other hand on his mouth to stop him. "You don't have to explain. My mom told me it was an accident. She told me how Dad and Yeager jumped you after your brother drove off and left you all alone with them." She sat back in the seat. "You must have been terrified."

Will took on a faraway look. The memory brought pain to his eyes, and Carla suddenly felt guilty, so she changed the subject. "Are you still writing songs?"

Will looked at her with genuine surprise, and she giggled again. "I remember walking by the ball field with some girlfriends one day during lunch, and you and Tommy were sitting on the bleachers playing guitars. He was singing the prettiest song. I wanted to stop and listen, but the other girls wouldn't hear of it, you being a dangerous criminal and all." Will blushed and she smiled. "I just couldn't get that song out of my mind so asked Tommy about it later, and he told me you wrote it."

Will smiled. "Tommy was the only real friend I had back then. Taught me how to play and always encouraged my songwriting." He laughed softly. "He always said we were going to make it big one day on those songs."

"Anything's possible," Carla said, raising an eyebrow.

"Yeah, right," laughed Will. "Now you're just trying get on my good side."

She cocked her head to one side. "Funny," I thought I already was."

He leaned in and gave her a kiss, which she let linger a while, then she pulled away. "But I really should get to bed. I have an early meeting with Corrine, and I have a feeling it won't be pleasant."

He walked her to the lobby entrance, and reluctantly said good night, but not before she agreed to meet him for lunch after her meeting. Part of him desperately wanted her to invite him up to her room, but he was somehow relieved when she didn't. The whole thing was all very confusing. He hadn't felt this kind of connection with anyone since…well, ever.

As he climbed back into his truck the printout Thumbs had given him pressed against his back pocket. He dug it out, leaving the door open so he could read by the ceiling light in the cab. There were several pages, each containing copies of newspaper articles. The first one, dated five years ago, showed the deputy atop a victory podium clad only in a baggy, day-glow bathing suit, a large trophy at his feet, spraying champagne all over the second and third place winners. The headline read: *Pacheko Takes Memorial Day Surf Championship*. Will had to chuckle at the photo. The hair was much longer and messier, but the goofy grin on his face was all Pacheko.

The article said he had bested some of the top surfers in the country and went on to give an impressive list of his other surfing accomplishments, some of which were further documented in two more articles. He couldn't help but wonder why the deputy had never mentioned any of this. Pacheko didn't seem like the type who would shy away from a little self-adulation.

The next article made his jaw drop. *Prominent Santa Cruz Family Murdered in Alleged Home Invasion*, blared the headline. The following piece read: *Surf Champion Son Held for Questioning*. And the last one: *Pacheko Released for Lack of Evidence*. He skimmed through the stories and then shuffled back to the one about the home invasion. He had skipped over the photograph of the murder scene initially, but a closer look at it sent shock waves through him. He started up his truck and roared out of the parking lot. Bad blood or not, Yeager had to see this.

CHAPTER 29

About a mile past Spring Meadows on the main road heading east out of Shambles, a poorly kept dirt road angled off to the right, disappearing into the inky darkness up Spruce Canyon. It dead-ended after barely a mile where a couple of long-abandoned cabins were tucked away in the thick trees, but no one went back there much anymore except the occasional elk or deer hunter.

Twenty years ago, Rod Yeager had planted his single-wide trailer in a small meadow he purchased about a hundred yards up from the turnoff. He chose it because he loved the solitude, or so he claimed. Most folks agreed it was a good fit for him because his personality matched the prickly Blue Spruce trees that dominated that section of the forest.

Will had just turned off the main road into the small canyon when he smelled the smoke, and when he rounded the sharp corner just before Yeager's place his headlights caught it billowing off the meadow. A numbing wave of déjà vu came over him as he turned onto the rutted double-track that constituted the Sheriff's driveway. Flames were crawling up the walls on the front end of the trailer, quickly spreading toward the back and lighting up the entire clearing.

The big Ford Excursion was parked a relatively safe distance away under a makeshift canopy rigged to provide some protection from the weather. Will skidded to stop, jumped out and ran towards the trailer, which sat smack in the middle of the clearing, thankfully far enough from the trees that the flames weren't reaching them. Yet.

"Yeager!" he shouted, leaping up the wooden steps and beating on the flimsy door. "Are you in there?" No answer. He tried the door, but it was locked. "Yeager, wake up!" The flames were moving his way fast. He put his shoulder into the flimsy door, and on the third try it gave way and he fell inside. The trailer was completely filled with smoke, instantly causing him to cough. "Rod? You in here?"

A loud crash spun him around as the heat shattered a pair of windows in the living room. Luckily, there was no sign of Yeager there, but flames were now working their way down both sides of the trailer with startling speed. He quickly grabbed a dishtowel from the counter and wet it in the kitchen sink, holding it to his face as he made his way toward the back past the tiny bathroom and into the bedroom at the far end. The smoke was so thick he could barely breathe even with the towel. He found Yeager lying unconscious on the bed in his underwear. Will shook him, but there was no response.

He figured the Sheriff was overcome by the smoke until he noticed the blood running down the side of his head. Was he already dead, or just knocked out? Surprised, Will lowered the towel and breathed in a lung full of smoke. He fought to control the coughing and realized he was starting to feel faint from lack of air. He looked back down the hall.

LOOSE ENDS

Flames were almost at the front door. He looked around for another way out, but the windows in the bedroom were too small. The front door was his only way out. He needed to get moving.

Using his free hand, he tugged on Yeager's arm but only succeeded in rolling him off the bed and onto the floor. The limp body was too heavy, he needed both hands. As soon as he dropped the towel he breathed in more smoke. His lungs tried to expel it with more coughing, but when he tried to suck in a little air all he got was more smoke.

He grabbed Yeager by the ankles and started pulling him down the narrow hallway. The heat was become more intense, and the lack of oxygen was sapping his strength. He groaned as he hauled Yeager's body down the narrow hallway, moving the dead weight only a foot or two at a time. He felt like he was passing out and dropped to his knees. He had to get out or they were both going to die here. That thought motivated him to give one more massive effort, which got him and Yeager almost to the end of the hallway, where he stumbled and fell back onto the floor. He tried to get to his feet, but there was no air left in his lungs. Everything was going dark.

Out of nowhere someone grabbed him. He was all but unconscious, but he thought he heard a voice urging him to get up and get out of there. A hand slapped him hard across the face and he revived enough to feel someone helping him to his knees and shoving him down the hallway shouting, "Move, move!" He turned back and saw the figure grab Yeager's arms. Will's survival instinct kicked in and he started crawling toward the open door, which was now ringed by flames, the voice behind shouting between gasping coughs, "Go, go, don't stop! You can make it!"

The flames were all around him now, and just as he felt himself ready to pass out again, his hand found the edge of the door. With his last bit of strength, he threw himself outside, tumbling down the wooden steps. Air! Precious oxygen stung his lungs, but pain never felt so good. Behind him someone pulled Yeager roughly down the steps and dragged him across the clearing. Will lay on his back, sucking in huge mouthfuls of fresh air, trying to clear his head. The flames now engulfed the entire trailer, making the heat unbearable.

If he stayed where he was, they would get him next. He tried to get up but couldn't seem to get his balance, so he just started rolling, trying to get as far away from the fire as possible. When he rolled against something solid, he looked up and saw a soot-streaked face wearing the goofiest grin he had ever seen.

"Damn," said Pacheko. "For a minute there I wasn't sure we were going to make it."

An hour later Will sat on the tailgate of his truck and watched an ambulance haul Yeager off to the hospital. The still unconscious Sheriff had inhaled a lot of smoke, and he had a nasty gash on his head, but he would most likely live. The volunteer fire department was mopping up the last of the hot spots around the meadow. The canopy garage had caught a hot ember and completely burned away, the heat peeling all the paint off the top and driver's side of the Excursion. There wasn't much left of the trailer, but they had managed to keep the fire from spreading to the trees. Luckily, it had been a wet spring. With the peak tourist season right around the corner, the last thing Shambles needed was a forest fire.

The paramedics had given Will a clean bill of health, but he was still feeling far from okay. They told him it would take a few hours for his breathing to return to normal, and his lungs would probably be sore for a day or two from the smoke inhalation. He kept sipping water to suppress the coughing that still erupted every so often. His hair had been singed a bit as had his arms and eyebrows. His face and arms were red and sore, but they told him those burns were only superficial and would be fine in a few days. He'd suffered worse wounds in IED explosions and firefights during his tours in Iraq and Afghanistan but that didn't mean these hurt any less.

As darkness began to settle over the meadow, Pacheko finished talking to the Fire Chief and ambled over to Will sipping from his own water bottle and wiping his face with a damp towel. "I'd love to see the look on Yeager's face when he learns it was you who saved him."

"You're the one who got the job done," said Will, "for him and me. I thank you for that."

Pacheko just nodded, eying him cautiously as he sat down on the tailgate and took a long drink. "Mind telling me what you were doing up here?"

Will froze. Up until that moment he hadn't realized how easy it would be for others to assume that he had knocked Yeager out and started the fire to kill the Sheriff, only to be interrupted by Pacheko's arrival. At the same time, he knew he couldn't tell the deputy the real reason he was here.

"I, uh, was headed out the east road when I saw smoke. I thought it might be one of those old cabins farther up. Figured I'd better check it out."

"You knew Yeager lived up here?"

"Sure, but I didn't know if he was home. I was plenty surprised when I saw it was his trailer that was burning."

"What did you do?"

"I started yelling and beating on the door. It was locked, and when I got no answer, I busted in and found him in bed unconscious. I tried to pull him out, but the smoke got to me. Lucky you came along when you did."

"Yeah," Pacheko said, "lucky." Something in his voice told Will he wasn't necessarily buying the story. He motioned to the end of the driveway. "Where's that road go, anyway?"

"Nowhere. It ends about half mile farther up."

"You said there are a couple of cabins up there?"

"Yeah, but I don't think anyone has lived in them for years."

"Seems like whoever set the fire would have had to pass you coming out."

"I didn't see any other cars."

"Trailers like this usually go up pretty fast. And the fire chief says it looks like this one had some help, just like the other two. How far along was it when you got here?"

The front end of the trailer was covered in flames. It would have been close, but I guess someone could have set the blaze and made it back to the main road before I got to the canyon turnoff. Or they could have seen me coming and headed up above, then waited until I was inside the trailer before they left. Or they could have ducked into Spring Meadows until I passed."

Pacheko pondered this a while. Any other side roads like this nearby?"

Will nodded. "About a mile or so further east, I think. I suppose he could have parked somewhere else and hiked over here?"

"Maybe," said Pacheko, but he still didn't seem convinced.

Will was getting more unnerved by the minute. "Look, Pacheko, let's quit dancing with each other. I know it looks like I could have done this, but the DNA evidence just proved I didn't do either murder, so why would I screw that up by going after Yeager now? God knows I've got plenty of motive to hurt the guy, but I swear I'm telling you the truth."

"Then why do I get the feeling you're not telling me the whole story?"

Will sighed. Pacheko could read him like a book, and right now the newspaper articles on the front seat of his truck were all he could think about. He needed to change the subject. "So, what brought you up here?"

"Yeager was so pissed after the DNA fiasco he stormed out of the office saying he was going down to the lab in Boise to make them re-run the tests. I came by to see if he found anything new."

The two men eyed each other warily.

"This has to be the same killer," said Pacheko. "Both Montforte and the Captain were beaten before they were burned up, and now Yeager." He smacked his hand on his knee. "Damnit, something's not right. I can't believe we've got two murders in this little town and no one has a clue who's behind them."

"And one attempted," said Will looking over at the smoldering trailer.

Pacheko stood up and started pacing, his face screwed up with frustration. "Yeah, yeah, I know."

"And now with Yeager out of the way, you're in charge, so it'll be up to you to solve them."

Pacheko stopped and stared at him, his eyes flashing. "What the hell's that supposed to mean?"

"Nothing," said Will, raising his hands. "I was just…"

"You smug son-of-a-bitch." He walked over and got right in Will's face. "Make no mistake, Hickock, you're not off the hook on this one yet. For all we know, the first DNA test was a fluke and the re-test will show it was you all along." He held up three fingers, one at a time. "Motive, means, opportunity, as far as I can tell you've got all three. I could haul your ass to jail right now. In fact, I probably should, because unless Yeager comes to and can tell me someone else is behind this, he'll probably fire me if I don't arrest you."

The tirade made him start coughing again and he stalked off draining the rest of the water from his bottle. Will just sat there stunned to silence by the attack, but he could feel the blood rising in his cheeks. He had never seen Pacheko go off like that. Maybe there was something to those newspaper articles. The deputy noticed Will staring hard at him and a sudden thought made his eyes go wild. He came at Will again, getting right in his face.

"You think I'd do something like this? Just for a damn Sheriff's job? In this podunk town? You've known me, what, a week? You have no idea who I am or what I'm capable of."

Will was pissed now, but he knew better than to lay a hand on a cop, so he instead of shoving the deputy away he just slid sideways off the tailgate and strode to the cab of his truck. "I might know a little more than you think, deputy." He spat the words as he grabbed the papers off the seat. "For instance, I know you won a few surfing competitions.

The deputy's eyes narrowed. "Yeah, so what?"

"I also know you're rich." Pacheko blanched. "Yeah, mommy and daddy were rolling in dough. So, what the hell are you doing hanging around this podunk town with us low-lifes when you could be back on the beach basking in the glory of all your fans?"

Will could see the slow burn building in the deputy.

"Maybe it's because your fans back in California all think you did this."

He shoved the newspaper photograph in Pacheko's face. The deputy stared at the three body bags being hauled out of a huge mansion that had burned to the ground. His eyes flared as bright as the trailer fire they'd just escaped. His breathing got heavier, and he started to tremble.

Will kept going. "Maybe it's because you liked it so much you came up here where no one knew you so you could keep on doing it."

The next thing Will knew, he was flat on his back in the dirt. His vision was going in and out of focus and the side of his face felt like he had been stung by about a dozen bees. He tried to sit up, but that only made his head swim. He hadn't been clocked like that since his last tour in Iraq, when one of the guys in his squad lost it on a night mission and imagined his buddies were the enemy. A stray thought drifted through the haze in his head, and he wondered what ever happened to that guy after they'd shipped him stateside.

The sound of an engine revving up cut through the fog, and he rolled up on one elbow just in time to see Pacheko's black and white cruiser roaring out of the clearing spewing dirt and rocks behind it.

CHAPTER 30

Marcia couldn't stop staring at the newspaper articles about Pacheko and his family. Will sat across the desk from her, watching her reaction, absently rubbing the large bruise that had formed on the side of his face. He'd gone home after his altercation with Pacheko, but he was only able sleep in fits and starts. He felt bad about accusing the deputy based on such flimsy evidence, but it *was* evidence, and it might possibly help to clear his name. By morning he decided he needed to tell someone in authority about the discovery. The problem was Pacheko was now the only authority.

His biking guide schedule was jam packed for the next two days, and Carla was embroiled in estate affairs with Corinne, so he stewed about what to do for another day while he led tours out on the trails. Finally, he decided to bring them to Marcia.

"I just don't believe it," she said, shaking her head. You can't think that fine, young man would do a thing like this. He's been busting his butt to solve these murders and prove your innocence, and God knows he hasn't gotten much help from his boss."

"But it all fits, Marcia," Will pleaded.

"What fits? If he wanted the sheriff's job, he could have just killed Yeager. Why kill Sheriff Linehart? He retired over a year ago."

"Maybe he figured with Yeager out of the way the Captain would step right back into the job. The Town Council would certainly want him over a young, inexperienced deputy. But with both of them gone, he'd be the only choice."

"That's a big stretch if you ask me. And what about Sam Montforte? J.D. didn't even know the man, much less have a reason to kill him. Nope, I'm not buying it. This all has to be connected to someone local somehow."

Will fell back in his chair, frustration and anger darkening his face. He let out a big breath. "Which brings it right back to me."

"That's not what I'm saying. Damnit, Will HIckock, don't you go feeling sorry for yourself. You were right, wanting to show these articles to the Sheriff. Even moreso since it was what saved his life. But you have to look beyond the circumstances and examine J.D. the man."

"Hell, Marcia, I don't even know the guy. No one does. He shows up here a couple of weeks ago as our new deputy and people start getting killed. Tell me that doesn't sound suspicious. Didn't Yeager do any kind of a background check on him?"

"Yes, he did. That's how I knew he was a surfing champ." She held up the article about the Pacheko family murders, shaking her head again. "If any of this other stuff came to light the Sheriff never said anything about it to me."

"It says right there Pacheko was arrested. Even if Yeager did the bare minimum, he had to know Pacheko had a record."

"Maybe there's no record because there was no arrest," Marcia said looking at the article again. "What It says here is he was questioned and released." She turned a fierce gaze on him. "Why are you so all fired anxious to pin these murders on J.D., anyway?"

Will sighed again and rubbed his face. "Truth is, I don't want to believe it any more than you do. Hell, I like the guy. I guess I'm just frustrated that the whole investigation has gotten nowhere. All we know is that it looks like both the Captain and Montforte were killed by the same person. And it looks like whoever that is just tried to kill Yeager, too. I just want people to know it wasn't me so I can get on with my life."

Marcia reached across the desk and squeezed his hand. "I hear you, Will, and I'm here to tell you that I know in my heart you're innocent. But just remember, J.D. doesn't know you like I do. All he has to go on is the evidence, circumstantial or otherwise. And he still gave you the benefit of the doubt even though Yeager is convinced you did them both. Maybe you need to show him a little of the same consideration."

Will had to admit she made sense. He thought back over his encounters with the deputy since this nightmare began a week ago. That night at Libbie's, right after the Captain was killed, Pacheko seemed more like someone offering condolences than a cop looking for information. And ever since then it seemed like he'd gone out of his way to become a real friend. Could it all have been just an act to set Will up? If Pacheko was guilty, why pretend to be helping Will? Why wouldn't he just go along with the Sheriff and let Will take the fall?

The door to the office opened, jarring him out of his thoughts, and the Pacheko walked in, stopping in his tracks when he saw Will, his face flushed. Obviously, his anger had not diminished over the two day hiatus. Will stood up, ready to defend himself and Marcia spun in her chair, a worried look on her face. When the deputy noticed she was holding the newspaper articles, his face fell.

"So now you know, too," he said to her.

"J.D., I'm so sorry about your family," Marcia said.

"And I'm sure he's told you all about how I'm the guilty one," he said, flicking a hard look in Will's direction.

Marcia looked from one man to the other as they stared each other down, her face darkening, then she slapped the newspaper articles down on her desk and stood up.

"Well, if this isn't a fine little pity party we've got going here."

Both men looked at her, startled by her vehemence.

"First Will comes in here whining about how he's tired of being the number one suspect, and now you're feeling sorry for yourself because it looks like the shoe might be on the other foot." She stepped out from behind her desk and stood between them. "Well, I'm not putting up with it. I'm not here to hold your hands and make you feel better. You've both got some skin in the game now, so I suggest the two of you get back to working together and get these murders solved so we can all have some peace and quiet around here."

Her last comment was directed right at Will, who hung his head. She looked back and forth between them once more, then grabbed her purse and headed for the door. "I'm going out for…ah, hell, just out!"

Will and Pacheko stared at her, their mouths hanging open. She was almost out the door when Pacheko spoke up. "Wait, Marcia!"

She looked back at him, scowling. He screwed up his face like he was considering something that really bothered him. Then he wiped his hand across his mouth as if to take the expression away.

"I only want to have to tell this story once. So, you better stay and hear it, too."

Will and Marcia exchanged a look, then she slowly walked back to her desk. They all stood in silence for several moments, then Pacheko stuck out his hand. "I'm sorry I hit you, Will. That was totally out of line. If you want to file charges…"

"No way," said Will, sounding annoyed that he'd even asked.

Marcia took in a deep breath and let it out as she sat back down at her desk. Will stepped over and shook the deputy's hand, then rubbed his tender jaw. Part of him wanted to stay mad, but Marcia's words had struck home.

"I guess I sort of blindsided you, too, with those articles," he reluctantly admitted. "But I figured you were about to arrest me again, and I'm getting damn tired of being accused of something I didn't do."

"I can't say I blame you," Pacheko said, walking over to his desk. Will noticed his face went sad, just like it had the night before at Yeager's when he confronted him with the newspaper articles. "You said the other day this puzzle needed some new pieces."

"You have to admit, it does look a little suspicious," said Will.

Pacheko closed his eyes and sat down in his chair, letting the weight of the situation settle on his shoulders. "You're right," he said with a sigh, nodding slowly.

Will continued. "But after you clocked me last night, I took a closer look at your family's murders. You were three hundred miles away when it happened, winning the surfing championship in front of thousands of people. You couldn't have done it."

"That didn't stop the police from hauling me in as a suspect."

"Welcome to my world," said Will, and they both shared a half-hearted laugh.

"But why?" asked Marcia. "You had a solid alibi."

"Because of the money," Pacheko said.

He said it so casually they were both taken aback. Their surprised expressions made the deputy blush. It was obviously a topic he was not comfortable talking about, but after a few moments, he continued.

"My father was a plastics manufacturer. He developed some of the first body armor for motorcycle racers. Then the military discovered it was better than anything they had at the time and…"

He shrugged and fell silent as his memories got the best of him. At a loss for words, Will looked to Marcia.

"Must have made him a lot of money," said Marcia.

Pacheko took in a deep breath and let it out slowly. "More than you can imagine."

"I don't get it," Will finally said, "what the hell are you doing living here on a deputy's salary? You must have inherited a boatload."

Pacheko looked back and forth between them, still hesitant to discuss what happened. Clearly, there was still a lot of grief under the deputy's happy-go-lucky veneer. Finally, he decided to tell the rest of the story. "When I started digging into the estate after they were…" His voice caught in his throat, and he took a moment to clear it. "…after the robbery, I found out there was nothing left."

"Nothing at all?" asked Will, incredulous.

Pacheko took a breath, collecting his thoughts, and forged on. "Mom liked art. The good stuff. And Dad would do anything to please her. Turns out they spent nearly every dime buying new pieces. Dad drained the company dry. That house could have qualified as a damn fine museum." Will and Marcia exchanged looks of wonder as Pacheko continued.

"They loved to entertain and show off their collection, which was probably what got us targeted. Whoever committed the robbery killed them both and took everything, cleaned us out completely, then burned the house to the ground. When it was all said and done there was only a few thousand left in the bank."

"Whew," breathed Marcia.

"You didn't know the company was broke?" asked Will.

"I had no idea. I was too busy surfing and partying to pay much attention to the family business, and after my brother was killed in Iraq, we grew even more distant. Besides, there always seemed to be plenty of money, and everyone was having such a good time."

"They never found out who did it?" Marcia asked.

Pacheko shook his head. "All the records on the house were destroyed in the fire," said Pacheko. "The company was belly up, everyone left to find new jobs. I had nowhere to start looking."

"What did you do?"

"Some of their friends weren't convinced I had nothing to do with it. I couldn't blame them, really. I wasn't exactly the prodigal son. And his business partners were plenty pissed, too. There was a lot of animosity floating around, mostly centered on me. So, I collected the insurance money, sold the property to the first buyer that came along and got the hell out of Dodge."

"Why Idaho?" Will asked. "We're not exactly known for our surfing."

He looked at Marcia. "You talk about self-pity, I wallowed in it for almost a year. I got real screwed up on booze and drugs, and I wandered a lot. Blew through a lot of money. I really don't know how I ended up in Boise. I guess it was just the next town along the road. Anyway, one morning I woke up in a seedy motel with the hangover from hell and decided if I was ever going to find whoever did this to my family, I'd better get my shit together. I found out Boise State has a first-rate criminology department, so I enrolled. Turns out I have a bit of a gift at forensic science."

"Obviously, you graduated," said Marcia, pointing to his degree on the wall above his desk.

"I had enough money left to pay for school, and an apartment. Got my four-year degree in three and my Masters in another year. Finished top of my class. I went back home, but the local police had nothing more than they did when it happened. I worked it for a while, but by that time the trail was way too cold. Then one of my professors from Boise State called me about this deputy job. Santa Cruz didn't have anything I wanted anymore, so here I am. If somebody had told me what I was walking into I would never have believed them, but sooner or later you've got to make a stand somewhere."

The deputy's words struck home, and Will realized he hadn't really let himself get all the way back home after he left the Army. His life in Shambles now was so different from when he left. He'd been a loner growing up because of circumstance, perhaps now it was because part of him resented the fact that he could never really go home again.

The old Shambles was long gone. But now maybe these murders were forcing him to take a stand of his own.

Marcia's voice brought him out of his reverie. "Doesn't it bother you that these killings are so much like what happened to your family?"

"That makes me want to solve them even more," said Pacheko. "Like maybe solving them will make up for not finding my family's killers. In a way, these murders are like my final exam. Only not for school, for life."

Will smiled. "I can see now why you've been going easy on me."

"I can relate a little, yeah, you lost your only family, too." He straightened up in his chair. "But don't think for a second I won't nail you if that's how it turns out."

"Fair enough," Will said. "But I'm telling you now, that won't be the case."

"I sure hope not. I was really starting to think you were all right."

"Okay, okay," Marcia chimed in. "Let's not get all mushy here. You boys still have two murders to solve."

"And one attempted," said Will. He walked over to Pacheko's desk, his hand outstretched "I'm sorry, too," he said, "about last night. I guess I got the cart before the horse on this one."

Pacheko gave him a half smile. "Yeager would be proud."

Marcia let out a cackle, and Will couldn't help but laugh with her, even though it made his jaw hurt like hell.

"Speaking of the sheriff," asked Marcia, "have you heard how he's doing?"

"I just came from the hospital," Pacheko said. "They've got him sedated. All that smoke and heat singed his lungs pretty good. They're going to keep him there until they make sure there are no complications, and his breathing gets back to normal. The good news is his throat is so parched he won't be able to talk for at least a week."

Another laugh circled the room.

"Will said he got a pretty good hit on the head," said Marcia.

"There's no fracture, but he definitely has a concussion. Hard to say if whoever did it was really trying to kill him, or just knock him out and hope he'd die in the fire. They're going to run some tests later today. That reminds me, does he have any family we should notify?"

"He was an only child," said Marcia. "His parents left town right after he graduated high school, but he stayed on. He never talks about them. I have no idea where they went, or even if they're still alive."

A thought struck the deputy, and he turned to Will. "Speaking of family, you think this DNA we've got could be from your father?"

Will just shrugged. "I have no idea. He took off right after I was born, and I haven't heard from him since."

"Good riddance, too," said Marcia. "That no account drunk left Will's mother with two small boys and not a cent to her name. She started a little seamstress business, but she had to take in laundry and just about any other kind of work she could find just to make ends meet. He left a bad taste in a lot of mouths around here. I can't believe he'd ever show his face again."

"Was he the type that might have had an affair and fathered another child?" asked Pacheko.

"Ha!" barked Marcia. "I don't know of any woman around here who would have given that ornery bastard the time of day, much less anything else."

"Ever try and track him down?" Pacheko asked Will.

"Nope. Never wanted to. I was only a few days old when he left, so I never knew him. All I ever heard growing up were stories about what an asshole he was and how much better off we were without him, so I had no interest in finding out anything more."

"Well, it's the only lead we've got at the moment, so why don't you start looking around, Marcia. See if you can locate anything on him. Check prisons, hospitals, obituaries, anything you can think of."

"Why would he come back here after all these years and start killing people?" Marcia asked.

"I guess we won't know that until we find him.' He looked to Will. "I'd like you to check at home for any documentation your mother might have kept that would help Marcia in her search."

"Look at you," said Marcia, "acting all Sheriff-like." Pacheko was embarrassed by the remark, and that made her break out a big grin. "Maybe we'll finally start getting some police work done around here."

"I may be able to help with that."

They all looked up to see Dolores standing in the open doorway smiling like the cat who at the canary.

CHAPTER 31

Will fell back in his chair and stared at the lab report, speechless. Even Marcia was stunned to silence.

"Are they sure about this?" Pacheko asked, his face a mixture of surprise and concern.

"They're sure it's not Will's brother in that grave," Dolores said assuredly. "They're just not sure who it actually is."

Pacheko took the report from Will and looked it over once more, then shook his head. "Well, this opens up a whole new can of worms." He gave his forensic protégé a nod. "Thanks, Dolores. I appreciate your help once again."

Marcia looked at him sideways. "Wait a minute. You knew about this?"

Will was oblivious to her question. He just sat there, completely gobsmacked by this new revelation, visions of his childhood and the payroll robbery swirling around in his head. Was it possible? After all these years, was Doc still trying to screw up his life?

Pacheko held a hand up to stop Marcia and exchanged a quick look with Doloires, who nodded in return. "After I dropped Will off at home the other night I got to thinking about the familial match on the DNA. I figured it was worth a shot to check Doc's grave, so the next morning I called a judge in Boise and got an exhumation order."

"Wait a minute," Will cut in, "don't you need some kind of family permission to dig up a grave?"

"Not when the only family member is a suspect in a murder investigation," said Pacheko. "The judge granted it based on exigent circumstances."

Will looked to Marcia, who just shrugged, then to Dolores.

"He's right," she said.

"I was on my way to meet her at the graveyard when I decided to stop by Yeager's and see if he had anything new on the DNA. You know the rest."

"I got tired of waiting for him, so I took some DNA samples from the body they dug up and drove them down to the State Police lab in Meridian," said Dolores. "The lab will need some time to make a positive ID, but it only took them a couple of hours to determine it wasn't your brother."

Will was more confused than ever. If that wasn't Doc in the grave, then who the hell was it? Pacheko seemed to read his mind.

"Anyone else go missing around that time?" the deputy asked.

Dolores and Marcia looked at each other, both having the same revelation at the same time. "Henry Latham," they both said at once.

"The smelter owner?" asked Pacheko. "The one who disappeared with all the gold?"

Dolores produced several photographs of the body. "They found what looks like a wedding ring on his left hand. It's a pretty distinctive design."

"Holy shit," said Marcia. "If that's true, Sarah's going to have a cow."

Pacheko looked confused.

"Sarah Latham, his widow," Marcia informed him.

"She's still around?" Pacheko asked.

"Still lives in the same house," said Marcia, "over on Highland. She'd likely be in her eighties now."

The deputy perked up. "Do you think she might still have anything around that would have a sample of his DNA?"

"I'm on it," said Dolores, already on her way out the door. "And yes, I'll ask her about the ring."

"Oh, my god," Marcia exclaimed, "that means Doc could still be…"

She stopped in mid-sentence and looked at Will, who was still staring at the report, though his eyes were glassed over, his mind clearly elsewhere.

"How could they not get a positive ID before he was buried?" asked Pacheko.

He was burned to a crisp," said Marcia. "And DNA science twenty years ago was a long way from what it is now. Besides, it all seemed so obvious."

"Just like he wanted it to," Will said, half to himself.

They both flinched at his voice, as if they'd forgotten he was in the room.

"You think your brother had the whole thing planned out?" asked Pacheko.

Will shook his head. "As far as I knew, we were just going to get the payroll and get out of town. Doc always used to say he had a plan for every job we did, but I don't think he ever really thought that far ahead."

"Except when it came to leaving you behind," said Marcia.

"Yeah," Will said with a sigh. "He knew I'd never see it coming, and he was right."

"The only good thing that little weasel ever did for you," said Marcia, reaching across her desk and taking his hand.

Will gave her a sad smile and squeezed hers in return. "You're right about that."

"I'm not buying it," said Pacheko. Marcia shot him a nasty look, but Pacheko hadn't been listening to their nostalgic reverie. "We're missing something here." hey both looked at him with blank faces. "You said the payroll was burned in the wreck, along with the body, which, for the moment, let's assume was Latham." Will nodded slowly. "All of it?"

"There was burnt money all over that mountainside," Marcia said. "They spent days picking up all the pieces. Sheriff Linehart said that near as they could tell there couldn't have been more than two or three thousand dollars unaccounted for. And that much could easily have just been scattered in the wind."

"But why would Doc burn up his big score?"

Realization dawned on Will. "Unless he had something bigger."

"You can't mean the missing gold." said Marcia, her eyes going wide.

"I never thought so. All he could talk about was how the payroll cash was going to be the biggest score he ever made. That alone would have been way more than anything we ever got before."

"But how would Doc even know Latham was skimming, much less where he kept his stash?" asked Pacheko.

Will thought about it. "You're right. It doesn't seem likely."

Another idea hit, and Pacheko straightened up. "Unless it wasn't gold." Will and Marcia exchanged a confused look. "The story goes that ten million went missing. That's a big pile. Probably weighs a few tons. How the hell was Latham planning to get it out of here?"

Will picked up on the thought. "He would have to convert it to something easier to carry."

Pacheko snapped his fingers. "I remember Yeager saying that along with the payroll cash there was always a locked briefcase they brought directly to Latham. What if he was converting the gold to cash, or bonds or something, and having them delivered along with each payroll? Just a little each week, so no one would notice. That would add up over the years."

Pacheko was pacing now, his brain in motion along with his body. "He leaves you holding the guards with a gun. He's got the payroll, and he's driving away when he spots the briefcase."

"Doc would definitely not have overlooked a locked briefcase," said Will. "He would have wanted to know what was inside."

"So, he opens it, finds the bonds, or whatever it was, and then Latham shows up."

"Why would he be there?" asked Marcia.

"The van was late because of the robbery. If the skimmed money was in the briefcase, he may have panicked and gone looking for it. Or maybe he didn't want to risk getting the briefcase at his office for some reason, so he arranged to meet the van somewhere on the road each week."

"Wouldn't the guards have been suspicious?" asked Will.

"Maybe, unless one or both of them were in on it."

"Yeager?" said Marcia with a laugh. "I don't believe that for a minute. He's never had a dime to his name. Always moaning about his salary and not having any money."

"Could be a cover. Could be he's got his payoffs stashed somewhere waiting for him when he retires."

"I'm with Marcia," said Will. He may be an asshole, but he's as straight arrow as they come. The main reason he hated Doc so much when we were kids is because he suspected we were committing those robberies. He just couldn't prove anything."

"Okay, what about Montforte?" He turned to Will. "You told me there's always been speculation about where he got the nest egg that started his real estate business."

Will and Marcia exchanged a look that said there could be something to that theory.

"Carla told me her mother always believed his story about hitting it big in Reno one night," said Will.

"Wouldn't be the first time a husband lied to his wife," Pacheko countered. "Maybe she found out, and that's why she left him."

"I don't buy it. If she left him because of that, why not turn him in? Besides, Carla told me…"

"Well, of course you're going to take Carla's side."

Will flushed. "That's not what I'm saying."

Marcia raised her hands. "Okay, okay. enough! This is nothing but speculation."

Both men took a deep breath and sat.

"Let me get this straight," she said, pacing herself now. "You're saying that after the robbery Doc somehow met up with Latham, killed him and substituted his body in the crash, then burned everything to fake his own death, took Latham's car and got away with whatever was in the briefcase?"

"It's the perfect cover," said Pacheko. "Everyone thinks Doc's dead and Latham took off with the gold."

"Only one thing wrong with that theory," said Marcia. "If Doc's out there with ten million dollars living the high life, why the hell would he bother to show up back here twenty years later and start killing people?"

"Only one reason I can think of," said Will. "He only got a small piece of the ten million."

Now it was Pacheko's turn to see the light. "And the rest of it is still here."

CHAPTER 32

Jimmy Villanova was famous for his spaghetti. Everybody in town loved it. He always won first prize at the annual summer cook-off in Shambles, where he spent a lot of his time mountain biking every summer. So, when the town started bustling with tourists, he quit his job as a clerk at the Elmore County courthouse down in Mountain Home and moved up to the mountains full time. He had his choice of empty buildings on Main Street, so he bought one from Sam Montforte and opened up an Italian restaurant called Jimmy V's.

His famous spaghetti topped the menu, of course, but he also cobbled together a few recipes from Italian cookbooks and bought a pizza oven. No one was too surprised when his other dishes turned out just as delicious as his specialty. And every Sunday his mother, who was raised on a farm in Nebraska, would come up from Mountain Home and cook up her fried chicken, complete with mashed potatoes and gravy, some fresh corn or lima beans, and home-made biscuits. Not exactly Italian, but, as she liked to say, everybody loves good comfort food, once in a while. Needless to say, her fried chicken soon became just as requested as her son's spaghetti.

Will showed up at Jimmy V's a few minutes after noon and found Carla waiting for him in a back booth. She looked pensive, but her face lit up when she saw him. "I was starting to get worried," she said.

He slid in opposite her, just as the waitress came by. Once they ordered, he filled her in on everything that had happened since he'd dropped her off the night before. She was glad to hear Yeager would be all right but showed a good deal more concern for Will's singed lungs, and his battle with Pacheko. Once she was satisfied that the two of them had gotten through their rough patch, he told her about Marcia's idea to dig up an old booking photo of Doc from the Ranch files and run it through the system.

"It's a long shot," said Will, "especially after all this time, but it's worth a try." He could tell she was bursting to talk to him about something, and he had a pretty good idea what it was. "So, how did it go with Corinne?"

Her relieved smile told him he was right on the mark. "Let's just say neither of us is a very happy camper right now. I'm not too sure everything she's been telling me is on the up and up."

"What do you mean?" asked Will.

"I've been doing some digging myself, and I found out Corrine has been trying to buy up oil and gas leases around here for over a year through a company Fitch owns that has a reputation for unethical practices. They picked up the ones on that foothills property just last month."

"They must have been the ones who scheduled the test drilling Dolores saw down there started not long after".

"I just can't believe my father would have gone along with this. He must have known what it would do to the town."

"How could she pull all that off without him knowing?"

"I wondered the same thing, until I met with Arvin Melville this morning."

"That's right, I completely forgot. What did he have to say?"

"A lot." She cracked a smile and squeezed Will's hand. "And you were right, he's quite the character."

Will chuckled, looking to her for more. "And?"

Carla sobered and leaned back in the booth. "He showed me Dad's will, and Corinne was right, he left almost the entire business to her."

"Damn, Carla," Will breathed. "I'm sorry."

"Don't be," she said shaking her head. "I didn't come here expecting anything. I didn't even know about all their success. She obviously played a big part in that, so if that's what he wanted, I can live with it."

"Just the same, I wish he'd…wait, you said *almost* everything."

She tried not to smile, but the twinkle in her eye gave her away. Will leaned forward in anticipation and she explained that, according to Melville, Sam and Corinne hadn't exactly been getting along the last couple of years. It got to the point where he was starting to regret letting her put everything in both their names over the years. But he apparently needed her skills to keep the business running, so he went along with it.

"According to Arvin," she said, "Dad had started working on some land deals without her knowledge. The foothills piece was one of them. He traded some forest land he owned before Corinne came into the picture to the BLM for it with the idea that it might be a way to expand the bike trails system down in the future. Corinne found out, and when he refused to put her name on it, she freaked out. Said she was going to do whatever it took to make her own fortune and get out of Shambles forever, no matter what it cost the company, or the town."

Will was impressed. "Wow, you've been busy."

"There's more," she said with a conspiratorial grin. "I found some plot designs for the land tucked away in my father's office desk that looked more like plans for a housing development than for oil or gas drilling." Will's eyebrows went up, asking for more. "I'm thinking he was planning on developing more than just an expanded trail system down there."

"And Corinne didn't like being cut out of the deal."

"Right. Melville told me that Sam thought it was all going smoothly until Fitch showed up. Apparently, he told Corinne that if she could figure a way to work around Sam's sole ownership of that land, they could make millions off the mineral rights. Somehow, Sam found out about their scheme, and was talking to Melville about what he could do to stop them just a few days before he was murdered."

"Sounds like motive to me," Will said when she was finished. "Except that Pacheko heard Corinne and Fitch talking the other day after your father's funeral. They were going behind Sam's back to do the test drilling on that land all right, but they needed him alive, and in the dark, until the results came back. The last thing they wanted was for this to go public before they were ready, which is just what happened when he was killed."

Carla frowned. "Damn. I guess that lets them off the hook,"

A sudden thought struck Will. "So, who owns that land now that he's dead?" Carla raised an eyebrow over a mischievous grin. "Seriously?"

Will laughed. "I guess your father was looking out for you after all."

"Seems that way."

Will hesitated. "Does this mean you'll be sticking around a little longer?"

She slipped her hand into his. "I really wish I could, but my boss wants me back in Minneapolis. I managed to hold him off for one more day, but then I've got to leave. I was hoping you could give me a ride to the airport," she said hopefully.

Carla's phone rang before Will could respond, and she looked surprised when she saw the screen. She answered, listened for a moment, then looked at Will in disbelief. "You don't have a cell phone?" Will stammered for a moment and she thrust her phone at him. "It's Marcia, for you."

Surprise and confusion flashed across his face as he took the phone.

"I figured I'd find you with Ms. Montforte," Marcia said, a sly smile in her voice. Will rolled his eyes, but as he listened, his expression grew dark.

CHAPTER 33

A pretty nurse topped off the large water glass on the table beside Sheriff Yeager's hospital bed. He was snoring deeply. She paused a moment, considering, then adjusted his pillow in an attempt to stop it, which worked just long enough for her to smooth his blanket and turn to leave. As the snoring resumed, Pacheko walked in the door.

"I've never seen him so peaceful," the deputy said with a grin. "He almost looks like a normal person."

The nurse gave him a scolding frown, glanced back a Yeager, then left.

"I heard that," said Yeager, his eyes now open and glaring at Pacheko. His voice sounded like he'd swallowed broken glass, and from the way he winced when he spoke, it looked like it felt that way. He immediately started to cough and Pacheko handed him the glass of water.

"Sorry, Rod. I didn't mean anything by it."

After choking down several difficult gulps, he tried to speak again but it was obviously too painful, so he just glowered at Pacheko.

"Yeah, it's probably best if you don't talk. Sounds like it hurts a lot." The sheriff scowled a moment longer, then raised an eyebrow to ask why Pacheko was there. The deputy took the cue. "First off, did you see who clocked you in your trailer?"

Yeager scowled again and shook his head, using his hand to indicate the blow came from behind. "Hickock?" he squeaked.

"No, we've ruled him out." Yeager started to say something else but his throat hurt too bad to get it out. Pacheko gave him another drink of water, using the lull to change the subject. "Don't worry, we're on it. Meanwhile, we've got some new information on the murders I thought you'd want to know about."

Yeager sipped on his water while Pacheko explained their theory about the body in Doc's grave, his face turning redder and redder as the story unfolded, until he looked like he was ready to explode.

"I got a phone call from Dolores on the way over here," Pacheko continued. "She said Sarah Latham positively identified the wedding ring on the body in Doc's grave as her husband's. It matches hers perfectly. Of course, we'll have to wait for DNA results to be sure, but at this point, it looks like a pretty good bet that it's him." Yeager's face screwed up as if he wasn't quite making the connection. "Either way," Pacheko continued, "it's a distinct possibility that Will's brother could still be alive."

As realization dawned on the Sheriff the color slowly drained from his face. He stared at Pacheko in disbelief. He tried hard to say something, but it was just too painful. Pacheko spotted a notepad and pen on the bedside table and handed them to him. Yeager scribbled furiously, then turned the pad to his deputy.

Killed Linehart and Montforte?

"Yes sir," he said after reading the note, "we think he could be our killer."

Yeager scribbled one word and a question mark, then shoved it at Pacheko.

We???

"You want to know who *we* is?" Yeager raised his eyebrows expectantly and the deputy scrambled for a way around telling him that Will had been helping with the investigation. "Well, that would be me, and uh, Dolores, um, Esperanza, the BLM Supervisor. She's been working right along with me on this. Marcia's been a big help, too."

Yeager started to write again, but Pacheko had already anticipated the question.

"No sir, Sheriff," the deputy said firmly, "Hickock has not been taking part in any investigation. We have, however, been keeping a close eye on him."

Yeager scribbled some more. *Your version?*

Pacheko took a breath. He remembered Libbie's words from the bar the other night, *in for a penny in for a pound*. "Do you remember those briefcases you said were part of every payroll delivery?" he asked. Yeager nodded, his expression asking what that had to do with anything. "You ever know what was in them?"

Yeager shook his head and wrote. *Always locked. Montforte delivered to Latham.*

"Only Montforte? You never delivered a briefcase?"

Yeager shook his head, but his face continued to show confusion. Pacheko hesitated, suddenly unsure whether he should play his final card. Yeager's cold stare told him he damn well better finish the story.

"Well, it's only a theory so far," said the deputy, but we thinking Latham was converting the missing gold into bonds or something, a little at a time so as not to arouse suspicion and having them delivered with each payroll."

The Sheriff's face went completely blank. Pacheko could see the wheels turning in his brain, but he couldn't tell from the look on his face if he was still trying to figure it out or whether he was surprised that he hadn't thought of it himself.

"You think Montforte could have been in on it?" Pacheko asked.

Yeager thought hard, considering the possibility, then gave a noncommittal shrug.

"We think it's possible that Montforte knew what was in those briefcases, and that Latham may have been paying him on the side to deliver them."

Yeager looked at him sideways, like he was trying to remember something from back then. He wrote again.

Real estate nest egg?

Pacheko nodded. "We think it could be. But we haven't found any proof of that. There was no briefcase found at the site where the van crashed, so we figure Doc got hold of it, and whatever was in it was enough to make him burn the payroll cash and use Latham's body to fake his death and disappear."

Yeager gazed out the window and his face relaxed, as though everything suddenly made sense.

"If that is, in fact, the case," Pacheko went on, "the only reason we can figure that Doc came back here is that whatever was in the briefcase represented only a part of the gold Latham stashed and now he's after the rest."

Pacheko waited, and after a moment, the sheriff started writing. *Why he tortured Sam.*

"We think so, yeah," said Pacheko."

Yeager's look went from skeptical to sad, then back again, and he wrote something else. *Tortured for what?*

Pacheko took the pad and read. "That's a damned good question, sheriff," he said, scratching his head. "No one seems to think Doc could have known about the missing gold before he disappeared. I agree he would have probably heard about it soon after. It was all over the national news. But I have no idea why he would wait twenty years to come back for it."

Pacheko's phone beeped with a text message. He looked at the screen. "It's Marcia. She wants me back at the office."

Yeager scowled and waved him off, then took a deep breath and reached for his water glass again.

CHAPTER 34

Marcia was beside herself when Pacheko walked in. "It's about damn time," she scolded, then a look of relief flooded her face. "Oh my god, J.D., you're not going to believe it." She grabbed his arm, pulling him over to her desk where Will sat studying her computer screen.

Dolores was pouring a cup at the coffee machine. She handed it to the deputy as he passed by.

"You might need this," she said, looking grim.

Pacheko took the cup and walked over behind Will, still staring at a pair of booking photos. The one on the left showed a young man about 17 or 18. He had cold eyes that seemed to look right through you, and a hard expression. His hair was long and tangled, and though he hadn't shaved in a while, there wasn't much of a beard. The photo on the right appeared to be of the same man, taken a few years later. The hair was cut short, and a fresh scar ran from his left eye down his cheek. The beard had filled in some, but what clinched the likeness were those same cold, hard eyes staring back at them.

"Doc?" Pacheko asked. Will nodded dumbly.

Pacheko read the booking information at the bottom of the photo. One Jimmy Columbo had been incarcerated in the Cottonwood Correctional Facility not quite three years after everyone thought Doc died in the crash during his escape.

"Isn't that the maximum-security prison up in north Idaho?" asked Pacheko.

Dolores peered over his shoulder at the photo. He must have made a real impression on the judge to get sent up there."

"Sounds like Doc, to me," said Marcia.

"What was he in for?" asked Pacheko.

"Armed robbery," answered Marcia. "Got fifteen years, but they tacked on two more for an attempted escape about eight years ago."

"He was released a month ago," added Dolores.

"They didn't have a more recent photo?" Pacheko asked.

"This is the one they matched to his juvenile picture," said Marcia. "Once we confirmed it was who we're looking for they said they'd send us his complete file. We should have it soon."

"Well, I'll be damned," said Pacheko, letting out a big breath. "I just finished telling the Sheriff everything we knew. He was practically apoplectic when he heard about Doc. This will put him right through the roof."

He walked over to his desk and sat down, relaxing into his chair and propping his feet up. He gave them a quick rundown of his conversation with Yeager.

"So, it all fits," he said, wrapping up, "Jimmy, or rather Doc, screws up and gets busted before he has a chance to come back and look for the rest of the gold. He spends the next seventeen years planning, then comes back for the big score."

The room was silent for a while as everyone ran through the events of the last week in their minds, the puzzle pieces falling into place.

Dolores spoke first. "Ok, we're assuming he doesn't know where the rest of the gold is, so I get why he would torture Sam to try and find out, but the Linehart just seems like overkill. Will shot her a look. "Sorry."

"Could have been pure spite," said Marcia. "He and the Captain had quite a few run-ins back in the day."

Pacheko spoke up. "Could also be he figured if anyone would recognize him after all these years, it would be Linehart. More likely it was just a distraction to keep us all occupied while he located the gold and got away."

"New faces," Will said, half to himself.

Pacheko's feet came off the desk. Dolores stopped pouring a cup of coffee for Marcia. Will looked to each one of them.

"Something you said right here the other day," he said to Dolores. "We couldn't think of anyone in town who would want either the Captain or Sam Montforte dead, so it had to be a new face." He turned to Pacheko. "When I mentioned it to Tommy, he thought of you."

Marcia frowned at him. "Not the brightest idea."

"Still, it makes sense," said Pacheko. "Shambles is small enough that a new face would stand out."

"Doc would have known that," Dolores chimed in, "and kept a low profile."

"And he would know just how to do that," said Will. "He knew every back alley and short cut there was. And he had lots of hiding places for the stuff he stole."

"But the town's changed a lot since then," said Pacheko. "A lot of those places are no longer there."

"Or they're hidden even better," Will said.

"Regardless," said Dolores, "everyone around here has been on edge since Linehart was killed. We've asked people all over town if they've seen anyone suspicious, but no one has come forward."

Pacheko leaned back in his chair again, looking stumped. Dolores finished pouring Marcia's coffee then sat down at the sheriff's desk. "What I want to know is, if Doc only got part of the gold, where the hell's the rest of it?"

"I don't suppose you asked Mrs. Latham that question when you talked to her," Pacheko said to Dolores.

"As a matter of fact, I did," she said. "She told me the same story she's told everyone all these years, that she had no idea her husband was doing any skimming, and that she never suspected a thing until the day he disappeared."

Marcia shook her head. "No help there."

"I also asked her if she ever thought he might have stashed it in their house. She'd wondered the same thing. Said scoured the place after he left and never found a dime. She didn't think he would have used their house anyway, since he wasn't letting her in on his secret. She said he spent more time at the smelter than he did at home, so anything of value would have been kept up there."

Pacheko snorted. "If there ever was anything of value in that rat hole it's long gone by now."

Will perked up. "Maybe not." He turned to Marcia. "When's the last time you talked to Stu?"

"Stu English? The realtor?" said Pacheko. "What's he got…"

"Of course," Marcia interrupted. "Another new face." She rummaged around on her desk and found a business card, then picked up the phone and dialed.

"Are you talking about that developer who wants to turn the smelter into a health club?" asked Dolores. "I thought he was from San Francisco."

"That's what he told Stu," Will said.

"Where's the key to the smelter?" asked Pacheko.

Marcia looked up from the phone. "Stu's got it. He was going to show the place to his developer and some designer last week. Never brought it back." Her attention jerked back to the phone. "Hang on, I'm putting you on speaker." She punched the speaker button and Stu's voice came through.

"…need to do that? What's going on, Marcia?"

Pacheko got to his feet and came over by the phone. Stu, this is Deputy Pacheko. I understand you have the key to the smelter."

"Yeah. Well, that is, my client has it. Looks like we'll be closing the deal in the next day or two. He went up to give the place one last inspection before he heads back to San Francisco."

"When was that?" asked Pacheko.

"About an hour ago. He said he'd drop off the key on his way out of town. Why?"

"This client," Will cut in, "what does he look like?"

"Will, is that you? Listen, once this deal closes, we really need to have a serious talk about your place."

"Just answer the question, Stu," said Pacheko.

"He's about average, I guess. Short grey hair. He's got this scar on his left cheek that looks like…"

Pacheko grabbed his gun belt off the table by his desk and looked at Will. "You up for a little drive?"

"Drive?" Stu said over the phone. "What are you talking about?"

Will jumped up and followed the deputy. "Marcia, don't let him out of that office until you out everything he knows about this developer," Pacheko called out as they disappeared out the door.

"Hello?" said Stu. "What's going on over there?"

CHAPTER 35

Pacheko's cruiser shot through town and tore up Latham Canyon Road. Will was too freaked out by Pacheko's driving to say anything until the pavement turned to dirt and the curves in the canyon finally forced the deputy to slow down.

"For a guy who doesn't think there could be anything of value in that rat hole, you sure seem in a hurry to check it out."

Pachcko didn't take his eyes off the road, but a slight grin crept over his face. "I've got a feeling about this. Besides, I don't get an excuse to really put the pedal down around here too often."

"You really think this developer could be Doc?" Will asked. "Stu seemed to think he was pretty legit." Will had to admit he was torn between wanting the developer to be legit so he wouldn't have to confront the brother who had deserted him twenty years ago and wanting him to be Doc so he could put this whole nightmare behind him once and for all.

"Yeah, but how much background checking do you think he did? As bad as he wants this development to happen it probably wouldn't take much to pull the wool over his eyes."

Will shrugged. "He's been pretty excited ever since this guy showed up."

"In my experience, that kind of excitement can make you overlook a lot of red flags. Besides, Stu wasn't even around when that whole payroll robbery thing went down. I'd be surprised if he even knew about it."

The radio crackled with Marcia's voice. Pacheko grabbed the mic and responded, then released the call button. Will cringed as the deputy strained to hold a sweeping curve with only one hand on the steering wheel. Marcia's voice came back. "Cottonwood sent a more recent photo of Doc. I just sent it to your phone, and to Stu."

"Ok, thanks," said Pacheko. He put down the mic and dug his cell phone out of his pocket. Will fought the urge to take over the steering wheel and hung on tighter as the cruiser careened around another curve. Marcia came back again o the radio. "There's something else."

He handed the phone to Will and picked up the radio mic again, pressing the talk button. "Go ahead."

"He's sick."

Pacheko's foot backed off on the gas pedal. He looked at Will as if to ask whether they had heard her right. Will's face went slack, and he eased back in his seat. "Say again? Who's sick?"

"Doc's dying. They sent his medical report."

"The TB," Will said softly as he brought up the photo on Pacheko's phone.

Pacheko gave him a confused look. "I thought you said he grew out of it."

Will stared at the picture, looking dazed. "They said there was always a chance it might come back."

He held out the phone so Pacheko could see it. In the latest photo Doc looked like he could be sixty. His hair was mostly gray, and the scar down his cheek had faded, but those cold eyes still bored right through you. Will stared at the photo, suddenly feeling sad. It surprised him that even after all Doc had put him through, he still felt a sense of compassion for his older brother.

Pacheko realized he was holding the talk button down and released it. Marcia's voice came over the radio in mid-sentence. "…symptoms about three years ago, and it's gotten worse the last six months. The prison doctor doesn't seem to think he has much time left."

The patrol car slowed further as they approached the smelter turnoff. The parking lot came into view, and they spotted a black Cadillac Escalade backed up next to the main entrance, its nose tucked up against the hillside and the tailgate open next to the smelter's open side door. Pacheko eased into the lot and stopped, scanning the area, alert for any sign of activity. The rear compartment of the Escalade was empty and there was no sign of anyone.

"Do me a favor." he said to Will, "Look in the glove box and see if there's a pair of handcuffs."

Will just stared out the window as if he hadn't heard him, the reality of the situation taking hold. He could almost forgive Doc for leaving him behind during the payroll robbery. In the end that had turned out to be a good thing for Will. But if Doc really did kill the Captain, that was something for which there was no forgiveness whatsoever.

For that, Will vowed then and there, Doc would pay dearly. His eyes began to smolder with long-buried anger, and he was suddenly back in Iraq, an invincible Ranger in full body armor and ready to go to war. He reached for the door handle just as Pacheko smacked him on the shoulder, bringing him back to reality.

"Will! Glovebox, handcuffs." Will opened it and pulled out a set.

"Being a little optimistic, aren't you?" said Will.

Pacheko snatched the cuffs away and tucked them into his belt. "I had this training officer in school who was always saying you can never be too prepared. He drove that into us every damn day."

The radio crackled again, and they both jumped. "I just heard back from Stu," said Marcia. "It's him, J.D. Positive ID. You boys be careful up there."

Pacheko dropped the mic on his seat and pulled the patrol car nose-to-tail right tight behind the Escalade, leaving it no room to maneuver.

"You stay put," he said to Will. When Will started to protest, the deputy cut him off. "He's probably armed, and he's damn sure dangerous. I don't need you getting killed on my watch along with the others."

Will bit back his anger and stayed put as Pacheko popped the trunk latch and slid out the door saying, "I'm going to get some more firepower."

Staying low, he snuck around to the trunk and slid a twelve-gauge shotgun out of a canvas case attached to the floor. He checked the magazine, which held a full complement of six shells. They were only loaded with birdshot, but it would have to do. He grabbed another handful of shells from a partial box strapped to the case and stuffed them into his pocket. Then he snuck back around to tell Will once more to stay put. The passenger door was open, and the car was empty.

"Damnit, Will," Pacheko swore under his breath.

He chambered a round in the shotgun and cautiously crept to the back of the Escalade. A pair of large black duffel bags lay on the floor in the back, but no one was inside. The bags looked full, but Pacheko didn't want to waste time checking them with Will walking into a potential killing field. He flattened himself against the corrugated aluminum wall next to the smelter door. He listened a moment. Hearing nothing, he took a quick peek inside. Sunlight filtered through the holes in the roof and the row of windows high up along the wall. The giant, hand-hewn support beams and metal catwalks cast a latticework of shadows across the walls and floor below. There was no sign of Will.

He took a couple of deep breaths then ducked inside, sweeping his gun left to right then back again as he moved across the open expanse, taking a knee in a dark shadow behind a pillar. As his eyes began to adjust to the dim light, he scanned the room again but saw no one. The wooden stairways that led to the offices and locker rooms at the far end of the building seemed a long way away. He slowly rose to his feet, his mind reflecting on his training.

They had taught them how to clear a room, but this was more like an indoor sports stadium, minus the seats. He had no idea where Will had disappeared to, but the look he'd seen on his friend's face back in the cruiser told him it was a pretty good bet Will was going after his brother himself. That left him all on his own. He cursed silently to himself. Not only did he have to track a murderer in a place that screamed ambush from a dozen different places, he had to keep from shooting Will at the same time.

Keeping the shotgun out in front of him, he swiveled his upper body checking in all directions as he scurried from shadow to shadow making his way down the length of the building. At the halfway point he took cover behind another pillar. He was breathing hard, more from nerves than exertion. A few deep breaths brought his heartbeat gradually back to normal, and just as he was about to start moving again, he thought he heard a noise and froze. Silence.

He waited for what seemed like several minutes, then broke cover and began moving farther down the building. The noise came again; a rasping sound, like something scraping over a rough surface. It sounded like it was coming from somewhere inside the office complex. Then it was silent again.

The stairway leading up to the offices was still a good thirty yards away, and there was no cover in between. He took one more look around but couldn't spot Will. He didn't dare call out. The noise came again. It sounded like coughing, the deep, wracking kind, he thought, like someone with tuberculosis might have.

"I hope you're not doing something stupid, Hickock," he muttered under his breath.

CHAPTER 36

Following the fresh that were now mixed with the ones Pacheko had left tracks across the landing beneath the warren of rooms along the back wall during their visit to the smelter almost a week ago, Will crept cautiously up the stairs from the landing to the first floor of offices. In the fine dust it was easy to recognize the prints had the same left foot twist he'd found outside the first time he was here. Suddenly, he realized that was what had been bothering him about the boot tracks at Montforte's house, too.

The coughing had drawn him this far, but by the time he'd reached the landing the sound had stopped. He peeked into the locker room, but it looked just as deserted as it was before. The tracks continued up the stairs to the third floor and down the walkway to a large room at the end. He moved slowly, testing each step to make sure a squeaky board didn't prematurely announce his presence. He knew he shouldn't have left Pacheko behind, but the urge to find out if Doc really was alive gripped him like a vice. Twenty years of mixed emotions churned inside him, making his head swim.

As he approached the last room, he stopped next to a rectangular hole in the facing wall where a window used to be and peered cautiously around the edge. His face registered surprise, then confusion, then shock, all in the space of a millisecond. He quickly drew back and flattened against the wall. He was sure the noise had been coming from this last room, and the tracks he was following led into it, but there was no one there. *Shit! Where the hell could he have gone?* Panic welled up inside him and his chest grew tight. He was vulnerable as hell standing there, three stories up, on a narrow walkway with a flimsy wooden railing. All it would take was one good shove.

He scanned the smelter floor below. Where the hell was Pacheko? Pretty stupid to leave the only guy with a gun behind. Apparently, the deputy was smart enough not to come charging in like the cavalry, but that didn't solve Will's immediate predicament. He took a deep breath to steady his nerves. There was no going back. He'd just have to trust that Pacheko had him covered. He crouched down as he crept slowly to the office door and, after one more quick check, ducked inside.

There was no one there, but what was equally strange was the room itself. Everyone always said that the widow's company had salvaged everything it could, yet what was almost certainly Henry Latham's office looked just as it must have two decades before. A huge painting of a mountain lake hung on the back wall above a large wooden desk. A set of old mining scales sat on one corner of the desktop and a pen set still occupied the other. The high-backed leather chair was turned slightly sideways, as if its owner had just stepped out for a moment.

A pair of wooden chairs sat against opposite the desk, beneath the window opening. The entire end wall was covered with a set of floor-to-ceiling bookshelves, still crammed with books, photographs, mementos and knick-knacks. Except for the thick layer of dust covering everything, it was as if Latham had never left.

Pacheko swore silently. He was just approaching the landing when he spotted Will creeping along the highest walkway. What the hell was that idiot thinking going after a killer unarmed? He waved, but Will didn't see him, and the next thing he knew, the idiot had disappeared into the big room at the end of the row. Pacheko started to climb, trying to make as little noise as possible.

It seemed like hours had passed by the time he finally reached the top floor. Sweat trickled down the back of his neck and he was out of breath, which didn't help with the staying quiet part. Two pairs of fresh tracks in the dust led him down the walkway toward the last room. He knew one set belonged to Will, which meant the other must be Doc's. He hadn't heard any coughing for some time now. The building was eerily quiet. Stopping at the window opening where he spotted Will, he steadied himself, then took a peek inside. What the hell? He'd seen Will go in there with his own eyes. He checked the tracks once more to confirm it. So how could it be empty?

He made his way to the door, and after making sure the room was indeed unoccupied, he stepped inside. It was creepy, like a museum that no one had visited in a long time. Dolores had told him that when Latham's widow was salvaging everything, she still held out hope that he might come back for her and couldn't bring herself to dismantle his office. Pacheko walked over and surveyed the desk. Given the thicknest of the dust that covered virtualy the entire room, nothing had been disturbed for a very long time. The same was true of the two chairs on the opposite wall. The bookshelves, too, looked as if nothing had been touched in decades. Then he noticed the footprints.

CHAPTER 37

Will followed the fresh footprints from outside the office directly up to the bookcase, at which point whoever had made them seemed to have disappeared. The only disturbance in the dust blanketing everything was on a large book at one end of the top shelf. He reached up and started to pull it out. As soon as it moved there was a soft click and one end of the bookcase swung free from the wall, the hinges making a low squeal. He cringed, stopping it when he had just enough room to slide through the opening.

He found himself on a small landing, with a wooden staircase descending into what appeared to be a vertical tunnel about ten feet square. It was dimly lit by a series of bare bulbs placed at intervals along an aluminum conduit running down one of the bare, sandstone walls that appeared to drop all the way to the bottom floor of the smelter. He felt a chill slither down his spine. It was the same feeling he'd had many times as a Ranger, always when danger was near. How could a secret passage not have something to do with stolen gold?

He took a step forward, letting go of the bookshelves. They began to squeal again, but before he could grab them, they closed with another soft click. He pushed hard against them, but they were locked in place. Forcing down the panic tightening his chest, he slowly started down the narrow steps descending in a series of short flights joined at right angles around all four walls. Judging by the age of the wood, this secret passageway must have been part of the original design, and he couldn't help wondering whether Henry Latham's grandfather, who had built the smelter, had planned the nefarious swindle from the very beginning.

Will slowly made his way down the last flight of stairs, his senses alert to anyone, or anything, that might be laying in wait for him. As he neared the bottom, he heard the coughing again. It was definitely coming from below, and it was muffled, like it was coming from another room.

At the bottom of the stairs, he found a closed door set into the sandstone. The rest of the walls were solid, making it the only way out, other than climbing back up the stairs. He cautiously tried the handle. Unlocked. He listened. It was deathly quiet. He noticed a light switch next to the door and turned it off, plunging the tunnel into darkness again. No sense making himself an easy target.

He eased the door open slowly, thankful the hinges did not announce his entrance and immediately determined the room was dimly lit. He quickly dropped to a crouch and scooted inside along one wall. He waited, but there was no sound. A lone, bare bulb hung from the ceiling of a room about twenty feet square revealing a low ceiling supported by stout wooden posts, and a dirt floor. Will could make out two waist-high rectangular shapes covered with tarps. The one closest one was about three feet by four feet, the other about half that size. A heavy wooden door at least eight feet across hung on an iron rail at the far end of the room.

He had barely taken a step toward the nearest tarp when a husky voice froze him.

"Well, hello Cowboy."

Will felt himself flush. Reason told him to flee, but curiosity wouldn't allow him to move. A gravelly chuckle spawned a brief spasm of the raspy cough that had led him here.

"Thought I heard someone on those stairs," growled the voice. "I have to say, I'm surprised to see you here. Thought it might be that damn deputy."

The cough came again. Will peeked out from behind the tarp scanning the dimly lit room in the direction of the sound and came face to face with his past.

The man leaning casually against the wall at the far corner of the room was almost invisible in the shadows. Will strained to see into the darkness, part of him hoping it wasn't Doc. The man stepped forward and the bulb cast a harsh light across his face, accentuating the scar and giving his steel-gray stubble an eerie glow. One hand held a half-empty bottle of whiskey, the other gripped a pistol aimed directly at Will. It took a while for the wracking cough to subside. He took a swig of the whiskey and looked Will over, a smile curling his lips.

Seething with anger but overwhelmed with curiosity. Will stood up slowly, ready to dive for cover should Doc start shooting.

"Look at you." Doc said with an evil grin. "All grow'd up."

Will forced himself to take a few steps closer, staring hard, trying to recognize the brother he remembered in this gaunt, tortured face.

The dark slacks and dress shoes conveyed his role as a businessman but made him look painfully out of place. His pale blue dress shirt had stains on the sleeves that looked too dark and blotchy to be dirt. More like blood, perhaps leaking from dog bite wounds. At his feet lay an open duffel bag.

"Is it really you, Doc?"

He grunted. "What's left of me." The cough threatened to start again but he quelled it with another pull on the bottle. "Been a while, huh."

Will felt his anger begin to overtake the curiosity. "Yeah, ever since you left me standing in that creek."

"What do you want me to say, I'm sorry?" Will didn't respond. "Don't look so pissed. You must have figured out by now the last thing I needed, or wanted, was to drag a little kid along with me."

"You got away clean, Doc. I got sentenced to fifteen years. That, and thinking you were dead, is what killed Mom."

The cold eyes softened ever so slightly. "I know, and I am truly sorry about that. She did her best."

"So why the hell did you have to come back?"

"For this," he said, pulling back the tarp he was leaning on. The light gleamed off a stack of gold ingots, each one a little bigger than a dollar bill and a couple of inches thick. Will's eyes went wide.

"Latham's gold," said Doc, grinning. He pulled off the other tarp to reveal an even bigger stack. "Ten million, so the story goes, but it looks to me like there might be a lot more than that."

Will's mind feverishly tried to compute the amount of money sitting in front of him. Realizing it was a futile effort, he shook his head and snapped back to reality. "So, what was in the briefcase?"

A smile lifted one side of Doc's mouth opposite the scar. "You found out about that, huh? Quarter million in bearer bonds. Imagine my surprise." He let loose a laugh. "Hell, I thought I'd died and gone to heaven. Turns out it was small change compared to this."

"So, you killed Latham."

"The fool damn near ran me off the road trying to get me to pull over. Finally drove me into a rock." His finger absently traced the scar running down his cheek. "Once he figured out what happened, he told me I could keep the payroll, all he wanted was the briefcase. But it was too late. I'd already opened it."

"And with a payday like that you still couldn't resist robbing a bank?"

"Hell, I blew through most of those bonds in a couple of years. Oh, I had me some high times, I can tell you," he said with a grin. Then he shrugged. "I needed some cash, and I figured security would be light in that little nothin' town." He shook his head. "Goddamn cops got me before I could even get past the city limits." His harsh laugh crumbled into another coughing spell. Will tensed looking for an opening to take him down, but Doc was still fifteen feet away and he held the gun steady. It took two long drinks of whiskey to get it stopped this time. He took a couple of deep breaths and went on.

"I thought the bonds were for the investors, you know, their cut or something. I was so busy spending the money I didn't even learn about what Latham was really up to until I was already in prison. You talk about motivation," he said with a cackle. "I worked on this plan for five years. Five years!" He took another swig. "It's okay, I told myself, you got time. Everybody thinks Latham took the gold and split. No one knows he's dead and it's all still sittin' there, ripe for the pickin's. Just serve out your sentence and you'll be a rich man."

"How's that working out for you?"

"I'm here, ain't I?" he scowled. "Cleaned up a few loose ends along the way, too." He laughed again, then quickly sucked on the whiskey bottle before the coughing could take hold. "Too bad you had to show up, Cowboy. Now I'll have to take care of you, too."

Will felt the anger rising in his chest. "Why the Captain?"

"Why the hell not? I needed a distraction so I could move around without being recognized, and I knew killing him would throw the whole town in an uproar. Besides, that son-of-a-bitch never gave me nothin' but grief. As far as I'm concerned, he deserved what he got."

Will took an angry step forward, but Doc took aim with the pistol. "Don't, Billy boy, you know I'll shoot you." Will stared him down, but didn't move, "I heard all about how he took you under his wing and raised you up all right and proper."

"You seem to know a lot for being gone the last twenty years."

"Nothin' much to do in prison 'cept read and cruise around the internet. And your pal Stu just loves to talk," he said with a laugh. "I swear, he knows everything about everybody in this town."

"And Montforte?"

"I read about his little windfall, and how he got rich bringin' this town back to life. I got to thinkin' that might have been hush money for helpin' Latham out somehow, and he might know where his private stash was. It didn't take long for me to work out of him that he delivered one of those briefcases every time they brought up a payroll."

"A lot of people thought Montforte was in on it," said Will, "including the Captain."

"He swore up and down he never knew what was in them. All he did was deliver them. I tried real hard to persuade him otherwise, but he stuck to his story. Finally, he remembered one time when he walked into Latham's office to deliver a briefcase and saw that bookcase cracked open. Latham closed it real quick and told him to keep his mouth shut or he'd be out of a job. Montforte said he didn't think anything of it at the time. 'Course no one knew about Latham's little scheme back then. Ol' Sam forgot all about it."

"And you believed him?"

"Trust me, he was in no position to lie," he chuckled. "Hell, you ought to thank me. If I hadn't come along and jogged his memory, no one ever would have known about that trick bookcase, and all this would have stayed down here for who knows how long."

Another coughing spell seized him. Will thought about making a move, then, just as quickly, he wondered if Pacheko had found his tracks, and figured out the bookcase. If so, he needed to stall for time until the deputy could get there. As he waited for the coughing to stop, he was surprised to find himself wanting to tell Carla that her father hadn't lied about his gambling windfall.

"How long have you got?" Will asked as the coughing slowly subsided.

"Hell, if I know," Doc rasped, trying to catch his breath. "I read about some experimental treatment down in South America. It's pricey, but this should cover it, with plenty left over." He waved the gun over the stacks of gold and grinned at Will, his teeth glowing gold in the light reflected off the ingots. "I may not live long enough to spend it all, but I'm sure as hell going to give it a try. I got kind of used to the high life with those bonds."

Keeping his gun leveled on Will, he tossed over an empty duffel bag. "Since you're here, you might as well make yourself useful. Help me load up some more of these and get them out to the car. I got two more bags already out there. I'll make it worth your while."

Will let the bag fall to the floor. "You really are crazy, aren't you?"

Doc resumed loading ingots into his bag. "So they tell me."

"You don't really expect to get away with all this, do you?"

"Who's gonna stop me?" Doc snarled. "The Captain's dead. That puke Yeager should be, too." Doc scowled at him. "I understand I got you to thank for him still being alive."

"Stu told you?" asked Will.

Doc nodded. "Like I said, that boy loves to talk."

"He's lucky I happened along. Even Yeager didn't deserve to die like that."

"Reckon you and me will just have to disagree on that."

Doc added a few more ingots to the bag at his feet, then stood up, straining to lift it. He looked over at Will, who hadn't moved. "Somehow I didn't think you'd be any help," he said, aiming the pistol at him again. "Guess the Captain ruined you, just like I figured."

"There's still Pacheko."

Doc snorted. "I did my homework, little brother. He's fresh out of school, only been on the job a couple of weeks. He don't know squat."

"I wouldn't count on that," said Will.

Doc laughed softly and slid back the wooden door next to him. Behind it stood a row of metal lockers. He pushed on the top corner of the end locker and four of them swung open just like the bookcase. Two more loaded black duffel bags sat on the floor just outside.

"Pretty slick, huh? Old man Latham had it all figured out." He took aim at Will. "Now I just finish you off and I'm long gone."

"Or you could just put down the gun and we end this without anyone else getting hurt."

Will jumped when Pacheko's voice came from outside the tunnel door, then instinctively dropped to the floor. Doc fired off a couple of hurried shots, each sounding like a stick of dynamite exploding in the small room, and ducked behind the largest ingot pile. Will looked around for a place to hide but before he could move Doc fired another shot into the post next to him and he froze. "Stay right where you are, Cowboy, I've still got you in my sights."

"Will?" Pacheko called out."

"I'm okay," Will shouted. "Stay put."

"I was wonderin' when you'd show up, deputy," Doc called out.

"I've got more men outside." Pacheko lied. "Put it down, Doc. You've got no chance of getting out of here."

Doc laughed. "I'd beg to differ. There ain't no other men. Now, I've got a dead bead on Billy boy here, and unless you toss your gun over this way right now, I'll put a bullet through his head. Then it'll just be you and me. Did I mention I'm pretty damn good with a handgun?"

"You'd shoot me?" Will asked.

"What do you think? But hey, it's not really up to me, is it?" He turned to the doorway. "What's it gonna be, deputy?"

"Don't trust him," shouted Will.

"Now that just hurts, Cowboy. You know I've always been a man of my word."

"You can't haul all this away in one load, there's too much," said Will. "And even if you get away today, you can never come back here after the rest." said Will.

"I don't have to," said Doc. "It's amazing the things you can learn on the internet. See, after the widow Latham and the others got everything they wanted out of this place, they declared the building salvage, which means they gave up their claim to anything left on this property. Once I buy it, everything in here belongs to me, including these little stacks of gold bars I'm leavin' behind. All legal and above board. Took me a few days to get it all set up with Stu and the bank after I found this little hidey-hole, but everything is finally in place."

"You'll never make it," said Pacheko. "We know who you are now."

"You may know who I am, but you don't know the man who's buyin' this building. I've made damn sure he's completely anonymous, and you two won't be around to cause any trouble."

"If you mean Jimmy Columbo, he's busted, too," said Pacheko.

"Nah," said Doc, he died up in Cottonwood. You must know how easy it is to set up a new identity these days?"

"If you kill us, they'll hunt you down no matter where you go," said Will.

"They'll never find me. I've got a foolproof plan to disappear for good. I've got people waiting at a bank right now. Once I deposit this gold, everything else can be done online. My lawyers will handle the final transaction and hire someone to salvage the rest of this gold. They get their cut, and the rest gets transferred to my offshore account."

"What happens when your lawyers find out you killed people to get that money?" said Pacheko.

"With what I'm payin' 'em they won't be askin' no questions. Besides, they're bound by confidentiality rules." Without warning, he fired another wild shot at Pacheko. "Enough talk! Come on, deputy, let's not make this any harder than it has to be. Make no mistake about it, I won't have any problem shootin' my little brother here, and if you don't show your face in the next five seconds, I'll do just that."

As a Ranger Will had faced situations like this many times but seeing his own brother's stoney stare brought on a different kind of fear. As the seconds ticked by, he began wonder just how good a friend Pacheko had become.

"Time's up, deputy," said Doc. "Say goodbye to your pal." He fired another shot into the post next to Will.

"No, wait!" Pacheko shouted. He stepped into the doorway, his hands raised, shotgun pointed toward the ceiling. Relief flooded over him when he saw Will still alive.

"Put it on the floor and kick it over here," said Doc.

Pacheko did as he was told, sliding the shotgun past Will.

"Smart boy. Now the pistol," he said, using his gun to indicate the deputy's sidearm. Pacheko removed it with two fingers and put it on the ground, kicking it towards Doc with his foot.

Doc picked it up and stuck it in his belt, then grinned at Will. "See, Cowboy, I told you he was a rookie." Doc fired again and Packeko cried out as he spun sideways and slumped to the floor, silent.

"No!" cried Will, lunging toward the fallen deputy.

Doc fired into the post again. "Back away from him, Billy!"

Will's anger overflowed. He let out a long yell and charged his brother. Doc fired again, but Will's momentum carried him forward and they both went down. They lay still for a breathless moment, then

Doc scrambled to push Will off and get to his feet. Will rolled over, clutching his leg and moaning in pain. Doc backed away holding the pistol on him, his hand shaking with anger. "You move again, and I'll put another one in you. I only said I wouldn't shoot you to get the deputy to show himself. Don't believe for one second that I won't put you down if I have to."

Will stared his brother down, then the pain took hold. He groaned, clutching his leg. He looked down and saw a dark hole in the center of his thigh and blood was flowing freely. Feeling around the back of his leg he found the exit wound. He'd seen more than his share of bullet wounds in the Middle East and he knew enough to recognize that the wound wasn't squirting like the bullet had hit the femoral artery. He also knew that because the wound was a through-and-through he was losing enough blood that he needed to get help soon. He pulled off his shirt and tied it around his leg, covering the hole, and pulled the knot as tight as he could, cringing at the pain. The shirt was quickly soaked with blood.

While Will was taking care of his leg, Doc retrieved the shotgun and emptied the magazine, dropping the shells into the open duffel bag and tossing the gun behind the gold stacks. Holding his pistol on Will, he crossed the room to where Pacheko lay motionless. He bent over the body lying face down and saw blood pooling under his head. "Well, looky there, a head shot the first time. Guess I'm better with this thing than I thought."

"Is he...?" asked Will.

He gave the deputy a tentative shove with his foot. When there was no response, he kicked him hard. Still nothing. "Looks like he won't be a problem anymore."

Rage surged in Will again. He tried to get to his feet but cried out in pain and fell back onto the ground. "You bastard!" he growled through gritted teeth.

"Sticks and stones, Cowboy, sticks and stones." Doc leveled the gun at Will, then his eye caught something on Pacheko. Well, looky here," he said with a grin. He plucked the handcuffs from the deputy's belt, then turned back to Will. He may have just saved your life after all." He waved his pistol. "Move over there and wrap your arms around that post."

Will scowled at him but did as he was told. Doc tossed the cuffs on the ground next to him. "Now cuff yourself to it."

"What for?" Will growled. "You're just going to kill me, too."

"Call me sentimental," Doc said with a grim grin. "Or maybe I just figure I owe you one after that day in the canyon. Look on the bright side, Cowboy, if you don't bleed out before someone finds you, you'll have one hell of a story to tell."

He walked over to make sure the cuffs were secure, and for the first time Will noticed he was favoring his left leg. That explained the tracks. The stains on his sleeves looked damp as well, the dog bite wounds must have re-opened during their tussle.

"Looks like Dusty did a pretty good number on you."

"If you mean that damn wolf that attacked me up at the Captain's, yeah, he gave it a shot, but it was his last one. I took care of him good."

Will decided to let that lie. Besides, the pain in his leg and the loss of blood was starting to make him light-headed. He watched as Doc filled the second duffel with the remaining ingots in the smaller stack, then zipped them both up and stood up to leave. "Oh yeah, I almost forgot." He walked over to Pacheko's body and rummaged around in his pockets, until he found a set of keys. He held up the handcuff key and winked at Will. "Just in case someone finds you before I have a chance to get clear this'll slow them down a bit more."

He stuffed the keys in his pocket and strolled back over to the duffel bags. "I have to admit, part of me hopes you make it out of this, Cowboy. If you do, have a nice life, you hear? I know I sure as hell will." He let out a loud laugh, and this time the coughing did not come. He cocked his head to one side and took in a deep breath. "Whattaya know, looks like that miracle cure is workin' already."

He tried hoisting one of the duffel bags onto his shoulder, but it was too heavy to lift. Finally, he grabbed the straps on each bag and dragged them out into the locker room, turning off the lights as he left. When he slid the wooden door closed the room went so dark Will couldn't even see his hands cuffed in front of him. A moment later, he heard the metal lockers swing closed with a bang, and then all he could hear was the sound of his own breathing.

CHAPTER 38

Doc barely made it through the locker room and down off the landing onto the floor of the giant smelter before he had to stop and rest. He'd picked up the two additional duffel bags waiting in the locker room and dragging all four was proving to be difficult. Dropping the four straps he bent over with his hands on his knees and sucked in big gulps of air, trying hard to stifle the coughing. He told himself he didn't need to hurry. Billy wasn't going anywhere soon, and the deputy, well, ever. Still, the fact that they'd caught up to him in the first place made the urge to flee almost overpowering.

As soon as his breathing began to return to normal, he bent and picked up the straps. Just the strain of dragging them a few feet more had him puffing again. He made it another thirty yards before he stumbled, twisting an ankle and dropping to his knees. Damned gold was heavier than he'd imagined.

He looked back at the locker room, disappointed with how far he had come, and a sense of urgency gripped him once again. He hoped that deputy was bluffing when he said he had more men outside. Rubbing his ankle, he grabbed the straps once more and started dragging with a vengeance. The scraping noise they made echoed loudly the enormous smelter, but there was nothing he could do about that.

It took him a full five minutes, stopping every few yards to fight down the coughing and catch his breath, to make it outside and back to his SUV. Relief flooded over him once he determined there were no other deputies waiting. He cursed Pacheko for boxing him in with the patrol car, but that wouldn't be much of a problem. The Escalade was much bigger and heavier. It demanded almost every ounce of strength he had left to heft the four duffels into the compartment along with the two already there. Once that was done, he stared greedily at his haul and allowed himself a smile.

The weight of the gold had the rear end of the big Cadillac riding low to the ground, but he wasn't in any particular hurry now. He breathed some air back into his ragged lungs as he closed the hatch. Turning back to the patrol car, he pulled out his pistol and put a round in both tires on the passenger side. The passenger door still hung open and he pumped two more rounds into the radio for good measure.

Will sat in the dark cursing himself for being so foolish. His impetuosity had not only gotten Pacheko killed, it was allowing Doc to get away. He felt a terrible surge of grief at the death of his newfound friend, and it struck him that, except for the Captain, he couldn't remember ever feeling that close to anyone before. He'd had friends in the Army, but like his romantic affairs, they'd either been shipped out to other postings or taken out by the Taliban. The latter was the primary reason he'd remained a loner even after coming home. He looked over at Pacheko's lifeless body and anger began to blend with his sense of loss until it finally boiled over. He let out a primal scream, jerking furiously at the handcuffs. His wrists screamed in painful protest, but the cuffs held fast.

The moment he quit tugging at the cuffs, his leg wound took center stage again, burning like hell. He knew he needed to get more pressure on it somehow or he was going to bleed out. Fighting the pain that any movement sent shooting through him, he felt around in the darkness with his good leg and finally caught a corner of a tarp that had covered one of the stacks of gold. The discovery buoyed him, and he dragged at it with his foot until he could grab an edge with one hand. The material was lightweight, and although it wasn't easy maneuvering in the handcuffs, he finally managed to rip off a couple of long strips. He worked his body around until he was straddling the post so he could reach his damaged leg.

Removing his blood-soaked shirt, he ripped it in two, folding the two halves into makeshift compresses. Placing those over the two bleeding holes in his thigh he then wrapped the tarp strips tightly around his leg. It was a pitiful field dressing, but it would have to do for now. All he could hope was that the added pressure would slow the bleeding somewhat.

All the while, he racked his brain for a way to get out of the cuffs, but he could think of nothing helpful. Frustrated, he slammed his fists against the pole. Surely Marcia had called for backup, but he realized it would take the nearest law enforcement at least an hour to get there, and by then, Doc would be in the wind. He tried to estimate how much time had passed since they'd left the office to determine when help might arrive, but his brain was too fuzzy from the loss of blood to think straight. He shook his head to clear it and tightened the dressing on his leg again, frantically trying to concentrate. He had to find a way out soon or he was going to join Pacheko.

A groan came from the darkness. Will stopped and listened, not sure if he was hearing things. It came again, and across the room he heard Pacheko stir. He felt a jolt of adrenaline and his spirits rose. "Pacheko?" he called out. Another groan. "Pacheko, please tell me that's you!"

"Where...what...can't see." His voice was mushy, like he was coming out of a fog.

"Damn, I thought you were dead."

"Not so sure I'm not.

"How bad is it?"

"Can't tell. I think I'm blind, though."

"No you're not. Doc turned off the lights when he took the gold and locked us in."

"How long ago?"

"Maybe ten minutes. He's probably long gone by now.

He heard Pacheko struggling to his feet, then falling. "Damn, can't get my bearings. Head's spinning like a top. Feels like it weighs a ton. Give me a hand, will you?"

"I would, but I'm cuffed to a post."

"You're what?"

"When Doc shot you, I went for him, but he got me first, in the leg. Then he got your handcuffs."

"Shit, you alright?" asked Pacheko.

"I've been better."

He heard Pacheko begin feeling his way around on his hands and knees.

"What the hell were you thinking, coming in here by yourself?" groused the deputy. "Didn't they teach you anything in the damn Special Forces. You always wait…"

Will cut him off, his voice tinged with regret. "For backup, yeah, yeah, I know. I couldn't help it. I just had to find out if it was really him."

"Well, it was. And now he's getting away. Again."

"I appreciate you not letting him shoot me," he said sheepishly.

"I'm starting to have second thoughts about that right now."

Two distant gunshots rang through the building and they both jumped.

"What the…?" said Will.

"Most likely our tires," Pacheko said." Moments later, two more shots followed. "And there goes the radio."

"You boxed him in pretty good. Maybe that will slow him down some."

"Are you kidding? That Escalade will push my cruiser out of the way like it was a toy. And I doubt he's worried about the rental insurance."

Will tugged angrily on the handcuffs, but they remained locked tight. He started thrashing his good leg around the floor.

"What the hell are you doing?" asked Pacheko, his voice closer now.

"I'm trying to find something that might help us get out of these cuffs." Will said.

The deputy continued to work his way toward Will, feeling around for obstacles. "What, you think you can smash them with a gold bar?" he said with no small amount of sarcasm.

Will shot a nasty look in the direction of his voice, immediately realizing it was lost in the darkness. "You got a better plan?"

"As a matter of fact, I do."

This time his voice was right next to Will, and it sounded like the deputy was taking off one of his boots. "What the hell are you up to?" he cried out.

"Remember that training officer I told you about? He was a real jerk. Always trying to trick us by putting us in situations he knew we couldn't get out of. One time he had the whole class cuff themselves to our desks and took all the keys. He told us there were instructions on how to pick a set of cuffs on the computer monitor at the front of the room. All we had to do was figure out how to get up there and read them. Then he told us he'd check back after lunch and left."

Pacheko got his boot off and Will could near him rummaging around inside it. "You know, this probably isn't the best time for story hour." he said.

"The desks were bolted to the floor. No one could get to the computer. The instructor came back a couple of hours later. He thought it was real funny."

Will heard the boot drop to the floor and then felt Pacheko fiddling with the cuffs. "Since then, I always carry a spare key."

A moment later, Will was free. He immediately felt his way to the light switch and flipped it on. He blinked hard, forcing his eyes to adjust to the sudden light. One look at Pacheko made him gasp. He looked like something out of a horror movie. The entire right side of his face was covered in blood, and it had seeped down his neck soaking his shirt. He tried to give Will one of his patented grins, but it came out even more lopsided than usual.

"That bad, huh?" he asked, as he staggered to his feet. Will took a closer look a look at the deputy's head. A sizeable crease ran along the side of his skull, front to back, and blood oozed from the wound. He picked up the torn tarp he'd used to bind up his own leg and ripped off another strip, tying it around Pacheko's skull. "I'm not going to lie," said Will. "It doesn't look good. We need to get you to a hospital."

The deputy grimaced when Will tightened the makeshift bandage and held onto Will for support. As soon as Pacheko steadied himself, Will sprang toward the locker room door.

"Hey!" shouted Pacheko. Will stopped and looked back at him. "What did we just talk about?"

"Ok, ok, I'm waiting."

Pacheko stumbled around looking for something. Will was about to ask what he was doing when the deputy reached behind the gold stack and retrieved his shotgun.

"What good is that?" complained Will. "Doc took all the…" He stopped talking as Pacheko pulled the extra shells from his pocket. He finished loading the gun and then stopped in his tracks, mesmerized by the pile of ingots. "Holy shit," he breathed. "This must be worth…"

"A hell of a lot," said Will. "Now will you please get your ass moving?"

CHAPTER 39

Doc slammed the Escalade into reverse and rammed the front of the patrol car. Because the front end was so close to the hillside there wasn't much room to maneuver. Metal screeched and the patrol car moved back couple of feet before the bumper on the big Cadillac slid up into the grill of the smaller car causing its rear wheels to lose traction.

Cursing, he pulled forward, jamming his front end as far into the hillside as it would go, then put it in reverse again and floored it. The Escalade hit the patrol car again, moving it several feet farther back, but still not enough to let him get around it.

"Goddamn cops," he swore. "Always fucking with me."

He shifted into low gear and powered forward, this time driving the big truck part way up the dirt embankment. Shifting back to reverse, he braced himself and hit the gas. The Escalade shot back, catching the patrol car on the front corner. This time the smaller car spun out of the way, and the Escalade scraped past it, roaring backwards into the open parking lot.

"All right!" Doc shouted gleefully. "I am outta here!"

Will and Pacheko heard the cars colliding as they raced across the smelter floor toward the exit, Will limping badly and Pacheko holding onto him for whatever support he could get, his balance still affected by the head wound. The second crash made them move faster, praying they would make it to the parking lot before Doc broke free and disappeared forever.

The third crash came just as Will ran through the door, Pacheko right behind him. The badly crunched patrol car was tilted sideways on its flat tires, doors hanging open. A few yards beyond, the Escalade slid backwards to a stop facing them. Behind the wheel, a look of surprise fluttered across Doc's face as he saw them emerge from the smelter. Then he smiled and gave them a middle finger salute as he punched the gas and spun the wheel, dirt and rocks flying back at his pursuers.

As Doc raced toward the road, the rear end of SUV almost dragging on the ground, Pacheko raised the shotgun and started firing at the escaping killer. One of the shots took out the rear window, but the Cadillac continued to gain speed. He fired off his last shot just it reached the end of the parking lot. All they could do now was watch as Doc fled with his prize.

The Escalade veered to the left, preparing to take the hard right turn onto Latham Canyon Road at full speed. By the time Will and Pacheko made it to town for help, he would be nearly impossible to find. All they could do was stand there and stare, pain and exhaustion creeping into their bones, along with the incredible frustration that comes with failure and the sure knowledge that Doc had actually gotten away with the murders and the gold.

The blast from a car horn shook them out of their brain fog. Their eyes refocused on the Escalade in time to see it swerve violently to the left to avoid running head on into another car coming up the road. Weighed down with the heavy bags of gold, the rear end of the SUV lost traction and started sliding sideways, inertia lifting the right wheels up off the ground. Pacheko took off running, frantically pulling more shells from his pocket. It only took Will a moment longer to follow, but his wounded leg hampered his progress considerably.

Miraculously, Doc managed to get the Escalade back on four wheels, but the momentum was too much. With all that weight in the back the rear end swerved hard the other way.

Pacheko was struggling to load the shotgun as he ran, dropping some of the shells, but still managing to get a few into the magazine. Will bent down and picked up the dropped shells as he followed trying desperately to ignore the pain in his leg.

Doc corrected again, and for a moment it looked like he'd gained control, but the big SUV was going too fast. It shot straight across the road and launched off the creek bank, sailing nose-down into McKinley Creek and crunching to an abrupt halt. The engine revved violently in the rushing water for a few seconds, then died.

Will stopped in his tracks, in shock over what he'd just witnessed, but Pacheko kept running toward the crash scene, pumping another shell into the chamber. "Stay back," he shouted at Will. "He's still armed."

As the dust began to clear, Will noticed the red Subaru stopped at the entrance to the parking lot. The door opened and Stu climbed out, looking dazed from his near collision with the Cadillac. Their eyes locked for a moment, Will's asking what the hell he was doing here and Stu's asking what in God's name was going on? Then they were both drawn back to the crash site.

Pacheko slowed as he approached the creek bank, the shotgun raised to his shoulder. "Doc! It's over!" he shouted at the wreck "Come out with your hands up!" There was no response.

The rear wheels of the Escalade continued to spin in the air, steam from the engine rising from the creek where it had nosed in. Still in shock, frozen where they stood, Will and Stu watched as the deputy disappeared over the creek bank around the side of the upended SUV.

Pacheko cautiously made his way down the creek bank and around the driver's side of the truck, shotgun at the ready. "You hear me, Doc?" Let me see your hands."

There was a long silence. The rear wheels of the Escalade slowly spun to a stop. Will was finally able to get his legs to move and started limping tentatively toward the crash. Stu followed, looking like he'd rather not but couldn't help himself. They reached the top of the creek bank just as Pacheko reappeared from behind the Escalade. He raised a hand to stop him, and slowly shook his head.

"The air bags?" Will stammered.

"They opened," Pacheko said softly. "Probably would have saved him, too. But all that swerving around must have ripped open one of the duffel bags." Will gave an involuntary gasp. "When he nosed down into the creek, a bunch of the bars flew up front," Pacheko continued. "One caught him in the back of the head. His skull's crushed." The deputy climbed up over the top of the bank and put a hand on Will's shoulder. "He never knew what hit him. I'm sorry, Will."

Exhaustion took over and they both collapsed on the embankment, staring down at the wreck in the middle of the creek. Stu looked over at them, a pained look finally eclipsing the shock on his face. "So, does this mean the smelter deal is off?"

CHAPTER 40

I'm all at loose ends
Nothin's workin' out for me
I'm all at loose ends
Guess that's just how it's meant to be
But I've got good friends
Lookin' out for me
And nothing but blue skies
As far as I can see

Will stopped singing softly to himself as he finished hammering home the last nail in a section of two-by-four wall frame and stood up to take a breather. The sun burned hot in the clear blue summer sky. He gazed around the small valley where the Captain's life had tragically and prematurely come to an end two months before, absently rubbing his leg where Doc's bullet had entered. The entrance and exit scars were barely sensitive anymore, but the thigh still protested mightily when he pushed himself too hard on his bike.

He finally felt good about the new melody he'd been working on for the last several weeks, but the lyrics had only come to him after Doc and Latham were finally buried again, this time with the correct headstones.

The two funerals had been held simultaneously, and as quickly as possible after Doc was killed. Two of Shambles' most prominent citizens had been laid to rest less than two weeks before, and no one felt much need to acknowledge simultaneous burial services for a pair of the worst criminals the town had ever spawned. Everyone agreed that it would be best to expedite the proceedings so they could start forgetting about them.

That's not to say the ceremonies weren't well attended. News reporters from all over the region flocked to Shambles for the event. Every national network covered the funerals and interviewed just about anyone they could get to talk. The widow Latham had shown up, accompanied by Stu English, but she refused to speak to anyone. They left as soon as she saw her late husband's casket being lowered into the ground, a look of good riddance on her face.

Will had laid low until it was all over. He chose not to attend either funeral, figuring Doc was finally right where he deserved to be, in the grave next to their mother. Good riddance, indeed. Instead, he hunkered down at home obeying doctor's orders to let his leg heal properly. He'd even avoided Libbie's for the most part, despite multiple pleas from Tommy to play with the band. Since he'd gotten back on his feet, he'd been so busy working on his new house and guiding bikers that he'd barely had time to sleep.

The carnage of the Captain's old ranch house had been completely cleared away, as had the burned out bunkhouses. The original foundation lay bare, save for several framed sections of wall that had begun to give shape to the new structure going up.

As he wiped the sweat from his face, a glint of sun reflecting off something down the valley caught his eye and he spotted a dust trail rising up from the road out of Latham Canyon. As it drew closer, he recognized the Placer County Sheriff's Department's big Ford Excursion at its head, the shiny, new paint job and the sleek, new red and blue lights on top gleaming in the midday brightness. What the hell could Yeager want with him now?

The giant SUV turned off the road and rolled across the old bridge over McKinley Creek that emptied onto the ranch property. As it wheeled up to the partially framed house and Dusty came running over from the barn, barking loudly at the intruder. Will kept his hammer in his hand as he walked over to greet the unexpected arrival.

The dog had been released from the vet a month ago and seemed to be fine, but he was hanging pretty close to the ranch these days. Will had fixed him up with a makeshift bed in the barn. With all the time he'd been spending on the house the two had finally begun to establish a friendship of sorts. Dusty seemed to sense that the rebuilding of the Captain's ranch meant he still needed to stick around and watch over it. But the big dog was still as leery of strangers as he'd always been.

"It's okay, Dusty," Will called out, walking over to stroke the giant dog's silvery fur, careful not to rub the still-tender side that had burned where the hair was just starting to grow back. "Quiet, boy, it's okay." The barking turned to a low growl as the driver's window hummed down, stopping halfway.

"I brought treats," said Pacheko, no small amount of trepidation in his voice. "Can I get out now?"

"Hear that, boy? He's got treats." Will was surprised to see the friendly face. Pacheko had offered to stop by and help out on the house today, but he wasn't expecting him to be driving Yeager's pride and joy instead of his vintage Malibu. Maybe he'd been waylaid by official business.

The growl became a whine and the big dog looked up at the new arrival, licking his chops. Will smiled and looped his fingers loosely under the thick, leather collar around Dusty's massive neck, not exactly sure whether the treats the dog was anticipating were of the canine variety, or the deputy variety.

The car door eased open and Pacheko tentatively descended, a package of dog treats extended in one hand, leaving the door open just in case he needed to make a quick retreat. Will was surprised to see he was wearing his civvies, not so surprised they consisted of his Forty-Niners jersey and electric blue shorts. The flip-flops, however, had been replaced with low-cut hiking shoes, a suggestion from Will when his friend offered to help work on the house. A new baseball cap with *Libbie's* embroidered across the front was pulled low to hide the bullet scar on the side of his head. Will noticed the hair was starting to grow back where the wound had been shaved.

"He going to be all right?" asked Pacheko, looking ready to jump back into the safety of the car at the slightest provocation.

"I think so," said Will, patting the dog's head. "See, Dusty, it's only Pacheko." The dog cocked his head to one side as if he was unsure whether he should relax or not. Will looked back at the deputy. "Give him a minute. It's been a while since he's seen you."

Pacheko held out the treats and approached the dog slowly. "Here you go, boy," he said, trying to smile away his fear. "You remember me, don't you?"

Dusty barked once and Pacheko froze. Will gripped the collar tighter. "Maybe if you actually gave him a few of those," he suggested, nodding at the package of treats.

Pacheko nervously started to open the bag. In his haste, the cellophane ripped and several of the treats fell to the ground. Dusty lunged forward, breaking free of Will's grip. But instead of attacking Pacheko, he gobbled up the treats and looked eagerly up at Pacheko for more. Now frozen with fear, he didn't respond, so the dog started licking the hand that held the bag. Pacheko swallowed hard and pulled a few more treats from the package. Dusty immediately sat down, waiting. Pacheko looked to Will, who only shrugged, almost as surprised as his friend at the dog's friendly behavior.

Dusty made a kind of half-whine, half-growl noise and looked at Pacheko expectantly. The deputy contemplated the dog a moment, then tossed one of the treats high in the air. Dusty leaped up and caught it, then sat again, waiting for the next one.

"Ha!" said the deputy, relaxing slightly. "You just want to play, don't you, big guy?" He tossed several more treats, and each time Dusty snatched them out of the air, then sat obediently.

"I'll be damned," said Will. "I never saw him do that before."

"The Captain must have taught him," said Pacheko.

"Must have."

"You just have to know how to handle dogs," Pacheko said, puffing out his chest in a show of confidence. Then he very cautiously reached out and patted Dusty on the head. The dog licked his hand again, then bobbed his head up and down as if asking for another treat. Pacheko tossed him one more, then spread the rest on the ground. Dusty dove in like he hadn't eaten in days.

"Damn, Hickock, don't you feed this animal?"

"He ate a huge bowl of food earlier this morning. Guess I'm going to have to up my grocery budget." Dusty looked up at him and barked in agreement, then snatched up the last of the treats and headed for the barn. Will glanced over at Pacheko's partially shaved head again. "How are you holding up?"

"You mean this?" asked Pacheko, lifting the cap up to show off his scar. "Another half inch and I wouldn't be standing here, but the Doc says I'll be fine. Lucky my head's just as hard as this guy's." He gave Dusty's head another rub.

Will looked over at the Excursion. "Yeager know you're driving that?"

"Nope. Why should he?" His face scrunched up when he saw the vacant look on Will's face, then it struck him. "You haven't heard?"

"Heard what? What's he done now?"

"Damn, you really have been incognito the past few weeks, haven't you?"

"Pretty much, why?"

"Pacheko opened the door and reached inside pulling out the wallet that held his badge. He flipped one side up and Will's mouth dropped open. The deputy badge had been replaced by a shiny gold star with Placer County Sheriff embossed on the face.

Will's eyebrows shot up, pulling his mouth into a big grin. A chuckle escaped as his eyes darted back and forth between the badge and Pacheko full of questions.

Pacheko smiled with him. "The town council called Yeager in last week after they found out he'd been feeding Corinne and Fitch information on ranchers they were after for their mineral rights. They didn't go into detail with me, but aside from the ethical ramifications some of his actions apparently crossed a few legal lines. Rather than go public and get the whole community in an uproar again, they told him if he retired quietly, they'd forget about any charges."

"And he did? Just like that?"

Pacheko cocked his head to one side and grinned. "There might have been some yelling and screaming, but bottom line, he gave up his badge. The next day they called me in and asked if I wanted the job."

Will shook his head, incredulous. "I can't believe it."

Pacheko looked at him with big, innocent eyes. "Why not? I did solve three murders and capture a wanted fugitive, all in the space of two weeks."

"Damned if you didn't." Will let out a laugh and Pacheko beamed with pride. Will grabbed his hand and shook it hard. "I can't think of anyone better for the job, and that's for sure." He pulled his friend into a hug and slapped him on the back, then took a step back to look at the big Excursion in a whole new light. "So, this is all yours now?"

Pacheko grinned proudly. "Picked it up from the shop down in Boise this morning and drove straight here. Looks pretty good for being half burned up, huh?"

"Will shrugged, stifling a grin. "As cop cars go, I guess." Pacheko gave him a playful shove. "This calls for a beer."

Pacheko retrieved a six-pack of Miller High Life from the Excursion. "You got someplace to cool these down?"

"I appreciate the contribution, but I'm way ahead of you," Will said, taking the beers over to a cooler resting next to a worktable that held his toolbox. He pulled two cold ones out of the ice and opened them while Pacheko put his six-pack on ice.

"So, how's he doing?" Will said, handing him a beer.

"Yeager?" Pacheko shrugged. "No one's seen him that I know of. Marcia said he packed up what belongings he had left from the fire and left town, just as cantankerous as ever. She said he still wasn't breathing too well. Apparently, his lungs got pretty fried. Said he kind of squeaks when he talks."

"Now that I'd like to hear." They shared a laugh and clinked their bottles together in a toast. "To the new Sheriff," said Will.

They both took a long drink, then fell silent, each contemplating what this revelation meant to the other. Will finally spoke up. "So, if you're the only law in town, how do you get a day off to come out here and help me? Shouldn't you be busy fighting crime?"

"Thankfully, things have been pretty quiet since our dustup with your brother. I've mostly been digging out from under the mountain of paperwork that and those two murders generated, not to mention Latham's resurrection after all these years. Last time I saw you was when you played at Libbie's. When was it, a month ago?"

"Their anniversary party, yeah," Will said, shaking his head. "I can't believe they've been married ten years."

Pacheko chuckled. "Time flies when you're having fun."

They walked over and stepped up onto the foundation. The outer walls were completely framed in, and some of the interior rooms were taking shape. A series of vaulted roof trusses rose up toward the sky across the front half of the new house resembling the mountain peaks surrounding them. "It's looking pretty good."

"Yeah, getting there. The crew has made good progress for just three weeks, and I pitch in on my days off."

"I thought you didn't get those this time of year."

Will smiled. "Not often enough, that's for sure. Tim says this is the biggest season yet. Had to hire two new guides. He's booked solid through September." He led Pacheko to the back of the house. "I appreciate you offering to help out. You ever done this kind of work before?"

"Oh sure," the deputy said nonchalantly. "I had a friend who owned a surf shop back home. I helped him build a few surfboard racks one time."

"Great," said Will, not bothering to mask his sarcasm.

"Hey," I know how to use a hammer as well as the next guy."

"You can show me by securing this new section."

They hefted the wall section Will had just finished into place and Pacheko confidently nailed it to the floor plate and the adjoining section.

"I stand corrected," Will said, as he added a temporary brace to the other end and. "Three more of these and I'll have a bathroom."

"Let's get to work then."

Two hours later they'd finished off the bathroom walls, and Pacheko called for a break. Will pulled another pair of beers from the cooler and they drank as he walked the new Sheriff through the interior of the new house, pointing out the various rooms. A ringing phone caused Pacheko to pat his pockets, only to realize he had left his in the car. When Will walked over to the toolbox and pulled out a new cell phone of his own, the exaggerated look of shock on the deputy's face drew a scowl.

"Wait, that can't be yours," Pacheko said, his hand grabbing his chest feigning a heart attack. "Don't tell me the famous loner has been dragged into the twenty-first century."

"Kicking and screaming," said Will. He answered the phone and immediately shot Pacheko an embarrassed glance, then walked away to talk in private.

Pacheko was curious, but he didn't want to butt in, so he gingerly approached Dusty, who'd been lying in the shade of his SUV watching them work. He held out a hand cautiously. The big dog sniffed it, then allowed him to pat his head. By the time Will came back a few minutes later, Pacheko was rubbing the thick fur like they were old friends. He tried to act like he wasn't interested in who was on the other end of the call, but Will didn't buy it.

"Carla says hi," he said grudgingly.

"Oh, so it's her fault you got finally got connected to the rest of the world. That makes a lot more sense."

"Keep it up and I'll sic the dog on you," Will said with a smirk.

Pacheko gave Dusty a hug. "Too late for that," he said with a grin. "Nice to know you two are still talking after you ran out on her at Jimmy V's that day. I thought that between her father's murder and her issues with Corinne Barker she would have been happy to put Shambles in her rearview mirror for good."

Will gave him a scowl and Pacheko responded with a laugh.

"She came by the hospital to see me before she left," Will said with a shrug. "I'll admit she was a little freaked out about everything that happened, but we parted on good terms. In fact, she's taking care of all the legal stuff on my inheritance, so we needed to stay in touch."

"Yeah, like that's the only reason. So, she went back to Minnesota or wherever?"

"She did. But you'd be surprised what you can do over the internet."

Pacheko laughed at the reference to Doc's scheme to salvage the gold. "You're into computers now, too? Who are you and what have you done with my friend Will?" Will just shook his head. "Besides, I thought Melville was your lawyer?"

"He's pretty much retired now that the Captain's gone. Besides, she offered."

"Pro bono, no doubt," chuckled Pacheko.

Will face screwed up into a smirk. "I'm paying her for her services, thank you very much, thanks to the reward money."

"Must have been a pretty healthy payoff for recovering all that gold."

"It'll take care of this," he said sweeping his arm across the construction site. "With enough left over to buy the resource rights for this valley."

"Don't you have to bid on those?" asked the deputy.

"Already did," said Will with a satisfied grin. "That's what Carla was calling about. Just got them locked up for the next five years."

Pacheko let out a whoop and raised his beer bottle in a toast. "Hot damn, Will, congratulations! That's the best news I've heard all week!"

Will clinked his bottle off Pacheko's. "Hell, all month."

"Corinne won't be happy to hear that. This property was the key to her whole plan with Fitch."

"Win some, lose some," Will shrugged. "What's the latest on her and Fitch anyway?"

"He hasn't been seen for the last few weeks. I don't know if he's gone for good or just taking a break. She's got her hands full anyway, just trying to keep the Montforte empire from falling apart."

"Yeah, I'll bet she's not too popular since her drilling deal went public. And once Carla found out that foothills land was hers, she was able to put a halt to the tests."

"She got any plans for that yet?"

"No, it's way too soon. She's hoping to get back out for a visit in a few weeks. You can ask her yourself."

"Sounds like you two have something in common now. What's she going to do with her father's place in Spring Meadows?"

"Sam had a pretty sizeable life insurance policy with her as the beneficiary. She's thinking about using it to build a summer home on his lot. But she wants to wait until things quiet down a little."

"I know what she means. Finding Latham's gold is all anyone's been talking about in town. Ever since the story got out the resort has been swarming with people. Stu's even booking tours of the smelter. I hear he's worked up some tall tale for the tourists about the long-lost gold and the notorious criminal who killed to find it, only to be undone by a daring Deputy Sheriff and his Army Ranger sidekick." Will cringed at the reference. "I guess he figures since he can't sell it, he might as well milk it for whatever he can get,"

"I would expect nothing less from him. I just wish he'd left me out of his story."

"Maybe you could make that a condition for selling him your mom's house. He begs me to ask you about it every time I see him."

"What's his hurry? I thought all that went up in smoke when his San Francisco developer didn't pan out."

"I wouldn't say that. All the press Doc's phony smelter deal got apparently spawned some interest from real developers."

Will laughed and shook his head. "Why am I not surprised? I'll bet they're already lined up outside his office trying to outbid each other."

"How'd you know?" Pacheko drained the last of his beer. "Guess we'd better get a roof over your head before he sells your other house out from under you."

Will tossed his empty in the direction of the cooler and stood up. "Hop to it, Deputy…I mean, Sheriff. We're burning daylight."

"Sounds like the title of one of your songs."

Will paused and thought a moment, then smiled as musical notes started dancing in his head. "It might be, Pacheko. It just might be."

The End

ACKNOWLEDGEMENTS

Thank you for taking a chance on the first Will Hickock mystery. I hope you enjoyed it. This book would not have been possible without encouragement of many people along the way. First and foremost, my beautiful wife, Cheri, whose steadfast belief in my desire to create stories out of thin air kept me plugging away to the finish, and whose critical editor's eye greatly improved the final product. In addition, many friends and writing colleagues listened patiently to my ramblings as the story developed and offered much appreciated feedback as well. You know who you are.

As you may have guessed, the town of Shambles, as well as Placer County, are fictional entities. I have endeavored to make them seem as real as the characters who inhabit them. It should be noted that several real county boundaries were shuffled by the legislature during the early days of statehood, which came in 1890.

History buffs among you will know that gold mining in the mountains of southwestern Idaho had its heyday in the late 1800s and early 1900s. I hope I can be forgiven for choosing to extend that heady and chaotic era a few decades in order to facilitate my story.

Any newly published author needs help getting the word out about his books, you would have my heartfelt thanks for any reviews you can offer on Facebook, Goodreads, Google, or any other platform you choose, as well as any referrals you may choose to offer your friends and families. You can find out all about me and my other books on my Author Page at Amazon.com or at rdcopsey.com.

The next book in the Will Hickock Mystery series, *Dead Man's Curve*, is now available on Amazon. I encourage you to take another chance as Will and his pal J.D. Pacheko track down a killer and end up working with the DEA to take down one arm of a Mexican drug cartel.